Helen Black grew up in Pontefract, West Yorkshire. At eighteen went to Hull University and left three years later with a tattoo her shoulder and a law degree. She became a lawyer in ham and soon had a loyal following of teenagers needing advice and bus fares. She ended up working in Luton, king predominantly for children going through the care em. Helen is married to a long-suffering lawyer and is the her of young twins.

e for Helen Black:

ark and gripping read that will have you on the edge of your *Closer*

ntastic first novel.' Jane Elliott on *A Place of Safety*

fic! A great read from start to finish.' Jessie Keane (author of *rd*) on *Dishonour*

pected and moving . . . *A Place of Safety* is written with sym thy and humour.' *EuroCrime*

Also by Helen Black, in the Lilly Valentine series

Damaged Goods
A Place of Safety
Dishonour

Blood Rush

Helen Black

Constable & Robinson Ltd
3 The Lanchesters
162 Fulham Palace Road
London W6 9ER
www.constablerobinson.com

First published in the UK by Robinson,
an imprint of Constable & Robinson Ltd, 2011

A copy of the British Library Cataloguing in Publication data is available from the British Library

ISBN: 978-1-84901-473-1

Printed and bound in the EU

1 3 5 7 9 10 8 6 4 2

To Joseph and Phoebe

Acknowledgements

My thanks must go to Krystyna Green and everyone at C&R. Lilly has found a new home and I'm sure she'll be happy.

Next comes a shout out to the Buckman posse, always watching my back.

I must also thank Lynne McA, who kindly agreed to give the very rough first draft of *Blood Rush* a read through. The turnaround was as impressive as her comments were helpful.

Last, but by no means least, are my fantastic family. If I say so myself, we rock.

Prologue

We've run the length of the estate and my breath comes out in weird little grunts. I glance at Malaya but she's staring straight ahead. Either she hasn't heard me or she knows better than to comment.

We slow to a jog, Malaya's bangles jangling up and down her doughy wrist. Three of them. All gold. When I next get some peas, I'm buying me some of those.

We stop outside a chip shop, panting. A woman comes out with a hot parcel under her arm. The delicious smell of steam and vinegar fills the air and my stomach growls. When we've done this thing I'm heading straight to KFC, man.

Malaya looks up at the pair of box-fresh Nikes, tied together by their laces, and dangling from the telephone wire. We've crossed into South Side territory.

'What will they do if they catch us?' Malaya asks.

'What would we do if we caught someone slipping into our ends?' I shrug.

She knows the answer to that one.

We set off again, past the Spar, already closed for the night, metal shutters down, and into the estate.

I can tell Malaya's bricking it. Her eyes are wide in her fat face. She wants to be part of the crew, course she does, but she wishes the entry ticket wasn't so expensive.

I remember my jump in. Fuck, man. I had to cut some girl's face. I was so pumped I nearly took her nose off.

We round the car park and arrive at a disused ground floor flat. The windows are boarded up providing a blank canvas on which the words South Side Massive are spray-painted in letters three-feet high.

Underneath are the tags of all the South Side members. Carmel, Chelsea and that crazy motherfucker Yo Yo, who would cut you open as soon as look at you. Then there's Michaela, Kadene and that slag Tanisha McKenzie. Plus a load of others I don't even recognise. Youngers.

For the first time I feel apprehensive and toss a spray can to Malaya. The South Siders are bad people and we don't want to get caught.

'Let's do it.'

Malaya begins to write next to the mural and I draw a massive arrow flanked by two footballs. When we've finished we step back to admire our handiwork:

South Side Massive suck . . . and a huge pink cock covering the whole front door.

I can't resist a laugh.

'Fucking sick, man,' says Malaya.

I nod and pull out my phone, take a picture of her grinning in front of it, her hand resting on top of an ugly bollock. Now we're both laughing.

'What's funny?'

I spin to the sound of the voice. Shit. It's that mental case, Yo Yo, barrelling towards us.

Malaya looks at me, her mouth opening and closing but no sound coming out.

I throw down my can. 'Run.'

We dart sideways, out of Yo Yo's path. I'm running hard now down the road and I can hear Malaya behind me, but I know

Yo Yo won't be far behind her. Up ahead I see the entrance to a swing park on the right. I crash through the gate, snagging my Adidas hoodie on a stray nail. Then I feel the sting and realize it's sliced through more than my top. I put my hand to the gash in the material and feel the wet of blood on my fingers.

A group of white boys are huddled under the slide but I can tell by their scabby mouths and the stink of them that they're glue-sniffers and won't give us any trouble.

I risk a look behind me and see Malaya following, but she's slowing down. Built for loving, not running. And Yo Yo is catching up, her teeth bared like the animal she is. Another girl follows. Then another. Shit, the whole crew are on our case.

I pound across the rec when I hear a thump and a groan. Either Malaya's fallen or they've caught her. Either way, I ain't stopping. No way. I'm right at the other end of the rec, at the fence, and I throw myself over into an overgrown garden. I hit the deck, smelling dog shit and the plastic tang of used condoms.

I keep my head down and listen good. No footsteps are chasing me. All I can hear is crying.

I hold open a couple of spiky branches and peep through a tiny gap in a bush.

Malaya is in the middle of the rec, lying on the ground, curled up like a baby in one of those ultrasound pictures. She's making a noise in her throat, somewhere between a sob and a choke.

Yo Yo stands over her. 'So what you got to say, girl?'

She jabs Malaya with her foot. Not real hard. Just enough to make Malaya groan.

'Cos I'm wondering what reason you got, coming into my area, disrespecting my people.'

Malaya doesn't answer, just covers her face with her hands.

Yo Yo's mouth twitches like she's done a pipe or something. But trust me, that girl don't need a stone to get riled.

'You ain't going to answer me, bitch?' she screams down at Malaya. 'Cos if you don't give me some explanation, I'm going to show you what I'm all about.'

Some of the other girls step forward to form a semi-circle around Malaya's head and I have to swallow my panic. I could call my own crew, get them over here. But they're on the other side of Clayhill, waiting on us. How long would that take? Enough time for the South Side to find me.

All I can do is lay low and hope Malaya can take it.

Then I see that slag, McKenzie, put her hand on Yo Yo's arm. 'Don't be vexing yourself, sister.'

Sister. I cringe at that. Back in the day, Tanisha and me used to roll together. Used to be like we was family. Not any more.

Yo Yo shrugs her off. 'You saying we should just leave it?'

Tanisha shrugs, picks her thumb nail.

Yo Yo nods. 'Maybe you're right and we should just send this piece of shit back to where she came from.'

Then she starts to walk away. I can't believe it. Malaya's one lucky bitch. When Yo Yo's taken two, maybe three steps, I allow myself to exhale.

Suddenly, she spins sharply and runs at Malaya. Lands a flying kick in her back. The thud of trainer against flesh makes me heave. Acid stings my throat.

I close my eyes, hoping a few lashes from Yo Yo will be punishment enough. Each kick is accompanied by a scream from Malaya. One, two, three, four.

Then silence.

I open my eyes, praying it's over. That someone has interrupted them and sent the South Side scattering back to the estate like the fucking rats they are.

But no. The park is quiet. Even the glue-sniffers have sloped away. The only sound is Malaya quietly crying and Yo Yo panting like a dog.

She steps back, wipes her hand across her mouth. The others look to her expectantly. I hold my breath. Please let this be it. Let Yo Yo get bored.

Then I see it. The flash in her eye. Like an electric current. She ain't bored. She ain't even got herself started. She throws back her head and yells at the night sky. Then she jumps on Malaya and stamps on her head. The others join her. Punching, slapping, kicking. Shouting, screaming, laughing. Hysterical.

Nothing will stop them. They got da bloodrush.

Chapter One

'You look terrible.'

Lilly fixed her son with a glare. It had been a long night. Long and draining.

Sam reached into the kitchen cupboard for a glass, leaving the door wide open. 'Do you want me to lie?'

She considered pointing out that telling lies and not telling the whole bald and ugly truth at all times were not one and the same thing. That there was no moral obligation to state the bloody obvious.

'What?' Sam helped himself to a carton of juice and nudged the fridge shut with his hip. He slurped his drink and wiped his mouth with the back of his hand.

'Nothing,' said Lilly, and mentally filed this battle with the countless others marked 'simply not worth it'.

Instead, she turned to Alice, who was smacking the tray of her high chair with a pudgy fist, and proffered a spoon of yoghurt.

'At least you haven't learned to talk yet,' she said.

Alice rolled her head from side to side, her baby curls jiggling like a halo of red snails.

'Come on, sweetie.' Lilly brushed the spoon against her daughter's lips. 'Eat your breakfast.'

Alice clamped her mouth closed. More cat's bum than Botticelli angel.

Sam leaned over, his fringe flopping into his eyes. He peered into the pot and wrinkled his nose at the white gloop.

'Maybe she doesn't like it, Mum.'

Lilly waved him away. 'Of course she does.'

She waggled the spoon and its contents enticingly. Alice watched the trajectory of her breakfast with caution, her eyes following it from left to right. When it came within a whisper of her face, Alice gave a gummy grin.

'She loves this stuff,' Lilly sang out.

Her eyes twinkling, Alice opened wide and raised her hand as if she were about to give Lilly a high five.

'See.' Lilly was triumphant. 'All babies love this stuff.'

The yoghurt wobbled as the spoon touched Alice's lips, causing her to laugh out loud. Then, without warning, she batted the spoon away, splattering Lilly in the eye.

Sam let out a hoot. 'Let's face it, Mum, Alice is just not like other babies.'

The doorbell rang and Lilly made her way through the hall, Alice under her arm. She carefully picked her way through an assault course of papers and wine bottles awaiting recycling and answered.

It was Jack. 'Mary, Mother of God, you look awful.'

'So would you if you'd been up all night.'

Alice held out her arms to Jack and Lilly passed her over.

'How's Daddy's little girl this morning?' Jack kissed the baby's sticky cheek. 'Are you pleased to see me?'

Alice gurgled and Lilly felt a familiar stab of regret. Alice was always pleased to see Jack. And he was always pleased to see her. How easy life would be if they could live like a normal family.

'I have to get ready for work.' Lilly spun on her heels and

clattered up the stairs before Jack could see the sadness written over her face.

When Sam and Lilly had left, Jack breathed in the silence of the cottage and let out a heavy sigh. It was a complete mess. Every flat surface was littered with bibs and toys. The sofa was entirely covered in clothes that had clearly been carried from the tumble drier but hadn't made their way upstairs. No doubt Lilly had been distracted by a phone call, or a question from Sam, or a leaf falling off a tree in a garden two miles away.

'What's the kitchen like?' he asked Alice, who chuckled into his leather jacket.

The answer was a rat's nest of toast crusts, unopened post and pans left to soak on the window sill. He'd been in crack dens cleaner than this.

He slid Alice into her high chair, reached for a dishcloth and sighed again.

God, he missed living here.

Daylight and noise spill into the dorm. Ten minutes ago, when the last bell for breakfast shattered the air like glass, the other boys had hauled themselves from their bunks, thrown on their crumpled shirts and blazers, and bolted to the dining room before the last rashers of greasy bacon could be cleared away.

Since then, Jamie has laid in his bed, unable to lift his head. His sheet is knotted and uncomfortable beneath him, but he doesn't care. He is concentrating every ounce of his being on not throwing up.

'What's this, Holland?'

Mr Prior stands at the door, legs apart, hands on hips. Tristan Saunders does a pukka impression of him that has everyone laughing their arses off. He's almost been caught in the act a few times, but he doesn't give a shit. Tristan Saunders doesn't give a shit about anything much.

'I don't feel well, sir,' Jamie mumbles.

Mr Prior enters the dorm, kicking shin pads and a hockey stick out of his way with a grunt. Anyone would think he was a general in the marines, not some poxy housemaster at a boarding school.

'Let's take a look at you,' he barks.

Half-heartedly, Jamie pushes back his duvet. The swoosh of cold air makes him shudder.

'Sit up, boy.' Mr Prior stands over Jamie, his five-foot-three frame almost blocking the light.

'I don't think I can, sir.'

'Don't be ridiculous, Holland,' says Mr Prior and grabs Jamie by the shoulders.

The sudden movement sends the room spinning and Jamie gasps. His head is banging and his stomach lurches.

'A shower is what's needed here,' says Mr Prior.

The pressure of his grip is agony. It's as if the housemaster's fingers are squeezing right through the skin to his bone. Jamie's throat tightens and he gives a strangled cough.

Mr Prior releases his hold and drops Jamie back on to his bed.

'Five minutes,' he bellows. 'Then I want to see you washed, dressed and in my office.'

As Mr Prior reaches the door, he turns and narrows his eyes at Jamie. They hold each other's stare for a few seconds until Jamie leans over the side of his mattress and empties the contents of his stomach on to the floor.

'Dear me, your pulse is racing.' Matron holds Jamie's wrist between her thumb and forefinger and checks her watch.

She's moved him to the sick bay, where there's always a smell of disinfectant and the beds have plastic under the sheets which crackle. Jamie once spent three uncomfortable days here with flu, sweating and sneezing into his pillow. At least it's quiet and Mr Prior will leave him alone.

Matron wipes his forehead with a damp flannel. It feels deliciously cool.

'Do you want me to call your parents, dear?'

'No.' Jamie answers far too quickly.

Matron squints at him, takes another swipe with the flannel.

'They'll be busy at work,' says Jamie, 'and I don't want to worry them for nothing.'

Matron eyes him for a moment longer, then nods.

'I'll leave this here.' She pats a metal bowl perched on the bedside table. 'Just in case.'

Jamie smiles weakly. He knows she's trying to be kind but he wishes she'd just give him some peace. When a day boy arrives with a blood-stained hanky covering his nose, Jamie can only sigh with relief and watch Matron bustle away to her next patient.

The room tilts and Jamie lowers himself on to the bed as gently as he possibly can. He closes his eyes and breathes in through his nose. Never has he felt this rough in all his life, and he swears on everything that is sacred and holy that he will never take drugs again.

Lilly pulled into the winding drive of Manor Park, her son's school. As usual, she was stuck behind an army of shiny, new four by fours, inching their way to the entrance. Every morning she swore she would set off five minutes earlier and beat the yummy mummies to it, but every morning something got in the way. Today it had taken longer than she'd expected to scrub yoghurt from her eyelashes.

'You won't be late,' Lilly told Sam, with more confidence than she felt.

He shrugged, without looking up from his iPod.

With fondness, Lilly remembered how the school run used to be a cacophony of singing and questions.

As they approached the main entrance Lilly could see the maintenance staff stringing Christmas lights around the imposing oak door and the ten-foot fir tree that stood outside the music room window.

'That's going to look beautiful,' she said.

'Last year you said it was no wonder the fees were so extortionate if they wasted money on stuff like that.'

'Well, last year I was Scrooge,' she said.

Sam's thumbs whizzed across the touchpad. 'And this year?'

'I'm the other one,' said Lilly. 'The one who loves Christmas.'

'Tiny Tim?'

At last Lilly managed to pull into a parking space, the Mini Cooper dwarfed on both sides by black Range Rovers.

'Not Tiny Tim,' she said. 'Bob what's his name.'

Sam opened the car door and slid out in one fluid movement. A blast of icy air smacked Lilly in the face.

'Bob Cratchit,' said Sam.

'That's the man.'

Sam rolled his eyes. 'So you're going to be the guy who is completely exploited by his boss, never speaks up for himself, and sells out for a goose.'

Lilly tried to think of a clever retort, but nothing came.

'Well, good luck with that,' said Sam and slammed the door.

As she watched him take the steps two at a time, she wound down the passenger window.

'Sam,' she called.

He turned and raised an eyebrow.

'Actually, I *am* the boss.'

He laughed and disappeared inside.

A dark-haired woman in her mid fifties, wearing a pillar-box-red overcoat and a scowl, was already waiting outside the offices of Valentine & Co. when Lilly arrived. She was stamping her feet against the cold and checking her watch at regular intervals.

Lilly smiled warmly. 'You must be the new secretary.'

The woman peered at Lilly over glasses that were perched on the end of what looked more like a beak than a nose.

'The agency told me you opened at nine,' she said. 'It's ten past.'

'The traffic was hideous on the A5,' answered Lilly.

'I see,' said the woman. Her frown matched the grey winter morning. Her coat incongruously cheerful.

Lilly smiled again and unlocked the door. This was the sixth secretary she'd welcomed through the doors in as many months. The previous five had left in various states of despair at Lilly's special brand of working practice.

Lilly had high hopes for this one. She'd come recommended from the agency as 'robust and flexible'.

'Let me show you around,' said Lilly.

The woman said nothing as Lilly gave the tour of reception, meeting rooms and kitchen, though there was an audible intake of breath when Lilly opened the door to her own office.

'I'm not the most tidy of people.'

Files were scattered across the floor and a brown apple core was discarded on her desk. Lilly scooped it up and catapulted it into an overflowing bin.

'I don't see clients in here.' Lilly tapped the back of the spare chair which was piled high with documents and law books.

The woman didn't put so much as a toe over the threshold.

'So what do you think?' Lilly opened her arms. 'I think you'll find I'm pretty easy to work for.'

The woman didn't speak.

'Any questions?'

The woman looked at Lilly as if she were completely mad. 'No thank you.'

The hospital room is completely bare apart from the bed and a chair pulled alongside. No pictures or posters on the grey wall. No books or magazines on the window ledge.

Demi looks from her grandmother's face to her sister's and back again. She can't say who looks worse, Malaya with her purple eyes, swollen shut, or Gran, her mouth pinched into a straight line.

'Why don't you get yourself a cup of tea, Gran?'

Gran glances up at Demi. But only for a second. She's been at Malaya's side ever since she got here and hasn't taken her eyes off her.

'What if she wakes up?' Gran asks.

Demi opens her palms. 'I'm here.'

Gran breathes through her nose, her nostrils flaring, unable to decide. She must be thirsty yet she can't bear to leave her poor girl.

'You need to stretch your legs,' says Demi.

Gran gives a tight nod and pulls herself to her feet with a groan. She backs to the door, still unwilling to let Malaya out of her sight.

'If anything happens . . .'

'I'll run and get you,' Demi interrupts.

Gran hovers in the doorway.

'Go,' Demi urges, shooing her grandmother away with her hand.

Finally, Gran leaves and Demi takes her seat. It's still warm.

Now she's alone, Demi's not sure what to do. She crosses her feet. Then she uncrosses them. Cross, uncross. Cross, uncross. She keeps time with the steady rhythm of the machine next to Malaya. It's attached to her by a viper's nest of wires. The nurse says the sound is her heart beating. Which seems incredible to Demi, because lying there, not moving at all, Malaya looks as if she's already dead.

Demi leans forward and places her hand next to her sister's. Malaya's is bigger than hers. Fatter. A ring sinks into the plumpness of her finger like a sausage tied in the middle. Demi tries not to think about all the times she's watched Malaya stuffing her face with fried yam and called her a pig.

'This is a terrible thing.'

Demi turns to the door and sees their neighbour, Mrs Mboko. Like Gran, she's at least eighteen stone, both their skins the anthracite black of the Igbo. At church on Sundays, dressed in their head wraps, they look like a couple of proud statues.

'They think she'll be okay,' says Demi, though as far as she knows no one has actually told them that.

'Your grandmother has already suffered so much.' Mrs Mboko shakes her head sadly.

'Yes,' says Demi.

Mrs Mboko kisses her teeth. 'These gangs are a wicked thing.'

It's only now that Demi sees Chika skulking behind her mother, kicking her high-tops against the door jamb. She's a few years older than Demi, and everyone on the estate knows her. She's part of the gang that runs things.

'You girls must concentrate on your studies and stay away from trouble.' Mrs Mboko wags her finger.

Chika mumbles something under her breath and Demi assumes they'll leave, but Mrs Mboko remains where she is, her eyes closed, her lips moving. Demi realizes she's saying a prayer. When she's finished, she crosses herself. Demi copies her. A reflex action.

'Remember me to your people,' says Mrs Mboko, and leaves.

Chika stays behind, her nose ring glinting in the striplights.

'She really going to be all right?'

Demi shrugs.

'That's harsh,' says Chika. 'But you need anything, you let me know, yeah?'

Demi nods.

'CBD look after their bredren, you get me?'

Demi nods again.

'Have the police been?' asks Chika.

'No.'

'They will.' Chika enters the room and lowers her voice. 'Say nothing, you understand me.'

'Don't have anything to say.'

A small smile plays around the edge of Chika's mouth. Then it's gone and something cold and hard settles.

'We're gonna sort this ourselves,' she says.

'How?' asks Demi and instantly regrets it.

Chika narrows her eyes. 'You fuck with our family and we gonna fuck with you.'

Lilly spun around in the swivel chair behind the desk in reception. She found that if she lifted her feet, she could make it almost 360 degrees.

Her would-be secretary had left without even taking off her coat. A record. The agency had promised a replacement by lunchtime. In return, Lilly had promised to tidy things up. And she would. Just as soon as she had made an entire revolution in the chair.

She held the edge of the desk and pushed herself from left to right to gain momentum. When she felt she had sufficient force, she propelled herself around, letting out a high-pitched squeal of delight.

'Excuse me.'

Lilly came to a juddering halt.

Another woman was standing in the doorway. Her hair was sticking out at odd angles and she wore a bright-orange waterproof. Her expression was puzzled, but at least she wasn't frowning.

Lilly leapt from her seat and held out her hand. She was determined to make a good impression. Spinning like a child was not a good start, she conceded, but still.

The woman shook her hand, her brow knotted.

'Annabelle,' she said.

'Lilly.' She grinned inanely. 'Let me show you around.'

She had already decided that her room was strictly out of bounds.

'This is the reception.' Lilly waved at the phone and computer.

Annabelle nodded seriously.

'I work on an entirely different floor.' Lilly let out a strangled laugh. 'Entirely separate.'

'Is that where you want me to go?' Annabelle asked.

'No, no, no.' Lilly shook her head. 'Me and my things need not bother you at all.'

'So where do you want me?'

Lilly gestured to the chair. 'Your domain. Completely free of my . . . stuff.'

Annabelle smiled and strode across the room, a rucksack jiggling on her shoulder, sat down and looked at Lilly expectantly.

'Why don't you log on to the PC and I'll make us a coffee,' said Lilly.

'Log on,' Annabelle repeated.

She seemed a little vacant but at least she was in the building.

'Milk and sugar?' Lilly asked.

'Er . . . yes, please.'

Annabelle's hands were poised over the keyboard. She looked back at Lilly, who smiled encouragingly, and headed for the kitchen.

When she returned with two steaming mugs, Annabelle was frozen in the same position, her fingers floating in mid-air.

'I don't mean to be rude,' she said, 'but I really don't think I should access your computer.'

'It's fine,' said Lilly. 'Anything case sensitive is password protected.'

'I'm still not comfortable.'

Lilly reminded herself to be patient. Perhaps Annabelle had never worked for a lawyer before. How was she meant to know what she could or couldn't be party to?

'Seriously, you don't need to worry.'

Annabelle didn't move to touch the keys.

'How else are you going to type?' Lilly joked.

Annabelle's face reddened. 'Oh, I can't type.'

Lilly took a deep breath. She had told the agency that she would be prepared to take on someone without any prior experience. Actually, they had said that only someone who had never stepped foot in a solicitor's office before might stand a chance of going the distance. Even so, there were some basic skills that any secretary needed to have.

'How were you going to manage case notes and things?' Lilly asked.

Annabelle reached into her rucksack and pulled out a biro.

Lilly stifled the urge to laugh. 'I'm sorry, Annabelle, I mean I really do need someone like you, but I don't think this is going to work out.'

'But you don't know what I'm going to say.'

Lilly smiled in what she hoped was a kindly way. 'Look, I'm sure you're hard working and that you have lots of excellent qualities if only I would give you a chance, but with the best will in the world I need a secretary who can at least type.'

Annabelle hung her head.

'I'm sorry,' said Lilly, 'it's nothing personal.'

The other woman buried her face in her hands and her shoulders began to heave.

'Oh please don't cry.' Lilly reached out. 'I'm sure you could go on a course or something.'

Annabelle let out a choking noise in her throat and rocked back and forth. Oh God, this was terrible. Lilly had to force herself not to relent and employ the woman. She bit her lip to stop herself.

At last, Annabelle let her hands drop and threw back her head. Her cheeks were puce and damp with tears. Lilly furrowed her brow. Annabelle wasn't weeping. She was laughing.

'Oh dear me.' Annabelle pressed her palms into her eye sockets. 'You think I want to work here.'

Lilly frowned in response which sent Annabelle into another volley of giggles.

'I'm sorry, but it's so funny,' said Annabelle.

'You haven't come for the job?' asked Lilly.

'No.'

'So what did you want?'

Annabelle fished a crumpled hanky from the depths of her pocket and blew her nose. 'Some legal advice, of course.'

'Oh shit.'

Jack balled a handful of tissues and aimed for the bin.

'Slam dunk,' he called out when they landed on target.

Alice gurgled in appreciation.

He aeroplaned around the now-clean kitchen, his daughter waving her chubby arms and legs.

'I used to be in the school basketball team.' Jack changed his voice to a vague imitation of Marlon Brando. 'I could have been a contender.'

He scooped Alice up from her high chair and swung her in the air. 'Now it's your turn, kiddo.'

She squealed, laughed, then burped as Jack pretended to line up his trajectory. He carried on pitching her high above his head until his mobile rang.

'McNally.' He slid his hiccupping baby back into her chair.

'Jack, it's the chief superintendent.'

Aye, aye, something was up.

'What can I do for you, sir?'

'I'm afraid there's been more gang violence. This time on the Hightown Estate.'

Jack wasn't surprised. The last six months had seen a rash of knife attacks on the bordering estates of Clayhill and Hightown.

'It's open warfare up there,' the chief muttered.

Jack grunted in response.

'The latest victim is a fifteen-year-old girl. Beaten, kicked, left for dead,' said the chief super. 'She's still unconscious.'

'Witnesses?'

'That's why I'm calling you, Jack. These kids won't talk to the police.'

'I hate to break it to you, sir, but I'm job myself.'

'Yes, but you have a way of gaining their trust, Jack.'

Jack wasn't convinced. 'These gangbangers are different to the kids I worked with in Child Protection. Another breed altogether.'

The chief super's voice became firmer. 'I'm getting a lot of heat about our success rate and the press are all over it.'

Jack sighed. This issue had been boiling for months but the top brass only got involved when the press and the politicians got themselves involved. Same old, same old.

'I'll come in later, sir, look at the file.'

'No time for that Jack. My secretary will text you the details and you can get cracking.'

Jack was about to explain that he really needed to read all the information but the chief super was in no mood for discussion.

'I'm putting you in charge of this investigation, Jack. Don't let me down.'

Then he hung up.

Penny Van Huysan greeted Lilly with a kiss on both cheeks. 'Hello, stranger.'

She smelled of Jo Malone cologne and lip balm. In the unfamiliar world of Manor Park with its talk of horseboxes and second homes in Tuscany, Penny was a much appreciated ally.

Not that Penny didn't belong to this world, she did. Her teeth gleamed and her hair shone. The understated handbag slung over her shoulder cost several thousand pounds. But she was kind and funny and real.

'How's business?' She linked arms with Lilly as they strolled from the car park to the quad where the pupils poured out in a river of green blazers.

Lilly groaned. 'I had another secretary walk out on me.'

'You're worse than Henry,' Penny laughed, 'and he's a complete bastard to work for.'

'It gets worse,' said Lilly. 'I made a client sit at the computer and ordered her to log on.'

'Why on earth would you do that?'

'I thought the agency had sent her,' said Lilly, still mortified by the misunderstanding. 'It turned out she was after legal advice for her foster daughter.'

'You need some help,' said Penny.

'No shit, Sherlock.'

Penny delved into the bag worth more than the GDP of most developing nations, and withdrew a leather-bound notebook. A slender silver pen was attached. If it had been Lilly's, the pen would have been lost within days, replaced by a chewed pencil.

'I met Carol at Pilates.' Penny scribbled down a number. 'A total godsend.'

'I need someone who can type, not bend me into impossible positions.'

Penny rolled her eyes. 'Carol is fantastic. Our paperwork has never been in such great shape.'

Lilly frowned as she imagined neat rows of taxi receipts and hotel bills from Henry Van Huysan's endless business trips to the Far East.

'For goodness sake, Lilly, why do you assume the worst in every situation?' asked Penny.

'I do not.'

Penny turned to her friend and pursed her lips.

'Okay, okay,' said Lilly. 'I accept I am not naturally an optimist.'

'Cassandra was cheerier than you, believe me.'

Lilly couldn't help but laugh.

'And I'm not even going to mention Jack,' said Penny.

'Then don't.'

As they waited for their children, Lilly counted in her head. One. Two. Three.

'All I will say is that he's a good man,' said Penny.

Lilly held up three fingers.

'And he's the father of your child.'

Lilly exhaled slowly. Penny was right. Jack was a good man.

'You two should be together,' said Penny.

'It's not that simple,' Lilly replied.

Penny waved at her son who, unlike Sam, was always one of the first day boys to leave. He bounded towards her, his braces glinting. Lilly squinted into the distance, searching for Sam. Why was he always last?

'Do yourself a favour, Lilly,' Penny put an arm around her son's shoulders, 'and don't make life so hard for yourself.'

Lilly had barely opened the cottage door when Sam pushed past her and headed upstairs mumbling about homework.

'Advanced PS3, I assume,' she called out.

He grunted and slammed his bedroom door. Lilly sighed. He'd given her the silent treatment on the journey home from school, declining to speak except to mention that he was quite capable of getting the bus. Being collected by his mother was 'totally embarrassing'. Lilly had pointed out that Penny still did the school run.

'Van Huysan is a complete loser,' said Sam. 'Everybody knows that.'

After that, she hadn't even bothered explaining for the six hundredth time that the bus was too expensive. Sam's dad paid the school fees but Lilly had to cover everything else, and since she was virtually passing Manor Park on her way home from work she wasn't about to cough up three quid a pop for his lordship to be taken home.

Instead, she'd flicked on the radio. The local news was full of the latest gang-related attack.

The police have confirmed that the victim was set upon by a group of assailants, which leaves the people of Luton asking when will something be done about these violent young people?

Sam had sneered at Lilly as if to say these were the kids she had always represented. Proud of yourself?

She had snapped off the programme, concentrated on the road ahead and wondered when would be the earliest she could allow herself a glass of wine.

Now, Lilly hung up her coat and went in search of Alice. She found her in the kitchen, asleep in Jack's arms.

'How's she been?'

'Grand,' he smiled.

Lilly flicked on the kettle while Jack kissed his daughter and hunted for his car keys.

'Coffee?' she asked.

Jack stopped in his tracks. Since Alice had been born they had developed a routine of one in one out. Any attempts by Jack to initiate more than civility had been rebuffed by Lilly and soon abandoned. He was welcome to spend as much time as he wanted with Alice, but Lilly made herself scarce.

'If you haven't got time,' Lilly didn't look at him, 'don't worry.'

He paused and Lilly felt the back of her neck redden.

'A coffee would be good.'

She reached into the cupboard and instinctively searched for Jack's usual mug in the shape of Gromit. Sam had given it to him as a present and the nose was supposed to light up on contact with hot liquid. It had only worked once and it now had a chip.

'So what are you up to at work?' She tried to keep her voice light.

'A GBH. The girl's still in the hospital,' he said. 'Looks like another gang thing.'

'I heard about that on the radio,' Lilly sighed. 'It's getting out of hand.'

'I know.'

She placed the drink in front of him and couldn't help notice him finger the now-defunct nose.

'You?' he asked.

'I took on a kid in foster care.'

Jack raised his eyebrows. 'I thought you weren't doing that work any more?'

'I'm not,' she said, 'but I felt obliged.'

He blew on his coffee and she knew exactly what he was thinking. So many of the other cases she'd taken on for kids in the care system had brought nothing but trouble. They took up too much time, and they were badly paid. Worse, they had placed Lilly in danger more than once.

She had sworn to Jack, Sam, and more importantly herself, that she was sticking to divorce work. Boring, yes, but safe.

'A quick guilty plea in the Youth Court for possession of class B,' she said. 'Ten minutes in and out.'

'If you're sure.'

'I am.'

A silence stretched between them until Jack smiled, drained his cup and stood. 'Best get up to A&E.'

She followed him to the door. He walked to his car and turned to her.

'I'm glad we were able to do that,' he said.

'Me too,' Lilly said. And she was.

She waited until he was sat in the driver's seat before stepping outside towards him.

'Jack,' she said. 'I don't want to fight any more.'

Demi would like to punch the policeman, with his lopsided smile and tatty leather jacket. He probably thinks his Converse make him down with the kids.

He's said all the usual stuff, like how sorry he is, and how he wants to catch whoever did this to Malaya. The same thing the police always say whenever Gran calls them about the boys on the estate smashing a window or nicking a car. Mostly, they don't even bother to come out.

'Has Malaya had any arguments recently?' he asks.

Gran tries to reply that she's a good girl, that she has lots of friends, but she's crying and her accent always gets thicker when she's stressed. Usually it embarrasses Demi if someone can't understand her, and she hisses a translation under her breath, but right now it's just making her angry at the policeman.

'Could you repeat that?' he says, and Demi balls both hands into fists.

Gran wipes her eyes. 'My granddaughter is not the type of girl to be fighting in the street, Officer.'

He nods but he's obviously unconvinced.

'What about you, Demi?' he locks eyes with her. 'Can you think of anyone who would want to hurt your sister?'

Demi stares back at him, refusing to blink. 'No.'

Eventually he looks back at Gran.

'Let's hope Malaya wakes up soon and she can tell us who did this to her,' he says.

Gran's face fills with hope. 'And then you will bring these terrible people to justice.'

The policeman smiles but promises nothing, and Demi can feel her nails digging into the palms of her hands until they draw blood.

Chapter Two

Lilly was late.

She was standing in the queue to pass through the metal detectors at Luton Youth Court, the two boys ahead of her refusing to put their mobiles on the conveyor belt.

One waved his Nokia under the guard's nose.

'If that machine wipes my contact list, I'm coming for you, man.'

The guard rolled his eyes and hitched up his belt.

'I'm gonna sue you for loss of business, you get me?' said the boy.

Lilly recognized him immediately. She'd represented him half a dozen times. Beneath the bravado was a brittle child slowly unravelling in the care system, making the inevitable descent into drugs and crime.

She tapped him on the shoulder. 'You might have all day, Jermaine, but some of us have to work for a living.'

His face lit up. 'What you doing here, Miss?'

Lilly opened her arms to encompass the bare brick walls, the stained carpet tiles and the crowds of young people pushing, swearing and ignoring the smoking ban.

'I fancied a day out.'

Jermaine laughed. 'Thought you said you weren't doing this work no more, Miss.'

'Just doing someone a small favour.'

Jermaine bounced back on his heels. 'How about doing me a small favour then, Miss? My brief is one useless mother. I swear I'm gonna end up inside.'

'No chance,' said Lilly. 'And if you don't get a move on I'll shove you in the cells myself.'

Jermaine kissed his teeth, but placed his mobile in a plastic tray and passed through into the court. Lilly followed suit, praying she didn't set anything off.

'Who you here for, Miss?' asked Jermaine.

Lilly fished in her jacket pocket and pulled out a scribbled note. 'Tanisha McKenzie.'

Both boys sucked in a breath and began dancing from foot to foot, flicking their wrists.

'I take it you know her,' said Lilly.

'Man,' Jermaine laughed, 'everybody knows Tanisha.'

Annabelle was waiting for Lilly by the vending machine. She was wearing the same orange waterproof and looked even more incongruous amidst the pandemonium of the Youth Court. Yet she seemed perfectly comfortable, her shoulders relaxed.

'Sorry I'm late,' said Lilly.

Annabelle shrugged and smiled. 'The lists are enormous. The usher says we won't get on before eleven.'

'You obviously know your way around,' said Lilly.

'When you foster teens this place is home from home.'

Lilly laughed. 'Where's Tanisha?'

Annabelle gestured towards a black girl sitting on the bench opposite, furiously texting on her phone.

Lilly could see where the boys' appreciation stemmed from. Tanisha was soft and curvaceous, wearing a skin-tight T-shirt declaring 'Holla if U want me'. Her banana-yellow baseball cap matched her enormous yellow hooped earrings, large enough to fit around a wrist.

Lilly took the seat next to her. 'Annabelle asked me to come here today to represent you.'

Tanisha looked up. Each eyelid was completely covered by turquoise shadow. Coupled with the yellow it ought to have looked horrific, but instead the effect was vibrant.

'Do you have any previous convictions?' Lilly asked.

'Some.'

'Such as?'

Tanisha shrugged. 'Threatening behaviour, common assault.'

'Is this the first time you've been done for drugs?'

'It was only a bit of weed.'

'It's still an offence, I'm afraid.'

Tanisha looked disgusted. 'When the police stop us they usually just keep it for themselves.'

Lilly didn't know whether to laugh or cry.

'I'll explain to the magistrates that you've had a tough time, but that you're settled in foster care now, trying to make a fresh start,' she said. 'Is that okay?'

'Whatever,' Tanisha yawned.

Back at the vending machine Annabelle looked apologetic.

'She does care, you know, she just doesn't know how to show it.'

Lilly nodded and put her hand on Annabelle's arm. 'It'll be fine.'

God, this place is a dump.

Jamie wanders through the Clayhill Estate. His mum always tells him not to look down his nose at 'those less fortunate' but it's hard sometimes.

He comes down here once a week and it never ceases to amaze him how many girls there are pushing buggies, the babies sucking on bottles of purple juice. Why are they here, circling like scraggy birds of prey?

Dump or not, it's better than Combined Cadet Force. At the beginning of each year everyone in the senior school has to sign up for community service. Most of the boarders went for the CCF and Jamie had followed without thinking. It turned out to be the worst mistake of his life. Being screamed at by some sergeant-major while you crawled on your belly in the mud was no fun at all. Jamie hadn't lasted the first term.

When his dad got his report he'd gone ballistic.

The worst cadet I have ever had the misfortune of meeting.

Talk about an over-reaction.

So Jamie had to sign up for the Duke of Spastic's Award Scheme instead. It's true that some of the leaders are complete tits but it isn't too bad. Not as bad as boot camp anyway.

The camping trips are always in boring places like Wales or Dartmoor, and there is never enough food, but every Tuesday morning he gets out of school to do some voluntary work.

Jamie has landed a spot in a Help the Aged in Luton. The old ladies that run it are pretty nice and once he's helped them lug boxes of smelly books from the back they usually let him go early, and he spends the rest of the morning mooching around.

He goes into the Spar and rifles through the latest magazines. Cheryl Cole has had a trim and Madonna has had a nose job. Yawn.

A girl appears next to him. 'All right.'

She pronounces it as if it were one great 'eye'. No Rs or a T. Mrs Rafferty, head of Speech and Drama, would have a fit: 'How we speak, and how we present ourselves say everything about us.'

What would she make of this girl in her camouflage parka with a furry hood, a gap between the ribbed edge and her tracksuit bottoms, where a roll of brown flesh peeps out?

Jamie's met her a few times now but doesn't know her name.

She flashes him a smile and she's got one of those diamonds stuck to her tooth. He's always wondered how they stay on. Why she doesn't swallow it when she's eating.

'You chasing, rich boy?'

He shakes his head. After the last time he's not touching that shit again.

'If you change your mind you know where to find me,' she says.

Jamie watches her walk away, her movements languid and lazy and he feels a little twitch in the pit of his stomach. Maybe he's being a bit hasty. The other night he took too much. Got greedy. If he takes it steady he should be fine. And Benjamin Hamilton-Hobbs is having a party on Friday night. A little taste would be just the thing.

As if she can read his mind, the girl turns with a sneaky smile and Jamie smiles back at her.

She shouts something to a boy on a mountain bike hovering in the doorway. He can't be more than twelve and he races off. Then she gestures for Jamie to follow her down the aisle where a woman in an apron is mopping up a pool of spilled milk. She looks up from her bucket and narrows her eyes, but the girl stares her down until she moves away.

The boy on the bike returns and skids to a halt in front of them, leaving a black rubber track mark on the newly cleaned floor.

The girl holds out her hand to Jamie. 'Twenty.'

Jamie fishes into his back pocket and pulls out a note. The girl snatches it and stuffs it inside her basketball boot. Then the boy pulls a wrap from his mouth and presses it into Jamie's palm. It's warm and wet.

'Catch you later,' says the girl and walks away, the boy on the bike idling by her side.

Jamie pushes the drugs deep into his pocket and rushes off to the bus stop, his heart pounding.

'Not a bad result,' said Lilly, as they filed out of the courtroom.

Tanisha yawned loudly without covering her mouth.

'I'll send you a letter confirming exactly what a supervision order entails,' said Lilly. 'But the reality is not a fat lot.'

Tanisha put her baseball cap back on, carefully arranging the peak. She pulled a small mirror out of her pocket and checked her reflection. 'What will happen to my grass?'

'Sorry?'

'The grass they arrested me for,' said Tanisha. 'What happens to it now?'

'I expect it gets destroyed.'

Tanisha let out a snort. 'More like it gets bagged up again and ends up back on the streets.'

The depth of her young client's cynicism was no doubt meant to make her seem tough, but it struck Lilly as painfully sad.

'Take care,' she said. 'And try to stay out of trouble.'

Tanisha didn't respond so Lilly smiled a goodbye to Annabelle and turned to leave. She needed to get back to the office and the pile of divorce petitions waiting to be drafted. If she picked up a sandwich on the way, she could work through the afternoon before she had to collect Alice from nursery.

She was mentally deciding between a BLT or a panini when she caught sight of Jack picking his way through the crowds towards her. Her stomach lurched and fear made her knees bend.

'Oh my God,' she called out. 'What's happened?'

Jack pursed his brow.

'Has something happened to Alice?' Lilly said.

'Not at all,' he replied.

Lilly tried to catch her breath and leaned heavily against him.

Jack put a strong arm around her shoulders and led her to the bench. He pressed her to sit down.

'I'm so sorry.' His arm was still in place. 'I should have realized you'd be worried.'

Lilly inhaled deeply.

'Oh God, this has nothing to do with Alice,' he said.

Lilly nodded, relief flooding her system. 'So what are you doing here?'

Jack cleared his throat and removed his arm. The moment of intimacy vanished.

'Business, I'm afraid,' he said, glancing at Tanisha who was now chatting with Jermaine, one hip jutting suggestively towards him. 'Social Services told me I'd find Tanisha McKenzie here,' he said. 'I need to have a wee chat with her about the girl in hospital.'

'She's my client,' said Lilly.

Jack exhaled slowly. 'Isn't it always the way with us?'

'So is this the sort of chat that involves coffee and a cake, or a full body search and a caution?' asked Lilly.

Jack's smile was relaxed. 'Just a few questions.'

Lilly sat up straight. Jack might be one of the most easygoing men she had ever met, but he was also a copper, and years of experience had taught Lilly that the laid-back approach was bullshit.

'What exactly do you want to ask Tanisha?'

Jack shrugged. 'Nothing specific. We think the injured girl was attacked by the South Side Massive and it's possible Tanisha knows something about it.'

The South Side were notorious. Lilly flicked a glance at Tanisha. The kid was bloody difficult but Lilly wouldn't have put her down as violent.

'What evidence have you got against her?'

'It's not like that,' said Jack. 'We just want to talk.'

No evidence then. This was a fishing expedition. Get Tanisha yapping and hope she would trip herself up.

'I don't think she'll agree,' said Lilly.

Jack opened his palms. 'We can do this the easy way or the hard way.'

'What?' Lilly narrowed her eyes. 'You'll arrest her even though you've got bugger all to go on?'

'A kid was almost kicked to death, Lilly. Who knows if she'll ever wake up or what state she'll be in when she does. You said it yourself last night, this gang stuff is getting out of hand.'

Lilly looked over at Tanisha who was laughing now, her head thrown back, white teeth showing. The kid was about to get caught in the middle of a shit storm.

'I'll get someone to represent her,' said Lilly.

Jack raised an eyebrow.

'I told you that I wasn't doing these cases any more and I'm not,' said Lilly.

The eyebrow rose higher.

'Listen, Doctor Spock, this was a tiny job at the Youth Court, nothing more,' she said. 'I'll make the call now.'

She couldn't be sure, but Lilly thought she saw the trace of a smile at the edges of Jack's mouth.

Demi frowns at the gas fire.

Gran only allows two bars. More than that and the key card runs out before pay day, plunging them into days without anything to cook on.

'Four bars may warm your feet,' says Gran, 'but not your soup.'

Demi wishes Gran were here now, lecturing and wagging her finger. She runs her thumbnail up and down the metal grille, as if she were strumming a guitar, and peers into the orange glow. She fancies some toast but there isn't any margarine left in the tub and Gran took the change from the dish in the kitchen to pay for a taxi back to the hospital.

Things didn't used to be this tight. Gran used to work in the café at the leisure centre. After school, Demi and Malaya would go down there and Gran would give them a hot chocolate. They'd wait for her while she finished wiping the tables and listen to her big laugh fill the room.

When her hip got bad and she couldn't do it any more, the manager gave her a big bunch of roses and everyone signed a card. Demi remembers Gran crying that night as she filled out some benefit forms.

'Never forget this day, girls,' she waved the papers at her granddaughters. 'Whenever you are tempted to stop listening to your teachers, think about this day.'

Demi sighs. Gran thinks the answer to everyone's prayers is 'a good education'. She never gets tired of telling them that back home school isn't free, and that kids will walk miles without any shoes for a single lesson. Demi imagines their bright smiling faces and blistered feet.

The trouble is Demi just isn't cut out for the whole school thing. Maybe the books are different in Nigeria, but here in England the letters jump around the page like black flies. No matter how hard she concentrates, the words don't make sense.

She used to dread the Friday spelling tests, fear solidifying in her stomach on her way to Miss Wilson's classroom. The humiliation when the marks came back. Two out of ten. Must try harder. She started to make excuses. A headache. A sore throat. She hasn't sat a test all term. No one seems to have noticed.

Demi's knees are so close to the fire they're smarting. But she doesn't move away. Instead she rubs the hot skin with the heel of her hand. She supposes she should get washed and head off for school. She might get there in time for lunch if she hurries.

Gran will be furious if she finds out Demi has sat at home all morning.

She stretches her limbs like a cat. Just a few more minutes.

Lilly tracked down Annabelle who was waiting patiently outside for her charge. Her cheeks were pink from the cold. As soon as she saw Lilly's expression the muscles of Annabelle's cheeks tightened.

'Everything okay?'

Lilly shook her head. 'The police need to interview Tanisha about an assault.'

'On who?'

'I don't know the girl's name, but she's in a very bad condition. If you could tell Tanisha what's happening I'll call someone I know to go to the station with you,' said Lilly, pulling out her mobile.

Before Lilly could punch in the number of a colleague at a nearby law firm, Annabelle had placed a hand on Lilly's wrist. Her grasp was surprisingly firm.

'I'd prefer it if you could come.'

Lilly nodded her understanding. She realized that was what Annabelle would want, but there was no way she could do it.

'I'm sorry,' she said. 'This sounds like it's pretty serious. You need someone who can devote the time to it and I'm completely snowed under at the moment.'

Annabelle didn't remove her hold. 'I asked around. Everyone told me you were the best person to help Tanisha. That's why I came to you.'

Lilly looked down at Annabelle's fingers, their grip was beginning to make her uncomfortable.

'The guy I'm about to call is excellent, and right now he has more resources than I do.'

Annabelle's grasp tightened until it hurt.

'I'm sorry,' said Lilly, 'but I can't help you.'

Annabelle's hand slid to her side, lifeless, and she turned away. Lilly rubbed the bracelet of red welts beginning to appear.

'Tanisha has no one to help her.' Annabelle spoke into the distance. 'Her mother's in prison and she's never known her father.'

Lilly felt her heart sink in her chest. She'd met lots of kids like Tanisha. Life was very cruel to them. It never ended well.

'She has you,' said Lilly.

Annabelle smiled politely. 'I'm not a lawyer, and you know as well as I do that if the police get their teeth into her, she's going to need more than a warm bed for the night.'

Lilly did know. Jack could dress it up however he wanted but she could smell pressure like smoke in the air. The establishment needed an arrest and by hook or by crook they would get one. A child like Tanisha was a gift. A mouthy, obnoxious, completely vulnerable gift.

'My colleague really will do a good job,' Lilly confirmed, as much for her own benefit as Annabelle's.

She thought of the waiting paperwork, the fact that she didn't have any help. Then there was Sam, almost a stranger to her. She desperately needed to spend time with him, break down his defences. And Alice, of course. The baby who never slept, the baby who needed bathing and changing and feeding. The baby who needed two parents. How were Lilly and Jack ever going to work things out if they were on opposite sides of a case like this one? Right now, they certainly didn't need anything extra to argue about.

'I understand,' said Annabelle, but she didn't. How could she? 'Let's go back and tell Tanisha.'

They trooped back through court where Tanisha was still flirting with Jermaine. They were listening to a track on his iPod, Tanisha grinding her backside against his groin. When she saw Annabelle and Lilly she scowled.

'What?'

'The police want to speak to you,' said Annabelle.

'I don't want to speak to them.'

Jermaine laughed and rested his chin on her shoulder. Tanisha stroked his cheek, her false nails improbably square, the tips gold. A gangsta French manicure.

'No choice, I'm afraid,' said Annabelle.

Tanisha kissed her teeth in disgust. 'What they say I done this time?'

Annabelle glanced at Lilly.

'A girl was attacked in Hightown by the South Side,' said Lilly. 'They want to know if you were involved.'

Tanisha's face dropped. 'I ain't done nothing.'

'Then you need to explain that,' said Lilly.

'What if I refuse?'

'They'll arrest you,' Lilly shrugged. 'Take you down the nick in a van. This is a serious offence and they're not going to play games.'

Tanisha's hands flew from Jermaine's face and wrapped around herself in protection.

'You can't let them do that.' The anger was gone from her voice.

'I don't think I can stop them.'

Tanisha's eyes pleaded with Lilly and then Annabelle. She shook her head in a quiet desperation.

'It'll be okay, Tanisha,' said Lilly.

Tanisha's mouth slackened. For all the make-up and grand-standing it was easy to see now that she was fifteen.

'Will they call Social Services?'

'I expect they'll inform your social worker,' said Lilly. 'Frankly, that's the least of your worries, Tanisha.'

The girl's eyes glittered with tears and she hugged her stomach tightly.

'No,' said Annabelle, 'that's Tanisha's biggest worry.'

Lilly frowned. 'How?'

Annabelle put an arm around Tanisha's shoulder. 'Are you going to tell her or shall I?'

Tears fell down Tanisha's cheeks in bright blue rivulets and stained Annabelle's waterproof.

'I'm pregnant,' she said.

The chief super set a cup in front of Jack. It was white china with a handle so small Jack could barely fit his finger into it. He rattled it against the saucer before giving up.

'We need a result on this one, Jack.'

'I'm doing everything I can,' he replied.

The chief super took a seat at the other side of his desk. On the wall behind him was a large photograph of the chief shaking hands with the new prime minister. They beamed at one another like children who had won all the prizes on sports day.

'These gangs have to be stopped,' said the chief super. 'And it starts here.'

Jack watched his boss cock his little finger as he brought his tea to his lips. He was tempted to mention that nobody had seemed to care very much up to now. He'd even heard rumblings in the canteen that if a bunch of blacks wanted to kill one another then why not just let 'em.

'So where are we with the investigation?' asked the chief super.

'It looks like the victim was on a jump in,' said Jack.

The chief super frowned.

'An initiation,' Jack explained. 'She was supposed to sneak into the turf of an enemy gang and spray-paint a mural.'

'How do we know all this?'

'Her hands were covered in the stuff,' said Jack, 'and we found her handiwork, less than five hundred metres from the scene. We can only assume she got caught.'

'Do we know who is in this rival gang?'

Jack shrugged. 'We've one or two names. Got one girl in the nick now, sir.'

'Any evidence to connect her to this crime?'

'Not yet,' said Jack. 'I've got uniform going through all the CCTV footage in the area and forensics going over the victim's clothes with a fine-tooth comb.'

'Door to door?'

Jack nodded. 'I've two officers over there now, checking if anyone saw anything.'

'Not a lot of point to that is there?'

'Not really,' Jack agreed. 'But we can't be seen to be doing nothing.'

The chief super smiled at him and Jack realized he had crossed the line. He was now one of them. He'd earned his stripes the hard way. A couple of murders, a kidnapping.

At last, it seemed, he was being taken seriously.

'You'll interview her yourself?' asked the chief super.

'Of course.'

'Very good. Let me know if you need anything else.'

Jack stood tall. 'I will, sir.'

The custody sergeant's lip curled at the man slumped in front of his desk.

'I can't help you out here, Terry,' he said.

The man's emaciated body curled in on itself. 'Please, Sarge.'

The custody sergeant shook his head and looked down at his paperwork.

'Just bail me till tomorrow,' the man whined. 'I'll be at court first thing in the morning.'

He leaned against the desk, his breath coming in rasps, scratched raw by years of smoking crack. Lilly watched him in pity. His face was gaunt, his cheeks sunk into the gaps where his back teeth had long since fallen out. It was impossible to even guess his age.

'You know I won't skip,' he begged.

The sergeant tapped his biro against an A4 pad and even that slight sound seemed to pass right through the prisoner, making him shudder. Without any gear he was in for a very hard night in the cells.

'I'll get someone to bring you a cup of tea.' The sergeant gestured to another policeman to take the man away.

As he was half carried, half dragged away, he began to sob. Lilly looked away and tried not to wonder if he had a mother who had loved her little boy, who used to hang his pictures on her kitchen wall. Did she jump every time the phone rang, wondering if he'd been arrested? Or worse?

The sergeant clapped his hands together, snapping Lilly from her thoughts.

'What are we doing here today?' he asked.

His brisk tone sprang Lilly to her feet.

'I'm Lilly Valentine,' she placed a card at his fingertips, 'and this is my client, Tanisha McKenzie.'

The sergeant nodded and ran a finger around the edge of the white card, allowing the sharp corner to dig into the flesh.

'We're here voluntarily to answer some questions,' Lilly said.

The sergeant began transcribing Lilly's details on to a form.

'My client is not under arrest,' she added unnecessarily.

'Officer in the case?'

Lilly coughed uncomfortably. She and Jack had attempted to keep their personal life just that, but there were some coppers who knew their story.

'Detective McNally,' she said.

Lilly thought she saw the sergeant's mouth twitch but ordered herself to stop being paranoid. She was a professional and so was Jack. There was nothing untoward about what she was doing. So why then was she dreading the very sight of him?

The sergeant punched a button on his phone. 'Jack? It's custody here. We've got a kid called McKenzie to see you. She's with her brief.'

Lilly felt a sliver of relief that he hadn't mentioned her name. Then again, it merely delayed the inevitable by moments. When Jack entered the custody area she felt her heart pound and she tried to melt into the wall behind her. At last, he was standing right in front of her and she had no alternative than to look at him. His face was utterly impassive.

When he didn't speak, Lilly was forced to. 'Could you tell me exactly what evidence you have in this matter and what you want to ask my client?'

'Of course.' Jack's tone was even.

He stretched an open palm towards the corridor and led Lilly into a side room.

'What the hell are you doing here?' he hissed.

'Tanisha needs representation,' Lilly answered.

'You said you were calling someone you knew.'

Lilly stood taller. 'My client was unhappy with that course of action.'

'Your client was unhappy . . .'

Jack turned away and ran his hand through his hair. He walked to the other end of the room and pressed his forehead against the wall. He took an audible breath and remained in the same position for what seemed like an eternity. Lilly didn't dare speak.

At last Jack faced her. His expression said it all. How can you possibly do this? Why would you possibly do this?

'Tanisha is very vulnerable,' Lilly whispered. 'She needs me.'

Jack looked deep into Lilly's eyes as if he were trying to find the answers to a thousand questions. He seemed bruised purple by her decision. For a moment she thought he might weep. Instead he blinked hard and looked away.

'Malaya Ebola,' he said.

'What?'

'The victim's name is Malaya Ebola. She was dragged to the ground by a gang of attackers and kicked until she was unconscious.'

Lilly swallowed hard.

'She has a fractured skull, a shattered pelvis and broken ribs,' said Jack. 'She's lucky to be alive.'

Tanisha unwrapped a piece of Hubba Bubba and slid it into her mouth. As she chewed, the air filled with the chemical scent of artificial strawberries.

Lilly watched her client's jaw move up and down seamlessly, and listened to the wet smack of her lips.

Conversely, Annabelle was pinched and nervous, her eyes darting between Lilly and Tanisha.

Lilly dragged a chair across the room and settled directly in front of her client.

'Do you know Malaya Ebola?' she asked.

Tanisha shrugged. 'I seen her around.'

'Are you friends?'

Tanisha snorted her answer. 'No, we ain't friends.'

'Did you assault Malaya Ebola?' Lilly asked.

Tanisha pushed her tongue through the wad of gum, the iridescent pink clashing against the riotous yellow of her earrings. She blew into the gum, making a perfect balloon which she popped with the sharp edge of her nail.

'Nah,' she said.

'Do you know who might have assaulted Malaya Ebola?'

'Could be anyone, innit?' said Tanisha. 'Hightown and Clayhill, them bad places.'

'The police think the attack was part of a long-standing rivalry between two gangs,' said Lilly.

Tanisha didn't answer, just sat back in her seat and chewed.

'Do you think it had anything to do with gangs?' Lilly asked.

Tanisha sighed, weary of those who clearly didn't understand the rules of the street.

'Like I say, Clayhill is a bad place, sisters gotta protect themselves.'

'By kicking someone until they're in a coma?'

Tanisha didn't miss a beat but pulled up her T-shirt to reveal the smooth, caramel flesh of her belly. A livid scar ran from her hip to the edge of her breast bone. Annabelle gasped but Tanisha continued to glare at Lilly.

'Here's where I got jumped for my phone when I was twelve.'

Lilly felt her mouth make the shape of an 'o'.

'Twenty-two stitches,' Tanisha said.

When she was satisfied with Lilly's reaction, Tanisha pulled down her top.

'It ain't easy out there, so we do what it takes to survive. I been looking after myself since I was six years old, you get me.'

'I know that,' Lilly could taste the metal tang of horror, 'but I need to know if you had anything to do with hurting Malaya Ebola.'

'I didn't touch her,' said Tanisha.

As they entered the interview room, Jack was still reeling. Not so much from the fact that Lilly had chosen to take this case knowing full well how difficult that would make things between them, but that her actions, even now, could shock him.

Throughout all the years he'd known her, she would never take the path of least resistance. And it was this lack of self-protection that had drawn him to her. She was the real deal.

But Lilly's refusal to avoid difficult situations didn't just affect her did it? She didn't stagger from one car crash to another in isolation. There was Sam, there was Jack, and now there was Alice to consider.

Mary, Mother of God, why couldn't the woman just act like everyone else?

He sighed as he took in the scene. His answer was in the question. Every other solicitor he had ever met sat opposite their clients, separated both physically and emotionally by their desk and papers. Reluctantly, they moved next to their clients when the interview began. Not a second beforehand. Not Lilly. She had placed herself inches from Tanisha, their knees almost touching, their eyes locked. Neither looked up at him.

'I'm going to record our discussion, Tanisha, so we both know exactly what's been said today,' he told her.

Wordlessly, Lilly rearranged the chairs so that Tanisha was flanked by her solicitor and foster-parent.

'This is the video camera.' Jack flicked it on.

Tanisha shrugged and chewed a mouthful of gum. It made a rhythmic clack that reminded Jack of the heart monitor attached to Malaya Ebola.

'Before we get started I'm going to read you the caution,' said Jack.

Lilly leaned forward. Jack could smell the perfume he'd bought for her last Christmas.

'This is supposed to be an informal chat,' she said. 'My client isn't under arrest.'

'That's true, but I'd rather Tanisha understand the implications of what she says today,' Jack replied. 'It's imperative that she tells the truth.'

Lilly turned to Tanisha and gave a whispered explanation as to what the caution meant, as if the kid hadn't heard it a hundred times before. Jack fingered Tanisha's rap sheet. She had almost as much experience as he did.

At last Lilly agreed to continue and Jack read out the caution.

Tanisha pulled at her gum with finger and thumb, drawing it into a ten-inch string, before stuffing it back in.

'Tell me about the South Side Massive,' said Jack.

'What?' Tanisha sneered at him.

'What do you know about the gang who call themselves the South Side Massive?'

Lilly held up her hand. 'Stop right there. Tanisha came here today to answer specific questions about an assault on *another* teenager.'

'I think it would be helpful to put that assault into context,' he replied calmly.

'Then by all means you should do that,' she said. 'Then ask your specific questions.'

He held her gaze. They both knew that this was going to get very sticky. Of course, Lilly refused to look away.

'All right,' he said. 'It's pretty common knowledge around the estates that one of the crews there is called South Side. It's also pretty common knowledge that you're a member.'

'Are you asking or telling?' said Lilly.

'I'm putting the assault in context,' Jack replied.

'And now you've done that, do you have a question for my client?'

Jack took a deep breath and reminded himself that all defence briefs were this spiky. It was just their job. Only last week some newly qualified solicitor had threatened to report him to the Police Complaints Authority. Water off a duck's back. Jack had personally given the number to the little tosser.

So why did it sting when the lawyer was Lilly?

'Okay, here's a question your client might feel able to answer. On Monday night was Tanisha with any members of the South Side Massive?'

'It might assist if you could be more specific,' said Lilly. 'Name the people you have in mind.'

Jack smoothed his tie. He didn't have all their names. 'How about if Tanisha tells me who she was with on Monday night.'

'Can't remember.' Tanisha shrugged.

'Come on, Tanisha,' Jack laughed. 'It wasn't long ago.'

Tanisha kissed her teeth. 'I hang out with a lot of people, I can't say exactly who was around and who wasn't, can I?'

'Fair enough,' Jack's eyes flicked to the camera, 'but can you tell me at least, where you *hung out*?'

Tanisha glared at him without blinking. Jack forced a smile.

'Did you go to a friend's house?' he suggested. 'Maybe you did your homework together?'

Tanisha still didn't take her eyes off him. 'Like I said, we hung out.'

Jack tipped his centre of gravity forward, ever so slightly, reducing the space between them. He let another minute of silence roll by, let the camera record it all.

'And did any of this *hanging out* take place in Hightown?'

Tanisha reached deep into the front pocket of her jeans and extracted a tissue. Slowly and deliberately she spat out her gum.

'I don't live there no more, do I?' she said.

'So you weren't there at all?'

'No.'

Jack knew that another copper wouldn't be able to suppress a smile, but all he could feel was overriding sadness as he turned off the camera.

The potato is so hard and cold, the butter won't even melt into it. Demi presses it into the flesh with her fork but it just sits there, in yellow, oily smears.

It said on the menu 'baked potato' but the thing on Demi's plate feels like it made friends with a microwave for a couple of minutes at the most. If she had a phone she'd take a photo of it and send it to one of those consumer programmes her gran loves. Demi hates the food in the school cafeteria. The only thing going for it is that it's free.

She abandons her main course and picks up her pot of jelly. It hasn't set properly and slips over the side of her spoon on to the table.

'Clean that up, you dirty bitch.'

The noise in the room is deafening, but Demi knows who is shouting at her. She carries on with her pudding, letting the cool gelatine slide down her throat.

'You wipe that up before I make you eat it.'

Demi doesn't look up. She knows Georgia Moore will be at the end of the table, sandwiched between the two cronies who laugh at every pathetic joke she makes.

'I know where you come from it don't matter,' Georgia shouts, 'but this is England and we don't put up with filth.'

Demi feels the heat at the back of her neck and stacks everything on her tray. She wipes up the tiny blob of jelly with a paper napkin and heads out into the playground. On good days Georgia gets bored and finds someone else to torture. But not today. She keeps step behind Demi, her cling-ons just behind.

'I saw on the telly that people in Nigeria don't use proper toilets,' Georgia laughs, 'that they just crap in the street.'

Demi hears the sniggering all around her as other pupils catch on to the fact that the Georgia Moore show is in full swing. A group of boys interrupt their football game to see what the fuss is about.

'Imagine the stink.' Georgia is enjoying the attention now. 'All that shit just sitting on the roadside.'

The audience hoots in appreciation and Demi imagines that this is what it must feel like to be on *The X Factor* and have Simon Cowell lay into you on national telly. She speeds up towards the gate.

'I don't know about you lot, but I can smell Demi Ebola from here,' Georgia shouts.

Unable to bear another second, Demi sprints into the street. Leaving school premises at lunchtime is strictly against the rules but Demi doesn't care. She needs to get away.

Outside, she takes a sharp left, her feet pounding on the pavement, but she can hear panting behind her. They're right on her tail. But she's had practice. Plenty of practice. If she can make it to the end of the road, she can lose them. If she can just keep going. Her heart hammers in her chest, but she can't slow down.

She can see the junction. She *can* make it.

Without warning, a white transit van backs out from a side street, blocking Demi's path. If she doesn't stop she will crash into its metal side. She screeches to a halt. For a split second she hesitates. Too late. That moment is all it takes and Georgia and her comrades are upon her.

Demi feels a hand grab a fistful of her hair and spin her around. She gasps as it tears away from the roots.

Georgia leers into her face. 'You're not just minging. You're completely stupid.'

Demi feels the tears well in her eyes. They're hot and they sting. She tries to blink them back.

'Leave me alone.'

'Leave me alone,' Georgia mimics.

The other girls laugh and crowd into her, Demi can feel their pizza breath on her face. Her arm is bent behind her back and the pain makes her wince. Once upon a time, she might have hoped a passer-by would intervene, today she knows that won't happen. A mother, out shopping with her toddler, crosses to the other side.

'You've put us to a lot of trouble, Demi,' says Georgia. 'What are you going to do about it?'

Demi squeezes her eyes shut. They stole her phone weeks ago and she doesn't have a penny on her.

Georgia yanks at Demi's hair, ripping it from its roots. Demi bites her bottom lip. Whatever they do to her she refuses to give them the pleasure of seeing her crumble. She waits for the hot slap of a hand against her cheek, or the kick of a heel in her shins.

'Is there a problem here, Demi?'

Demi's eyes shoot open to find Chika standing less than a foot away, some of her friends behind her.

She lifts a chin at Demi. 'Everything all right?'

Chika's shoulders are relaxed and she bobs from foot to foot in a casual dance. Her friends lounge against one another. Yet something in their stance makes Georgia loosen her grip on Demi's hair.

'This ain't your business,' says Georgia, but something in her tone is unsure.

Chika checks her friends and they all laugh as if Georgia has just told the funniest joke.

'You don't get to tell me what is and what ain't my business.'

Chika's body is still loose, but she takes a step towards them.

'I don't see why you care.' Georgia is pretending to hold her ground, but Demi can hear the trace of fear in her voice. 'She ain't nobody to you.'

Chika takes another step so that she's now face to face with Georgia. The two cronies melt into the background.

'Just so you know, this girl's sister is my bredren,' Chika squares up to Georgia, 'which makes her family, you get me?'

The other girls call out their agreement.

'And when someone is beating up on a member of my family, that vexes me.'

Georgia releases Demi. 'Fine. Whatever.'

She tries to move away but Chika is blocking her. She has to physically push past, clearly frightened that Chika might hurt her.

Chika doesn't move until Georgia is touching her, then she opens her mouth, bares her teeth and hisses like an angry cobra.

Georgia lets out a squeak and runs away.

'Stay in touch,' Chika shouts, as Georgia reaches the other side of the road and hurries back in the direction of school.

Everyone is in fits of laughter when she finally disappears, and Chika puts an arm around Demi's shoulders.

'You on your way to visit Malaya?'

'Yes,' she says, though that hadn't been her immediate plan.

'We'll come with you,' says Chika.

'Can we eat first?' a girl with waist-length braids grumbles. 'I'm starving.'

Chika turns to Demi, her arm still heavy and protective. 'You okay with that?'

Demi tries not to smile. It's been a long time since anyone cared what she thinks about anything.

She nods and allows herself to be steered into a fried chicken place. On a sticky chair, stuffing her face with chips and ketchup, listening to the girls shout at the owners and laugh into their mobiles, Demi notices how warm it is inside.

The black granite kitchen surface was cold to the touch. Lilly ran her finger along it, feeling the pleasing smoothness. It ran the entire length of Annabelle's kitchen, punctuated only by a deep butler sink, and there wasn't a single crumb or drop of water on it.

'Is that an end to this business, now?' Annabelle loaded a tray with teapot, cups and milk in a jug.

Lilly see-sawed her hand. Something about Jack's questioning bothered her. Not so much what he'd asked, but what he hadn't.

Annabelle carried the tray to an enormous oak table that could easily seat ten, and began to pour the tea.

'They didn't seem to have any evidence against Tanisha at all.' Annabelle's tone was bright.

Lilly didn't want to worry her so she took a seat next to Annabelle. 'You've got quite a place here.'

Lilly had expected a modest semi, or a cottage like her own. She'd pictured knick-knacks and wellies by the door. In fact, Annabelle's home was palatial. An enormous old rectory, set in acres of woodland. Through the kitchen window, Lilly had spotted an outdoor swimming pool and a tennis court beyond.

'It's a touch too big for my needs,' said Annabelle.

Lilly nearly spat out her tea. There had to be at least eight bedrooms in a place this size. The triple garages outside could have housed a small family.

'Is that why you foster?' Lilly asked.

'No,' Annabelle said, but offered no further explanation.

They sipped tea in silence until Tanisha breezed in. She was barefoot, her toes painted the same gold as her fingers, and she was wearing earphones, listening to an iPod.

'Can I get something to eat?' She spoke too loudly.

Annabelle smiled and got up from the table. She opened an American-style fridge and pointed to a shelf of smoothies and yoghurts.

Tanisha wrinkled her nose so Annabelle gestured to a wooden bowl, overflowing with fresh fruit.

'Can't I have some crisps?' Tanisha shouted.

Annabelle leaned forward and removed one of the ear plugs. 'You need to take care of yourself.'

'But I don't like all that shit,' said Tanisha.

'You need to take care of the baby,' said Annabelle, pressing a palm on Tanisha's stomach.

Tanisha rolled her eyes but reached for an apple. 'They're hard to chew.'

'Cut it up,' Annabelle laughed.

Tanisha grabbed a knife from a block and hacked the apple into four pieces before replacing the ear plug and dancing out of the kitchen.

'She's a great kid,' said Annabelle. 'She's had to cope with a lot of problems in her life.'

Lilly thought about the girl lying in the coma, and the look in Jack's eye as he had turned off the video camera. She had a dreadful feeling that Tanisha's problem's were about to get a whole lot worse.

Chapter Three

The thing about parents is that they don't remember what it was like to be young.

They start sentences with the words, 'when I was your age', then go on about how really great they were.

'When I was your age, I ate whatever was put in front of me.'

'When I was your age, I wouldn't have dared to argue with my father.'

They don't have any idea about how things are today, and they certainly don't ask.

Then again, maybe they do. Maybe other kids' parents actually listen. Maybe they all sit and eat together (having taken the trouble to find out what their kids like) and chat.

But Jamie's parents don't do anything like that. They work. They read the Sunday papers. They go out to restaurants. If Jamie were ever to dare mention that he might have a problem, Dad would frown over his half-moon glasses.

'What on earth can a chap of your age have to worry about? These are the best years of your life and don't you forget it.'

Anyway, Jamie aims for minimum contact with his dad. Most of the time he's at school, so it's easy, but even during the holidays he stays in his room a lot of the time.

Mum's better. Well a bit, anyway. She usually calls him on Friday mornings from the train. They don't have much to say to one another, but it's a habit neither of them can break.

The dorm is a pit as usual, with clothes spilled over the floor. Jamie rummages through the piles until he finds his trousers. They're crumpled and dirty but he doesn't care and pulls them on, dragging the waistband low on his hips. Then he reaches over to his bedside table, plunges his fingers into a pot of wax and pushes a handful through his fringe.

'Waiting for Mummy to call?' shouts Tristan from the bed next to Jamie's. 'So sweet.'

Jamie flips him the finger and pulls out his phone.

Rule one in boarding school is never, ever show your feelings. You will be teased mercilessly by your housemates, but if you express the tiniest of feelings, it will get worse.

He heads down to the dining room, grabs a tray and helps himself to bacon and toast. A lot of the kids here moan about the food, but Mum only ever opens packets from Marks and Spencer so Jamie hardly feels deprived.

A communal jug of orange juice is in the middle of a table. Jamie pours himself a glass and takes a seat at the furthest end of the hall. When the mobile rings he answers immediately and faces the wall. Phone calls are only allowed in the evenings after prep and if any of the masters catch him he'll get a detention.

'Jamie?' Mum asks.

Honestly. Who else is she expecting?

'Hi Mum.'

'Is everything okay?' she asks.

Jamie wonders what she'd do if he told her the truth.

'I'm fine, Mum.'

He can hear the sound of train wheels on the track. The countryside whooshing by as Mum heads into London. He wishes it were him, escaping into the city.

'Exeat this weekend,' she says brightly. 'Any plans?'

'Ben is having a party on Friday night,' Jamie says. 'I told you last week.'

'I remember now.' Mum has clearly forgotten. 'What time will you be back?'

'I'll probably stay over at his place,' Jamie shrugs.

'No rugby match on Saturday?'

Jamie sighs. He's never been picked for the rugby team. Ever.

'Have you got everything you need?' Mum asks.

Jamie pats his back pocket. He has the only thing he needs.

'Have fun,' says Mum. 'I expect you'll be fighting off the girls.'

Jamie rolls his eyes and wonders how she can be so stupid.

'Clever girl,' Lilly smiled at the empty bottle Alice had just polished off.

'Now let's put you down here while Mummy gets ready for work.'

Lilly pressed the baby across her chest, patting her back in a soothing rhythm and moved slowly across the bedroom floor. She hummed softly, a song she remembered her own mother singing, and one Sam had always loved.

When she reached the cot, Alice stiffened, her fat little legs as rigid as metal poles and Lilly told herself to remain calm. Alice hated her cot and bedtimes were often dramatic affairs with the sort of screaming that would put any banshee to shame.

Every parenting manual in the bookshop sat in a pile by Lilly's bed. There was nothing Gina Ford or Supernanny advised that Lilly hadn't tried. Be firm. Keep lighting low. Sprinkle lavender oil on the sheets. None of it worked and as soon as Alice felt herself being lowered into her cot, she would crank up for action.

'It's not bedtime, sweetheart,' Lilly sang out. 'You just need to lie here while Mummy has something to eat and a shower.'

Lilly reached out with one hand to start the mobile toy attached to the side of the cot. It had been a present from Penny and had no doubt cost a fortune.

'She can't be held twenty-four hours a day,' Penny had chided. 'She needs to know who's boss.'

Three pink bunnies began a gentle circle to the tune of 'Oranges and Lemons'. Alice turned her neck to the tinkling sound and smiled.

While she was distracted, Lilly seized her chance and lay Alice down. Alice was mesmerized, seemingly unaware where she was. Lilly touched her cheek then silently began to back out of the room. When Alice let out a murmur, Lilly froze, but it was nothing more than appreciation for the music. Lilly could picture the look of satisfaction on Penny's face when she told her.

Once out of the door and on the landing, Lilly breathed a sigh of relief and crept downstairs to grab a drink. Sam was in the kitchen, cleaning his rugby boots in the sink with a knife. He prised away each clod of earth around the stud and flicked it towards the plug hole. He watched Lilly open the fridge and take out the milk.

'Aren't you missing something?' he asked.

'Yes,' said Lilly. 'A glass.'

'A very small person with curly hair.'

Lilly poured herself a drink and took a sip. 'Alice is lying quietly in her cot.'

Sam laughed. 'Did you drug her?'

'Very funny.' Lilly poked out her tongue. 'I simply told her who was boss.'

Sam snorted and went back to his boots.

'Is Dad coming over for you?' Lilly asked.

Sam nodded. On Friday mornings her ex-husband, David, would take Sam to school and collect him afterwards. They spent the night at his place, watching a movie, and on Saturday mornings they would go together to Sam's school rugby matches. Lilly was certain that this arrangement didn't please David's girlfriend, Cara, but watching their son being pummelled into the mud by boys twice his size seemed to bring out the man in David, who had stood his ground.

On cue, the doorbell rang.

'Get it quick before Alice hears,' Lilly shrieked.

Sam held up his dirty hands like a surgeon waiting to be gloved. He looked around him as if in a strange place.

The doorbell went again so Lilly flung down her milk and raced to the door, vaulting the recycling. As she threw it open David's finger was poised over the bell to try again.

'No,' Lilly hissed and batted his hand away.

'Ouch,' David complained.

'Alice is in her cot,' Lilly whispered, 'and if you disturb her I'll have to kill you.'

David gave her the same smile that had won her over all those years ago in university. She had thought him an arse. Another public-schoolboy with a sense of entitlement almost as big as his ambition. He'd made a joke about her accent in a Latin tutorial and she'd considered punching him. Then she caught the twinkle in his eye and couldn't help laughing.

He followed her through the cottage. 'Is Jack here?'

'You know full well that Jack and I aren't together.'

'But he's here a lot,' David opened his arms, 'and you do change your mind like a stripper's knickers.'

The urge to punch him returned, but before Lilly could connect, David slipped past her and clapped Sam on the back.

'We're going to thrash Oak Hill tomorrow,' he said.

'We?' Lilly asked. 'I thought it was just Sam getting a pasting.'

David leant in to Sam and stage whispered. 'Women will never understand the importance of sport, son.'

'But we do understand the importance of staying alive,' Lilly retorted.

Father and son stood side by side and sighed at her.

'Why don't you get your sleepover bag, Sam,' she suggested, and flicked on the kettle. 'Tea?'

'Thanks.' David smiled.

He accepted a cup and took an appreciative gulp.

'Cara still got you on the wagon?' Lilly asked.

David curled his top lip. He was regularly forced into his girlfriend's latest health craze and had previously suffered a macrobiotic diet, daily skin brushing and Ashtanga yoga to name but three. Her latest fad was a ban on caffeine.

'Apparently taking the pledge reduces your chance of cancer, heart disease and strokes,' he said.

Lilly raised her glass of milk. 'Here's to living for ever.'

David groaned and drained his tea.

'Before we leave I need to give you this,' he pulled a letter from his pocket and handed it to Lilly.

She spotted Manor Park's school crest on the headed note paper immediately and skimmed the first paragraph.

Thank you for your enquiry about boarding facilities at Manor Park School.

We are pleased to confirm that there is currently a place in Seymour House . . .

'Don't even go there.' She held the letter between her thumb and forefinger as if it had been dropped in a puddle.

'I went boarding when I was younger than Sam.'

'And look how you turned out.'

David ignored the crack. 'It would make perfect sense now you have Alice and the new office. It can't be easy.'

Of course it wasn't bloody easy. The house was a shambles, the office work was out of control and she didn't even want to consider the new case she'd just taken on. But the solution did not lie in Sam living at school.

'Is everything okay?' Sam poked his head through the door.

'Everything's fine,' said Lilly and helped herself to another glass of milk.

David held out his car keys. 'Put your stuff in the boot, Sam, I'll be out in a second.'

Sam took the keys and sloped away.

'It's only twenty minutes away,' said David. 'You could pop in any time to see him.'

'I don't want to make an appointment to see my own son,' Lilly replied. 'He needs to be here with me and Alice, like a normal family.'

At that moment Alice began to scream.

David looked up at the ceiling. 'If you say so, Lil.'

Demi's eyes blink open as she is ripped from sleep by the sudden removal of her quilt.

'What do you think you are doing?' asks Gran, her eyes sparkling like they're filled with diamond dust.

Demi shudders in the sudden blast of cold air. 'What time is it?'

'Time you were up and ready for school.'

Demi squeezes her eyes shut, as if she can escape the onslaught, but Gran's heavy footfall to the window and the swoosh of the curtains opening tell her Gran is in no mood for an argument.

'I want to come with you to see Malaya,' she tries.

Gran pushes out her lower lip. 'No my girl, you will do your lessons and meet me at the hospital afterwards.'

Demi gropes for the duvet but Gran pushes it out of reach.

'And don't bring those friends of yours again,' Gran orders. 'They are not nice girls.'

Demi realizes she has no choice but to get up, so she swings her legs to the floor. She rubs her big toe against the spot where her rug is wearing through. The strings of matting that poke through are rough to the touch.

A year ago, one of her classmates had a birthday party and everyone was invited, even Demi. The carpet in the girl's bedroom was creamy coloured and as thick as Demi's thumb. While the other girls danced to the CD player, Demi watched their feet disappear into the soft pile. Gran suggested Demi ask the girl over for tea, but she didn't.

Demi hovers for a second, listening intently. She can hear Gran plod down the corridor to the bathroom. A moment later comes the flush of the toilet and the whoosh of water running down the pipes. She imagines Gran washing her lined hands. The water is so icy in the mornings that it stings, but that won't stop Gran from rubbing soap between every finger, before a thorough rinse.

At last she hears more steps, then the tell-tale thud of the front door. Gran has left and Demi is alone. She waits another second, to be sure, then pulls the quilt back on to the bed and enjoys the warmth and the silence.

School is for losers. Everybody knows that.

It was unbelievable how something as small as a baby could make so much noise. In better circumstances Lilly might have laughed.

After David and Sam left, Alice had screamed until she was completely puce and each curl on her head sodden. It was as if she'd realized that she'd been tricked by Penny's mobile toy and needed to make up for lost time. Lilly sang to her, waggled a teddy at her, made funny faces, but to no avail. Alice was incensed and determined to make her point.

When the sobbing had subsided to mournful hiccups, Lilly had tried to at least brush her teeth, something she could do with one hand, but as soon as she reached for the tap, Alice took it as another call to arms.

'I'll say this for you,' Lilly told Alice, 'you've got stamina.'

She checked the time. Jack was late. He'd said he'd give Alice her breakfast, then take her to nursery.

The phone rang which seemed to increase Alice's annoyance. She bellowed at the receiver.

Lilly had to shout above the din. 'Hello.'

'Christ, woman, what did you do to Alice?' said Jack.

'We disagreed about the best Doctor Who of all time,' said Lilly. 'She's not a fan of David Tennant.'

He chuckled, but it was polite not warm. 'I'll get straight to the point, Lilly, I can't get over to you today.'

Lilly felt her stomach lurch.

'Is this because of the McKenzie case?' she asked.

'No. Well sort of.'

'I know you're mad at me for taking it on, Jack, but I'm shocked you'd let your feelings come between you and Alice.'

He paused for a second as if he was measuring his words. 'Nothing will ever come between me and Alice.'

He let that statement hang in the air.

'Something's come up at work that I can't ignore,' he said.

'Something on the McKenzie case?' Lilly asked.

'Yes.'

'Can you tell me what?' she asked.

'Not at this time.'

'This is me you're talking to, Jack.'

He sighed. 'You made this official, Lilly. You drew the line in the sand.'

She opened her mouth to argue but knew there was no point. For one thing, it was entirely true.

'Okay then,' she said, 'let me know when you have any information you can pass on.'

'I will.'

Lilly hung up the phone and pressed her lips together. Jack's position was clear and she had brought it on herself.

'Let's get you to nursery.' Lilly kissed Alice who had finally run out of steam.

A shower would have to wait.

She arrived outside Little Daisies half an hour later, Alice still in her sleep suit encrusted with baby rice, Lilly wearing a coat over her pyjamas and a ski hat to cover her unruly hair. A stray and frizzy ringlet tickled her nose and she blew it upwards in short blasts. She'd thrown a suit in the boot of her car and would change at work.

Nikki came to the door. At twenty-two she was the senior nursery nurse, and never failed to make Lilly feel inadequate. She could smell out an empty nappy bag at ten paces.

'Hello Mrs Valentine.' She blinked at Lilly's appearance.

Lilly was about to explain that she wasn't a Mrs but she stopped herself. Instead, she held Alice out like a parcel.

'Ooh, she doesn't look very good, does she?' said Nikki.

'Just sleepy,' Lilly laughed. 'She's worn herself out screaming.'

Nikki squinted at Alice's floppy body, her neck lolling to one side.

'Is she running a temperature?' She held a palm to Alice's forehead.

Lilly shook her head. Alice had wolfed down a bottle. She couldn't be ill.

'She's fine.'

Nikki took Alice from her with a doubtful frown. 'If you're sure.'

Lilly smiled in what she hoped was a confident manner. This girl hadn't yet had a child of her own. This was Lilly's second and she knew when a baby was or wasn't sick. She turned to leave, waiting for Alice to start howling. Instead she heard something worse. A bovine moan followed by the splash of liquid as it hit the tiles. Alice had thrown up over Nikki's shoes.

After the fresh winter wind outside, the smell of disinfectant was overpowering. Jack instinctively put his hand to his mouth.

'You get used to it,' the nurse clucked from the ward desk.

'How?' Jack choked.

She waved her hand in the direction of an old lady being led by the hand to the bathroom, the flaps of her gown wafting open at the back, exposing her arse.

'The alternatives are worse.'

Jack shivered. He loathed the thought of growing old. Never thought he would. Occasionally he'd allowed himself the luxury of imagining the future with Lilly. He'd been an eejit to ever think it could happen.

'How can I help you?' asked the nurse.

Jack flashed his warrant card and she smiled. 'Copper eh?'

'I got a call about Malaya Ebola.'

The nurse's face straightened. 'Tragic isn't it?'

Jack nodded.

'Something's got to be done about these gangs,' said the nurse. 'They're a law unto themselves.'

'I'd like to speak to Malaya's doctor if I may,' said Jack.

The nurse leaned towards the computer and tapped a few keys.

'Mr Stephenson,' she said. 'But he'll need to speak to the family first.'

'Of course,' said Jack.

He took a seat next to the desk and waited. He tried not to think how he'd feel if it were Alice laying on that hospital bed.

A moment later, the buzzer to the ward doors sounded. The nurse answered and released the lock.

'It's the grandmother,' she said.

Jack breathed deeply as Mrs Ebola puffed her way towards them, each footstep heavier than the last. She was wearing thick surgical tights and her swollen feet were squeezed into sandals. His ma had been the same, wearing her Scholls whatever the weather. There were prima ballerinas with fewer bunions.

When the old lady recognized Jack, her eyes opened in alarm.

'What has happened?' She was out of breath.

Jack jumped up. 'Take a seat Mrs Ebola.'

She flapped her arms against her sides, and began to groan. Jack tried to push her into a chair as her knees began to give way.

'Oh my Lord. Oh my Jesus,' she whimpered.

Jack felt the full bulk of her collapse in his arms. He was terrified he wouldn't be able to take her weight, that they'd fall to the ground together. He tensed both his arms and his back, holding her as best he could.

'Why are we punished like this again?' she moaned. 'Why have you forsaken us?'

Sweat prickled Jack's back and just as he thought his knees would buckle the nurse sprang around the desk and wedged herself under Mrs Ebola's left arm. She was surprisingly strong and Jack felt immediate relief. Together they managed to lower the desperate old lady into the chair where she slumped backwards, still praying aloud.

Jack fell to his knees at Mrs Ebola's feet and took one of her hands in his. It was huge and lined, yet smooth between the deep furrows.

'It's okay, Mrs Ebola, it's okay.'

He looked at the nurse and gestured to the phone on the desk. 'Better get the doc.'

She gave a single nod and hurried to make the call.

Jack turned back to Mrs Ebola. 'It's going to be all right. Everything's going to be all right.'

Mrs Ebola looked at him as if he were completely mad. He noticed that her dark brown eyes shone with an intense brightness, like shards of broken mirror.

'Malaya is dead and you think everything will be all right?'

Jack frowned. Then in an instant he understood why Mrs Ebola had reacted as she had. She wasn't having a heart attack, she had seen a copper and thought the worst. Mary, Mother of God, he had nearly killed the woman.

'She'd not dead Mrs Ebola. Malaya's not dead.'

Mrs Ebola's entire body went rigid. 'Not dead?'

Jack shook his head.

'Are you sure?' She blinked at him in incomprehension.

'Absolutely.'

'Then why are you here?' she asked.

'Because the hospital rang me to say Malaya had woken up.'

The thumping on the door is so loud that Demi jumps out of bed.

Shit. Her first thought is that Gran is back from the hospital. She'll be furious when she finds out Demi hasn't gone to school. Maybe Demi can say she felt sick. But will Gran believe that?

And why is she knocking on the door? Why doesn't she just let herself in?

Demi's heart pounds as the thumping continues. She can hear from the sound that whoever it is, is using the side of their fist and not their knuckles. Thump, thump, thump. Both the door and Demi's heart.

She rubs her bare arms in the cold and tries to think straight. Perhaps it is Gran and she's lost her key. But why knock? She thinks Demi is out at school, so who could answer? And Gran would never hammer like that. She tells the girls off whenever they clatter down the corridor, or slam a cupboard door. 'The world does not need to share our every move.'

Not Gran, then. So who?

If she just keeps very still and waits, whoever it is will have to go away. She holds her breath as if the person at the door might be able to hear even that. Another rally of thumping makes Demi start.

Whoever you are, just go away.

Then it stops. Silence.

Demi listens very hard for the sound of shoes moving away from the door. She's tempted to creep to the window and try to see who it is. But what if they look up and catch her? No, that's a stupid plan. She'll just remain completely still until the coast is clear.

Just when she thinks enough time has elapsed and it must be safe, she hears the tell-tale scratch of someone lifting the letter-box as they peer inside.

'Demi,' a voice calls out, 'you in there?'

Shock roots Demi to the spot. It's a girl's voice and for a moment she thinks it might be her sister.

'It's me,' the girl shouts. 'Chika.'

Demi's eyes widen. Yesterday, Chika had promised to check on Demi every day.

'It's the least I can do for Malaya, innit.' She stuffed the last of her chicken burger into her mouth, her lips greasy with mayonnaise. 'Family and that, gotta stick together.'

It had made Demi smile, even though she hadn't believed it. Yet here she is, true to her word.

Demi grabs her school sweatshirt from the floor, pulls it over her pyjamas and races to the door. She can see through the frosted glass that Chika has begun to move away, her outline disappearing. She pulls open the door.

'Chika,' she calls.

Chika has reached the end of the walkway and turns to Demi's voice. She's wearing a hoodie pulled over her baseball cap and dark glasses, despite the greyness of the morning.

'You sagging school?' Chika slides back towards the flat.

Demi hopes she's not going to get a lecture and shrugs. She needn't have worried, Chika just laughs.

'Your Gran's gonna beat your arse.' Chika wags her finger.

'She's at the hospital,' says Demi.

Chika leans her hip against the balcony wall, one arm dropping into mid-air. 'You hungry?'

Demi nods.

'All right.' Chika looks away from Demi, out over the estate. 'Meet me in Dirty Mick's in half an hour.'

Demi must look clueless because Chika rolls her eyes. 'The caff on the corner.'

Demi wants to say thank you, to tell Chika how much she appreciates her kindness, but she's already walking away towards the stairwell.

Lilly carried Alice in her car seat from the car to the office. She plonked it on the step as she rummaged for her keys. Since Alice had projectile-vomited at nursery, and Lilly had been forced to beat a hasty retreat while Nikki rubbed her shoes angrily with kitchen roll, Alice had shown no other signs of ill health.

'You,' Lilly pointed down at her with the key, 'are a fraud.'

Alice gurgled back at her.

Once inside, Lilly went straight to the kitchen. The answer phone was winking wildly and she really needed to change into her suit, but she was completely famished. She rummaged in the fridge and pulled out a Twix. Not the healthiest of breakfasts, but needs must.

She handed Alice a rice cake, which she sucked until it disintegrated into wet sludge under her chin, and went back to reception to check her messages. Several clients were baying for her blood, or their divorce documents at least. She had to get those out today or they would sack her for sure. She logged on to the computer and sighed. Fifty-three unanswered emails.

She smiled at Alice. 'We're going to be here till midnight, kiddo.'

Lilly looked down at herself. She really did need to change out of her PJs, but she'd do an hour's work first.

She pulled out a file and started to type. Mrs Clayton wanted to file for divorce under unreasonable behaviour. Her husband, she said, was mean, and would only pay for a housekeeper four days a week.

'How am I to manage at weekends?' she'd asked.

Lilly had tried not to laugh as she imagined her own cottage, where Sam's bicycle lay in three pieces on his bedroom floor.

'You might need to give me something a little more serious,' Lilly said.

Mrs Clayton had thought hard. Her husband had also suggested that visiting the hairdresser twice a week was excessive.

In the end, Mrs Clayton had been forced to admit that the unreasonable Mr Clayton had been having an affair with his secretary for over two years.

'Then let's cite adultery,' Lilly offered.

Mrs Clayton baulked. She was a size six, with a wardrobe Gok Wan would have been proud of. She worked out every morning and had her teeth whitened in Harley Street. She had so much botox in her forehead she looked like someone had melted a candle over her face. She did not want the world to know that her husband had chosen another woman. Particularly not a 'fat tart from Essex'. Lilly imagined Mr Clayton tucked up in bed with a curvy blonde. Who could blame him?

'I will not have that woman mentioned.' Mrs Clayton tossed her professionally blow-dried hair. 'I have my reputation to consider.'

Lilly's fingers hovered over the keyboard. How on earth could she word the divorce petition in a way that would not make any judge fall off his chair laughing?

'The Respondent, despite a huge income, deliberately kept the Petitioner short of money,' Lilly read aloud as she typed. 'He resented her having any luxuries.'

Alice, who was still in her car seat, began to cry.

'I know it's a pile of crap, but what can I do?' Lilly laughed.

Alice continued to cry. Lilly put her head in her hands. Could the day get any worse?

'Hello.'

Lilly looked up. She had forgotten to lock the door behind her and a man in his mid thirties was standing on the step outside, peering in.

Lilly cringed. After Annabelle had made her entrance in exactly the same way, you'd think she would have learned. She pushed her chair firmly under the desk to hide as much of herself as she could, and yanked off her hat. She felt her hair spring out like a nest of coiled snakes.

'I'm sorry,' she said. 'We're closed.'

He looked at her with a puzzled frown, then at Alice, who was bawling like a mourner at an Indian funeral.

When he took a step inside, Lilly saw that he was tall with dark skin that seemed to gleam. His shoulders were almost the width of the doorframe.

Lilly coughed and tried not to notice how attractive he was. 'I said we're closed.'

'Penny told me you needed help.' His accent was African. 'She was not wrong.'

Penny? What did this have to do with Penny?

'You're not a Reiki master are you? Or an aromatherapist?' she asked.

Penny was a fan of alternative therapies and was convinced the chaos that was Lilly's existence could be alleviated by the judicious application of essential oils.

The man laughed, making creases around brown eyes. 'I do administration, typing, help with paperwork.'

'I thought that was a lady called Carol?' said Lilly.

'Or a man called Karol, perhaps.'

Lilly was stunned.

Karol gestured to Alice. 'Do you want to go to the baby?'

Lilly reddened. If she got up he would see the full glory of her grubby nightwear, but what could she do? She pushed back her chair and put her chin up, as if it were the most natural thing in the world to be in her pyjamas. She picked up Alice and shushed her.

'This is Alice,' she said.

Karol nodded. 'I think you and Alice really do need my assistance.'

Mrs Ebola wasn't listening to the doctor.

Jack didn't blame her. The relief was written across her face in shocking simplicity. Right now, all she could concentrate on was the fact that her granddaughter was going to live.

She held Malaya's hand in her own and rocked back and forth, whispering, 'Oh sweet Lord, oh sweet Lord.'

Mr Stephenson stood on the other side of the bed, scribbling on Malaya's chart with a heavy-looking fountain pen.

'Malaya regained consciousness two hours ago,' he said. 'She hasn't spoken yet, but we think she's out of the woods.'

'When do you think she might speak?' Jack asked.

Mr Stephenson frowned. 'You won't be able to grill her just yet, I'm afraid.'

Jack put up his palms in surrender.

'Not a grilling, Doctor, just hoping for anything that might help us catch whoever did this. Experience tells us that we have to move fast.'

'And when that time is appropriate I'll let you know,' said Mr Stephenson. 'Now I think we should leave the family in peace.'

Jack nodded and got to his feet. He passed his card to the doctor who immediately pressed it into his pocket without looking at it. Jack sighed. A little chat couldn't hurt, could it?

He was about to leave when a rasping sound came from the bed. Malaya's mouth was open and the noise came again. It was painful to hear, as if the skin inside her throat was cracking apart. Mrs Ebola poured water from a jug into a plastic cup and put it to the girl's lips. As Malaya took the tiniest of sips, her eyes didn't leave those of her grandmother. Then Mrs Ebola put the glass back down and wiped Malaya's mouth with huge yet gentle hands.

'There my baby, there, there,' she soothed.

Malaya opened her mouth again and this time found her voice. It was faint, and hoarse. Jack couldn't catch the words.

'What did she say?' asked Jack.

'Really, Officer,' Mr Stephenson sighed. 'My patient is in no condition for this.'

Malaya tried again, but all Jack could hear was a small scratching sound.

'You must leave now,' said Mr Stephenson and pressed the heel of his hand into Jack's back to direct him outside.

When he reached the door, Jack took one look back. Mrs Ebola was bent towards Malaya's head as if she were kissing her cheek. Then she turned to Jack and pierced him with those glittering eyes.

'She says to speak to Chika Mboko.'

Demi fingers the hoodies lined up on the market stall.

'These are fake, man,' Chika shouts at the guy selling them.

He's got a fag hanging out of the corner of his mouth and looks at her through the blue plume of smoke.

'No shit.'

She kisses her teeth at him and prepares to walk away until she sees Demi entranced by the thick black material and the gold lettering embossed on the front. D&G.

'They ain't real, sister,' says Chika. 'That's why they're cheap.'

Demi shrugs. It doesn't matter. She can't afford one, real or not.

Chika's face softens and she thumps Demi playfully on the arm. 'Try one on.'

Demi shakes her head.

'Come on.' Chika pulls the nearest one out, toppling the pile.

'Watch it,' says the man.

'You wanna sell any of this tat or not?'

He grumbles under his breath and sorts out his stock. Chika holds the hoodie against Demi, nods and pulls it over her head. When Demi has it on Chika takes a step back and peers over her dark glasses to admire.

'Not bad actually.'

Demi turns to look at herself in the old mirror propped up against the side of the stall. There's a crack running right through the middle, but Demi can still see how she looks. She can't hold back a smile.

'We'll take it,' Chika pulls out a wad of twenty-pound notes from her back pocket and peels off two. 'And one of those.'

Demi follows Chika's finger to a baseball cap at the back of the stall. Like the hoodie, it's black with matching gold lettering. Chika plonks it on Demi's head and laughs.

'You are looking fine now, sister.'

As they walk away, Demi feels a lump in her throat, like a piece of bread has got stuck. She tries to gulp it down.

'Thanks,' she whispers.

Chika shrugs. 'Like I told you, bredren gotta look after each other.'

Demi doesn't know what to say. It's like a dream. She's had breakfast bought for her. A fried egg sandwich and two cups of tea. Now she's strutting through the market in the best clothes she's ever owned in her life. She only hopes they bump into Georgia. Then she remembers that she'll be in school and the thought makes her smile even wider.

'It's like this, Demi,' Chika says. 'I do something for you and another time maybe you do something for me.'

Demi nods. She has no idea what she could possibly do for someone as sorted as Chika, but she knows that nothing would stop her from trying.

The scent of burnt oranges filled the room as Lilly poured an indecent amount of aromatherapy oil into the bath. It was a gift from Penny, meant to help clear the mind. Lilly was agnostic as to the efficacy of such things, but either way, it smelled good enough to eat.

A bit like Penny's other present, Karol. Now he really *was* good enough to eat.

Lilly chuckled at her own naughty thoughts. The man was ten years younger than her and looked like he spent half his life in the gym. She held her arms out to Alice, who was lying naked on a towel. The baby lifted her head and squealed in anticipation. She loved bath time and would happily remain immersed in the warm water until her hands were as wrinkled as month-old apples at the bottom of the fruit bowl. In this, she and Lilly were as one.

Lilly dropped her bathrobe, scooped up her daughter and stepped into the bath. She lowered herself down and perched Alice on her knees, swirling the delicious water around them. Alice let out an audible sigh of appreciation. Lilly followed suit.

A day that had started with disaster had steadily improved. Within minutes of entering her office and life, Karol had taken control, ordering Lilly into her office to work while he got on with the administration. She had acquiesced in a way that had surprised her. Even Alice had fallen under Karol's spell, finishing a bottle he expertly gave her and rewarding him with a loud wet burp.

In barely an hour, Karol came to find her, carrying coffee and a typed copy of Mrs Clayton's divorce petition. Lilly scanned it and smiled. It was impeccably worded, putting a spin on it that would make Lilly's client the happiest of bunnies.

'This is genius,' she said.

He didn't answer, just smiled and grabbed an armful of paperwork to file.

When Lilly's stomach told her it was lunchtime, she made her way back to reception. Karol looked up from the computer and gestured to the suit Lilly had changed into.

'A more conventional look for the office,' he said.

Lilly laughed. 'You have to admit my PJs had a certain style.'

'It might catch on and we can all come to work in our nightwear.' There was a twinkle in his eye. 'Of course, I always sleep naked.'

Lilly laughed again. If anyone else had said something like that, she would have thought it crass, but Karol was so natural, so comfortable in his own skin, it was impossible not to play along.

At the end of the day they had agreed that he would come every morning until the office was under control.

'I'll see you tomorrow,' he said, pulling on his coat.

'I'll look forward to it,' Lilly replied.

Back in the bath, Lilly mussed Alice's curls and tapped her wet little nose.

'Mummy is being very silly.'

Alice beamed, as if to say, 'Yes, you are.'

Chapter Four

'Are you a virgin?'

Tristan leers at Jamie over a plate of spaghetti hoops on toast.

'Shut up,' says Jamie.

'Course you are,' Tristan continues. 'I bet you've never even copped a feel.'

Jamie shakes his head in disgust.

The trouble with boarding, well, one of them, because there were so many that if asked for a list Jamie could fill pages of a notebook, is that there is nowhere to escape your tormentors.

Every school has them don't they? The kids who seem to get a kick out of torturing anyone they think won't fight back. It's just that when you live there, you can't get away from them. They find you in lessons, in the dorm, in the dining room, when all you want to do is eat your fucking breakfast in peace.

It's all just one continual session of pain and humiliation. Jamie remembers that episode of *Big Brother* that the papers went mental about. The one where the girl who died of cancer and some old singer bullied the Bollywood star. Well, the *Daily Mail* should get a load of Manor Park if they want to see some real action.

Tristan spears a hoop on each prong of his fork and waves it at Jamie.

'You're a mummy's boy, Holland.'

Jamie's tempted to point out how daft a remark that is coming from someone who's eating what's basically food for toddlers. But he doesn't. He doesn't need a punch in the face.

Every time there's a party, it's the same. The girls whip themselves up into a frenzy over the latest Jack Wills catalogue, and the boys brag about who they got off with last time and how far they got. Casual requests to borrow a johnny make everyone paranoid that they're the only one who hasn't 'gone all the way'.

If it wasn't for the fact that Jamie's only alternative is to go home to his parents, he wouldn't bother with the party at all.

When Tristan realizes he isn't going to get a reaction from Jamie he rams the last of his breakfast down his throat and goes off to find another victim. Jamie sighs in relief, and thanks God that he didn't stick to his 'no drugs' policy. At times like this, looking forward to a small taste of freedom is all that stops him from doing himself in. Even if his body has to live in this cage, he can let his head fly away.

Jack opened the car window to let in a blast of air. He had barely slept the night before, tossing and turning, until his mind was as tangled as his sheets. He needed to sharpen up.

From the look at the medical evidence, there was no doubt that the attack on Malaya was a GBH, possibly an attempted murder. He knew which one the chief super would plump for. If there was going to be any chance of the right result on this one he needed to keep his wits about him, and lying awake in the early hours fretting about Alice and Lilly wasn't a good start.

He reached for his bottle of Diet Coke and took a long glug.

The only lead was the girl, Chika Mboko, but Malaya had given nothing more than the name. Jack needed to know how and why she was involved.

A quick look on the database told a colourful story. There was a kid called Mboko living in the next block to Malaya's. She had been in and out of care since the age of ten, when her mother claimed to be unable to control her. She'd been in trouble with the police for almost as long. Last year she had been arrested on a robbery charge where the victim had been pulled to the ground and stamped on. The case had fallen through, but not until a psych report had been completed.

Jack read it with a shudder.

Chika Mboko is a very angry young woman. She has a history of school refusal and rebellion towards any form of authority. She admits to having persistently disobeyed her mother and foster carers but blames them, stating the rules they attempted to apply were unreasonable. Her last placement broke down when Chika set fire to her duvet. She states this was an accident and points out that she was the only person hurt.

She is now back with her mother, but to all intents and purposes is living independently.

She is of above average intelligence yet has little concentration. She is very easily bored and has no aspiration. When asked what she intended to do as an adult, Chika replied, 'stay alive'.

When asked about the future, she could not envisage herself having a job or a family. When asked if she feared the possibility of prison, she simply shrugged.

I concluded that Chika does not fear punishment. Indeed, Chika does not appear to fear anything.

A few years ago, Jack would have been tempted to just bring Chika in. She fitted the profile exactly. But these days he knew it paid to be canny. Malaya had only said Chika's name. She hadn't accused her of anything. And since he could be guaranteed to get sweet FA out of Chika herself, he needed to see if he could find out anything that might help.

'Hello, Jonjo, fancy seeing you here.' Jack smiled at the skinny kid snaking out of the flats, his eyes darting from side to side.

Jonjo clocked Jack and sighed.

'Nice to see you too,' said Jack.

Jonjo hunched his shoulders and scowled. His jacket was too thin for the weather and had a large red stain down the front which could have been ketchup, but could just as easily have been blood.

'I'm a bit busy right now, Jack.' Jonjo dithered in the drizzle. 'I've got my routine. You know how it is.'

Jack nodded. He did know how it was. They'd met five years ago when Jonjo smacked a stolen Fiat Uno into the side of Tesco's. He was lucky that it was four in the morning and the only injury was to Jonjo's front teeth, which got left in the dashboard. Jack had sat with him while he got his lips sewn up in A&E. Jonjo's parents didn't even turn up.

For the next couple of years, Jack kept an eye out for Jonjo, bollocking him when he got arrested, slipping him the odd fiver, but it was only a matter of time until he slid into the gear. Now Jonjo did the same as every other junkie: whatever he had to. And that included providing information to Jack.

Jack gestured with his head. 'Get in.'

Jonjo groaned and hugged himself. He badly needed his morning fix.

'Give us ten minutes, Jack.'

Jack shook his head. He knew Jonjo was suffering, but if he let him score first, he wouldn't get any sense out of him for an hour. Jonjo swore and circled the car. He stepped in and slammed the door shut.

'Fucking hell, man, I'm in agony here.'

Jack exhaled slowly. Jonjo was only eighteen but looked a decade older and weighed less than someone half his age. His fingers were coated in the black residue left from smoking rocks, and the thumb on his right hand was swollen from too many digs with a needle in the same spot. His life was spent getting high and dealing with the comedown. Jack wondered how long he would actually last.

'Tell me about Chika Mboko,' he said.

Jonjo shrugged. 'Nasty little bitch.'

'Violent?'

'Man, these girls are all violent. It's fucking mayhem on these estates.'

'What about Malaya Ebola?' Jack asked. 'The girl who was attacked in the rec.'

Jonjo paused for a moment, a thick sheen of sweat breaking out across his forehead.

'Is she the fat kid?'

Jack winced but nodded all the same.

'Haven't seen her about much,' said Jonjo. 'She ain't dealing, I know that much.'

Jack nodded. If anyone knew all the local dealers it was Jonjo.

'I heard she was on her jump in,' said Jonjo. 'They always send the youngers to other gangs' areas, to prove what they're made of. Fucking suicide, really.'

Jack thought about Malaya's swollen face, the eyes closed over. Suicide was about right.

'Was Chika Mboko part of it?' Jack asked.

'Oh, she was part of it, for sure,' said Jonjo.

Jack suppressed a smile. Jonjo's word wasn't hard evidence of course. No jury in the world was likely to believe what a sweaty addict was prepared to say for the price of a bag. But it was something Jack could build on. A start. And where there was a start there was always a finish. He held out a twenty and Jonjo snatched it.

Jack watched Jonjo get out of the car and didn't waste his breath advising him to try for a place in rehab.

'Take care,' he called through the window.

As Jack watched Jonjo scuttle around the bonnet, his back bent like an old man, he decided to head back to the hospital. Whether Mr Stephenson liked it or not, Jack needed to ask Malaya if Chika Mboko was one of the perps. If the victim confirmed it, he was halfway there.

Jonjo was about to head off to his man when he stopped and turned, leaned towards Jack's open window.

'She never done it though.'

'Who never done what?' asked Jack.

'Chika,' said Jonjo. 'She never hurt the fat kid.'

Jack felt as though he'd been slapped. 'You said she was part of it.'

'Yeah. She was part of the jump in.'

'I don't understand.'

Jonjo muttered something under his breath. 'Malaya was on her jump in for the CBD. Chika's one of the olders so she would have been part of that, you know, helping to set it up and that.'

'How can you be sure Malaya was joining?'

Jonjo spread his arms wide so that his dirty top rode up, exposing painful hip bones.

'This is Clayhill, man, Clayhill Bitches Dem rule these streets.'

The road outside Lilly's office was clean and bright. Always well tended by Harpenden Council, it sparkled in the morning frost.

Lilly unlocked the door and smiled. It was a far cry from the sink estate where she grew up, the pavements littered with empty fag packets and dog shit.

'You look happy.' Karol dropped his briefcase next to the computer and slid off his coat.

'Alice slept for five hours last night,' said Lilly.

Karol pursed his lips. 'Five hours is good?'

'Five hours is cause for celebration,' Lilly answered.

She slipped into her office and sighed with pleasure. Karol had cleared the decks, repatriating loose papers with their files and housing those files in the correct drawers. Her desk was empty apart from a plastic pot filled with pencils and biros and a typed list of things to do. Outside in reception she could hear him whistling as he went through her emails.

She pulled the laptop from her bag and placed it at the dead centre of her desk. A feeling that anything was possible filled her.

Even the situation with Tanisha could be resolved. The police were under pressure to get a result, but they had nothing on her.

'These gangs have ruined your sister's life.'

Gran grunts as she buckles up her shoe. It's been years since she could reach her feet by bending forwards and she's devised a way of doing them up by stretching her leg out to the side and flicking the strap with her finger.

Demi sits at the kitchen table, stirring sugar into her tea with one hand, resting her chin on the palm of the other.

'But now she's awake, the doctor said she could make a full recovery.'

'I pray to Lord Jesus that is the case.' Gran crosses herself, and attempts her other shoe.

'Well then,' says Demi.

Gran lifts her head and fixes Demi with one of her looks. Demi has never been able to beat the look. It makes her feel like a small child. She concentrates on her tea, sucking up a spoonful noisily.

'I just mean we should try to stay positive,' she mumbles.

'I suppose that is what your new friends are telling you,' says Gran.

Demi moves back slightly in her chair. Chika says the streets are dangerous, that sisters get hurt all the time. That's why they have to stick together.

'I suppose they say that what happened to Malaya is all right,' Gran pushes herself to her feet and reaches for her coat which is hung on the back of her chair. 'That these things happen.'

Demi shakes her head, stung. 'They're gutted. Really upset.'

Gran buttons up her coat and lets out a little snort through her nose.

'You don't know anything about them,' Demi says.

'I know that Malaya was a good girl before she got involved with them and started wearing rings in her nose like a cow.'

'What's that got to do with anything?' asks Demi.

'Good girls don't put holes in themselves or cover themselves in tattoos.' Gran reaches for the door handle. 'And good girls don't get involved in gang fighting.'

Demi feels her cheeks go hot and she pushes away her tea, sloshing it over the table.

'You don't understand what it's like, Gran. Things aren't easy for us.'

Gran kisses her teeth. 'You young ones don't know how much you have here. Back home there is real suffering, people have real problems.'

'We have problems here, Gran.'

'I'm talking about life and death, Demi, not whether you can afford new trainers.' Gran raises her hand to show the conversation is at an end. 'Let's not forget the reason why we came here in the first place.'

Demi looks down at the table and chases a pattern in the spilled tea with her thumb. There's no point trying to talk to Gran. She doesn't understand.

'Clear that up, Demi, and go to school,' says Gran and closes the door behind her.

When she's sure Gran is safely off the walkway, Demi lets the tears spring into her eyes and smacks down her hand, spraying tea across the table. She's so angry. Gran of all people should know that you have to protect yourself.

She checks her watch. It's time to leave for school. Instead, she puts on her new D&G hoodie and pulls the baseball cap low over her eyes.

Then she heads out for Dirty Mick's, leaving the mess on the kitchen table behind her.

Jack drained the last dregs of the bottle of Diet Coke and wiped the back of his hand across his mouth.

From what Jonjo had said, it was clear that Malaya Ebola and Chika Mboko were members of the same gang, which in turn meant it was highly unlikely that Chika had anything to do with the attack. So why had Malaya named her?

Maybe she didn't know the names of her attackers and thought Chika might. But did Malaya really believe Chika would help the police? Perhaps the poor girl couldn't think straight. It was hardly surprising in the circumstances.

Jack turned the key in the ignition. He'd go back to the hospital, try to get more information.

He was about to pull out when his mobile rang. Caller ID told him it was the chief super. Shit.

Jack snapped open the phone. 'Sir.'

'Any progress, Jack?'

Jack sighed. He hated having the boss breathe down his neck. The report of the interview with Tanisha had been typed and sent to the chief super. He knew the score.

'The victim has given me a name, but it doesn't look like she had anything to do with it.'

'Are you sure?' asked the chief.

'Not one hundred per cent, but I don't think she's our perp,' said Jack.

'Have you brought her in?'

'No reasonable cause, sir,' said Jack.

The chief coughed. 'The victim named her.'

'Not as her attacker.'

'The clock is ticking here, Jack,' the chief snapped. 'You know the serious pressure we're under.'

Jack sighed. He did indeed know the score. The police needed to be seen to be following every lead, even those that would lead nowhere.

'There ain't nobody that can tell me what to do, you get me?'

Chika takes the straw out of her milkshake and wags it at Demi. It's green and white striped. Demi and Malaya always argue over who gets the red one. Gran tells them to stop being so silly, but it doesn't seem silly at the time.

'I especially ain't listening to no teacher chatting their shit at me.' Chika sticks the straw in her mouth and chews the end flat.

Demi smiles and takes a slurp of her own milkshake. She could listen to Chika's stories all day.

'Battle of Hastings, blah, blah, blah.' Chika opens and closes her hand like a beak. 'Capital of China, blah, blah, blah. Tell me something I need to know and I might fucking listen.'

The workmen on the next table look over. They're big, with shaved heads and dirty hands, but Chika's not scared.

'What are you staring at?' she shouts.

They shake their heads and go back to their bacon sandwiches.

'See, people will try to disrespect you,' Chika tells Demi, 'so we show them that they can't mess with us. That they need to take us serious, you understand?'

Demi nods. She's always being told what to do and where to go, being pushed around.

'That's why we got each other's backs,' says Chika.

She puts up her fist and Demi touches it with her own.

'Safe,' says Chika.

She's about to launch into another story, when a black Mercedes pulls up outside. Even from inside the café Demi can hear the deep base of a hip-hop tune. Chika mutters something under her breath and slams down some coins on the table before moving towards the car.

Demi's not sure what to do, so she just follows.

Outside in the cold, the music is even louder. The low thuds make Demi's stomach flip. As the passenger window lowers, the sound fills the street. Demi wonders how the people in the car can tolerate it. Chika stands a little way off from the car, and for the first time Demi thinks she seems nervous. But that can't be right. Chika isn't afraid of anything or anyone.

A man's face appears at the window, a cigarette clamped between his lips so that most of his face is hidden in a cloud of smoke. He jerks his head at Chika.

'Danny.' She takes a step forward.

'On your own?' The man called Danny speaks without removing his fag, so that his words come out in a rush of white smoke.

'I'm with one of my homies,' Chika nods at Demi.

Demi feels a thrill at hearing herself described that way, but it's short lived as the man looks in her direction. Something in the way Chika is standing, all stiff, tells her to be very wary.

'What you called?' the man asks.

Demi watches the ash on the end of his cigarette move up and down, getting longer and longer. It's going to drop if he doesn't flick it.

'Her name's Demi,' says Chika. 'She don't say much.'

'Come 'ere,' says the man.

Demi daren't move. She feels like she's been glued to the spot.

The man drops his voice. 'I said come 'ere.'

Chika nods and Demi forces herself forwards. When she's a foot from the window, the man removes his cigarette and throws it at her feet. She watches it roll into the gutter. As the smoke clears she can make out more of the man. He's almost as dark as Gran and wears a thick gold chain with a crucifix that glints against his skin.

After a second, she can fully take him in and she gasps. The left side of his face shows he is a handsome man, but the right side bears a scar from the edge of his hairline to his chin, dissecting his eyebrow along the way. In his right eye socket his eye is nothing more than a milky white marble.

'You don't find me pretty?' the man laughs, but it sounds cold and harsh.

Demi doesn't know what to say. She realizes her hand is covering her mouth.

'You don't want to stroke my handsome face?'

'Come on Danny,' Chika interrupts. 'Leave her be.'

He glares at Chika, his dead eye boring into her.

'She's just a younger,' says Chika. 'She don't know nothing yet.'

The man turns back to Demi, making her shudder. Demi is terrified he'll ask another question. At last he nods, as if accepting what Chika says, and Demi feels relief flood through her. She wishes she could sit down.

'Babylon crawling all over the estates,' the man says to Chika.

She bends down at the waist so her face is level with his. 'It's because of what happened to Malaya.'

Demi is surprised to hear her sister's name.

'It's very bad for business,' says the man.

Chika nods. 'It'll soon blow over. You know how it is, man.'

'Not this time,' he says. 'Papers, politicians, they all looking for someone to be locked up.'

Chika leans her arm on the top of the car, but the man lets out a low growl and she removes it.

'This is a bad mess,' he says. 'A very bad mess.'

'I'll sort it,' says Chika.

The man puts another cigarette between his lips and pulls out a lighter. He shields the flame with his hands and lights up. He breathes in and out until his face is once again shrouded.

'No more fuck-ups, Chika.'

Then the electric window rises and the car pulls away.

Karol peeped his head around Lilly's office door.

'There's someone to see you.'

Lilly frowned. There were no appointments in the diary.

'She says it will only take a moment,' said Karol with a smile. 'I think you might be interested.'

In reception, Annabelle had taken a seat, most of her face hidden by a bouquet of flowers. Tanisha was by her side, engrossed with her phone.

When she saw Lilly, Annabelle jumped up. 'These are for you.'

The flowers were exquisite. Tiger lilies held together in an organza bow.

'These are beautiful,' Lilly gasped.

'A small thank you,' said Annabelle. 'Since we were passing.'

Lilly held them to her face and took in the perfume. Representing children in care had not involved many gifts over the years. A grunted acknowledgement was as good as it got.

'We know you weren't keen to take on Tanisha's case and we want you to know how much we appreciate it,' said Annabelle. 'Don't we, Tanisha?'

Tanisha didn't look up from her phone but managed a nod.

'Let me put those in some water,' said Karol.

He took the flowers and headed to the kitchen. Tanisha lifted her head and watched him.

'He your man?' she asked Lilly.

'No.' Lilly gave a nervous laugh. 'He's doing some work for me.'

'He's sexy, innit.'

'Tanisha,' Annabelle chided.

The girl shrugged. 'Just saying.'

Annabelle sighed and a sadness passed over her face. She clearly wanted to say something else to Tanisha but settled for rubbing her knee.

'So what brings you down here?' Lilly asked.

Annabelle instantly brightened. 'Tanisha's scan.'

Lilly hid her surprise. There was only one hospital in Harpenden and it was private. Annabelle must be paying for Tanisha's ante-natal care.

'Do you have the photo?' Lilly asked.

Tanisha fished into the pocket of her hoodie and pulled out a small black and white picture, already crumpled around the edges. Lilly took it and smiled. It was impossible to make out more than an egg-shaped blur.

'Do you think it's a boy or a girl?'

'A girl.' Tanisha pointed to a tiny swirl that might be the head. 'Cos you can see she's going to have a pretty face.'

'A beautiful baby girl,' Annabelle said, her eyes shining.

'You got any kids?' Tanisha asked.

Lilly nodded. 'A boy called Sam and a baby called Alice. She's only five months old.'

'Ain't you a bit old to have a baby?'

'Tanisha, what have we said about manners and keeping things to yourself?' whispered Annabelle.

Lilly threw back her head and laughed. 'Don't worry. You're right. I'm far too old.'

When Karol came back into the room, Tanisha gave him a sly smile and shifted in her chair, arching her back.

Annabelle coughed and got to her feet.

'We'd better be off,' she said. 'Lots to do.'

Tanisha stood too, taking the opportunity to jut her hip in Karol's direction.

'We haven't heard anything from the police, so hopefully the whole matter is closed,' said Annabelle and ushered Tanisha out of the door.

The bedroom is a complete mess with tops and jeans scattered everywhere. The floor is covered in CD cases and bracelets and at least ten pairs of high-tops are thrown in a pile in the corner, their laces tangled together.

If Demi kept her room like this, Gran would have a fit. Then again, Demi doesn't have half the stuff that Chika does. Not even a quarter. Her school uniform and church outfit hang in the old wooden wardrobe. The other clothes she owns are mostly passed down from Malaya.

Chika catches Demi's eyes, round as plates, as she clocks the window sill covered in a rainbow of different eye shadows and pencils and sticky tubes of lipgloss. There are six bottles of Charlie Pink and Black.

'Take one,' says Chika.

Demi's hand hovers in mid-air.

'Go on,' says Chika and reaches for a roach sitting in an overflowing ashtray.

Demi picks up the nearest can. The metal is cold to the touch. She pops off the plastic lid and smells the nozzle. It reminds her of sherbert.

Chika flicks her lighter and takes a deep lungful of weed.

'Where's your mum?' Demi asks.

'Out.' Chika holds the roach at arm's length for Demi to take.

Demi has never smoked before. She's seen kids at school huddled in corners sharing a joint, smelled it in the toilets too. She always thought it must be nice to share a secret like that with a friend.

'Thanks.' She takes the roach between her fingers. It feels hot, in contrast to the Charlie in her other hand. She puts it to her lips and takes a small puff. The smoke burns her tongue and she spits it out, as if it were solid. Chika laughs and Demi laughs too, handing back the roach. That's the difference with Chika and the other girls in the crew. When they laugh at you, it's not like they want to make you look bad.

Demi wonders if she dare ask Chika about Danny, the man outside the café. Everything about him frightened her. His voice, his eye, and the way Chika behaved around him. As soon as he left, Chika shrugged her old self back on, like a coat, and suggested they come back to hers before hooking up with the other girls. The swagger was back in her step and the smile back on her face.

She seems totally relaxed now, blowing smoke rings at her ceiling.

Demi opens her mouth to speak when the doorbell rings. Chika leans to the window to see who is down below.

'Shit.'

Demi's heart leaps. Is it the man with the scar? She hopes to God it's not. It was bad enough standing next to his car. She wouldn't want to be in the same room as him with no way to escape. She joins Chika by the window, trying to make out the figure. Definitely a man.

'Who is it?' Demi's voice sounds choked.

Chika takes a deep drag and exhales a plume of smoke. 'Police.'

'How do you know?' asks Demi.

Chika raises her eyebrow to the question.

Demi gasps. The thought of the man was bad enough, but being caught by the police smoking drugs is a whole lot worse. Gran will explode with fury.

'What are we going to do?' asks Demi.

Chika stabs out the roach among twenty others and reaches for a discarded pack of chewing gum.

'I'm going to find out what he wants.' She pops a stick of gum in her mouth.

'But what if he wants to come in?' Demi hisses. 'What if he smells the dope?'

Chika opens the draw of her bedside table and pulls out a freezer bag full of weed. She hands it to Demi.

'Put this down your trousers.'

Demi stands there with her mouth open like a fish. Chika sighs, yanks at the waistband of Demi's jeans and pushes the package down.

Demi gulps, feeling the plastic wad pushed against her pubic bone.

'What if I get caught?'

Chika pulls at Demi's hoodie, smoothing it over the obvious bump. 'You're only thirteen, he ain't gonna strip search you.'

'But what if he does?' Demi grabs Chika's arm. 'What if he arrests me?'

'Listen to me, yeah, he's not going to touch you.' Chika puts her hand over Demi's and looks into her eyes. 'But if he comes into the house and finds that stuff, he's gonna haul my ass to jail, innit.'

Demi can feel the muscles in her nostrils pulsing as they open and close.

'I've got a record so they can send me away for a long time, you understand me?' says Chika.

Demi feels like she might cry. She's terrified of being caught, but Chika is her friend. No one has looked after Demi like she does, no one else cares. The doorbell rings again, making Demi jump.

'Are we family?' asks Chika. 'Cos you gotta decide.'

Demi swallows hard, her eyes hot with tears.

'Yes,' she whispers.

Chika nods and hands the ashtray to Demi. 'Flush this while I answer the door.'

Demi's hands are shaking as she carries the ashtray carefully to the bathroom. It feels like the time she was one of the wise men in the nativity play at primary school. She had wanted to be an angel like all the other girls, but Mrs Thomas said she had a regal look about her, whatever that meant, and anyway, none of the white dresses would fit. So Demi, Rory Carney and Joel Evanson had been dressed in some old dressing gowns and paper crowns. Demi had been the third wise man and her job had been to carry a box of Ferrero Rocher to the manger, before delivering her only line: 'I bring you Myrrh.'

Unfortunately, Demi's hands were shaking so much she dropped her gift for the baby Jesus, scattering chocolates wrapped in gold paper across the stage. Everyone had laughed and Demi had wet her pants.

Today she won't make any mistakes. Her sister is relying on her. She carries the ashtray across the landing to the bathroom with both hands. She doesn't spill a single flake of ash. Then she shakes it into the bowl and flushes the chain. The sides of the ashtray are covered in a thin film, like a layer of dust. Can the police do tests on that? Demi's not prepared to risk it and tears off a square of toilet roll. She scrunches it into a ball and wipes the ashtray thoroughly before flushing the paper away.

The doorbell rings again and Demi hears Chika swear before thundering down the stairs to open the door.

Demi strains her ears to listen.

'Chika Mboko?' The policeman's voice is low and quiet. He has a strange accent.

'Who wants to know?' asks Chika.

'My name is Detective Jack McNally, and I need to ask you a few questions.'

Demi slumps on to the side of the bath. His words sound like something off the telly. She knows this must be serious.

Something just didn't feel right. Jack couldn't put his finger on it, but there was a feeling gnawing in his gut.

The girl sitting on the other side of the table, her left leg slung over the arm of her chair, so that her groin almost shouted at him from inside her jeans, looked as if the interview room at the police station was her second home. From the list of previous convictions detailed on the print-out, it more or less was.

Jack hadn't come across Chika before, but he knew a hundred girls just like her. Angry. Resentful. Fearless.

She pulled a packet of Marlboro from her pocket and took out a cigarette.

'Got a light?' She held it between her teeth.

Jack pointed to the no smoking sign on the wall.

'I thought there was an exception in jail,' she said.

'You're not in jail.'

Chika removed the cigarette from her lips and rolled it between her thumb and forefinger.

'What if I go mad without my nicotine?' She smiled.

'I think you'll manage.'

Chika held his gaze, then leapt forward with a scream, slamming her hands down on to the table, crushing the cigarette in her palm. The door was flung open and a uniform jumped into the room.

'Everything okay?' His eyes darted around.

Jack nodded. 'Just this one messing about.'

The uniform shook his head and left, while Chika settled back into her chair, chuckling.

Jack brushed the strands of tobacco on to the floor. 'You finished?'

'Just a little joke.' Chika was still laughing. 'To brighten things up.'

'How about we leave the comedy to Michael McIntyre, and you and me get on with this,' said Jack.

Chika wagged a finger at him. 'You ain't no fun.'

Jack watched Chika carefully. Everything about her was what he would have expected. The body language, the piss-taking. And yet.

'Tell me where you were on Monday night,' he said.

Chika shrugged.

'It was the night Malaya Ebola was attacked in Hightown,' he said.

Chika didn't reply.

'Malaya's a friend of yours, isn't she?' asked Jack.

Again, Chika said nothing.

Jack sighed. Non-cooperation with the police was as natural to these kids as breathing. If Chika's own mother had been beaten up, she wouldn't have volunteered any information.

'Listen,' he said, 'I'm not accusing you of anything.'

Chika tossed her head back. 'So why you come to my house and bring me down here?'

'Because I need to talk to you.' Jack leaned forward. 'Malaya told me you knew something.'

Chika's eyes opened wide. 'What she say?'

Jack put his hand on the table and splayed his fingers. He may as well be honest.

'She didn't say anything, just your name.' He saw Chika's

shoulders relax. 'All I want to know is if you know anything at all about it.'

Chika's tongue poked out from between her lips, a startling pink against her smooth, dark skin and she blinked at him. He was wasting his time. She had no intention of telling him anything at all.

'If you don't help me, this assault on Malaya will go unpunished, and everything will just carry on as normal.'

Her tongue was still resting on her bottom lip, obscene and slippery. Jack gulped.

'Until it all happens again,' he said, 'and maybe next time one of you will die.'

She didn't react, her body still, her breathing even. She didn't care. Life, death, it was all one and the same.

'All I need is a name,' he said. 'I'll do the rest.'

Almost imperceptibly something in the air between them changed. Chika's mind changed gear. He could almost see it. Then, like a bubble, it burst.

'A name.' His voice was hoarse.

She stared at him for a long time, her tongue mocking him.

'Tanisha McKenzie,' she said.

The panini was hot and soft to the touch, dusted with flour and oozing with mozzarella. Lilly took a bite, basil-infused oil sticking to her lips. She had sworn off these calorie-laden little devils after Alice reached four months and the baby weight was showing no signs of leaving its home on Lilly's hips and thighs. Today, though, she'd allowed herself a treat. It felt like life was going her way and she deserved it.

She took another huge bite when her mobile rang. She answered with her mouth full of food.

'Lil, it's Jack.'

She chewed frantically. Please God, he was calling to make peace and arrange to see Alice.

'Hi.' Her voice was muffled by the food.

'Everything okay?' he asked.

She forced the sandwich to the back of her mouth and swallowed. 'Yeah. It's good to hear from you.'

He didn't respond. Knowing Jack, he was embarrassed. She wondered if she should offer to cook him some dinner as a peace offering.

'Lil,' he said at last, 'I'm afraid there's a bit of a problem.'

'What's that then?'

Jack coughed. He always did that when he was thinking what to say next. Lilly imagined he would be smoothing down his tie too, if he was wearing one.

'Your client, Tanisha McKenzie,' he said, 'we need to speak to her again about the attack on Malaya Ebola.'

Lilly's heart sank.

'We've evidence now, that she was involved,' he said.

'What evidence?'

Jack coughed again. 'I'll fill you in when you get down here.'

'Get down where?'

'The station,' he said. 'Uniform are bringing McKenzie in now.'

Jesus. This was serious.

'I thought I'd just . . .' He paused. 'I thought I'd just give you a heads-up, so you can arrange things.'

'Right.'

Lilly prodded her panini. It had gone cold, the cheese like white plastic. She pushed it away, her appetite gone. At least it was good for her diet.

Chapter Five

'What on earth's going on?'

Annabelle leapt out of her chair as soon as Lilly entered the interview room. 'We'd barely got back home from your office when the police came to the house and arrested Tanisha. They insisted on bringing her here in a squad car and I had to follow behind.'

Lilly led Annabelle back to her chair and smiled at Tanisha who was sitting quietly in the corner.

'We've been stuck in here for over half an hour and no one will tell us anything.' Annabelle's cheeks were crimson. 'It's a barbaric way to treat a child.'

Lilly nodded. There was no point explaining to Annabelle that the police had every right to place Tanisha in a cell and make Annabelle wait outside.

'They say there's evidence that Tanisha attacked that girl, but they won't say what,' Annabelle gabbled. 'I tried to explain that this was all a terrible mistake but they just don't want to listen.'

Lilly held up her hand to calm the situation.

'I've spoken to the officer in the case and he tells me that a witness has placed Tanisha at the scene.'

As soon as Lilly had arrived at the station, she'd tracked Jack down for details. All he'd been able to tell her was that another girl had stated that Tanisha *had* been at the rec on the night of the crime.

'Is that it?' Lilly had been astonished.

Jack had coughed. As well he bloody might.

'That's hardly firm evidence,' she told him.

'A girl nearly died,' he said. 'Would you expect me to just ignore it?'

Of course she didn't expect that, any more than he expected Lilly to be happy about it.

'This witness is apparently very clear that, on the night of the attack, Tanisha was present,' Lilly informed them.

Tanisha and Annabelle both looked at Lilly in surprise.

'That's not possible,' said Annabelle. 'There must be some mistake.'

Tanisha narrowed her eyes. 'Who made the statement?'

Lilly checked her scribbled notes. She could barely read her own writing.

'Chika something,' she said.

With a roar, Tanisha got to her feet and punched the wall.

'That fucking bitch,' she screamed.

She pulled back her arm to punch for a second time but Annabelle crossed the gap between them and caught hold of the girl's fist. The force pushed Annabelle's own hand into the plaster. The knuckle crunched but Annabelle didn't flinch.

'No, darling, stop that,' she whispered.

Tanisha's eyes were bright with tears and she snorted hard through her nose. Annabelle, her hand still wrapped around Tanisha's balled fist, led her away from the wall, back to the chairs.

'We can explain all this to Miss Valentine,' she said.

'Explain what?' Lilly asked.

Annabelle turned to her, but didn't let go of Tanisha. 'The girl in question is called Chika Mboko. She and Tanisha were in care together. They have a history.'

Lilly raised an eyebrow.

'She's a liar,' Tanisha shouted. 'She'd do anything to get me.'

Annabelle gently placed Tanisha's hand in her lap. Her own knuckle was bleeding.

'There was an argument between the girls,' she said. 'Chika harbours a lot of ill will against Tanisha.'

'Enough to lie to the police?' asked Lilly.

'I'm afraid so,' Annabelle nodded. 'Chika isn't an honest person. She's been in trouble many, many times.'

'To be fair, so has Tanisha,' said Lilly.

'That's true,' Annabelle's eyes widened with sincerity, 'but with a baby on the way, she is trying to change her life. Chika, on the other hand, has no interest in anything but drugs and violence.'

'She's poison,' Tanisha said.

Lilly pressed her lips together, weighing the options.

'This is what we're going to do. I'll explain that you weren't present, but you say nothing.' She fixed her eyes on Tanisha. 'You answer no questions whatsoever.'

Annabelle was shaking her head, her hair waving around like wild grass.

'But shouldn't she explain why Chika would make all this up?'

'I'll do that.' Lilly jabbed herself with her thumb. 'I don't want Tanisha saying anything that will make matters worse.'

She let the proposal remain in the air for a second, then nodded.

'Anything the officer says, you answer *no comment*.'

Tanisha shrugged. 'Suits me.'

'Okay, then,' said Lilly. 'Let's put this nonsense to bed once and for all.'

Jack angled the camera at Tanisha and read out the caution. She kept her head down, her eyes in her lap. The vicious striplight above bounced off her scalp, exposed by a parting so straight it could have been drawn on with a ruler.

'Do you understand, what I've told you, Tanisha?' he asked.

She tilted her head towards Lilly, her nose ring glinting.

'Tanisha?' he repeated.

Lilly placed a notepad on the table in front of her and cleared her throat. It didn't bode well.

'For the sake of the tape, I'm going to read out a short statement on behalf of my client,' she said. 'But I need to make it clear that I have advised her not to answer any of your questions.'

Jack sighed. 'Fine.'

'My client wishes to make it clear that she was not present at the rec in Hightown where we understand this crime was committed. You say that you have a witness who has stated otherwise, but the defence has not been afforded a copy of their statement.'

'There hasn't been time . . .' Jack tried to interrupt, but Lilly put up her hand.

'And in any event,' she continued, 'it is our contention that *any* evidence provided by this particular witness is unreliable.'

'On what basis?' Jack asked.

'She has been convicted of many criminal offences, including matters of dishonesty, as you well know.'

Jack felt scarlet heat begin to travel around the base of his neck. Tanisha's record was far from squeaky clean, but if he wanted this interview to have any chance of standing up in court, he had to avoid mentioning it, otherwise Lilly would have it excluded as prejudicial.

'More importantly,' Lilly went on, 'this witness and my client have a history of animosity, so I think we have to ask ourselves whether anything she says against my client is motivated by something other than social conscience.'

Jack didn't speak. He knew from experience that Lilly was far from finished.

'Frankly, I'm surprised the police didn't bother to check these facts before bringing my client back in for questioning,' she said.

'What makes you sure that we didn't?' Jack pushed his finger under his collar.

Lilly gave a small smile. 'Because that would mean you knew all this but decided to ignore it, and I have too much respect for the police to believe that.'

Jack almost laughed. Lilly was a consummate performer.

'What do you have to say, Tanisha?' he asked.

'I've already explained that my client will not be answering your questions,' said Lilly.

Jack ignored her. 'Come on, Tanisha, are you really telling me you don't want to set the record straight?'

'I've already explained . . .'

This time it was Jack who put up his hand. 'Whilst I have as much respect for you as you do for the police, Miss Valentine, you know full well that I am entitled to put a few things to Tanisha.'

Lilly narrowed her eyes but nodded.

'Are you seriously expecting me to believe that Chika just made it all up?' he asked.

'Are you seriously saying that Chika isn't a born liar?' said Lilly.

Jack felt the warmth seep across his cheeks. 'The question was to Tanisha.'

Tanisha kept her head down. 'No comment.'

'Sure, you might have had a little falling out, but would that be enough for her to try to get you locked up?'

'No comment.'

'Because that's what could happen, you know?' said Jack. 'You could be locked up for a very long time.'

'No comment.'

He paused. It wouldn't matter how long he carried on, Tanisha wouldn't crack. Lilly was a great lawyer and would have advised Tanisha on all the tricks of the trade. It was time to end the interview.

'So as I understand it, you're saying you were definitely not at the rec in Hightown on the night of the attack upon Malaya Ebola,' he said.

'That's correct,' said Lilly.

'Thank you.'

Lilly made a brief note of the interview. The police would send her a copy of the tape, but she liked to keep written notes too. Often the legal advice not to say anything was as important as what actually was said.

'Is that it?' Annabelle whispered.

'I think so,' Lilly replied.

Jack had brought things to a close, leaving them in the interview room.

'I expect the officer has gone to check on Chika's record,' Lilly told them.

'That evil bitch is a liar,' said Tanisha. 'When I next see her she better run fast.'

Annabelle patted Tanisha's knee.

'I mean it.' Tanisha squared her shoulders. 'I'm gonna fuck her up good style.'

'Hush now,' said Annabelle.

Tanisha was about to say something else when the door opened and Jack strode in. Behind him a young WPC was pushing a grey plastic table on wheels. On top was a television and remote control.

'This is Carla Chapman.' Jack's tone was breezy. 'She's been working on some of the evidence surrounding the assault on Malaya.'

The WPC smiled at them. She had an overbite and freckles on her nose.

Lilly felt suspicion tickle the back of her mind. 'What's going on?'

'Would you like to explain, Carla?' He gestured to the WPC, who tried to hide her excitement.

'Jack, I mean Detective McNally, asked me to check whether there were any CCTV cameras covering the area of the attack.' Her voice was girlish.

'And were there?'

'Not inside the rec, no,' said the WPC, plugging in the TV. 'Well actually there is one, but it was out of order on the night in question.'

'Typical,' said Jack.

The WPC laughed, but seeing Lilly's scowl, recovered quickly.

'But there is a camera at the entrance,' she said.

The tickle of suspicion in Lilly's brain became an insistent tap, as the WPC flicked on the television.

The screen filled with the grainy image of a road, the pavement flanked by parked cars. Halfway along the road was a pair of gates. They looked metal.

'You can see the entrance to the rec here.' The WPC pointed to the gates.

Lilly checked the clock at the bottom of the picture. 22:10:33; moments before Malaya was attacked. She looked over at Tanisha but couldn't interpret her expression.

The picture remained inactive, the only movement the digits of the clock ticking away. 22:10:45.

Then a figure entered the picture from the far right and ran down the road. When she reached the gate she didn't stop, just swerved into it at full speed, her hands out to push it open. Then she disappeared through it into the rec.

'That's Chika Mboko,' said the WPC, 'and after her comes the victim.'

Lilly watched with a growing sense of the inevitable. She could hear the sound of Jack breathing behind her. She could smell the lemon tang of his aftershave.

22:10:57. Another figure entered the picture, following the first. She was much heavier and lumbered behind. When she reached the gate, she barged it with her shoulder and also disappeared inside.

'That was Malaya Ebola,' said the WPC. 'And here are the group of attackers.'

22:11:01. This time a group of girls sprinted into the picture. Lilly counted six. When they reached the gate, the WPC punched a button on the remote and the screen froze.

The image was grey and blurred. A number of the girls were completely unidentifiable, their faces little more than a smudge.

But there was no doubt about who was in the centre of the group, her face exposed directly to the camera, almost as if she were looking into it.

It was Tanisha.

'Start talking.' Lilly glared at Tanisha.

Tanisha refused to even look at Lilly, causing dyspeptic fury to burn her throat. She had taken this case believing Tanisha a vulnerable child.

'You lied to me.' Lilly put a hand over her mouth, not trusting herself to say anything more.

'I don't think we can draw any conclusions from that.' Annabelle flicked her wrist at the television. 'The picture wasn't clear enough to prove anything, beyond reasonable doubt.'

Lilly groaned. Was there anything worse than people who thought they could twist the law?

'For one thing, that picture is very high quality and we could all see perfectly bloody well that it was Tanisha,' she said. 'But it's not just about the film is it? They have a witness too.'

'A lying bitch of a witness,' said Tanisha.

'Who no one will believe,' Annabelle added.

'On her own maybe,' said Lilly. 'Just like that film on its own might not be enough. But if you put the two together, it's a whole lot more convincing. Then there's the fact that you lied. You told me you were not at the rec, for Christ's sake, you let me read out that stupid statement.'

The room fell silent and Lilly closed her eyes. This was a bloody disaster. Jack must be laughing up his sleeve.

A moment later, her thoughts were interrupted by the sound of crying. She looked up and was shocked to see it was Tanisha. Once again the mask had slipped, and a frightened girl was revealed.

'Will they send me to jail?' Tears streamed down her cheeks.

'That depends on what you tell me,' said Lilly.

Tanisha wiped her eyes with the back of her hand.

'I was there,' she said, 'but I didn't do nothing.'

Lilly inhaled deeply. It was so predictable it made her nauseous.

'Seriously.' Tanisha leaned towards Lilly. 'I followed her into the rec and that, but I didn't touch her.'

Tanisha met Lilly's gaze. Everything was open, pleading.

'So you didn't push her?'

'No.'

'Hit her?'

'No.'

'Kick her?'

Tanisha shook her head violently. 'I didn't do nothing to her, honestly.'

'So why were you there?' asked Lilly.

Tanisha shrugged. 'I dunno. I was hanging out, innit.'

'Why?'

Tanisha looked puzzled. 'They're my friends.'

'Not good enough,' said Lilly. 'These girls set out to commit a violent crime. When they chased after Malaya, you must have known exactly what would happen.'

Tanisha didn't deny it.

'So why were you with them?'

Tears shone again in Tanisha's eyes, but Lilly knew she had to pursue this.

'Why didn't you hang back, refuse to get involved?'

'I couldn't do that.' Tanisha's voice was soft. 'They're my people.'

There it was. Breathtaking in its horrible simplicity. The police might not understand that, indeed a jury might not. But Lilly did.

'The police will have combed every inch of Malaya for forensic evidence, so if there is one hair from your head on her, one tiny piece of fingernail, they will know you are lying and that you did take part in the attack,' she said.

'There won't be anything,' Tanisha's voice was firm, 'cos I never laid a finger on her.'

They stared at one another.

'Tell me one good reason why I shouldn't just walk out of here right now,' said Lilly.

'Cos you're all I got.'

The weight of Chika's arm around Demi's shoulders makes Demi want to cry.

'What's up with you?' Chika yanks her closer.

Demi's cheek presses against the heat of Chika's chest and she shivers.

'You been waiting out here in the cold for me the whole time?' asks Chika.

Demi nods. As soon as Chika went off with the policeman, Demi pulled up her hood and ran all the way to the station. She took up a place against the metal railings and waited, her breath white in the freezing cold wind as she blew on her hands. A few coppers gave her a funny look, but she didn't care.

She doesn't think she has ever been so glad to see anyone. There was the time the immigration people took Gran away for a whole afternoon. Malaya had wailed the whole time, only stopping when a social worker had given them both a Penguin. Demi remembers not feeling hungry and hiding it in her pocket for later. When she went to eat it after Gran got back, the chocolate had melted. But she'd been young then and couldn't imagine what might happen to them alone in the UK without Gran. This time she could imagine exactly what her life would be like without Chika.

'Respect to you.' Chika laughs and kisses the top of Demi's head before playfully pushing her away.

'You got that stuff safe for me?' she asks.

Demi smiles and reaches to her waistband. Chika jerks her head towards the station entrance behind them.

'Not here, fool.'

Chika's eyes flash with anger and Demi knows it was a stupid thing to do.

'Sorry,' she murmurs.

'Look,' Chika scowls, 'if you want to be hanging with me and the CBD you gotta get some smarts, you understand?'

'Yes.'

Chika stares at Demi for a second and once again she feels like crying.

'All right then.' A smile snaps across Chika's face. 'Let's get the fuck out of here.'

Four o'clock. Last lesson. French.

Jamie detests French.

Every second in Mademoiselle La Mielle's class is pure torture.

Like having his eyes gouged out with a rusty spoon. He saw a scene where that happened in *Slumdog Millionaire*, but the kid was asleep. French lessons are like being awake through the whole thing.

Mademoiselle sashays between the desks, unaware that every boy's eyes are fixed on her arse. Or perhaps she knows perfectly well, which is why she wears those tight skirts that hug her cheeks. She hovers over Jamie and places last week's prep on his desk. There are hardly any corrections and at the bottom, in Mademoiselle La Mielle's flourish of red pen, is an A.

'*Très bien*, Jamie.' She smiles at him, her bottom lip, plump and glossed. '*Une bonne pièce*.'

He mutters something incomprehensible and buries his face in his paper.

When Mademoiselle moves forward to the next desk, Jamie feels a thwack as a book hits the back of his neck. He turns around to see Tristan waggle his tongue up and down, in what the stupid tit no doubt thinks is a good approximation of oral sex. The other boys snigger.

Not finished, Tristan strokes his hands over his chest and rubs his nipples through the ink-stained pockets of his school shirt. It's always the same in Mademoiselle La Mielle's class and Jamie wishes to God that they still had Mr Anderton with his brown teeth and cigarette breath.

His mum had been totally impressed when Manor Park wrote to say Mr Anderton was on leave of absence with 'personal issues' and that a young French student would be helping out. Little did she know that every lesson had been turned into a re-enactment of a soft porn movie.

The bell sounds and Jamie scrambles to put away his books. He can't escape fast enough. As he and the other boys dash for the door, Mademoiselle holds out a hand and catches Jamie lightly on the wrist. Her skin's hot against his.

'Could I have a little moment, Jamie?' she asks, in her thick French accent.

He cringes, knowing what will happen. 'Okay.'

He makes the mistake of catching Tristan's eye as he is leaving the room. He's cupping his dick with one hand and blowing Jamie a kiss with the other. Embarrassment flushes Jamie's cheeks.

When everyone has left, Mademoiselle turns to Jamie and motions for him to sit. Then she leans against her desk. This close, Jamie can smell her, a confusing mixture of perfume and toothpaste. She cocks her head to one side and gives a tiny smile.

'You have a talent for *le francais*, Jamie,' she says.

He doesn't smile back. 'Thanks.'

'I think,' she says, 'you can do very well.'

He thinks saying thanks again might sound stupid so he just nods.

'But,' Mademoiselle lifts a finger, 'I think something is troubling you, *non*?'

'*Non*,' Jamie shakes his head. 'I mean, no.'

Mademoiselle cocks her head further so it is almost resting on her shoulder.

'I know you English are very,' she pauses, struggling for the word, 'reticent to talk about private matters, but I sense you are not happy.'

Jamie gulps. 'I'm fine.'

'You know you can come to me, if you are having any problem,' she says. 'Perhaps I can help.'.

Jamie flicks a glance towards the door. Through the glass panel, Tristan is leering in, pulsing his tongue against the inside of his cheek so it bulges. Jamie feels sick.

He looks back at Mademoiselle. 'Honestly, I'm fine.'

She holds his gaze for a long moment that makes him stop breathing. He can hear his heart thudding in his chest.

'Okay.' Mademoiselle stands and the spell is broken. Jamie exhales noisily.

'Just as long as you know that you can come to me any time,' she says.

'Thanks.'

He nods his head and makes his escape.

Lilly found Jack in the station canteen. He was nursing a can of Diet Coke, laughing with WPC Chapman.

'Something funny?' she asked.

'I guess you had to be there.' The WPC smiled up at her, a relaxed hand stirring her tea.

Lilly narrowed her eyes. Was it an innocent comment, or a dig?

'Can I have a word, Jack?' she asked.

He opened his palms.

'In private,' said Lilly.

'I'm part of the investigating team,' said the WPC. 'We're all working closely together on this.'

A dig, then. Definitely a dig.

'I only deal with the senior officer in the case,' said Lilly.

Jack nodded at the WPC, who gave a little snort and scooped up her cup, sloshing tea on the table. Lilly watched her stalk to a nearby table, where she took up a place and scowled.

'She's a real charmer.'

Jack shrugged as if he hadn't given it any thought.

'So what's your client saying now?' he asked.

'That she was at the scene but took no part.'

He laughed. 'No shit.'

'Seriously. She says there will be no forensics.'

'That doesn't prove much,' he said.

Lilly leaned in. 'I'm not the one that has to do the proving.'

'What about Chika Mboko? She says your client was one of the main perps.'

'Like I told you, she's a liar with a grudge.' Lilly tapped the table with her fingernail. 'And let's be honest, you don't have a statement from her.'

Jack pressed his lips together. Lilly could almost hear his brain ticking over. No doubt Chika had been strong-armed into talking to Jack at all. If she'd fingered Tanisha, she did it verbally. There was a good chance Chika would never come back to the station to sign anything, less chance still that she would actually turn up at court to testify.

'Without Chika, you only have the film,' she said.

'And the fact that Tanisha lied about being there at all,' he retorted.

Lilly risked a glance at the WPC's table. She was still glaring at them. The police wanted a result on this, but the evidence wasn't concrete. Without a material witness, the case might get chucked out before it came to trial. Jack had to know Lilly would push for that.

'I'm willing to roll the dice,' she said. 'Are you?'

The chief super pushed aside a plate of lasagne and chips. The fork fell on to his desk, leaving a silver splash of grease.

'Does anyone actually eat this rubbish?'

Jack didn't feel it necessary to confirm that he had virtually lived off canteen food for most of his life as a copper. Apart from the short interlude when he'd lived with Lilly, and eaten like the proverbial king, it was his main source of nourishment. On his days off he usually had a take-out.

'So where are we, Jack?' the chief super asked. 'Any closer to resolving this mess?'

Jack see-sawed his hand. 'I can prove the McKenzie girl was at the scene with CCTV footage, but I can't prove she did anything while she was there.'

'I thought you had a witness?'

'Pretty dodgy,' said Jack.

'So what? Every grass turning Queen's is a thief or a dealer,' said the chief. 'If I know one thing, it's that there is no honour among the criminal classes.'

'I'm not convinced we can even rely on her to get to court, sir, and without her, I'm skating on very thin ice.'

'Then do a deal.' The chief waved a dismissive hand. 'She must have something she wants to go away.'

Jack gulped down his distaste. Bartering with the likes of Chika Mboko was not high on his wish list.

'I mean it, Jack,' said the chief. 'We need this nailed and you'll just have to do whatever it is that you need to do.'

The custody sarge yawned loudly, revealing a mouthful of silver fillings.

'Sorry,' he muttered. 'It's been a long shift.'

Lilly nodded in agreement. She was exhausted, desperate to go home and cuddle up with Alice in the bath. Then she planned an enormous glass of Sauvignon Blanc.

Lilly looked over at Tanisha who was slumped on the bench opposite the high custody desk, eyes closed. She checked her watch. Eight o'clock on a Friday night.

'Any chance of getting a wiggle on?' Lilly asked the custody sarge. 'I'd like to get Tanisha out of here before the drunks start polling up.'

'Officer McNally is reviewing the evidence against her,' he said.

'Trying to work out if he can justify a case.'

'I couldn't possibly comment.'

'And can he?' Annabelle asked Lilly, her cheeks pinched.

'Depends how much heat he's getting from the top brass,' Lilly replied.

At last, Jack arrived. Lilly tried to read his expression, but all she could see were the dark circles under his eyes. She smoothed down her suit jacket, straightened her spine.

'Well?'

Jack's face gave nothing away.

'Jack?' she said.

Then she caught it. That flash of discomfort.

'I'll be charging your client with attempted murder,' he said.

Annabelle gasped. 'You can't do that.'

'I'm sorry,' he said. 'I have no choice.'

Annabelle's eyes were wild, animalistic, flicking back and forth. She was shaking uncontrollably as they stood outside the station.

'We shouldn't have left Tanisha in there.'

'I've already explained that we have no choice here,' said Lilly.

Annabelle shook her head. 'You should have made them see that this is all wrong. You barely said a word.'

Lilly sighed. Fortunately the wind was loud and Annabelle didn't hear.

'Tanisha will be taken to court first thing tomorrow morning and that will be the time to put forward arguments,' said Lilly. 'Once the police decide to charge, there is absolutely nothing the defence can do. The same with bail. I can talk till I'm blue in the face, but there's no way on God's earth that a custody sergeant on the end of his shift is going to release someone on an attempted murder. You must see that.'

But Annabelle couldn't see anything. Her eyes were open yet completely blind.

'You should have told the police that she was pregnant,' Annabelle said.

Lilly pulled up the collar of her jacket against the cold. She wanted to go home.

'We've been through all this,' she said. 'It wouldn't have made any difference to tonight's decision, so we'll keep it back for tomorrow.'

Lilly glanced at her watch. She'd sneaked a call to Penny asking her to collect Alice from nursery, but it was getting late and Penny would be waiting. She couldn't spend another half an hour going over and over the same ground with Annabelle.

'I'm going to need to prepare for the hearing,' she said.

'But what are you going to say?' Annabelle's voice was almost a wail. 'How are you going to make them understand?'

Lilly's tone was brisk. 'Look, Annabelle, I need to tell the court that Tanisha's current placement with you is steady, that you're both reliable and responsible, so what you need to do for me right now is to remain calm. Go home and find anything you can for me to prove to the magistrate that Tanisha has changed.'

Annabelle raked her fingers through her hair, from the scalp to the tip, as if she were trying to throw off her desperation.

'I just want to make everything right,' she said.

Lilly nodded. She understood the sentiment, but over the years she'd learned the hard way that some things were broken beyond repair.

A horrible R&B track blasts out from the speakers, followed by a chorus of whoops from the girls who start gyrating furiously.

Jamie detests this sort of music.

'Come and dance,' the girl next to him giggles.

She's been sitting by his side for twenty minutes, banging on about spending the summer in Rock, because, it's 'like totally crazy, yeah'. She says her name's Melody and wears loads of those rubber bands around her wrist.

'What's this for,' Jamie points to a white one.

'I'm, like, totally against globalization,' she says.

Jamie takes in her Converse trainers, her Jack Wills micro mini-skirt, and several Hollister vest tops layered over one another.

'Right,' he says.

Someone turns up the volume until Jamie feels like his ears might bleed.

'Dance,' Melody mouths and holds out her hand.

'I can't stand this mass produced shit,' says Jamie.

'What?' Melody shouts.

Jamie points to his ear and shakes his head. Another boy sidles over. He's wearing what looks like a skiing helmet with a plastic cup taped to the side. A rubber pipe runs from the cup to his mouth and he constantly re-fills the cup from a two litre bottle of Merrydown cider. Jamie's tempted to ask why he doesn't just drink from the bottle, but presumably that's not the point and he thinks his home-made contraption is hilarious. From the look on Melody's face, he's spot on. She leans into the boy's arm, doubled up with laughter. Jamie watches them take to the dance floor, then heads off for the toilet.

Sometimes, especially when he's at these parties, watching everyone staggering about, grinning at one another, completely wrecked, he wonders if he'll ever fit in. Scratch that. He knows he'll never fit in.

When he reaches the bottom of the stairs, he stops short. On the second step is Tristan, wrapped around some girl, sucking her face off. Can he sneak past without being noticed? Or should he make his way out into the garden? No doubt it's pretty busy out there. The bad weather won't be enough to deter the shaggers, but there's bound to be a dark corner he can make his own.

Before he can make up his mind, Tristan looks up.

'Jamie, Jamie, Jamie,' he sings.

Jamie nods hello.

'Enjoying the party?' Tristan's voice is fuzzy around the edges. 'Cos I am having a fucking ball.'

The girl he's with giggles. She's wearing denim shorts over thick black tights and her thighs are just a bit too chunky.

'This is Kate,' Tristan leans towards Jamie. 'Completely top girl.'

She giggles again.

'And this,' Tristan takes a step down to Jamie, loses his balance, so that he falls into him, 'is my good mucker, Jamie.'

'Hi Jamie.' The girl is equally hammered and gives a small burp.

Tristan puts his arm around Jamie's shoulders, as much to hold himself up as to show friendship. He smells of beer and sweat. Kate's saliva glistens on his mouth and chin. Jamie gives an involuntary shudder.

'So Jamie, how are you getting on tonight?' asks Tristan. 'Seen anyone you fancy?'

He and Kate both laugh. Jamie joins in.

'Lost your cherry yet?' They double over as if it's the funniest joke.

'On my way to the toilet actually,' says Jamie and pushes his way past. Behind him, he can hear them calling him back, but he's not stopping. When he finally gets to the top, he throws himself in and locks the door behind him. The little room stinks. Someone's been sick. They've flushed the chain, but there are strings of purple mucus sliding over the side of the bowl. He flicks the lid with a finger and it clatters down. He reaches for some loo roll, but the holder's empty and there are no spares anywhere. No doubt some twat is setting fire to them outside.

He decides to brave the lid and sits down. Through the locked door he can hear the muffled sounds of the party in full throttle. Beyoncé has been replaced by Cheryl Cole, and a group of girls run down the corridor, pumps thumping on the wooden floor boards, as they sing along.

Jamie reaches into his back pocket and pulls out the packet. Carefully, he opens it and peers at the white powder. For twenty quid it looks a miniscule amount, but he knows it will be enough to do the trick.

He reaches into his other pocket and takes out a sheet of tin foil that he begged from one of the dinner ladies at school. He told them that he wanted to wrap up a biscuit for later. The dinner ladies all live in the council houses in the village and either hate the boys, or feel sorry for them. This one had not only given him some foil, she'd made him a ham sandwich. He hates ham, but didn't like to tell her.

Jamie smoothes out the foil on his lap and taps the ice into a small, neat pile. Finally he takes out a lighter and a metal tube, the width of his index finger. He pops the tube in his mouth, his lips making the shape of an 'O' and sparks up the lighter. The flame burns bright as he passes it under the tin foil.

Within seconds the powder begins to turn and he greedily sucks up the vapour. He remembers the first time he took crystal meth. He'd been in Luton doing his Help the Aged thing, when the black girl offered him a smoke. He'd scored a bit of weed from her before but as soon as he took a puff of her spliff he was knocked off his feet. He'd been worried it was heroin. Everyone knows how bad that is, how you end up stealing cars to pay for it, or dying of Aids. The girl just laughed and told him it was 'glass'. Even from that little taste, the rush had been incredible, and he knew he wanted more.

As soon as the smoke hits his throat, Jamie feels the huge wave of energy flow through him. It makes him laugh out loud. All those stupid thoughts and worries melt away and he knows he can take on the world.

When half the powder is gone, Jamie throws open the toilet door, smacking it against the wall behind. It leaves a small black mark that would send his mum apoplectic. He doesn't even try to wipe it away with a licked finger, but heads down the stairs.

Tristan is still on the bottom step, though Kate has disappeared. He's leaning against the wall, sweating.

'Tristan,' Jamie booms, and throws his arms around his neck.

'Feeling a bit rough, to be honest, mate.' Tristan sounds forlorn. 'Think I need to sit down for a bit.'

'Fuck that,' Jamie shakes his housemate hard. 'Let's party.'

Chapter Six

'There is no way on God's earth that I will agree to your client being given bail.'

Kerry Thomson went back to the stack of files on the desk in front of her. It was Saturday morning in the Magistrates' Court and she had taken over the whole advocates' room. She was the prosecutor Lilly most dreaded. Kerry seemed to dislike Lilly and not only because they were on opposite sides of the fence. It was personal. If she could make her life difficult, she would.

'I'm not trying to be difficult,' Kerry didn't look up from her papers, 'but this is a serious case and your client should remain in custody.'

Lilly stood her ground and stared at Kerry. She'd lost more weight since the last time they met and the shoulders of her suit jacket sagged like loose skin.

'The evidence against Tanisha is piss poor and you know it,' Lilly said.

Kerry sighed and placed her finger on a page to mark her place. 'Tell it to the magistrate.'

'I will.' Lilly gave a tight smile. 'I'll also tell him your main witness has got a past like Paris Hilton.'

Kerry waved her hand as if Lilly were an annoying insect.

'I don't know about you, Lilly, but I've got better things to do, so let's do this in court and go home.'

Lilly knew it was pointless to argue, turned on her heel and left.

Being Saturday, the court was almost deserted. Only suspects nicked on Friday night were brought over. There was just one woman slouched in a chair, two inches of dark root showing on either side of her parting, as if someone had chopped at her skull with an axe and her head were coming apart.

'Are you here for Terry May?' she asked Lilly, her voice as dry and cracked as her lips.

Lilly shook her head and the woman sighed.

'He promised me he'd put all this behind him, that he was off the gear for good.'

The woman's eyes were beyond sadness, they were empty.

'His dad's given up on him, says he's washed his hands,' she continued. 'But a mother can't do that, can she?'

'No,' Lilly whispered.

When the woman turned away, defeated, Lilly made her way to the stairs and headed down to the cells. She wasn't surprised to find Annabelle waiting for her at the thick, metal door.

'I've been up all night, trying to get as much information as possible for you.' She pushed a sheaf of papers into Lilly's hands. 'There are the last three social services reviews which show Tanisha is doing really well. And all the doctor's notes on her pregnancy, of course.'

'Thanks,' Lilly muttered and pressed the buzzer with her thumb.

She heard the tell-tale clank of the locks inside and the door opened.

'Morning ladies.' The security guard was cheerful. Saturday mornings meant double time.

'Tanisha McKenzie,' Lilly smiled back.

The guard led them through to cell three. 'Not had a peep out of this one. She can come again.'

Annabelle opened her mouth to speak but Lilly placed a warning hand on her arm.

'He shouldn't talk like that,' Annabelle hissed.

'He's probably spent most of the morning being sworn at by junkies doing their rattle, he's allowed a little joke,' Lilly replied. 'And trust me, you need to keep these guys on side.'

He opened the cell and Lilly stepped in. Tanisha was curled up on the bench, a grey blanket pulled up to her chin.

'You okay?' Lilly asked.

Tanisha sat up. 'I'm starving.'

'Haven't they fed you?' Annabelle was appalled.

'I ain't eating their muck,' Tanisha said.

Annabelle pushed past Lilly, sat close to Tanisha and put her arm around her shoulders. 'As soon as we get you out of here, I'll make you some fruit and toast.'

Tanisha glared at her and she laughed. 'Okay, bacon and pancakes.'

Lilly's stomach growled. She hadn't had time for more than a cup of tea.

'Will they let me out?' Tanisha asked.

'Of course they will,' Annabelle said.

Lilly moved further into the cell. Tanisha was tired, her eyes rimmed with red. A Friday night spent in the cells wouldn't have been relaxing.

'The CPS are refusing bail,' she said.

'What?' Annabelle almost screamed. 'How can they do that?'

'The prosecutor says it's too serious,' said Lilly. 'She'll lay it on thick for the magistrate.'

'But Tanisha didn't do it,' said Annabelle.

'Obviously I'll tell the court that,' said Lilly. 'But it's not going to be easy.'

'Once you tell them about the baby, they'll have to let her out,' Annabelle said.

Lilly was about to admit that this was probably her trump card when Tanisha spoke.

'No.'

'What do you mean, no?' Lilly asked.

'I mean,' Tanisha's eyes flashed, 'that you can't mention the baby.'

'Tanisha . . .' Annabelle pleaded.

Tanisha pushed her away. 'I don't want the police or the court or Social Services knowing about this baby. Not any of dem.'

'You haven't thought this through,' said Lilly.

'Yes I have, I been thinking about it all night,' she shouted. 'And you're my brief, right?'

'Right.'

'So you gotta do what I say.'

'You give me your instructions, yes,' Lilly said, 'but I also have to give you my best advice.'

Tanisha nodded. 'Well you've given me that advice and now you gotta take my instructions. And I'm tellin' you not to breathe a word about this baby.'

Kerry patted her belly. It was definitely getting smaller. The waistband on her skirt was loose. She couldn't wait for next Tuesday's weigh-in at Flab Busters, sure she'd get a round of applause.

She pulled a Golden Delicious from her bag and took a bite. Soon she'd be the same size as Lilly Valentine. Ha. She took another vicious bite, juice and pulp running down her chin. She loathed that woman, all wild curls and low-cut tops.

Her thoughts were interrupted when Jack McNally, the officer in the case, opened the door and poked his head inside.

'Ready to go on the McKenzie case?' he asked.

Kerry narrowed her eyes at him. For as long as she'd known

Jack, he had been a scruffy no-hoper, working on small fry in child protection. When he got Lilly Valentine pregnant, she was sure she'd seen the last of him, that he'd be transferred to traffic. Instead he got a promotion to the MCU and here he was heading up an attempted murder.

'I'm surprised to see you here, Jack.'

'It's my case,' he replied.

Kerry gave a sly smile. 'It's all a bit tricky, though, with Lilly representing the defence.'

Jack entered the room and slid the door shut behind him.

'Miss Valentine and I are both professionals.'

Kerry shrugged. 'Of course you are.'

'I will do my level best to win this case and no doubt she will do hers to secure an acquittal.'

'No doubt at all,' said Kerry. 'She's already been in here demanding bail for her client.'

Jack's tone was even. 'And what did you say?'

'I told her to take a hike, that this was a serious case. Don't you agree?'

His Adam's apple bobbed as he swallowed hard. 'Naturally.'

'So do you have anything for me to make sure Lilly's case is dead in the water?'

He paused for a second, then reached into his briefcase. The photograph he extracted was of the victim. Kerry allowed herself a smile. It was horrific.

'And here's the list of injuries.' He handed her a printed sheet.

A litany of wounds and broken bones. Kerry nodded in satisfaction. There was no way the defendant was getting bail.

Lilly was hurrying up the stairs to the court room, when she saw Jack. Her stomach lurched. She'd known he'd be there but actually seeing him in the flesh still set her synapses into a frenzy.

'Morning, Lilly.' His jaw was tense and he smoothed down his tie.

'Jack.'

Their formality seemed ridiculous, yet how else could they behave?

'Who's got Alice?' he asked.

'Penny.'

'That's kind of her.'

'It is.'

They stood together for another moment, neither knowing what to say. At last the list caller announced the case and Lilly gratefully scuttled into court.

'Court rise,' the usher called.

Lilly jumped to her feet, pulse racing. She had been away from the criminal courts for six months and she felt nervous, out of touch. Jumping back in with such a serious case wasn't ideal.

The door between the magistrates' chambers and the court room opened and a white-haired man appeared. He had a pronounced stoop and it took time for him to make his way to his desk. Lilly had read on the court list that his name was Andrew Manchester. He was new and Lilly prayed he was nice.

'What's been holding things up?' he snapped.

Lilly groaned inwardly.

'This is the last case on a Saturday morning,' he eyed Lilly like a hawk. 'Everyone is waiting to go home.'

'I'm sorry, sir,' Lilly kept her tone even, 'but I had matters to discuss with both my colleague for the prosecution and my client.'

Mr Manchester gave a humph, clearly unconvinced that Lilly hadn't been spending the morning brushing her hair in the toilets. He waved a bony finger at the usher. 'Call the defendant up.'

The usher mumbled into a phone on her desk and moments later another side door opened and Tanisha was led through by two security guards who pointed her towards the dock. Tanisha hesitated.

'For goodness' sake, what is the matter?' Mr Manchester barked.

Lilly cleared her throat. 'Actually, sir, my client is a child and has no experience of the adult courts.'

Mr Manchester rolled his eyes. 'I suppose you want her next to you?'

Lilly swallowed her annoyance. She might be out of practice but this man was taking the piss.

'It's not a case of what I want, sir, the rules for young offenders are laid out very clearly.'

Mr Manchester glowered at Lilly, but she refused to look away. Their eyes remained locked for several seconds until the magistrate growled. At last he nodded at the guards who led Tanisha to the seat next to Lilly.

'What are we here for today, Miss Thomson?'

Kerry pulled herself to her feet. Lilly could see a gap between her neck and the collar of her shirt. She tried not to imagine the rolls of skin that must drip off Kerry like melted wax, after so much fat loss. Next to her, Jack kept his eyes fixed firmly on the magistrate.

'Tanisha McKenzie is charged with attempted murder, sir, and I ask that this case be transferred straight to the Crown Court,' Kerry smiled sideways at Lilly, 'where she will sadly have to become accustomed to the procedures of the adult courts.'

Mr Manchester gave a humourless snort and Kerry followed suit. Jack's face remained motionless.

'Before you make the order for transfer, sir, I would ask you to deal with the issue of bail,' Lilly said.

'Bail?' Mr Manchester narrowed his eyes as if he'd never heard the word.

'Indeed,' said Lilly. 'I understand that the issue comes up often in both the youth court and the adult courts alike.'

He leaned forward so Lilly could see the papery thin skin of his throat. 'Be very careful here, Miss Valentine.'

Lilly tossed her head. Magistrate or not, the man was a bully and she would not give in to bullies. She clenched her fists so her hands wouldn't shake and pressed them into the table until her knuckles turned white.

At last, Mr Manchester whipped his glare at Kerry. 'What do the prosecution have to say?'

'This case could not be more serious, sir, and if convicted the defendant would serve a custodial sentence whatever her age,' said Kerry.

She extracted a photograph of Malaya from the inside cover of her file and slid a copy under Lilly's nose. Lilly checked her urge to gasp. The poor child's head was swollen unnaturally, like an overripe melon left out in the sun. Both eyes were closed and purple. Her lips were split grotesquely into four separate sections.

Lilly watched with trepidation as Kerry passed the photograph to the magistrate. She could well guess what his reaction would be and decided to meet the challenge head on.

'This was indeed the most horrific of crimes,' she said. 'Utterly heartless and brutal.'

'Then why are you still making an application for bail?' Kerry sniffed.

'Because, quite simply, my client isn't guilty and I can see no good reason why she should spend any time in custody for something she hasn't done.'

Mr Manchester shook his head. 'This isn't the place to assess the evidence. Your client will have a full trial in due course.'

'But that could take many months, sir, and in the meantime Tanisha, a fifteen-year-old girl, shouldn't be forced to spend it in prison.'

'I'm sure a place will be found for her in a secure unit,' said Kerry.

'It's not like booking a room in a hotel,' said Lilly. 'A free place has to be found. Who knows how long that might take, could be weeks, even months. Whichever way you cut it, if bail is not granted this morning Tanisha will go straight from here to jail, then she'll be locked up and forced to slop out like everyone else.'

Mr Manchester sighed. 'Miss Valentine, I am not the architect of our system.'

'But this morning, sir, you are the arbiter. You can decide that where the prosecution have little more than circumstantial evidence, you will not be responsible for sending a child to custody.'

She scanned the magistrate's face for any sign of compassion. She knew she was pushing it but all she could think of was Tanisha and the tiny baby growing inside her.

'I don't need to tell you, sir, that women's prisons are soul destroying places. Suicides are common, violence an everyday occurrence.' Lilly pressed on. 'And it would be an unconscionable act to send a child there when the CPS know perfectly well that they have very little chance of winning this case.'

'We know nothing of the sort,' Kerry interrupted. 'We can place the defendant at the scene of the crime with CCTV and we have a witness who says she saw her take part in the attack.'

Lilly slapped the desk with her open palm. 'This so-called witness has a list of previous as long as my arm and you don't even have a written statement from her.'

For the first time, Mr Manchester looked interested. Lilly decided to push harder.

'The witness isn't an innocent bystander.' She looked at Jack. 'She's well known to the police as a local gang member.'

Mr Manchester looked at Kerry. 'Is this true?'

Kerry leaned in to Jack and whispered a question, but Lilly steamed on.

'Not only that, the witness has a history of personal dislike towards the defendant. There's bad blood between them.' Lilly's voice rang clearly across the courtroom. 'She's made an allegation to the police knowing full well the trouble she can cause, but we all know she won't turn up at court when the time comes and the prosecution case will collapse.'

'We'll get an order for her attendance,' said Kerry.

Lilly waved a hand at her. 'And that will be the first order she's ever obeyed in her life. Good luck with it.'

Kerry pushed back her chair and got to her feet. Her shoes were just like a pair Lilly had bought for school when she was around thirteen. They'd been £13.99 from Freeman, Hardy and Willis.

'Miss Valentine is making a lot of supposition about our witness, but as far as the Crown are concerned there is nothing to suggest our witness is unreliable.' She put a podgy hand on Jack's arm. 'This is the officer who spoke to the witness and he assures me that things are in order.'

Lilly watched Jack run a finger down the length of his tie, a sure sign that he was stressed. He knew the score. Chika Mboko was a wild card.

'Then he should get a sworn statement or get the girl in question to court, but in the meantime, this child,' Lilly pointed at Tanisha, 'should not be left to rot in prison.'

'Sit down both of you.' Mr Manchester's voice was sharp.

He paused, lips pressed together, while Lilly and Kerry both took their seats.

'I understand that this is a difficult situation but this is not the time or the place for this particular argument.' Lilly opened her mouth to speak but Mr Manchester silenced her with a hand. 'I am not prepared to make any judgements on the strength or otherwise of this case.'

Lilly felt her stomach clench.

'The defendant is of course very young,' he said, 'and custody is entirely the wrong environment.'

Lilly held her breath and willed him to do the right thing.

'But I simply cannot ignore the severity of the charge.' He held up the photograph of Malaya. 'The public must be protected from whoever did this, and I cannot take any risks.'

Lilly's heart sank and she glanced at Tanisha. Her face was impassive. If Lilly could just tell the court how vulnerable she really was, perhaps she could change the decision.

'Before you pronounce, sir, may I take instructions?' she asked.

Mr Manchester shrugged.

Lilly took Tanisha's hands in hers.

'I know you don't want me to mention the baby, but it might be your only chance of going home today,' she whispered.

Tanisha shook her head.

'I mean it,' Lilly hissed. 'He's going to send you down if you don't let me explain.'

Tanisha closed her eyes, thinking. Her lips moved as if she were praying.

'Tanisha, please,' Lilly pressed.

'If you tell them,' she said, 'I will kill you.'

Jamie can't stop laughing. All around him are sleeping bodies crashed out on sofas or in sleeping bags on the floor. Tristan is curled up next to him, his face in an ashtray. The room stinks of stale smoke and staler sweat.

Jamie's legs are knackered. He danced for six hours solid, crashing into people, knocking drinks out of their hands. Some prick called Nathan threatened to deck him, but his girlfriend pulled him away. He's been grinding his teeth so hard his jaw aches and the inside of his cheek is like pulp. He pushes his tongue against the flaps of skin and is taken over by another fit of the giggles.

'Shut the fuck up,' someone groans from the other side of the room.

Jamie puts his hand over his mouth and lets out a snort. He sounds like a pig. A little piggy wiggy with a curly tail. He's laughing so much now he can hardly breath. Oink, oink.

Tristan stirs beside him and mumbles something. Jamie hopes he wakes up. He wants to talk to someone. He smiles down but the other boy's eyelids flutter and he soon returns to sleep. Disappointed, Jamie nudges him with his toe. Tristan smacks his lips together and flings out an arm, his hand landing on Jamie's lap.

Jamie's laughter stops instantly.

He stares down at the hand, the fingers long, the nails bitten to the quick, the grazes at the knuckles from rugby. He can feel the heat through his jeans as if their skin were touching. He moves a fraction and Tristan's hand wobbles slightly. The intensity stuns him.

Last Thursday in RS, they'd discussed free will. Some woman had been arrested for fraud after she'd told a load of men that she was dying of cancer so they'd buy her stuff. Her solicitor said she had a personality disorder and couldn't help herself. The class had laughed at that, but Jamie can now understand how she felt cos what is about to happen is completely out of his control.

He watches with a mixture of horror and fascination as his groin expands. A small hump grows with frightening speed until a full hard-on is stretching the denim of his jeans.

He glances down at Tristan. He's still fast asleep, oblivious to the throbbing cock millimetres away from his hand. Jamie knows that if he shifts even the tiniest bit they will touch. Cock and hand together. The thought bounces through his brain like a silver ball in the pin-ball machines he always plays when they have school trips to Brighton. Cock and hand. Side to side. Cock and hand. Faster and faster. Ping. Ping. Cock. Hand. Five hundred bonus points.

He holds his breath. Got to keep still. Cannot move. He feels a shiver at the top of his spine. Tries to check it. Tries to push it back in. Can't. It snakes down his back.

As if in slow motion he sees Tristan's hand wobble. Back and forth like a glass of water in a thunderstorm. His eyes open wide, waiting for the moment of impact.

'What the fuck?'

Tristan is still lying down, the look on his face moving from puzzlement to horror as he takes in Jamie's erection and its proximity to his own hand.

Jamie has no idea what he should do. Could he turn it into a joke and end up slapping Tristan on the back? Or should he feign indignation? After all, it's not his hand wandering in someone else's lap is it? Instead, he just sits exactly where he is, motionless except for the slight shake of his shoulders. He stares at Tristan. Tristan stares back. The thought as to what is actually happening here stretching between them like a string of chewing gum.

At last, Tristan breaks the silence, his voice steady and low.

'I always knew you were a fucking fag.'

Jamie shakes his head. He can't think of an answer.

'You know I'm going to break every bone in your body,' says Tristan.

Jamie blinks, taking in the threat. He knows what his housemate is capable of. He's seen the bloody noses and the bruises from almost casual elbow jabs. He heard Harry Chambers gasping for air as Tristan pushed his head down the toilet in the cricket pavilion.

Jamie leaps to his feet, like a cat, and makes for the door, tripping over sleeping bodies and discarded cans and bottles.

'You better run fast, queer boy,' Tristan shouts behind him.

Outside, the air is cold, and Jamie can feel the wind sting his cheeks. He keeps going, running faster than he's ever done in his life. He doesn't stop until the party, the house and the street are far behind him. It enters his head that Dad would be pleased to see his son displaying such speed and stamina.

Then there's a strange noise in the air, like a wheezy dog barking. Jamie looks around, trying to locate it. Then he realizes it's the sound of his own hysterical laughter.

'And where is it exactly that you think you are going?'

Gran looks up from the sewing box. It's an old Quality Street tin full of odd buttons and bits of cotton.

'Out,' Demi shrugs.

'Out where?'

It's not like Chika gives her a timetable, is it?

'Just out,' she mumbles.

Gran pulls out a pin cushion in the shape of a strawberry. Malaya made it for her in primary school. It's lived in the sewing box ever since, becoming studded with a collection of pins and needles.

'You don't want to visit your sister?' Gran asks.

'I'll meet you at the hospital later,' Demi replies.

Gran narrows her eyes. 'If you are not too busy with your new friends.'

'That's not fair.'

Gran doesn't answer. She pulls out a needle, checking that the eye is big enough. Why is she so against Demi having some friends? Doesn't she want her to be happy at last? Or would she prefer it if Demi stayed upstairs all day long in her room?

She watches Gran suck the end of a piece of white cotton to flatten it. Her glasses are perched on the end of her nose, but she got them for seventy pence in Help the Aged and they're worse than useless. She peers down at the needle.

'Do you want me to help with that?' Demi asks.

Gran waves her away and stabs the end of the cotton at the eye of the needle, missing by miles. Stupid old woman. Why won't she just let Demi do it?

'Right then,' Demi pulls on her hoodie, 'I'll see you up there.'

'Hmmm.' Gran holds the cotton up to the light bulb.

Stupid old woman.

Chika finishes her milkshake and leans back against the window, balancing her chair on two legs. Dirty Mick's is emptier than usual because it's a Saturday. No workmen. He keeps it open anyway.

'What's up with you?' she asks Demi.

Demi shrugs. She's still riled about her argument with Gran, but doesn't think Chika will be interested.

'You worried about Malaya?' Chika asks.

Guilt floods over Demi and she coughs into her tea. To be honest, she hasn't given Malaya a second thought.

'Don't worry,' says Chika, 'she's tough.'

Then she turns her head and looks out of the window. A wind has whipped up the rubbish from the gutter, sheets of newspaper and cigarette packets flying down the street. Demi's feeling deepens. Not only has she not given her poor sister any head space, she hasn't even told Chika that Malaya is on the mend.

'The doctor says she's going to be okay,' Demi whispers.

Chika swivels to stare across the table at Demi.

'She's woken up anyway,' Demi swallows.

Chika doesn't say anything for a few seconds, just continues to stare at Demi.

'Did you talk to her?' she asks.

To Demi it sounds like an accusation.

'I'm going up to visit her this afternoon.' She hangs her head, frightened of how Chika will react.

Finally, a smile spreads across Chika's face and she pushes her empty glass aside.

'I'll come with you.'

Gran won't be happy to see Chika. Not happy at all. But Demi is just grateful that Chika isn't annoyed. Anyway, Chika has already scattered coins across the table for Mick. It annoys him when she does that and he always grumbles that she should just pay at the till like everyone else. She doesn't care, just winks if she's in a good mood, swears at him if she's not.

'We need to get her something.' Chika is already out of the door. 'Chocolates and that.'

Demi thinks about the splits in Malaya's mouth, how the doctor said a lot of her teeth had been kicked out. Then there's the money issue. Demi has about thirty pence in her pocket and no way of getting any more.

As if she can read Demi's mind, Chika pulls out a wad of twenty pound notes. 'I got peas, if that's what you're worried about.'

Demi takes in the cash. There's at least a few hundred pounds. More money than Demi has ever seen in her life. It makes her feel hot, and a bit sick.

'I can't keep letting you pay for everything.' Demi is trotting alongside Chika.

Chika stops dead in her tracks. 'We're family and we share what we've got.'

The litter is still flying around in the wind, like dirty kites. Chika catches a burger box with her toe and crushes it.

'Respect to you though, sister, for wanting to make your own way.' Chika gives Demi's arm a gentle punch. 'So how about I let you start making a little bit for yourself?'

Demi raises her eyebrows. How can she make any money? She's not good at anything.

'You can do a few little t'ings for me, innit.' Chika cocks her head to one side. 'Okay?'

There's nothing Demi would like more, than to help her friend and repay her for all the kindness she's shown. And to earn something into the bargain. Unbelievable. She imagines how the notes will feel in her pocket. How she'll peel them off, one by one, when she goes to buy some new trainers. High-tops, like Chika.

'Flowers.' Chika points to a florist with buckets of roses outside and marches across the road. 'That's what we need for Malaya.'

There's a lovely smell inside, like grass and meadows. A woman with her hair tied in a bun and a pair of glasses on a chain, is threading pins through a tray of carnations. She glances up at the two girls.

'Can I help you?'

Before they can answer, a man crashes through the door. He's wearing a coat with a long tail, and one of those things round his neck that's not a tie, but not a scarf either.

'I'm late,' he laughs. 'Are they ready?'

The woman behind the counter smiles up at him and places the last carnation on to the tray. 'All done.'

As the man pushes past them and reaches for the tray, Chika kisses her teeth.

'So I'm invisible now, am I?' She raises her voice. 'You can't see me or nothing?'

The man turns to her. He's still smiling but he looks puzzled.

'I'm waiting to be served here,' Chika tells him. 'So you can't be just barging in front of me.'

He gives a nervous cough. 'Sorry about that, but I'm best man at my brother's wedding and if I don't get these to the church in ten minutes I'm dead.'

Chika stares at him as if she couldn't care less if he were late to save his child's life. Demi holds her breath, the back of her neck tingling.

'Sorry,' the man mumbles.

Demi bites her lip. The power Chika has is making her dizzy.

'My friend is in hospital,' Chika tells the woman with the bun, 'and I need a big bunch of flowers for her.'

The woman puts her hand out towards a pretty spray of chrysanthemums.

'I said a big bunch,' Chika hisses.

The woman nods and goes out to the back of the shop. While she's gone, Demi, Chika and the man stand in uncomfortable silence, punctuated by the impatient tap of Chika's foot.

When she comes back, the woman is carrying a huge bouquet wrapped in silver and gold paper.

'This is the largest I've got.'

Chika eyes the shiny ribbon tied around the stems. 'It'll do.'

'Seventy-five pounds,' says the woman.

Demi's mouth falls open. Seventy-five pounds? Gran doesn't spend that on her fortnightly trip to Aldi. Chika reaches into her pocket and throws four twenties on to the counter, then she snatches the bouquet.

When she reaches the door, she flicks a disdainful glance back into the shop and snarls, 'Keep the change.'

Had she done the right thing?

Lilly asked herself the same question over and over as she sped back to Harpenden.

If she had just mentioned the pregnancy, the outcome might have been different. Mr Manchester had been wavering at one point. It might have been enough to tip the balance.

Prison was no place for a kid, least of all a pregnant kid.

When she pulled into Penny's drive her thoughts were interrupted by the sound of a baby screaming. Somewhere inside her friend's converted barn, Alice was attempting to demolish the cool stone walls with the power of her lungs.

Before Lilly had a chance to ring the bell, the front door swung open. Penny had clearly been waiting for her.

'Lilly.' Penny's voice was slightly hysterical and a blob of something white and viscous nestled in her usually sleek hair.

'Hi.'

She followed her friend down the corridor to the orangery at the back of the house. Lilly loved this peaceful room, bathed in sunlight, a huge table covered with a Cath Kidston cloth. Today the floor was littered with toys and books and paper aeroplanes. Alice lay howling in the corner.

'So how was court?' Penny's tone strained to remain cheerful.

'Shit.' Lilly scooped up her daughter. 'Another child sent to prison.'

'Anything you can do?'

Lilly thought about Tanisha's baby.

'I'm going to visit her first thing tomorrow to try and talk some sense into her.'

She jiggled Alice on her hip and the bawling calmed to an annoying whine. 'I don't need to ask how things went at this end.'

'I don't know what went wrong.' Penny let out a false laugh that bounced from wall to wall. 'I tried every trick in the book.'

'Don't worry, it's not you.'

Penny opened her mouth to speak and then bit her lip.

'What?' Lilly asked.

'Nothing.'

'Penny, this is me.'

Penny pursed her lips. 'I've just been wondering if Alice is okay. If, you know, everything is okay.'

'What do you mean?'

'I don't know. It's just that she seems so unsettled all the time.'

Lilly ruffled Alice's hair. 'She's just a bloody handful, that's all.'

'If you're sure.' Penny looked doubtful.

'I am sure.'

It's almost four o'clock and the light is fading.

Jamie's been walking for hours, round and round in circles, and he can no longer feel his legs. It's getting really cold now, a biting wind stinging his skin, and he left his coat at the party. He pulls the sleeves of his sweater over his fingers and buries his hands in his armpits.

He hasn't eaten or drunk anything since last night and his mouth is so dry he can barely swallow. Crusted flecks of blood have gathered in the corners, but he can't be bothered to pick them off.

It's time to go home. But he can't. Images of Tristan's hand in his lap and the snarl on his lips when he woke up, pound through Jamie's head. He can still feel the way his cock had throbbed uncontrollably and the raw, violent anger that ran through Tristan's body.

He doesn't want to think about what's going to happen next. How Tristan will tell everyone what happened. By now it will be all over Facebook.

Jamie's phone makes him start and he fumbles in his pocket. He has a text.

Where are you, J?
Mum x

Tears spring into Jamie's eyes. Mum's been worrying about him. Surely that means she does care. That if he told her about what was happening she'd listen. He wipes his face with his sleeve. He tries to picture having a proper conversation with Mum. He's sitting on his bed and she's in the chair by his desk. She's put her phone and BlackBerry away, and she's concentrating on what he's telling her. Jamie's temples ache with confusion.

He realizes he's only ten minutes from home. If he runs he can make it in five. His heart leaps into his mouth and he can almost taste it. He stabs out a reply.

Home very soon
J x

A smile breaks across Jamie's face. Mum will understand. She'll help. She'll sort out this fucking awful mess he's got himself into.

He points his feet in the right direction when his phone bleeps again. Another text.

Dad and I going out now.
Help yourself to food in the fridge.
Mum

Jamie cries out as if he's in physical pain. It's like Tristan has punched him in the stomach. The force knocks Jamie sideways. He staggers towards the nearest lamp-post and clings to it as if it were the mast on a sinking ship. A drop of fresh blood falls from his open mouth and splashes on the pavement at his feet.

He is completely alone. Even as a young boy he knew this. In a world crammed with people and crowds, Jamie is utterly separate.

'Are you all right?'

Jamie looks up to find an old man stood over him. His white hair is neatly cut. His scarf is wrapped around twice.

'Are you all right?' he repeats.

Jamie, both hands still holding the lamp-post, opens his mouth to speak. Another drop of blood escapes. The old man's eye line follows it, until it hits the ground and opens like a flower.

'Are you ill?' He pulls out a mobile phone. 'Can I call someone for you?'

Jamie doesn't answer. Every cell in his body is aching and screaming. But who can he call? Who can help? There's no one. No one at all.

The old man frowns. 'Do you need anything?'

Need? He pushes himself up the lamp-post and straightens his back.

'I need to get out of here,' he tells the old man. 'I need to get to Luton.'

Lilly beat together sugar and butter with a wooden spoon. The repeated circling of her wrist was soothing. She cracked three eggs on the side of the bowl and let them slip into the mixture. Alice sat in her high chair, mimicking her mother with a plastic plate and a breadstick.

After the disastrous morning in court, Lilly had been baking. The air in the kitchen was a chocolatey fug she could almost bite.

Sam poked his head around the door and sniffed. His eyes widened at a plate of muffins cooling next to the oven.

'They're still hot,' Lilly told him.

He shrugged and helped himself to two. Lilly chuckled indulgently and reached for a cup of melted chocolate, dark and glossy. As she poured it in with the other ingredients, the door bell rang.

'I'll get it,' Sam offered, his mouth full.

'Blimey,' said Lilly, 'those muffins must be bloody good.'

He wrinkled his nose at her but left to answer the door. While he was gone, Lilly dipped her finger into the cake mixture and held it to Alice's mouth. The baby licked it off with a wet smack of her lips.

'See,' Lilly muttered to herself, 'there's nothing wrong with you at all is there?'

When Sam returned he was scowling. 'There's some man here for you.'

'Who?'

Sam shrugged.

Lilly shook her head in despair and made her way out to the front door, her flour-covered hands held out in front of her like a sleep walker. It was Karol.

He glanced down at her old jogging bottoms and flowered apron. 'Am I interrupting?'

'Not at all.' Lilly pushed the hair out of her eyes with her forearm. 'Come through to the kitchen.'

She cringed as he followed her through the sitting room, the sofa piled high with case papers. In the kitchen, he smiled at the dozens of bowls and utensils that littered the surfaces.

'I'm baking.' She laughed and kicked a cupboard door shut with her bare foot.

'It smells great.'

There was an uncomfortable pause where Lilly noticed how muscular his arms were and how badly her toenails needed cutting. Sam glared at them both.

'This is my son,' Lilly said at last.

Karol held out a hand. 'I work for your mum.'

Sam's didn't take his hand. 'What as?'

'I answer the phone and do the administration.' Karol leaned over and stage whispered. 'Have you seen the state of her office?'

'Crap job.' Sam's face relaxed slightly.

Karol threw his head back and laughed. 'Someone has to do it.'

'Suppose.' Sam gave a half smile and reached for another muffin before heading back to his room.

'Nice boy,' said Karol.

'If you like moody unreasonable teenagers,' Lilly answered.

'Fortunately, I do.'

There was another pause before Lilly coughed back her embarrassment.

'So what brings you to Casa Valentine?'

Karol pressed his lips together and took a breath through his nose. 'I spoke with Penny and she told me you were upset by the court case this morning. I wondered if I could do anything to help.'

Lilly sighed. 'How long have you got?

The plate in front of Karol contained nothing more than a few left over crumbs, which he chased with his finger.

'You are a very good cook, Lilly.'

Lilly smiled. 'I find refuge in my kitchen.'

'And what are you hiding from, may I ask?' Karol cocked his head to one side.

There were so many, many things. The situation with Jack. Sam's moods. Alice being Alice. But Lilly was sure Karol would not want to hear her long list of personal difficulties.

'Work can be very stressful,' she conceded.

'The McKenzie case?'

She nodded. 'I promised I wouldn't represent any more kids. I swore to everyone that I was done.'

'So why did you take Tanisha on?'

Guilt? Concern? Sheer bloody-mindedness?

'Because she needs my help,' said Lilly.

Karol leaned back in his chair. It creaked slightly under his weight. 'Then you have done the right thing.'

'I wish it were that simple.'

'When someone stretches out a hand to us, we can ask a hundred questions and listen to the opinions of a thousand people. We can tie ourselves up in knots.' He opened his palms. 'Or we can take that hand in our own.'

Lilly smiled. Karol was right. She reached for a muffin and took a bite.

'The problem now is that Tanisha's been sent to prison.'

'What?'

'She didn't get bail,' Lilly said. 'And the one thing that might help her get out of there, she won't let me use.'

Karol considered for a moment.

'She is a child, so you must decide for her,' he said.

'She told me this information in confidence,' Lilly replied.

'You said yourself that she asked for your help,' Karol held Lilly's gaze. 'It is you who must decide how best to give it.'

It's a cold evening. Chika and the other girls take it in turns to stand under the lamp-post in an alleyway on Clayhill. A tower block looms on either side reaching up into the black sky. Demi blows on her hands to warm them and puts up her hood.

Earlier, at the hospital, Gran had told her that it made her look like a 'hooligan'. Demi sighed and pushed it back, but Gran still wasn't satisfied, glaring at Chika until she left the room. She hadn't even been pleased with the flowers.

'Where did you get the money for those?' she demanded.

Honestly, it's like she wants them to be poor or something.

And Malaya wasn't much better. She didn't even look at them as Demi searched for a vase. She didn't say anything either. Just stared at Demi.

Well they can both do what they like. Demi's not paying any more attention. Here she is tonight, working with her crew, and it feels great. She looks up the length of the tower blocks. First the one to her left, then to her right. All those windows glowing yellow. How many girls are in there, hiding away? She wants to shout out to them all and tell them not to be afraid. That there are friends who will watch out for them.

A boy comes scurrying out of the shadows towards Demi. She can see the whites of his eyes, wild in his face. Chika's told her not to be scared. People like this might look mad, but they know exactly what they want. And they know Demi and the rest of the CBD have got it.

The boy stops in front of her, hopping from foot to foot. She stares him down, just like Chika showed her.

'Yeah?' She nods aggressively at him.

'Glass,' he answers. He sounds posh. Not from round here.

She signals to a boy called Sean on a BMX, who cycles off to get the gear. This is the worst part; while they wait.

'Don't talk to them, or listen to any rubbish, you get me,' Chika warned. 'If they try to tell you that they'll pay tomorrow or that they've only got three days to live, let them jog on.'

'Okay,' Demi replied.

'And if you think for even a second that they're gonna try to rob you, use this.' She pressed a can of pepper spray into Demi's hand.

At last, Sean is back and hands the man his wrap. But only after he's given Demi the money. She can't help smiling.

Chapter Seven

The ground was still covered in frost when Lilly arrived at HMP High Point, and the white blanket, stretching out across the cavernous car park and surrounding wasteland, made the dark prison walls even more foreboding.

A recent escape by a suspected trafficker had resulted in an extra layer of razor wire, circling the building itself like a crown of thorns. The fact that the woman in question had got out by knocking her solicitor unconscious, changing into her clothes, and sauntering through the front door, appeared to interest no one.

Lilly stamped her feet against the cold as she waited for reception to open.

She had spent the weekend barraging the prison with demands to visit her client. When the administration office had informed her for the fourth time that she would need to make a request in writing, Lilly had demanded to speak to the governor in person.

'Tanisha McKenzie is a juvenile,' Lilly had railed.

Mrs Loveland had sighed. 'Look, Miss Valentine, I'm no more keen to have her here than you are, but I wasn't given the choice. So while she is here, we have to follow the rules of procedure.'

'She's on remand,' Lilly pointed out, 'which means technically she can have visits every day.'

'Social visits, not legal ones,' said Mrs Loveland. 'For a start, we don't have the facilities and we're fully booked for a week.'

'Then I'll take a social visit.'

'You sure you want to do that?'

'Definitely,' Lilly answered.

In the freezing gloom of morning, with her breath alive in the air, Lilly envisioned attempting to interview Tanisha in the crisp-strewn visitors' centre.

By the time Lilly had passed through security and set off the scanner twice, the visitors' centre was full. Toddlers ran around in circles, screaming and laughing. They windmilled their arms, sending Cheesy Wotsits flying across the room. Their dads and grannies swore at them through the thick fog of cigarette smoke.

She took a seat at the last available table, her papers sticking immediately to the brown stain splashed across it. Lilly prayed it was Coke.

At last the door that connected the centre to the prison opened, and the inmates began to stream through. They scanned for their loved ones, then sprinted over, hugging and kissing them. Some couples lingered in their embrace, their tongues slurping and their hands groping.

The man at the adjacent table held his wife's face tightly in his hands, their open mouths locked together. Lilly winked at the little boy sat next to them, ignored, swinging his legs and picking a scab on his chin. When they finished and sat down, Lilly tried not to notice the fresh bulge in the woman's cheek.

'Can I have some sweets, Mum?' the little boy asked.

The woman didn't speak, but waited for the guard to pass by before removing a plastic bundle from her mouth and pushing it down the front of her jeans. She pushed her pelvis forward, wrinkled her nose and finally looked at her son.

'Course you can.'

Lilly sighed. Prison life.

When Tanisha appeared at the door, Lilly waved and stood to greet her. Her client ambled rather than hurried, but at least gave a tight nod of her head.

'How are you?' Lilly asked.

Tanisha took the seat opposite Lilly and shrugged. 'All right.'

'You sure?'

Lilly's client put her elbow on the table and pushed her face into her palm, pressing her cheek flat. Her hair was scraped back from her face and held in an orange band. Without make-up or jewellery she looked younger.

'Who are you sharing with?' Lilly asked.

The right cellmate could make all the difference in jail.

Tanisha gestured with her head to a woman on the other side of the room. The circles under her eyes were almost as black as her teeth.

'And?' Lilly asked.

Tanisha sighed. 'And she spent last night crying until she shat herself.'

Lilly shuddered.

'I don't know what you want me to say.' Tanisha closed her eyes. 'You must know what it's like in here.'

Lilly did know. 'I'm going to make another application for bail.'

'What's the point? The magistrate ain't gonna change his mind.'

'I'll go to the Crown Court,' said Lilly. 'A judge will be much more likely to listen to reason.'

Tanisha opened her eyes. 'Yeah?'

'Yes.' Lilly paused, weighing her words. 'A judge will give proper weight to the lack of police evidence and all the other issues.'

Tanisha narrowed her eyes. 'What other issues?'

'Your age and the fact that it's completely inappropriate for you to be here.'

The couple at the next table had begun to argue and their little boy watched them in distress. He bit his lip, clearly trying not to cry.

'I ain't gonna fight with you about that,' said Tanisha. 'What else?'

'I'll take Annabelle along and get her to testify about her home and your placement there.'

Tanisha looked uncertain. 'She can be a bit, you know, flaky.'

'Sure, but she cares about you. That much is obvious.'

Tanisha opened her mouth to speak but changed her mind and simply nodded.

'And you know the last thing I'm going to say, don't you?' said Lilly.

'Surprise me.'

Lilly leaned in to Tanisha. 'I need to tell them about the baby.' She waited for Tanisha to react. Instead, there was nothing but the noise of the room. 'I know you don't want me to because you're worried about Social Services finding out, but you'll be showing soon enough anyway,' said Lilly. 'At least this way you can be at home, rather than stuck in prison.'

It was impossible for Lilly to read Tanisha. She could only hope she was being swayed.

'I've seen too many women have their babies behind bars.' Lilly placed her hand on top of Tanisha's. 'I want to make sure that doesn't happen to you.'

Tanisha didn't move a muscle. Her skin was cold to the touch.

'Let me do this,' Lilly urged.

Tanisha didn't blink. 'Ain't gonna happen.'

The house is completely still as Jamie pads downstairs to the kitchen. His stomach is so empty it hurts, but he's not sure he'll be able to keep anything down. The fridge is stocked with ready meals. No doubt Mum did her usual ram raid on Marks & Spencer, but even the thought of putting food in his mouth makes Jamie heave. He settles on a glass of orange juice and needs two attempts before he can let it spill past his lips.

'Aah.' The acid burns his ripped gums. 'Fuck.'

He leaps to the sink and spits, running the tap over the blood-stained juice. He cups his hand under the flow and brings it to his face, lapping the water like a dog. Even that hurts.

He sinks down to the floor, feeling the cold tiles under him. His knuckles press against their hardness. This is beyond shit. Way beyond.

When he finally got home in the early hours of Sunday morning, Dad muttered something under his breath about binge drinking. He didn't seem to care that Jamie had been missing. And he certainly didn't care when Jamie spent the day in bed.

Mum did her best to show concern. She popped her head around his door every couple of hours and made cooing noises or offered to bring cups of tea.

'You're not going back to school tomorrow, darling,' she repeated again and again, her hands on her hips, as if he were arguing. 'You've obviously got a virus.'

This morning she even threatened to stay with him, but she was already dressed in her work suit, her hand clamped around her BlackBerry.

'I'll phone to check on you as soon as I'm in the office,' she called up the stairs.

Jamie glances at the clock on the kitchen wall. Half past ten. Mum hasn't rung.

He lets his head fall back against a cupboard door and remains on the floor, trying to think. The house is deserted and the garden beyond the window is silent, but it's so hard. When he's on the gear his mind is clear and he has the answer to all the questions. Not as if he could go on the telly and win *Who Wants To Be A Millionaire?* It's more like he knows what he wants and where he's going. Like the energy and happiness fill him up and there's no room for any doubt.

He knows when it starts to wear off because the tiny fears return, like worms burrowing into him. At first, they don't hurt but he can feel them wriggling. Soon they're everywhere, taking him over. Infesting him. If he has another hit they disappear as quickly as they arrived, taking cover in their worry holes. Trouble is they haven't gone. They're just waiting.

But Jamie's not stupid. He knows you can't keep going like that. Carry on taking it and you'll soon be addicted. Last night, over on the estate in Luton, he'd seen them. The junkies. They're dirty and desperate and there's no way he will let that happen to him.

All he has to do is sit tight. He just has to get through this until he starts to feel better.

He pulls himself to his feet and floats through the house like a ghost. He flicks on the television to distract himself but the sound rakes at his ears. Maybe he should just go back to bed. If he could get a few hours' sleep.

The stairs seem impossibly steep as Jamie drags himself back to his bedroom and he flops headfirst on to his duvet. There's a sharp smell but he ignores it and closes his eyes. Even a moment's unconsciousness would be welcome.

He tries to push aside every image fighting for air time and concentrates on blackness.

Sleep, sleep, sleep. He can do this. He can give himself up to nothing. And when he wakes, this will all be behind him.

When his phone beeps, Jamie isn't sure if it's a dream. When it sounds again, he knows it's not.

'Shit.' He opens one eye.

The mobile is on his bedside table staring accusingly at him. It could be Mum.

He reaches over for it with one hand and brings it close to his face. It's not from Mum.

U fucking queer.
U can stay off as long as U like but this isn't over.

Jamie drops the phone on the floor. How did he think a quick snooze could solve anything? Tristan, Mademoiselle La Mielle, Manor Park, Mum, Dad, everything. Nothing's changed.

He beats his forehead with the heel of his fist, as if this could chase away his demons. But they're all still there, deep inside, banging a louder drum.

There's only one escape.

The station canteen was busy. Coppers finishing a long shift. Coppers getting breakfast before the start of theirs. Coppers grabbing something to eat between calls.

Jack ordered a bacon sandwich and a mug of tea before settling at a free table. At the far side, WPC Chapman was sharing a joke with some guys from the team. Like all young and pretty policewomen she attracted the attention of her male counterparts like flies around shit.

She looked up, caught Jack's eye and waved. He took a bite of his sandwich and nodded hello. His mouth was still full when she appeared in front of him.

'Jack.' She smiled.

He swallowed. 'Morning, Carla.'

'I've been through the CCTV footage again.'

'You're keen.'

'I got one of the techies to enhance the image,' she said. 'And it's definitely McKenzie.'

Jack let out a low whistle. 'That was quick. Who did you have to kill?'

Carla pushed her lips into a pout. It reminded Jack of a little pink rosebud.

'You catch far more bees with honey than vinegar,' she said.

'But you need to be careful that the little buggers don't sting you.'

Carla raised an eyebrow. 'You don't seem happy about this case, Jack.'

'Let's just say I'm waiting for McKenzie's next move.'

The phone in Jack's pocket vibrated. He took it out and read the incoming text.

'Bang on cue,' he said. 'The defence have listed another application for bail.'

Carla wrinkled her forehead. 'I thought your ex tried that in the Magistrates'.'

Jack winced. He'd never officially moved out of Lilly's place. There hadn't been some dramatic bust-up where he limped down the drive with a cardboard box in his arms.

'My ex,' it hurt even to say the word, 'has listed the case at the Crown Court.'

'When?'

'Late this afternoon.'

'I thought I was quick off the mark,' Carla frowned. 'How did she manage that?'

'Lilly Valentine is a very persuasive person. Some might say, tunnel visioned.'

'Is that a good thing?'

'It is if you're Tanisha McKenzie.'

Lilly rang Annabelle's doorbell for a second time, but there was still no answer. Lilly slapped her forehead. Of course she should have telephoned, checked Annabelle was home, before hightailing it over there.

When she'd asked the Crown Court to list Tanisha's application for bail urgently, she hadn't expected the list office to act on the same day. She'd gone on the offensive, assuming the best she'd get would be a hearing in a day or so. What was the old saying Elsa was so fond of? Be careful what you wish for.

She groaned and checked her watch. How on earth was she going to get everything she needed together in a couple of hours? And more importantly, where was her star witness, Annabelle?

She stabbed the bell again, knowing it was pointless, and was about to give up, when she heard the low thud of music. From her position on the porch, Lilly could see a Mercedes pull up, windows blacked out and a private reg. DK 639. Sam called them pimpmobiles. The car of choice for a drug dealer, more like. What was it doing here in the leafy environs of the Hertfordshire commuter belt?

Lilly was surprised to see Annabelle get out. Her hair stuck out as usual as she closed the passenger door and bent to look inside the window. The glass lowered but Lilly couldn't see inside.

'I want you to think over what I said.' Annabelle's tone was cold.

'Of course.' It was a man's voice.

'Thank you.'

Annabelle turned and took a step towards her house. The car window began to rise. When it had reached halfway, Annabelle spun on her heel. Her back was very rigid.

'You owe me,' she said.

The man didn't answer but Annabelle remained where she was, staring in his direction. Finally, she nodded and turned again. Behind her, the Mercedes' engine gunned angrily and the car shot away.

When Annabelle reached the porch, she spotted Lilly.

'I didn't see you there.' She couldn't hide the tremor in her voice.

'Is everything okay?' Lilly asked.

'Everything's fine.' Annabelle reached into her pocket for her key but, when she put it in the lock, Lilly saw her hand shaking.

Once inside the kitchen, Annabelle made tea. She breathed deeply as the teacups rattled in the saucers. Something was very wrong. Lilly glanced at her watch again, she simply didn't have time to worry about it now.

'Leave that, Annabelle,' she said, 'and sit down please.'

Annabelle gave a tight smile and did as she was told. She smelled strongly of cigarette smoke and she held the edge of the table with both hands.

'I've made another application for bail,' Lilly said.

'That's good.'

'It is,' Lilly agreed. 'The only problem is, it's been listed this afternoon.'

Annabelle's eyes widened.

'So I need to get all my evidence together immediately,' said Lilly.

'I gave you all the paperwork.'

'I know, and it is all very helpful, but nothing can beat the personal touch.'

'Such as?'

'You.' Lilly paused to let the idea sink in. 'I want to put you in the box to tell the judge what sort of set-up you have here and how well Tanisha is doing.'

Annabelle gulped and ran a hand through her hair till it stood on end. Lilly tried not to notice.

'I need you to explain exactly how Tanisha has changed and how you're helping,' said Lilly. 'Can you do that?'

'Yes.' Annabelle's voice was shrill.

'Why not write it all down and have a practice?' said Lilly.

Annabelle nodded and Lilly eyed her nervously. This wasn't how she'd pictured things at all.

'I have to go now and try to dig up as much muck as I can on Chika Mboko,' said Lilly. 'I'll meet you at the Crown Court at four.'

'Fine,' Annabelle whispered, and Lilly left her still holding on to the table as if her life depended on it.

* * *

'How does she do it?' The chief super shook his head in disbelief.

'Black magic,' Jack said.

The chief frowned. 'This isn't a laughing matter, Jack. Getting a case listed on the day of the application is unheard of.'

Jack didn't argue but leaned against the top of the chair opposite the chief. It wheeled away from him, making him bend in an awkward manner. What could he say? He'd never understood how Lilly managed most of the things she did. Black magic wasn't far from the mark.

'Call the CPS and make sure we get a decent barrister on to this,' the chief barked. 'I don't want some part-time solicitor from the Luton branch screwing this up.'

'Right.'

'And what about the Mboko girl? Do we have a statement yet?'

'It's been the weekend, sir.' Jack knew it sounded lame.

'Then you'd better track her down, Jack.' The chief pointed at him. 'By hook or by crook we need her.'

The air in the office smelled thick and peppery. Lilly sniffed and smacked her lips.

Karol looked up from a bowl and smiled. 'Egusi soup. You want?'

'I do.' Lilly puffed out her cheeks. 'But sadly I don't have time.'

Karol looked her up and down. 'You don't seem like a woman who would turn down home-cooked food.'

'You mean I'm fat,' Lilly laughed.

'Not at all.' Karol gave an appreciative grin. 'Where I am from we like some meat on the bones.'

Lilly patted her stomach. 'Plenty of that here.'

'Go and start your work.' Karol waved her away. 'I will heat some soup for you.'

At her desk, Lilly picked up the phone and steeled herself as she dialled the number. Kerry Martin picked up on the first ring.

'Hello.'

'I'm just checking you know about the hearing this afternoon,' said Lilly.

Kerry didn't respond immediately and Lilly could hear her breathing down the receiver.

'Yes, I know about that,' Kerry said slowly.

'That's good. I just wanted to ask you to bring a few things to court.'

'Such as?'

'Chika Mboko's statement of course, and a list of her previous convictions. In fact any information you have on her, I'd like.'

Kerry sighed. The noise swished into Lilly's ear.

'It isn't a trial, Lilly.'

'I didn't say it was.'

There was another pause and Lilly could just make out the faint tapping of computer keys.

'I'll bring the previous but if you want anything else you'll have to ask Social Services,' said Kerry.

Lilly banged down the receiver as Karol entered the room carrying a bowl of soup. Steam rose into his face.

'Problem?' he asked and placed it in front of Lilly.

She screwed up her nose. 'I need info on a witness but the prosecution are playing silly buggers. I can try Social Services but it takes them a bloody week to answer the phone.'

He shrugged and gestured to the soup. Lilly took a spoonful. The sweet taste of oxtail, followed by the punch of spice, hit the back of her throat.

'This is fantastic.'

Karol smiled and placed a yellow Post-it note on Lilly's desk. His handwriting was round and neat.

Annabelle called – speak to the Bushes about Chika and Tanisha.

'You beauty,' Lilly yelled.

'Good news?'

Lilly took another celebratory mouthful of soup. 'I might not be able to get anything out of the CPS or Social Services, but the Bushes is another story.'

She let her fingers fly through the Rolodex Karol had set up for her and pressed in the numbers.

'The Bushes,' came the reply.

'Miriam, it's Lilly Valentine.'

'Oh my God, I thought you were dead.'

'Like Mark Twain before me, rumours have been greatly exaggerated,' Lilly laughed.

'So how are you, girlfriend?'

'Long story, Miriam, but I need a favour.'

'Naturally.'

'I need to know everything there is to know about Tanisha McKenzie and Chika Mboko,' said Lilly.

'Why don't you just apply for the files?' Miriam asked.

'Cos I'm in court this afternoon.'

'Naturally.'

'So what do you say? Can you help?'

'Get your arse over here and I'll see what I can do.'

Jack hammered on Chika's door for a second time. When there was no answer he opened the letterbox and peered inside.

'Chika, move your backside and open up now,' he shouted.

There was no response, no movement inside. In frustration, he thumped on the wooden frame again and the door next to it flew open.

'For Christ's sake, knock it off, will you.' A young woman in her early twenties glared at him. 'It's obvious they ain't in.'

She was wearing a velour tracksuit and her hair was pulled tight in a ponytail on top of her head. A stud glinted in her tongue as she spoke.

'How can you be sure?' Jack asked.

'Because you've been out here banging for God knows how long.' She nodded inside with her head. 'You'll have the baby awake if you carry on.'

Jack thought about Alice and how it was when she cranked up. 'Sorry.'

The young woman sniffed and went to close the door.

'I don't suppose you know where I can find Chika?' Jack called after her. 'It's urgent.'

He expected the door to shut in his face, but instead the young woman peered around the gap.

'What's she done this time?'

'Nothing. I just want to speak to her.'

The woman snorted. The residents of the Clayhill Estate believed nothing they were told. Especially if the person doing the telling was a copper.

'Seriously, I just need a word.' He knew he was losing her. 'What about the mother?'

There was a grating sound as the woman ran the metal in her tongue against her top teeth.

'You ain't telling me *she's* in trouble?'

'Like I say, I just want a wee word.'

She squinted at him, trying to weigh him up. At last she sighed. 'She's in the lift, cleaning it out.'

'What?'

'You heard me.'

'But why?'

The woman stuck her chin out at Jack. 'Cos some dirty bastard puked up in there and Mrs Mboko's one of the few decent people left around here.'

With that, she slammed the door as if he could never understand. In truth, he knew he never would.

Jack wandered to the end of the walkway to the lift. When he'd arrived earlier, he'd bypassed it and headed straight for the stairs. They were always out of order and even when they weren't you wouldn't pay your worst enemy to put a foot inside.

The doors were being kept open with a brick on either side and a large black woman was mopping the floor. The air stung the back of his throat with disinfectant.

'Mrs Mboko?'

The woman looked up at him briefly, but immediately returned to the steady rhythm of the strokes of her mop.

'I'm Jack McNally.' He flashed his badge.

She reached the end of the mop into the far corner and ran it along the edges in a square movement.

'I need to find your daughter.'

Mrs Mboko finished another circuit of the perimeter, then placed her mop in the bucket. With a grunt she bent for the handle.

'What makes you think I have any idea where she might be?'

'You're her ma.'

'And you are the police,' she squeezed her bulk past him, 'so you know full well that I have no control over Chika.'

Jack watched Mrs Mboko move slowly down the walkway to her flat. The water sloshed over the side of the bucket, splashing her leg.

'She's not in any bother,' Jack called.

Mrs Mboko didn't stop, but Jack caught the flinch in her shoulders.

'Quite the opposite,' he continued. 'In fact she's been helping me out.'

Bucket still in hand, Mrs Mboko turned. There was a glimmer of something in her eyes. Hope, maybe.

'You know the girl who was beaten? She was called Malaya Ebola,' Jack said.

'I know the family very well. Her grandmother and I go to the same church.'

Jack thanked the god of lucky policemen. 'Well, your girl is making sure that we put the person who did that behind bars.'

Mrs Mboko placed the bucket on the ground with a heavy groan, water pooling around her feet, and stared at him in disbelief.

'I just need to know where she is,' said Jack.

There was a clear choice for Mrs Mboko. Protect herself from yet another disappointment or drop her defences.

Tears shone in her eyes. 'The café on the corner of Queen Street.'

Jack watched her walk away, her tread slow, wet shoes leaving footprints on the concrete.

The front door was open as Lilly screeched into the car park of the Bushes Residential Home for Children. She double-checked her central locking had kicked in. She'd spent enough years visiting care homes to know that most of the kids living there would nick anything not nailed down. And for the rest, they'd bring a claw hammer.

Miriam came out to greet her. 'Look what the cat dragged in.'

She'd aged in the last three years, grey hair sprouting from her scalp to the edge of her extensions, her forehead furrowed with lines. Some things, though, never changed; Miriam still wore her Birkenstocks, despite the frost.

She held out her arms and enveloped Lilly. Another thing that never changed.

'I heard you had a baby.' Miriam smiled, her teeth large and white.

'Can you believe it?' Lilly laughed. 'The oldest swinger in town.'

Miriam pushed Lilly aside playfully. 'Tell me what you need.'

'I represent Tanisha McKenzie.'

Miriam clicked her tongue three times. 'I thought you weren't doing this work any more.'

'Don't you bloody start.'

Miriam cocked her head to the door. 'Let's get out of the cold and I'll see if I can help.'

Inside her office, it was as if Miriam had never been away. The room was jammed with papers and the computer entirely circled by Post-it notes. Lilly moved a pile of files from a chair and took a seat.

'So what do you know, Glasshopper?'

Miriam perched on the end of her desk. 'Tanisha stayed here on and off between foster placements.'

'And?'

Miriam opened her arms. 'And what can I tell you? The mother never got in contact and the poor kid had no other family. Eventually she got in with the wrong crowd.'

It had the inevitable familiarity of a fairy tale. Without the happy ending.

'What about Chika Mboko?' Lilly asked.

'Truth?'

Lilly nodded.

'She had everything going for her. The mother seemed to genuinely care,' Miriam let out a long sigh. 'But somewhere along the line that kid got seriously damaged.'

'Violent?'

Miriam bit her top lip, thoughtful. 'She was one of only a handful of kids I was ever really scared of.'

Lilly sucked in a breath. Miriam had been a social worker for fifteen years and had run care homes for another ten. Lilly had seen her slotting herself between two crack-deranged teens brandishing knives at one another. She'd seen her holding a six-foot lad in a headlock, while the ambulance arrived to take him to the secure wing of a mental hospital.

'So what's the story between Chika and Tanisha?' Lilly asked.

Miriam raised her arms then let them drop to her sides with a slap. 'Who knows? They were as thick as thieves, shared a room here and everything. When their key worker landed them a foster placement together, they were cock-a-hoop.'

'What happened?'

'Neither of them would ever say. The foster-carer reported that it had something to do with a stolen phone but I never bought that,' Miriam said.

Lilly nodded. Miriam's instincts about kids in care were rarely wrong.

'What I do know is that when they came back here it was all-out war,' Miriam continued. 'Chika did everything she could to get Tanisha kicked out and Tanisha did the same. One night there was a huge fight and Tanisha ended up in hospital.'

'Was Chika charged?' Lilly asked.

Miriam shook her head. 'Tanisha wouldn't play ball, but after that we got her out of here.'

'It sounds like it got pretty bad.'

'To be honest,' Miriam said, 'I was worried that one of them might get killed.'

The café on Queen Street served shocking food. The state of the kitchen was more shocking still. It wasn't a shock that its nickname was Dirty Mick's or that Health and Safety had tried to close it down three times.

Jack opened the door and the smell of a deep fat fryer, full of filthy oil and carbonized food, hit him. He scanned the tables and clocked Chika in the corner, sitting with a younger girl. When she saw him, Chika scowled. He moved across the greasy floor and stood over her.

'I'm busy,' she said.

The other girl looked up at him. Something about her was familiar.

'Are you deaf?' Chika shouted.

'No, Chika, I'm not,' Jack replied.

'Then why you still here?'

'Because Tanisha McKenzie's case is back in court this afternoon,' Jack said.

'And you think I'm interested?' Chika sucked her teeth. 'Cos I think you must be mistaken about that.'

Jack stood his ground. 'Thing is, Tanisha's got herself a shit-hot brief.'

'Is that right?'

'Afraid so, and this afternoon her brief is going for bail.'

'Let them,' said Chika.

'She's going to tell the judge what Tanisha said happened on the night Malaya was attacked,' Jack said, 'and I won't have anything to say she's lying.'

Chika blinked at him.

'If she's successful then Tanisha's getting out of jail,' Jack narrowed his eyes. 'And something tells me you don't want that.'

When she didn't answer, he smiled and turned on his heel. He got as far as the door, when Chika called after him.

'Wait for me outside.'

The policeman leaves and Chika leans over to Demi.

'I gotta go.'

Demi doesn't understand. 'With him?'

'It's complicated,' says Chika.

You bet it's complicated. Demi has had it drilled into her by Chika that whatever happens, you sort it yourself. You don't need the police.

Demi's head spins. Everything is topsy-turvy.

'You've got to trust me,' says Chika.

Demi flops back in her chair.

'While I'm gone I need you to do something for me.' Chika opens her eyes wide.

Demi will do anything for Chika. Surely she knows that.

Chika brandishes a key. 'I need you to let yourself into my house, understand me?'

'What if your mum's there?'

Chika waves away Demi's concern. 'She ain't gonna stop you. Go to my bedroom right, and in my top drawer you'll find something.'

'What?' Demi asks.

Chika glances to the door where the policeman is hovering. 'Just something. You gotta pick it up and take it to sixty-three B Clancy.'

'Sixty-three B Clancy,' Demi repeats.

'Right. Danny will be there.'

Demi feels her heart race at the mention of the man with the scar.

'Do I have to?'

'He's expecting a delivery around six,' says Chika.

'He scares me,' says Demi.

'Trust me, you'll be a lot more scared if he don't get what he wants.'

Chapter Eight

Jack glanced from the windscreen to his passenger. Chika was utterly still, staring straight ahead into the road, yet she fizzed with latent energy. She reminded Jack of an animal about to spring.

He tapped the steering wheel with his fingernails. Whichever way he turned it, he couldn't fit the pieces into the jigsaw.

'Why are you doing this, Chika?'

'Doing what?' she grunted.

'Helping me.' Jack jabbed a thumb at his chest. 'I'm a copper. The filth, the feds, Babylon. Whatever you call us these days.'

'So?'

'I'm the enemy, remember.'

'You telling me not to bother?' Chika clicked her seat-belt free and put her hand on the door handle. 'Cos I'll gladly fuck off.'

'Chika,' Jack warned.

'I'm serious.' She threw the door open, narrowly missing a man waiting to cross the road. He dodged out of the way, swearing and shaking his fist.

Jack slammed on the brakes. 'Shut the door, Chika.'

Chika stared at him, refusing to move. The car behind blared the horn and gunned its engine. Passersby stopped to look at the commotion.

'I just want the truth, Chika,' Jack said.

'I've told you the truth.'

The whole road was at a standstill, all eyes focused on Jack and Chika. The driver in the car behind got out and began to shout at them. Jack ignored them all, concentrating on his witness's face. Was it possible she could put aside her hatred and prejudices?

'All right,' he said. 'Tell me again what happened.'

Chika dragged the door shut and Jack pulled off.

'Me and Malaya was on her jump in,' said Chika, 'and we goes to Hightown to have bit of a laugh, do some spraypainting and that.'

Jack nodded. This much he knew was true. 'What did you do?'

Chika spat out a laugh. 'We legged it, innit.'

'Why?'

'Cos we're slipping in their area, and if they catch us they're gonna hurt us for real,' she said.

'Where did you run to?'

'You know that, man. We go to the rec thinking we can outrun 'em, get through the fence on the other side.'

'But you couldn't?'

Chika shakes her head slowly. 'They're right on our tail, understand, and Malaya ain't no Olympic athlete. They catch her pretty much as soon as she gets in there.'

'What about you?' Jack signalled and turned left into the car park for the Crown Court.

'I got hid in some bushes.'

He parked and pulled on the handbrake. 'But you could see clearly?'

'Yeah,' Chika said, 'and hear dem.'

The car park was almost empty. Court sessions had finished for the day. Only this case remained.

'That must have been hard,' said Jack.

Chika looked out of the side window into the growing shadows. 'I didn't know what to do.'

For the first time since Jack had met Chika, she sounded like any other young person would.

'What happened to Malaya?' Jack asked.

'She was on the floor and at first it was just one of them, shouting at her, putting the boot in a bit.'

Jack winced, imagining a fifteen-year-old lying helpless as she was kicked. Mr Stephenson had confirmed that the fractures to Malaya's forearms meant she'd tried to protect her head and face.

'I thought maybe they might leave her, you know, after she got a bit mashed.' All trace of anger and arrogance had disappeared from Chika's voice. 'That's what I was hoping anyways.'

'But it didn't happen like that?'

She wrinkled her nose. 'They all joined in, gave her a proper beating. Well, you seen the state of her.'

He had. Witnessing horrific injuries was a part of every copper's job. Traffic accidents, shootings, stabbings, Jack had seen the lot. It didn't get any easier, and the sight of Malaya Ebola's face was imprinted on his brain.

'Was Tanisha McKenzie there?' Jack asked.

'Yeah.'

'Are you sure it was her?' Jack said. 'It was dark and you were hiding.'

'I'm telling you for real, she was there. Me and Tanisha go way back and I'd know her anywhere.'

Outside, the sun was sinking and without the engine on, the temperature in the car had quickly dropped.

'Did Tanisha take part in the attack on Malaya?'

Chika didn't hesitate. 'Yeah.'

'Are you absolutely sure because she says that although she was there, she didn't take part.'

'I seen her punch Malaya in the stomach and I seen her kick her in the head.'

'Tanisha says she didn't touch her.'

Chika shivered and wrapped her arms around herself. 'She's lying.'

A trickle of sweat ran down Lilly's back. She was completely flustered, running late for court and stuck in horrendous traffic.

She pounded her fist on the steering wheel. 'Come on!'

She was wondering if she should take a detour when her mobile rang.

'Lilly Valentine.'

'It's Nikki from the nursery.'

Lilly's heart sank.

'I'm afraid we need you to collect Alice.'

'What's wrong?' asked Lilly.

'She's been unsettled all day' – Lilly could hear Alice screaming in the background – 'and now we just can't get her to calm down.'

'I'm working,' Lilly offered desperately. 'You know how she is.'

Nikki sighed. 'Yes I do, and we just can't deal with her this afternoon. I really think she needs to see a doctor.'

'She's not ill.'

There was a silence until Nikki spoke. 'You really do need to collect her.'

Lilly hung up and dialled Jack's number.

'Lilly?'

'Hi Jack, where are you?' Lilly asked.

'Court.'

'Why?'

'We have a case on this afternoon. Is the name Tanisha McKenzie ringing any bells?' he said.

Lilly didn't have time to joke. 'I meant why are *you* at court? It's only a bail ap. Couldn't you send Miss Teen Sensation?'

'If you mean Carla, no I couldn't. You know full well how important this is, Lilly, and you were the one who told me to either get a statement or bring my witness to court.'

'You have Mboko there?'

'Large as life and twice as ugly.'

Lilly groaned. Not only could Jack not pick up Alice, he had just decimated the central plank of her application. She thought frantically. Dare she ask Penny again? After Saturday's fiasco she wouldn't be keen, but perhaps if Lilly begged. She dialled Penny's number and got voice mail.

'Shit.' Lilly threw her mobile on to the passenger seat, where it bounced and fell on to the floor. Within seconds it rang. She reached over, flapping her hand towards it. When she couldn't get it she leaned from the waist, her side digging into the gear stick. The car swerved and bounced off the curb with a thud. She straightened the wheel with her left hand and wiggled the fingers of her right. As she finally touched the phone, the car thumped the pavement again.

'Penny?' she shouted into the phone.

'Sorry, no.'

'Hi, Karol.' Lilly's voice was flat.

'You seem very disappointed,' he replied.

Lilly forced a laugh. 'Not at all, it's just that I was hoping Penny could collect Alice from nursery. Her dad can't do it and I should have been in court five minutes ago.'

'Penny is in London. I believe she and Henry have tickets for a West End show.'

Damn. Lilly had thought it funny when Penny had told her she and her husband were instigating date nights once a month, 'to keep dialogue open'. It had been years since Lilly had been on a date. Then again it had been years since she had had any dialogue with anyone.

'I can do it,' said Karol.

'What?'

'I can pick up your daughter.'

'You can't do that.'

'It would be my pleasure,' he said.

Lilly was stunned into silence.

'You have been kind enough to give me work when many will not,' he said. 'Where I am from we try to repay such kindnesses.'

'Thank you,' was all Lilly could manage.

A scowl was painted across Annabelle's face as she waited on the steps of the court.

'Where have you been?' she demanded.

'The Bushes,' Lilly replied, 'and it's a good job I did.'

She strode through the building with Annabelle scuttling after her. If Chika was going to give evidence, Lilly would have to hurl everything she'd learned from Miriam in her face. It wasn't going to be pretty.

As she hurried across the atrium she caught sight of the prosecuting barrister and stopped dead. He was in conversation with Kerry, making notes on his brief.

'Jez Stafford QC, no less,' she called out. 'What brings you to sunny Luton?'

He beamed at her, displaying straight white teeth. 'When I heard you were defending I couldn't resist.'

'Your charm has no effect on me,' Lilly smiled.

He kissed her on both cheeks. 'There was a time I remember when that wasn't the case.'

'Once.' Lilly held up a finger. 'A long time ago. And I was very pissed.'

He tossed his head back and laughed. Lilly noticed Kerry looking longingly at him.

'So what are we doing today?' Jez rubbed his hands together.

'The usual,' said Lilly. 'You tell the judge that a fifteen-year-old should be locked up indefinitely for a crime she didn't commit and I tell him that's a pile of shit.'

'We have a witness, Lilly, she's here at court.'

'Have you met her?'

'Not yet.

It was Lilly's turn to laugh. 'Good luck with that.'

Demi taps gently on the door and listens. There's no answer so she slides the key Chika gave her into the lock and lets herself in. She's glad Mrs Mboko isn't at home.

She hurries up the stairs to Chika's bedroom. It smells of her, all lipgloss and weed. There's a set of drawers at the end of Chika's bed with a Nigerian wrap draped over the top like a cover. It's purple and grey batik. Demi runs her finger along the beautiful design before reminding herself to hurry.

The top drawer doesn't open easily. It's packed with so much stuff, the runners have buckled. Demi jerks it out as far as she can. There are at least twenty vests and T-shirts crammed inside. Not so long ago Demi would have been stabbed by envy.

Gran says being jealous is a sin. Thou shall not covet thy brother's goods. But it's so hard not to when everyone seems to have so much and you don't have anything at all. Does Jesus think that's fair?

Today she just smiles because Chika's good fortune is also her own. Demi's earning money and will soon have a drawer full of her own clothes to choose from.

She yanks the handle again, trying to get a look at the back. Whatever Chika has sent her to find is well hidden. She lifts the cotton tops and slides a hand under, her fingers brushing along the wooden base. Nothing.

She pushes out her bottom lip. Could Chika have made a

mistake? Could she have put whatever it is somewhere else and forgotten? Demi looks around the room at the messy chaos. She doesn't even know what she's looking for.

One thing Demi does know is that she doesn't want to be caught. She'll have another rummage and then she'll leave. Chika will be pissed off but there's nothing Demi can do. She pushes the contents of the drawer aside, fingers searching. At last she hits on something firm. She rifles through until she finds a small envelope. One of those padded ones with bubble wrap inside. Gran sometimes gets them from back home and Demi likes to roll each bubble between her finger and thumb and squeeze until it pops.

The envelope is sealed but there isn't an address on the front, as if it hasn't been sent anywhere. Inside, she can feel something angular and hard, like a little metal tin. Demi grabs it and propels it under her hoodie and into the waistband of her jeans. She shoves the drawer shut but it doesn't move so she nudges it with her side. The object in the envelope pushes into her hip bone.

When the drawer is nearly closed, Demi leaves it, and heads back for the stairs. The job is almost done. She's halfway down, a smile on her face, when she hears the unmistakable sound of a key in the lock. Demi's blood pounds in her ears. Mrs Mboko. What if she calls Gran? Or the police? She looks behind her, wondering if she should dart back into Chika's bedroom and hide. Before she can make a move, the door opens and Mrs Mboko's vast frame enters the flat. Demi freezes as if she can blend into the wallpaper and somehow Mrs Mboko won't see her.

She watches in horror as Chika's mother drops her small brass key into a bowl on the table in the hallway and turns to check her reflection in the mirror hung above it. Her face is sad and angry. Demi holds her breath and hopes Mrs Mboko heads straight into the kitchen, then perhaps she can sneak out without being seen.

It seems as if her prayers are answered when Mrs Mboko does indeed move towards the kitchen door. But as one fat foot passes over the threshold, she pauses, then takes a step back. Demi is gripping the banister so tightly her wrist hurts. Mrs Mboko looks up and their eyes meet.

'Demi?' Mrs Mboko frowns.

Demi doesn't answer. She's still holding on as if she's afraid she might fall.

'Is Chika with you?' Mrs Mboko asks.

Demi shakes her head.

'Is it true what the policeman said?' Mrs Mboko's mouth is tight. 'That she's assisting him?'

Demi nods and tears spring into Mrs Mboko's eyes.

'Oh my girl, oh my good girl,' Mrs Mboko mumbles and leans heavily against the table, making it sway and creak.

Demi seizes her opportunity, bolts down the stairs past Mrs Mboko, her hand pressed against the package in her waistband.

'Don't you worry, Demi,' Mrs Mboko calls after her. 'Chika will soon help the police catch the people who hurt your sister.'

As the guards led Tanisha from the cells to the dock, she blinked at Lilly.

Lilly approached the rail and whispered to her client. 'Don't be frightened.'

'I'm not,' Tanisha replied, but the look on her face told another story. There was a stain on her prison sweatshirt and she picked at it with her thumbnail.

'Have you had any second thoughts about . . .' Lilly gestured to Tanisha's stomach.

'None.'

Lilly sighed and went back to her seat. Kerry gave her a little smirk and took the place behind Jez. He was a bloody good barrister so this was going to be an uphill struggle.

'All rise,' the usher called and Lilly got to her feet.

Her Honour Judge Josephine Bevan glided through the side door and nodded politely. Lilly thought her eyes lingered just a little too long on Jez's handsome face but she chided herself for being paranoid.

'Since your client is a minor would she prefer to sit with you?' the judge asked Lilly.

Lilly smiled. 'I'm sure she would.'

The guard unlocked the dock and Tanisha shuffled over to Lilly.

'She seems all right,' Tanisha hissed.

'Don't be fooled. She's not about to give us an easy ride.'

The judge took a swift glance at her papers before turning to Jez. 'So what do you have to tell me, Mr Stafford?'

Jez leaned his thighs lightly against the desk, a hand in his pocket. The first time Lilly had seen him in action she'd marvelled at his coolness and today she was bowled over all over again. Why wasn't he ever nervous?

'Your Honour, I won't bore you by rehashing the details,' he purred, 'but suffice it to say that the prosecution strongly objects to the application for bail made by the defendant.'

'On what grounds?' the judge asked.

Jez shrugged as if he could barely bring himself to repeat it. Behind him, Kerry was almost drooling.

'Given the seriousness of the case there has to be a flight risk, particularly as this young woman has no real home. Then there's the possibility of her reoffending whilst on bail. Her list of previous convictions hardly fills us with confidence in that regard.'

'I've read the transcript of Miss Valentine's application at the Magistrates' Court,' the judge placed the nib of her pen on one of the papers in front of her, 'and the main thrust of her argument seemed to be that the prosecution case was weak.'

Jez turned to Lilly and gave her the sort of liquid smile that had led her into that cloakroom with him, many moons ago.

'And I have to say,' the judge continued, 'I have a fair deal of sympathy with that position.'

Jez held up his hands. 'It's true that at that point we didn't have a statement.'

'And I still don't seem to have one today,' the judge replied.

'Fortunately, Your Honour, we can go one better.' He paused for effect. 'We have the witness here at court.'

The judge raised an eyebrow and Lilly cringed.

'I think, Your Honour, you'll be very interested in what she has to say,' Jez said.

'Yes indeed.'

Tanisha leaned in close to Lilly. 'What's happening?'

'They're bringing Chika in,' Lilly replied.

'Here?' Tanisha was horrified.

Lilly grabbed her client's hand. 'Don't say a word. Don't even react. Let me deal with her.'

Behind them, the entrance door opened, and Lilly heard the rustle of clothes and the pad of feet. She and Tanisha resolutely stared dead ahead, their backs ramrod straight, their necks stiff. At last, out of the corner of her eye, Lilly caught the dark outline of a figure and allowed herself to cast a glance. Immediately she regretted it as she met Chika's gaze full on. The intensity crackled like electricity. Startled, Lilly had to look away.

When Lilly had gathered herself enough to raise her eyes once more, Chika was being helped into the witness box by Jack. He gestured to the seat and gently pressed Chika into it. All trace of the raw energy that had unnerved Lilly had disappeared. In its place was the same look of confusion that had been evident on Tanisha's face.

Lilly took a deep breath and tried to clear her head. Everything she'd been told about Chika had lead her to expect a monster. Instead, here was another frightened child.

* * *

The windows and front door of 63b Clancy are boarded up with metal grilles. There are loads of flats like that around the estate. Gran's always complaining about them.

'People all around the world are living in tents and shanty towns. It's a disgrace to let perfectly good homes stand empty or to let the vermin take them over.'

'Rats?' Demi asked.

'Worse than rats,' Gran replied.

Demi lifts her hand to rap on the door. She wonders if there's anyone inside, and if there is, how they'll hear her through the thick steel. She doesn't need to worry. Her knuckle is still touching the cold metal when the makeshift flap cut into the door slides open.

'Yeah?' a voice comes from inside.

She's practised what to say all the way over here, but now her throat has gone dry.

'I need to . . .' She coughs and gulps. 'I need to give something to Danny.'

'What?' the man asks.

Demi's hand flutters to the hidden envelope. 'I don't know. Chika sent me.'

'Chika?'

'Yes.'

'Fine. Hand it over.'

Demi reaches into her waistband and passes the package through the slot. Her hand is shaking as it is grabbed from her.

'Wait there.'

Demi has to snatch her hand clear as the flap slams shut. She takes a step to the side and leans her back and head against the stonework. As she concentrates on breathing, she can feel the bricks prickling her scalp. At the far end of the walkway a woman leaves her flat. She's got a toddler with her, most of his face masked by a dummy. They glance up at Demi and scramble in the opposite direction.

At last she hears the scrape and clank of metal, but instead of the flap, it's the door that swings open. A man with dreads to his shoulders pokes his head outside and checks up and down the empty walkway before grunting at Demi.

'Come.'

Like a bird, she hops inside and feels the whoosh of air as the door is wrenched close behind her. She tries not to panic as she hears the bolts being locked and peers into the shadows beyond. There is no light in the hallway and the air smells of chemicals. The man doesn't even look at her as he leads her to the sitting-room door.

'Danny wants to see you.' He jerks his head and pushes the door open.

The smoke and brightness make Demi blink as she passes into the sitting room. Then she blinks again in surprise. The room is twice the size she expected. An enormous cave lit by bare bulbs. In the dead centre is a huge square coffee table, surrounded on all sides by mismatched sofas, where a group of men are playing cards. As Demi shuffles into the room, they ignore her, but she can see Danny leaning back into the dirty, sagging cushions, a cigarette clamped between his lips.

When she's crossed a few feet she can see why the room is so big. The central wall has been knocked out, leaving a jagged, gaping hole. Demi is looking at the sitting rooms of 63b and next door.

Without warning Danny looks up at her. His milky eye, smooth as a peeled lychee, makes her shudder now as much as the first time she saw it.

'All right?'

No. She's not all right. She's locked in a disused flat with one of the scariest men she's ever met in her life.

'Fine,' she says.

He nods as if this news is important to him, then lays down his cards in a fan on the table.

'Read 'em and weep, brothers,' he laughs.

The others all shout together.

'Motherfucker.' The man next to Danny throws his hand across the floor, where a six of diamonds lands among the cigarette butts.

Danny is still laughing as he rakes a pile of money towards him with the side of his palm. Demi's eyes open wide as she mentally counts at least three hundred pounds. Then she sucks in her breath. There's a gun. It's laid casually amongst the phones and the ashtrays, but it's definitely a gun.

Danny catches her clocking it and picks it up, holding it next to his cheek, in line with his scar.

'Thanks for this, Demi.' He pauses, watching her reaction. 'What? Did Chika not tell you what you were bringing for me?'

Demi clenches her mouth shut, determined not to show any emotion. Inside the envelope she had felt something small and hard. She'd thought it might be a tin of cash. Or drugs. Then again, she'd known it was too small. The gun glints silver in the windowless gloom.

Danny kisses his teeth. 'She's a crazy bitch that Chika. Or maybe she thought if she told you, you'd bottle it.'

'I wouldn't.' Demi can feel the heat in her cheeks.

The men laugh and click their wrists. The only one not smiling is Danny.

'Good girl.' He blows out a plume of smoke. 'Now I need you to do something else for me.'

Demi nods. It's the last thing she wants to do but she's hardly about to say that.

'Just another delivery,' he says.

Her heart is beating so loudly she's certain they must be able to hear it. It's like a drum in her own ears.

'Rocky,' Danny calls out of the room.

The man with dreads appears at the door, a container of chow mein in one hand, a white plastic fork in the other. 'Wha?'

'Give the sister here the gear for Solomon Street,' says Danny.

The man forks in a mouthful of noodles, soy sauce dripping down his chin. He sucks them up with a smack and snorts at Demi as she follows him to the kitchen. She's glad to escape from Danny but the sight of the kitchen fills her with horror.

On the stained work surface, where Gran keeps the bread bin and her Lean Mean Grilling Machine, are lots of large bottles with yellow labels. Demi might not be able to read too good, but she knows the symbol for *flammable* and she knows what it means. Nearby, in fact far too near, is an old formica table covered in a series of pipes and funnels joined together by plastic piping, bubbling away on top of three Bunsen burners all attached to a Calor gas canister. It looks like a joke version of the chemistry lab at school.

The smell makes Demi feel sick. Like a mixture of glue and bleach. Rocky doesn't seem to care and continues slurping up his noodles.

'In the corner.' Rocky points with his fork.

Demi steps gingerly around the table towards a tray full of pills. The round white ones that are supposed to dry up a cold. Gran swears by hot water and lemon laced with chilli, but Demi's seen these tablets in the chemists.

'Not those,' Rocky rolls his eyes. 'The baggies, dem.'

Demi casts her eye around and sees a shoe box in the corner full of twenty-pound wraps of glass. She scoops it up, pushes down the lid and shoves it under her arm. She could be carrying a new pair of trainers rather than two thousand pounds' worth of drugs.

'Solomon Street,' Rocky tells her. 'Ask for JC.'

'What number?'

Rocky gurns at her. There are bits of food stuck between his teeth.

'Unless you serious stupid, you're gonna know.'

Throughout Chika's testimony, Tanisha didn't move. She didn't even lift her head. Instead she concentrated on her nails, peeling away the painted tips and letting the flakes of varnish fall, until her legs were covered in what looked like gold leaf.

When Chika mentioned her by name, Tanisha flinched but didn't look up.

Lilly made studious notes. Not because she needed to but because she needed to focus. Not on Chika's words, but on her own reaction to them. How was she going to undermine her? Which card should she choose to nudge so that the whole pack collapsed? Or should she just sweep away the deck in one move?

When she was finished, Chika moved to leave the witness box.

'Please remain seated, Miss Mboko,' said the judge. 'No doubt the defence have some questions for you.'

A shadow passed across Chika's face and she looked over at Tanisha and Lilly. There was a glimpse of the intensity Lilly had seen earlier as Chika entered court. Something powerful, yet trapped. As if sensing Lilly could see, it fled, but not before Lilly made a mental note of how to proceed with her cross-examination.

'Thank you for coming today.' Lilly gave a warm smile as she got to her feet.

Chika shrugged. 'It's all right.'

'Quite a way for you,' said Lilly.

'Not really.'

'Come now, it's a two-bus journey at least, and we all know how frequent they are these days in Luton.' Lilly gave a small laugh. 'You did come on the bus, didn't you?'

'Nah.' She nodded at Jack, who had taken a seat to the side of the court. 'He brought me.'

'That was very kind of him. Did you arrange to do that over the phone?'

Chika shook her head.

'Then how did you sort things out?' Lilly asked.

'He came and got me.'

Lilly paused as if she were puzzled. 'How did he know where to find you?'

'Dunno. Tracked me down, innit.'

'So you didn't volunteer to come,' said Lilly. 'The police, as you put it, had to track you down and bring you here themselves?'

Jez pulled himself to his feet. 'With all due respect, Your Honour, this application was listed at such short notice there was no way the witness could have known anything about it.'

'It's a fair point,' the judge said to Lilly.

'Then I'll put it another way.' She narrowed her eyes at Chika. 'I don't think you would have come here today of your own accord and I don't think you'll come again in the future.'

'Is there a question coming?' Jez rolled his eyes.

Lilly ignored him and kept her own eyes trained on Chika. 'Frankly, I don't think anything you've told the court today is true.'

'You calling me a liar?' Chika glared back.

'Yes,' said Lilly.

'Your Honour,' Jez called out. 'Who is giving evidence here? Miss Mboko or Miss Valentine?'

Lilly pressed on regardless. There was something dangerous about Chika and she needed the judge to see it.

'I think you made this whole story up.'

Chika pushed the tip of her tongue between her lips and pressed them around it.

'I think you hate Tanisha McKenzie and you saw this as an ideal opportunity to make trouble for her,' said Lilly.

'Your Honour,' Jez raised his hands so that they framed his head.

'Miss Valentine, I can see where you're going with this,' said the judge, 'and I'm asking you to stop.'

But there was no way Lilly was going to stop. She could see the colour drain from Chika's tongue with the pressure she was placing on it. Her nostrils flared as she used every ounce of her willpower to restrain the fury that was fighting to be set free.

'I think you didn't always feel this way about my client. You used to be the best of friends. But something happened and everything changed.'

'Miss Valentine, I am now *telling* you to stop this.' The judge raised her voice.

Despite the warning, Lilly continued. 'I think, Chika Mboko, that you are a violent criminal with a grudge against Tanisha and that there is no reason that this court or anyone else should believe anything you say.'

'Enough,' the judge bellowed.

Chika jumped to her feet in the witness box, her entire body shaking. She bared her teeth at Lilly. This was it. The reaction Lilly had been searching for. The rage.

'I . . . am . . . not . . . lying,' Chika whispered.

In that instant Lilly knew she had lost.

Jamie staggers down the street, hooting hysterically. He can't remember when he last had such a laugh. His new mate Trick, or is it Track, no, definitely Trick . . . anyway, he's a blast. He bumps into a litter bin overflowing with rubbish and ricochets sidewards, slipping on a discarded box of chips.

'I'm a stunt man.' Trick writhes around on the pavement. 'Roll the fucking cameras.'

They met a couple of hours ago in a swing park. Jamie had just scored from some girl on the Clayhill. Not the usual one. He'd walked around a bit, looking for her, when another one called over to him.

'You chasing?'

He wasn't sure. The other girl's gear was always good. He's read on the internet that some dealers cut it with all sorts of things. Rat poison and stuff. At least he knows the other girl's drugs won't kill him.

When she began to walk away he decided it didn't matter. It's probably only injecting it that can do you any harm. After all, they put loads of chemicals in cigarettes and you don't see people keeling over when they light up.

So he scored a wrap and set off to find somewhere to take a puff. Finally, he found himself in a park. It was pretty rundown, with graffiti sprayed over the roundabout and the tyre swing was melted where someone had set it on fire.

It was then he saw Trick. Their eyes met and he knew. They were the same. He darted under the slide and Jamie followed him.

Underneath, it was dark, but not cold. They had to crouch to fit. It reminded Jamie of a summer spent in Tuscany. Mum and Dad hired a villa and invited all their friends to visit. The adults spent their days around an enormous table by the pool, drinking Chianti, while Jamie sheltered from the sun under a slide in the garden.

Trick pulled out a bag and a piece of tin foil, and patted his pockets for a lighter. Jamie took out his own drugs and together they did their thing. He was nervous about getting high with someone else. Would it be the same, or would it spoil that delicious rush? He needn't have worried. It was even better. Somehow their shared secret intensified the moment.

'See that?' Trick pointed to a dark stain a few feet away. 'That's blood, that is.'

'No way,' Jamie exclaimed.

Trick nodded. 'Some black girl got proper battered.'

They both looked at it with serious faces. Then Trick started to giggle, and soon he and Jamie were coughing and spluttering with the humour of it.

As Jamie helps Trick to his feet now, he can't believe how much they have in common. Okay, they're from totally different backgrounds, but it just doesn't matter. The government are always banging on about how the middle classes shouldn't shut themselves off from the rest of society, how they should mix with the other members of their community. Well here is Jamie, well and truly mixing and loving every second of it. Maybe he should write to the prime minister and suggest he get all the kids together and throw them in a room with some meth. That would do wonders for his social cohesion policy. Jamie is laughing so hard he has to stop and bend forward from his waist to catch his breath.

Trick brushes the chips from his jeans. 'Shall we have another hit?'

See, that's what Jamie means, they're virtually reading each other's minds.

He looks around him. There are people milling up and down the street.

'Don't worry.' Trick puts a hand on Jamie's arm. 'I know a place.

The game was up. As Chika was led out of court by Jack, she gave Lilly a sneaky smile. She had won.

Lilly did a quick calculation. Her application had rested squarely on the assertion that the prosecution's case against Tanisha was built on sand. That Chika wouldn't turn up and shouldn't be believed. Sadly, she hadn't been able to prove that. Chika's evidence now lay on the table together with CCTV footage of Tanisha chasing the victim into the park, and of course, the fact that Tanisha had lied to the police.

There was no way the judge was going to grant bail.

'Your Honour,' Lilly said, 'I should like Annabelle O'Leary, to give evidence.'

The judge frowned at Lilly. She had not been amused by Lilly's refusal to stop her cross-examination of Chika.

'I am telling you now, Miss Valentine, that this had better not be a repeat of your previous spectacle.'

'Your Honour, I think it's important that you hear about Tanisha's current foster placement. From the horse's mouth, so to speak.'

'Very well.'

As Annabelle was brought into court, Lilly winced. Annabelle had clearly not been able to follow the instructions to calm herself down. She was bleached of all colour and her eyes darted around in an almost paranoid fashion. When she picked up the Bible to be sworn in, she dropped it, then banged her head against the rail as she bent to pick it up. Even Tanisha sighed. There was no way anything Annabelle had to say would impress the judge.

Tanisha was going back to prison.

Lilly took up her pen, scribbled a note on her legal pad and pushed it on to Tanisha's lap.

I'm sorry.

'I wonder if you could help the court with something,' Lilly asked Annabelle.

'Of course.' Her voice wavered.

Lilly took a deep breath. 'Is Tanisha McKenzie pregnant?'

Annabelle's mouth gaped, but before she could speak, Tanisha whipped up her head.

'No,' she shouted.

'I'll ask you again, Mrs O'Leary,' said Lilly. 'Is my client pregnant?'

In a split second, Tanisha leapt to her feet and crossed to the witness box.

'You don't have to answer.' Tanisha grabbed at Annabelle's arm, her fingers scrabbling to grip her waterproof jacket. 'You don't have to tell them nothing.'

The guards raced to Tanisha and held both her arms behind her back.

'Please, Annabelle, you promised me,' Tanisha screamed and struggled to get free.

Annabelle looked wildly from Tanisha to Lilly and tears tumbled down her cheeks when the guards dragged Tanisha back to the cells, the door slamming closed behind them.

A silence settled. No one seemed to breathe.

'Miss Valentine,' the judge's voice rang across the room, 'it appears you have just breached your duty of client confidentiality.'

Lilly put the palm of her hand over her mouth and breathed into it. She bit back a wave of nausea.

'Your Honour, I do have a duty to my client, but, because of her age, I have an overriding duty to the court and in these circumstances I felt it would be impossible for you to make such a life-changing decision without all the facts.'

The judge looked grim. 'Then you may repeat your question.'

'Mrs O'Leary,' Lilly could barely find her voice, 'is Tanisha expecting a baby?'

'Yes,' Annabelle sobbed. 'Yes, she is.'

The tissue that Annabelle used to wipe her nose was in shreds. White flakes clung to her nostrils. She had wept her way through the rest of her evidence.

As she and Lilly waited to be let into the cell area, she tried desperately to dry her eyes.

'How long before the judge makes a decision?' she asked.

'Not long,' Lilly replied. 'With any luck, Her Honour's gone off to find out what sort of facilities an adult prison has for a pregnant teen.'

The vast metal door clanked open and the guard smiled at Lilly.

'Who pissed on your client's chips?' he asked.

'That,' said Lilly, 'would be me.'

She knew Tanisha would be angry, but hoped she could make her understand that it had been necessary. She had hated betraying the girl's trust, but Karol's words had rung in her mind. *It is you who must decide.*

When they reached Tanisha's cell door, Lilly took a breath and began to speak as soon as she entered.

'I'm sorry, Tanisha, but you have to understand . . .'

Before she knew what was happening, Tanisha flew at her.

'You bitch.' Tanisha landed a punch on Lilly's mouth, the force throwing her off her feet. 'You fucking bitch.'

Lilly crashed backwards, banging her head against the stone floor. The impact rang her skull like a bell. She remained sprawled as the guard tackled Tanisha and pushed her face first against the wall of the cell.

'The baby,' Annabelle wailed. 'Don't hurt the baby.'

Lilly tried to sit up, her ears booming and the taste of blood in her mouth. Tanisha screamed, her cheek pressed flat against the cement.

'You're supposed to be on my side.'

Lilly attempted to speak but found her mouth numb. Nothing moved as it should. She leaned to her side and spat out a crimson string of mucus.

'I am on your side, Tanisha.' Her voice was muffled by swelling.

'You need to hear me now.' Tanisha's eyes blazed. 'I'm gonna kill you and that piece of shit, Chika.'

'I was just trying to get you out of that place.' Lilly struggled to her feet. 'That's my job. That's what I do. I'm your solicitor for God's sake.'

'No you ain't.' Tanisha squeezed her eyes shut. 'You're sacked.'

Chapter Nine

Outside the court room the silence was unnerving. Jack fiddled with his phone as they waited for the judge's decision.

The spectacle of Lilly performing her legal tight-rope walk had left him with a familiar knot in his stomach. Part horror, part admiration. What was it about her that needed to commit so fully to her work? Perhaps there was some dark secret in her past she'd never told him. Or maybe she was just bloody difficult.

When the doors to the corridor opened with a creak, the sound ran towards him in the emptiness. It was Lilly, her shoulders slumped, her head down. Jack's stomach contracted tighter.

She stopped a foot away, looked up and tried to smile. Jack gasped. Her mouth was bloody and swollen, the bottom lip split.

'What the hell happened to you?' He moved to her, his hand out.

As his fingers almost touched her mouth, she flinched and ducked backwards.

'Let's just say Tanisha was unimpressed with my performance,' she said.

'You should have her nicked.'

Lilly shook her head. 'Don't be such a copper.'

He didn't know what to say. He *was* a copper.

'I have to get Alice,' Lilly said. 'Look out for Tanisha for me.'

As Jack watched her head off, he turned and kicked the wall. Would there ever come a day when that woman didn't tear him apart?

Jez peeped out from inside the courtroom. 'The judge's back in.'

Thank God. Anything to take Jack's mind off himself and Lilly bloody Valentine.

They shuffled to their places, Lilly's empty seat screaming for attention.

'Can anyone tell me what's going on?' The judge raised one eyebrow.

Tanisha slumped down in her chair, refusing to meet anyone's eye. Jez looked around the court as if Lilly might be hiding in a corner. Jack sighed.

'You Honour, perhaps I can help here,' he said.

The judge peered at him from her platform. 'I'm all ears.'

'I understand that Miss Valentine has been disinstructed.'

Jez and Kerry looked at one another and Kerry couldn't hide a smirk of satisfaction.

'Is that correct, Miss McKenzie?' the judge asked Tanisha.

'I don't want her nowhere near me ever again,' Tanisha replied.

'She is a very capable and experienced solicitor,' said the judge.

'I don't care.'

The judge nodded and began to write out the draft order. 'No doubt someone will inform Miss Valentine that I am indeed granting her client's application for bail.'

Tanisha sat up. 'Serious?'

The judge stopped writing and leaned forward, her eyes narrowed. 'Young lady, you need to know that there is one reason and one reason alone why I am not sending you back to prison, and that is the fact that you are carrying a child. You will remain at your current foster placement and you will sign on at your nearest police station every morning and evening. At seven pm, you will be subject to a curfew until seven am the next day. Do I make myself clear?'

Tanisha nodded, a smile stretched across her face.

'Believe me when I tell you that if you put one foot out of line, I will revoke bail in an instant.' The judge pointed at Jack. 'And no doubt Officer McNally will be watching your every move.'

Another trickle of blood fell down Lilly's chin as she rang Karol's doorbell. She seemed to be re-opening the cut on her bottom lip every time she changed facial expression.

When Karol answered, his own mouth fell open.

'You should have seen the other bloke,' Lilly smiled.

'A man did this to you?'

'I'm joking.' Lilly waved her hand. 'It's nothing.'

'It most certainly is not.'

Karol showed her through his tiny house. It was a new build. One of the hundreds of rabbit hutches that the developers had thrown up five years earlier and now couldn't sell. It was like toy town, with ceilings so low Karol's head almost skimmed them.

'How's Alice?' Lilly asked.

Karol gestured to the car seat in the corner where the baby was fast asleep. She was swaddled tightly in a towel, the tip of her nose, like a bud, peeping over. Her curls framed her face and she was daisy pretty.

'Come.' Karol led Lilly by the arm to the kitchen. 'Let me look after your lip.'

'Honestly, it's not a problem,' Lilly mumbled, but didn't resist.

The kitchen couldn't have been bigger than fifteen by ten. It housed very little. A cooker. The old-fashioned, free-standing sort with a grill hovering above the gas rings. Along one wall was a bar-cum-work surface with a high stool tucked underneath. Karol pulled it out and guided Lilly on to it.

'How did the court hearing go?' he asked, reaching into a small fridge and retrieving an ice cube tray. Expertly, he popped out two cubes with his thumb into a piece of kitchen roll and wrapped them.

'Bloody awful,' said Lilly.

Karol nodded, placed the cold compress against her mouth and pressed Lilly's own hand against it.

'As firmly as possible,' he said.

'It hurts.'

He rolled his eyes and opened a drawer. The contents put Lilly to shame. Every drawer in her kitchen was crammed with a miscellany of debris. The one nearest to the washing machine was notorious for providing a resting place for tea towels, not necessarily clean, an assortment of scented candles, a wooden implement her mother had called a meat tenderizer, but which Sam used to bang in tent pegs, and three pairs of broken sunglasses.

Karol's drawer was a marvel of efficiency. Lined with old wall-paper, it contained only a first aid kit and a torch. He took out the green box marked with a red cross, flipped the lid and extracted cotton wool, antiseptic, surgical scissors and tape.

'Quite the professional,' said Lilly, who would struggle to put her hand to a plaster.

'I trained to be a doctor.' He smiled.

'Really?' Lilly hadn't meant it to sound so rude. 'I don't mean that you don't look like you could be a doctor, just, you know, you never said . . .'

Karol was still smiling as Lilly trailed off.

'What you really mean,' he removed the ice pack and dried her lip gently, 'is why am I working for you?'

Lilly was glad she couldn't speak.

'I began my training back home.' He squirted antiseptic on to a ball of cotton wool and dabbed the cut. It stung like hell. 'But my father decided that I should finish my studies here, where the hospitals are the best in the world.'

He must have seen the doubt cross her face at the thought of the grubby Luton General with its outbreaks of MRS. 'You British do not know what a gem you have in your NHS. Where I am from most of the people do not have access to medicines and doctors at all. The hospitals we do have are very primitive. Having an operation there is a dangerous thing to do.'

With the scissors, he snipped two thin slivers of tape and smoothed them on to Lilly's lip. It felt much better, the throbbing almost gone.

'So what happened?' Lilly asked.

'I still had eight more months of training to go when violence broke out in my home state.'

'I'm sorry,' Lilly said, softly.

'My father had to take refuge with family in the south,' he sighed. 'He had to leave behind his home and the business he had spent thirty years building.'

'That's terrible.'

'In many ways he is lucky. Our friends and neighbours are still being attacked. Most are dead. He is safe, as am I.'

His optimism brought a lump to Lilly's throat. Her days were so often filled with worries and troubles but the not the life and death variety.

'What will you do?' she asked.

He replaced the first aid kit in the drawer. 'I will work as hard as I can, send as much money to my father as I can, and one day, when I have enough, I will finish my training.'

Pink shame slipped around Lilly's collar. Karol had such quiet dignity. She was glad she had taken his advice and revealed to the court that Tanisha was pregnant. It had caused a rift, but it had been the right thing to do.

She was about to tell him, when her mobile bleeped with an incoming text from Jack.

Bail granted.

Solomon Street is on the edge of the Clayhill. A row of old three-storey houses with those big bay windows on the ground floor. It doesn't look like it belongs with the concrete tower blocks of the estate, as if someone stuck it on afterwards. Or maybe it was there before the flats were built. Imagine that. You're living in a nice-sized pad with a garden and everything, and someone from the council comes along and builds those monstrous fuckers behind you.

Demi wants to live in a house one day. Though nowhere near the Clayhill if she can help it. Maybe in the country, with trees and that.

She clutches the shoe box full of meth tightly under her arm and hopes Rocky was right, that she'll be able to work out which house she needs.

The first one is completely burned out. No glass in any of the windows. The paintwork is charred and black. The front door has disintegrated and the hole yawns like a huge mouth. Demi wonders if anyone was inside when it happened.

Next door looks inhabited. There are bins outside anyway, fighting for space next to a tangled thorn bush that has rubbish trapped in it. A small face appears from behind a ragged piece of material hung as a makeshift curtain. It's a girl, a bit younger than Demi, her hair covered by a headscarf. Some girls at Demi's school wear one. She can't remember what it's called but it shows they're good Muslims.

A lot of Africans don't like Asians. They call them Pakis and say they're dirty, or terrorists. Gran says you can't generalize, that there's good and bad everywhere. The next time Demi sees Chika, she'll ask her what she thinks, find out for sure.

The next one along looks more promising. It's boarded up. Then again, so's the next one, and they're both completely deserted. The way Rocky talked it was like she's supposed to pick out the right one straight way. She pulls a face, unsure what to do, when at the far end she spots a man with a pit bull, sitting on a wall. The dog is straining against his lead, barking viciously at a group of kids trying to get past. The man yanks the dog back, but he's soon making for the kids again. Demi can tell instantly from the slump in their shoulders and the way they dodge around the snarling dog, that the kids are junkies.

She makes her way up the street and when she can see the house with the dog outside, she understands what Rocky meant. The garden is ankle deep in crap, the windows are covered with frayed net curtains and the light of flickering candles leaks out. Someone else approaches the house. It's a woman. Skinny and shaking. The dog goes for her. The man drags it back, swearing, and the girl slips past.

When Demi is alongside the man, the dog bares his teeth. Demi steps into the road.

'I'm looking for JC,' she says.

'You Demi?'

She nods and the man stands. As the lead loosens, the dog takes his chance and lunges for Demi, his teeth snapping. She screams and nearly drops the shoe box.

'For fuck's sake.' The man gives the dog a hard kick.

It yelps and the man kicks it again.

'In the kitchen,' he tells her.

As she tries to pass, the dog growls, but when the man pulls back his foot for a third time, it stops. Demi takes her chance and sprints up the path. Once inside the door, she skids to a halt. The stench is unbearable. Like a thousand public toilets. She puts her sleeve across her nose and mouth and coughs into it. The carpet in the hallway has been ripped away in clumps and the walls are covered in graffiti. The first door is on the right. It's closed shut, but everything is so filthy, Demi doesn't even want to touch it, so she taps it with her foot.

The smell inside the room is worse than the hall and Demi nearly throws up on the spot. She swallows hard. It's been gutted, even the radiator ripped away from the wall, leaving only a ghostly imprint on the wall. A hole in the ceiling with a few loose wires dangling down is all that's left of the light fitting.

The only furniture remaining is a dank mattress pitted by cigarette burns. A white girl lies across it, her head in the lap of a boy perched at the end. At his feet, three candles are burning, stuck to the floorboards with melted wax. Their flames illuminate a blanket of uncapped syringes, bloody cotton balls and blackened strips of tin foil. There are piles of discarded crack pipes: small plastic bottles, their bases sliced off, coke cans punched with holes. And two larger bottles, labelled blackcurrant squash, now full with yellow liquid that Demi is sure must be pee, lean precariously against the wall.

'Either come in or fuck off.' The boy's voice is hoarse as he ties a length of rubber cable around his upper arm.

Demi stares. She knows about drugs. She's met enough of the losers who get themselves into this state. But actually seeing it like this, a few feet away, in full colour, is different.

'I told you to fuck off,' the boy shouts, reaching for a syringe full of brown liquid.

Demi knows she should leave, but watching is hideously fascinating, like when cars slow down to check out a crash. The boy gives her a disgusted grunt but is too engrossed in getting his fix to take action. Instead he pulls at the cable with his teeth, until it's tight enough to make a vein pop up. Then, the cable still clamped between his lips, he pushes the needle into his flesh. He peers intently into the barrel until he sees the scarlet plume of blood, then he plunges the gear into his body with a moan.

In the candlelight, the boy's eyes roll back into his head until only the whites show. It reminds Demi of Danny and she shivers. Soon, he lolls forward, his chin touching his chest, his back bending, until his forehead meets the girl's in his lap. They look like they could be kissing. The needle is still in his arm.

'You Demi?'

Demi spins to the voice behind her. The figure is large, dressed in a nylon tracksuit, hair shaved close to the skull. The voice is low and as Nigerian as Gran. Only a swelling in the chest tells Demi this is a woman.

'I'm JC.'

Demi holds out the shoe box in front of her like a gift.

JC nods but doesn't take it. 'Come to the kitchen.'

They make their way through to the end of the hall and through the far door. Surprisingly, it's recognizably a kitchen with sink, fridge and a table. There are several camping lanterns dotted around the work surfaces.

JC nudges the door shut with her hip. 'Keep the animals out.'

Demi laughs nervously.

'I don't joke, sister,' says JC. 'This is a zoo and we provide our animals with what they need, but they have to stay in their cages.'

Demi gulps and places the shoe box on the table. 'Danny asked me to bring this.'

JC flicks it open with her thumb. She wears a huge watch so loose that it sits on her hand and not her wrist. The movement makes it rattle. She peers into the box, as if she's checking.

'It's all there,' says Demi. 'Everything Danny gave me.'

'I don't doubt it.' JC smiles at her. 'But you know how it is.'

Demi has no idea how it is. She can't imagine anyone having the nerve to try to cheat someone like Danny. As if reading her mind, JC gives a chuckle.

'You'd be surprised how very foolish some youngers can be.'

Satisfied, she closes the box and reaches under her tracksuit top for a key on a chain. She squats and uses it to open a cupboard that has been padlocked shut. Her top rides up to reveal the silver handle of a gun resting in her waistband. This time, Demi isn't shocked. Anyone would need protection in a place like this.

On a shelf inside the cupboard, where there might once have been tins of baked beans, are rolls of bank notes. JC peels off a few and re-locks it.

She holds the notes out to Demi. 'For your trouble, sister.'

There are four twenties, but Demi doesn't know if she should take them. 'Danny didn't mention money.'

JC takes a step forward and presses them into her hand. 'He didn't need to. We are none of us doing this for the fun, eh?'

Gratefully, Demi pockets the notes. 'I'd better be off.'

JC smiles again and they move out of the kitchen to the front door. As they reach the first room, Demi can't resist another peep inside. The girl is still asleep on the stained mattress but the boy is standing, his back turned to the door, his hand on the wall for support. The gurgling sound of a bottle filling tells Demi she was right. The bottles in the corner are filled with piss.

Outside, Demi takes a greedy lungful of fresh air. The dog is snapping at a group of Asian women on the other side of the road. They pull their head scarves under their chins and hurry along.

'So you got Chika's job now?' The man wraps the lead around his hand twice.

'No,' Demi says. 'She's just busy right now.'

The man gives one of those long, slow, continuous nods. 'If you say so, sister.'

* * *

The chief super cleaned the handset of his telephone with an anti-bacterial wipe. Sometime last year Jack had received a packet. Every copper in the nick had. Hell, every copper in the land for all Jack knew. They'd come inside a glossy information pack about desk hygiene. Apparently, research had shown that telephones harboured more germs than toilet seats. Jack doubted that the author of the report in question had ever seen the toilets in Lilly's cottage. Or in his own flat, for that matter. Either way, Jack had filed the pack in the bin and the wipes had long since been buried under a mountain of paperwork. The chief super was the only person Jack had ever seen actually using them.

The chief ran the corner of the wipe around the key pad with his thumbnail. 'What happened, Jack? What went wrong?'

He was referring to the bail application, of course.

'The girl's pregnant.' Jack shrugged. 'When the judge heard that, she wasn't prepared to let her stay in jail.'

The chief dropped his wipe in the bin and replaced the receiver carefully. 'Ridiculous.'

Jack didn't answer. After hearing Chika recounting the night of Malaya's attack, both in his car and again in court, he was convinced Tanisha was guilty, but he wouldn't have wanted to be the one to send her back inside. He'd once had the misfortune to accompany a terrorist to the birth of his son, in a high security unit. The woman, accused of harbouring her husband from the RUC and the British Army, had been handcuffed to the bed throughout. Watching her try to push while unable to move had been heartbreaking. When the terrorist wept, Jack didn't know if it was in joy at the sight of his first born, or in pity for his poor wife.

'This girl is a risk to the public,' said the chief.

'There are pretty tight restrictions attached to her bail,' Jack replied.

'And if she breaches them even once, we come down on her

like a ton of bricks.' The chief reached for another wipe and began cleaning his fountain pen. 'In the meantime, we prepare our case against her scrupulously.'

Jack nodded. He had Chika's statement. He had the film. He had Tanisha's taped denial.

'I'm going to speak to the victim again, she might be well enough to talk to me properly by now.'

The chief squinted at his pen, as if searching for errant microbes. 'You do that, Jack. Whatever it takes, we must ensure this girl is punished.'

Jamie lifts the net curtain and peers outside, but the layer of grime is so thick he can only see outlines. He licks his finger and rubs in a circle until there's a small porthole in the dirt. Now he can see the guy with that horrible dog talking to a young black girl.

Trick leans over his shoulder, his breath sharp in Jamie's nostrils.

'I'll get supplies,' he beams, showing his brown teeth.

Relief floods over Jamie. The taste in the park has started to wear off and he really isn't comfortable in this place.

When Trick brought them here, and they were terrorized by the pit bull, Jamie almost ran away. Only the promise of more meth and a quiet spot to take it, made him sidestep the jaws dripping with saliva.

He pulls out the last of his money and slaps it into Trick's outstretched palm, then watches him scuttle off to score. Without Trick, the room is silent and still. They're on the third floor where, according to Trick, no one can be arsed to come. From the floor below, Jamie can hear talking and footsteps. Outside the dog is barking.

Jamie puts his hands over his ears and crouches. On the window sill beside him is a syringe and a blackened spoon. Clearly some people do make it up the creaking stairs.

At last, he hears the thud of Trick's return and he smiles as Trick bursts into the room and joins him by the window. Trick tries to clear away some of the rubbish with his foot, dragging the toe of his trainer against the used matches and empty lighters. Satisfied, he kneels.

Quickly, they prepare their drugs and inhale.

Instantly, the cloud of uncertainty lifts and Jamie's shoulders relax. As smoke streams out of his mouth he looks around the room and can see now that it's not that bad. A bit mucky, but then his dorm at school is no *Homes & Gardens*. Trick gives him one of his cheeky grins and once again they're both laughing.

'You should see the bird downstairs, serving up,' Trick snorts. 'When I say bird, I can't actually be sure.'

'What d'you mean?' Jamie asks.

'She's dressed just like a geezer, with a shaved head and that.'

'How do you know it's not a man?'

Trick draws a pair of breasts with his hands and gives a whistle. Jamie cracks up and leans against his friend for support. They giggle together for what seems like for ever. As soon as he stops, Trick sets him off again.

At last, Trick gives a long contented sigh. 'You got a girlfriend, mate?'

'No,' Jamie murmurs. 'You?'

'Don't think anyone would have me.' Trick's laughter turns into a wracking cough.

Jamie claps him on the back. 'Of course they would.'

Trick wipes his sleeve across his mouth, leaving a trail of bloody mucus. He turns his head and looks into Jamie's eyes. 'You're a good person to say that.'

'I mean it.'

Trick gives a small smile, the cracked teeth now tinged with red. Then he leans forward and puts his mouth to Jamie's. In the darkness and the stench, among the filth and the dirty needles, they kiss. And it is the sweetest kiss Jamie has ever had in his life.

The glass of sauvignon blanc was cold and spritely, the onion tart hot and oozing. Lilly let them both salve her frazzled mind and body. She re-read Jack's text for the umpteenth time and smiled. Tanisha had been granted bail. Tonight she would sleep in a proper bed that wasn't bolted to the floor, safe under Annabelle's protection.

No doubt Tanisha would instruct another solicitor who would help her through the trial. Lilly had done her job to the best of her ability and could do no more.

When she had finished the last creamy bite of tart, she pushed the plate aside and poured herself another glass of wine.

There was of course an upside to being sacked. A few, if truth be told. She could spend more time with Alice and Sam. She might also be able to salvage something with Jack.

At this point, Lilly paused. She did want to make their relationship easier. They were Alice's parents and being at war was never going to help matters. But did she want more than that? The longer she considered it, the more she couldn't help thinking about Karol and how attractive she found him.

She told herself to stop being so idiotic, drained her glass and headed off for her own bed.

Chapter Ten

Demi's at school. She's been here all day.

Last night the head called Gran and asked if Demi was okay.

'I know Malaya's accident must be upsetting her greatly.'

Gran tried to point out that what happened to Malaya was no accident, but the head was already banging on about unauthorized absences and OFSTED reports.

'If Demi has to have any more time off, she will need a doctor's note.'

Demi expected fireworks. She thought Gran would hit the roof, dragging up all the stuff from the past, telling Demi how she's wasting her chances. Instead she just sat quietly, shaking her head.

'I'm worn out, Demi,' and she looked it. 'I can't fight with you any more.'

This was worse than a row. Much worse. If Gran had started shouting at least Demi could have yelled back about how horrible school is. How none of the lessons make any sense, and the teachers ignore her, and the other pupils pick on her, and they steal her bus money so she has to walk home in the rain.

But Gran didn't shout. She cried. So Demi cried too and said she was sorry and promised to go to school.

Nothing changes. Mrs Patel is droning on about fractions and decimal points. She sounds like a bee in summer, climbing up and down a pane of glass, trying to escape. At the end of the lesson she collects the maths homework set last week, but doesn't bat an eyelid when Demi just shrugs.

'Hand it in tomorrow, Demi,' she says.

Yeah, right.

She catches sight of Georgia in the corridor, surrounding some other poor sod with her cronies. They're joking and laughing in her face. Demi thinks about intervening, but she can't be arsed. She doesn't know the girl. She isn't family.

By lunchtime, Demi's had enough. She gets changed in the toilets and heads out of the gate. Anyone could see her but she doesn't care.

When she reaches Dirty Mick's, she peers through the window. Her heart soars at the sight of Chika nursing a Coke. She bounds inside and throws herself into the chair opposite.

'Wanna get your nails done?' Demi asks.

Chika splays her hands on the table. Her fingernails are bitten short, the nail varnish chipped. 'I'm brassic.'

Demi pulls out some cash. 'I'm not.'

'Where you get that?'

'I dropped that parcel to Danny, like you said, and he asked me to do another delivery for him to Solomon Street.'

Chika barks with laughter. 'Man, that place is a serious dump.'

'Tell me about it,' Demi smiles. 'It's like that film *Evil Dead*.'

'Yeah, the Army of fucking Darkness.'

Still in stitches, they wander down the street to American Nails. Demi has no idea what's American about it, since everyone that works in there is Vietnamese. The receptionist hands them a board. Fifty or so fake nails are stuck to it, each with its own design. Demi likes the one with a sunset, Chika points to the one sporting a gold dollar sign.

'How much for a full set?' she shouts.

It's funny how people do that. Shout when someone can't speak English. It's not like they're deaf, is it? You'd think Chika would get that.

Soon, they're sat side by side at the nail bar, their hands invisible inside the dryers.

'I should go see Malaya,' says Demi.

'I'll come with you,' Chika replies.

Demi pulls her hands free and admires her manicure. A riot of oranges and yellows. She gestures to the receptionist.

'Can I get one of dem.' She nods at the tiny tooth jewels, lined up like shards of coloured glass.

Outside, she grins at Chika, showing off the new 'ruby' glued to her tooth. She runs her tongue over it, pleased by its sharpness.

'You really one of us now, sister,' says Chika.

At the bus stop, they make their plans. They'll visit Malaya then go back to Clayhill. A bit of dealing and then there's a party in some warehouse. The other girls are heading up there. It'll be a laugh.

They're interrupted by Chika's mobile phone. She reads an incoming text, her face dropping.

'Everything all right?' Demi asks.

Chika nods. 'Everything's cool. I just gotta take care of a bit of business. I'll meet you at the hospital in an hour.'

Demi gets on the number forty-six and takes a seat at the back. As it pulls away, she watches Chika, head down, hunched over her phone, texting. When she's almost out of sight, Chika briefly looks up and they catch each other's eye. Then the bus turns the corner.

Malaya's hand was heavy in Jack's, her skin hot.

'She looks much better,' he commented to Mrs Ebola, who was fussing with a vase of flowers.

She gave a tight smile. 'Mr Stephenson says she is getting there.'

Jack studied Malaya's face. The swelling was gradually reducing, the bruises turning canary yellow. She was now recognizably a girl, rather than a smashed cantaloupe melon.

'She drifts in and out,' Mrs Ebola added. 'With all the medication.'

He nodded. Every five minutes a nurse seemed to arrive, checking the monitors and sending more drugs into Malaya via her cannula. He rubbed his thumb in her palm. Poor wee thing.

As if nudged into consciousness by the movement, Malaya's eyes flickered and she tried a small smile.

'Hello, my angel.' Mrs Ebola leaned over and kissed her granddaughter's cheek. 'How are we today?'

Malaya's mouth twitched but she settled on a nod. Soon her eyes turned to Jack.

'Hello, Malaya.' His voice was gentle.

'You remember Mr McNally.' Mrs Ebola poured a tumbler of water for Malaya. 'He's the policeman on your case.'

Malaya gave another nod, then pushed out her lips to take a drink. Even the light touch of the glass made her flinch and she grasped Jack's hand a little tighter.

'You'll be pleased to know we've charged someone with your attack,' said Jack.

Surprise flittered across Malaya's brow.

'I spoke to Chika Mboko and she's been a lot of help.'

Surprise turned to out-and-out shock.

'I know it's not the way things are usually done on the estate, but she's given a statement,' Jack told her. 'She told us what happened at your jump in, that she was there and saw it all. She's named one of the girls as Tanisha McKenzie. Do you know her?'

Something else flashed in Malaya's eyes. Not surprise or shock. Something Jack couldn't put his finger on.

'Can you confirm that Tanisha was one of the girls who attacked you?'

Malaya's lips parted and Jack strained his ears, but all that came out was a long slow breath as Malaya's eyelids closed again.

When Jack got up to leave he saw another girl in the doorway. It was Malaya's sister. She stared at him, her hatred hot and obvious. Then, without a word, she left.

The coffee was made with beans from the Ivory Coast. Karol had ground them earlier, leaving the delicious earthiness wafting through the office.

It was strong, sweet and very good. Lilly was buzzing. She took another sip and signed off the pile of letters Karol had printed. He clicked his tongue appreciatively and slipped them into envelopes.

'We are a very good team, Miss Valentine.'

'Yes we are,' Lilly laughed.

She had felt light and free as soon as she woke. Alice had had a peaceful night but it wasn't just that. It was Tanisha's case. Or the lack of it. She realized that it had been hanging around her shoulders like a yoke. Even when she wasn't working it had laid heavily on her, dragging her down. Today, she felt ready for anything.

'Let me cook dinner for you, Karol,' she said. 'To say thank you for all your help.'

'It's not necessary,' he replied.

Lilly's smile slipped. She'd overstepped the mark.

'But it would be lovely,' he smiled back at her.

Jamie wakes up desperate for a drink. His throat is raw and bloody.

He and Trick spent the night in the crack house taking drugs, kissing, touching one another, taking more drugs. Finally he fell asleep, completely spent, at dawn.

He struggles to sit, pushing up from the stained mattress that served as their bed. He blinks into the stale room and sees Trick stood at the window, shivering.

'Are you okay?' Jamie's mouth feels like someone rubbed it down with sandpaper.

'Got any money?' Trick doesn't turn towards him.

Jamie pats down his pockets and finds a few coins. 'Not much.'

'Shit.'

Trick's whole body shakes. Even his knees knock. Jamie's heard people say that and thought it was just a figure of speech. But Trick's knees are indeed beating against one another, making a slight click as the bones meet.

'What's wrong?' Jamie crosses the room, stands next to him.

'Sick.' Trick's stomach contracts in and out. 'You know how it is.'

Jamie lifts a hand to touch his friend but leaves it in mid-air, unsure. Then Trick turns his face, cheeks wet with tears, his wretchedness complete.

'My mum ain't due her Giro til Thursday,' he says.

Jamie has no idea what that means, but he nods.

'And there ain't nothing left to sell,' Trick continues. 'Telly, CD player and that lot, it's all gone.'

A small bubble of snot forms under Trick's nose. Strangely, it doesn't make Jamie feel sick, only sad. He's got money at home. Fifty quid at least. His godfather sent him a hundred from Beijing. Jamie hasn't seen him in years, but Uncle Theo never forgets his birthday. A card with a few scribbled lines saying they must catch up soon, and a postal order. He's bought a couple of games but the rest is still sitting in his bedroom drawer.

'I can get some cash,' says Jamie.

Trick's eyes light up. 'When?'

Jamie doesn't have anything for a taxi so he'll have to take the bus home. 'An hour and a half.'

'I can't wait that long, Jamie.'

Tears stream down Trick's face and he falls against Jamie, sobbing. Jamie wraps his arms around him and holds him tight. He rubs his hand up and down Trick's bony back, his watch strap catching on his shoulder-blades. That's it. His watch. Dad's always moaning at him for leaving it face down by the bathroom sink. At this age, Jamie should have learned to respect things. Especially things that cost such a lot. Money doesn't grow on trees. Blah, blah, blah.

'Wait here.' He races for the door.

Trick looks uncertain. He wants to trust Jamie, but his need has stripped him of anything but hopelessness. Jamie nods and bolts down the stairs. He hears retching from another room. Trick is not alone in his sickness. When he gets to the kitchen door he hammers on it.

'What the fuck?' The door is thrown open by an angry black man. Then Jamie sees his chest. The man is actually a woman, just like Trick told him.

'I need some meth.' Jamie is out of breath.

The man-woman glares at him. 'And you think you can just come demanding it like this?'

Her accent is very strong, the sound of the words strange and exotic.

'My friend is ill,' says Jamie.

'Everyone in this place is ill.' She draws a circle around her temple with her forefinger. 'Sick in the head.'

Jamie hops from foot to foot. He has to help Trick.

'This is worth a lot.' He pulls off his watch. 'I'll give it to you for ten wraps of glass.'

The man-woman takes it from him and inspects it. 'Five wraps.'

'It cost at least four hundred pounds,' Jamie pleads.

'Then take it to a shop.'

The man-woman drops it back into his hand and reaches to

shut the kitchen door. Jamie's heart lurches. His dad will kill him when he finds out the watch is gone. That won't change, however much he gets for it. He has to help Trick.

'Okay,' he breathes, 'five wraps.'

She narrows her eyes at him and snatches the watch back. Then she disappears into the kitchen and returns with five baggies.

'Enjoy.' She laughs and slams the door.

Jamie takes the stairs two at a time and falls into the room where he left his friend. Trick is squatting in the corner, the wall behind splashed brown. He looks up at Jamie in abject misery.

'I've got it.' Jamie holds up the bags of meth.

He leads Trick back to the mattress, as much to get away from the shit as anything else, and presses him to sit down. Then he taps out the powder and lights it for Trick, holding the empty barrel of a biro to his lips. Trick accepts, like an invalid being fed soup. He inhales the white smoke once, twice, three times, until the softness returns to his pretty face. Soon, he's completely himself, grinning wickedly at Jamie. He lifts a hand, but doesn't take the foil or the pipe. Instead, he sneaks it between Jamie's legs.

'You want a little action?'

Jamie smiles. He does want some action. As soon as he's had a hit.

Jack had a heaviness in his chest as he left the hospital. An acid discomfort that burned. Malaya hadn't been able to offer any help about what happened in the rec, leaving him with Chika as his main and only witness.

He played the bail hearing over and over in his mind. Chika's evidence had been solid and she'd held up well under Lilly's questioning, but something was missing, though he wasn't sure what.

Dark clouds had gathered and Jack put up his collar against the wind. A storm was on its way.

His mobile rang.

'Jack?'

'Yes.'

'Jez Stafford here. I've been thinking about that bail hearing.'

'You and me both,' said Jack.

'Something wasn't quite right.' Jack knew exactly what he meant. 'Something in the back story.'

That was it. Chika had been word perfect recounting her version of the attack, but she hadn't said a thing about what had gone before. Why she and Tanisha had fallen out.

'We need to know why our witness hates our defendant,' said Jez.

'I'm on it.' Jack flipped his phone shut.

Why hadn't Jack tackled this before? He'd been so busy dancing around, building a case, he hadn't dug in the dirt.

A cold spot of rain hit Jack's cheek. He wiped it away with the back of his hand and called Chika.

'Let's meet and you can tell me it all, from start to finish,' he said.

Chika groaned. 'Again?'

'Again,' said Jack.

Chika paused, groaned again. 'I got something to do right now, but you can meet me in Dirty Mick's in forty-five.'

'I'll see you there,' said Jack.

'Get me a chocolate milkshake,' she ordered and hung up.

Jack took his time driving to the Clayhill, listening to the wall-to-wall Christmas songs being played on the radio. He wished to God he'd written one of those things. Imagine the royalties when it was played year after year. Now that would be a legacy to leave Alice.

He pulled up outside Dirty Mick's. The café was almost deserted. A family in the corner getting their tea before heading back to a noisy homeless hostel. A couple of scallies, making a few dodgy quid over a bacon roll. He locked the car and headed inside.

'What can I get you?' the owner shouted from the till. By the look of his oriental features there was little chance he was called Mick.

Jack surveyed the menu on the wall. For so many reasons he should order nothing more than a Diet Coke.

'Double egg, chips and a cuppa,' he said. 'And a chocolate milkshake.'

Mick disappeared into the kitchen and Jack took a seat at the table by the window, watching the rain smack against the glass. Moments later, a greasy plate was plonked in front of him. He squirted brown sauce on the chipped edge, and plunged a steaming chip into one of the yolks.

Outside, a gang of girls scooted past, hollering at one another, jostling with their elbows. Jack looked out for Chika but she wasn't with them. He went back to his food. One of the things he missed about Lilly was her cooking. Mother of God, it was to die for. Sometimes he would get home from work and the cottage would be alive with the smells of a chicken roasting or cinnamon cookies. And she would look up at him, her nose covered in flour and offer him a taste. What he wouldn't do to go back to that.

He forced his mind from Lilly, ate the last of his food and drained his tea. Chika's milkshake stood untouched. He checked his watch. Half an hour late.

He pulled out his phone. No missed calls, texts or messages. He called her number but it went straight to voicemail. Damn.

'Don't suppose you know Chika Mboko?'

Mick took the ten pound note Jack was holding out and slid it into the cash register.

'She was in earlier, giving me all the usual grief.' He tossed Jack's change on to a stained saucer and pushed it towards him, the coins rattling.

'Any ideas where I might find her?' Jack asked.

Mick sniffed once, then turned away.

Jack pocketed the cash and set out for the block where Chika lived. It was bloody freezing, but the car was safer outside the café than by the tower blocks. The last thing he needed was to spend half the night looking for Chika, only to find his car on bricks. He pushed on at a lick, padding through the darkness to the quad at the foot of Chika's block.

She better have a bloody good explanation for standing him up.

He held a hand above his eyes to shield them from the downpour and looked around for any sign of Chika. The quad was empty apart from a girl hovering by a parked car. She stared at him through the gloom, holding up her hood against the wind. It was hard to make her out. He thought he recognized her but couldn't be sure.

'Do I know you?' he called out.

'Yeah.'

He took a few steps towards her and saw she was shivering without a coat. She lifted a hand to her mouth and blew on it. Each nail was painted a headache-inducing mess of oranges and yellows. Jack was sure she had a connection with Chika but couldn't remember.

'How do I know you?'

The girl looked at the ground. Jack took another step closer.

'I'm Malaya's sister.'

That was it. Jack recognized her now from the hospital. The family lived in the next block.

'Well now, Malaya's sister, you look like you need to get indoors.'

The girl nodded and turned to walk away. Then suddenly she stopped. Jack watched as her back went rigid and she lifted her chin towards the night sky. He followed her eye line to the tenth floor, sheets of water hitting his face. He blinked.

There was a figure leaning over the side of the walkway, as if she were trying to attract their attention. He couldn't be sure, but the hair and jacket seemed familiar.

'Chika?' Jack took several steps forward, until he was directly beneath the walkway.

It *was* Chika, stretching down towards him, her mouth open. He strained to hear what she was saying.

'What the hell are you playing at, Chika?' he shouted up at her.

Again she didn't answer but her hand reached out to him.

'Chika?' Jack had a very bad feeling.

He watched in horror as she slid over the side and dropped. There was a moment when she seemed to levitate in mid-air, and Jack's scream was lost in the wind. Then she plummeted through the sky and landed with a crunch of skull and a splash of blood at Jack's feet.

Chapter Eleven

'You look terrible.'

Phil Cheney, handed Jack a forensic suit. It was white and papery, trying to blow away in the night wind.

Jack and Cheney went back years. Their friendship survived on a diet of beer and banter and this was Jack's cue to take the piss. But tonight, Jack couldn't manage it. He was exhausted and brittle, fingering the suit, listening to it crackle, oblivious to the drilling rain.

Cheney raised an inquisitive eyebrow. Jack was a copper. Bodies and death were his stock in trade.

'I was here when she jumped,' Jack explained.

Cheney remained unimpressed, and ducked under the yellow police-tape that cordoned off a twenty by twenty rectangle surrounding Chika's body. Someone had covered her in a brown blanket. Jack hadn't seen who.

He watched Cheney approach. If he'd been a plant, the FI would have been a cactus. Round and plump, not fat, just sort of juicy. And, like a cactus, he was covered in spikes. Metal bars pierced the skin of his ears, nose, lips and tongue. During a pub crawl in Brighton, as he tried to impress a couple of seventeen-year-olds in skirts so short you could see the colour of their knickers, Cheney had lifted up his jumper to reveal rings through each nipple. Now that was a sight Jack wished he'd never been party to.

'Are you coming or what?' Cheney called.

Jack put up a finger. 'Give me a minute.'

'Take your time, girlfriend.' Cheney shook his head, throwing off rivulets of water like a dog. 'I'll take a look and see if we need the tent.'

An icy shiver ran through Jack as Cheney lifted the blanket, and he had to turn away. He couldn't get it out of his head that he was responsible for this. He had known Chika was damaged, had spotted from the off that she was on the edge. Yet he'd pressured her to make a statement, pressured her to attend court. Hell, he'd dragged her there himself. Then, earlier tonight, he'd pressured her again, insisting they meet so she could spill out painful memories over a glass of chocolate milk. What had he been thinking? That it was okay to mess with someone's mind to get a conviction? Did the end really justify the means? Remembering the sound as Chika hit the concrete, Jack knew it did not.

'You need to get over here, mate.' Cheney wiped rainwater from his eyes.

Jack sighed. He didn't want to do this.

'I don't need the suit,' he shouted back, 'I'll be all over the scene.'

He snuck under the tape and tried not to look at the body.

'I sat with her until the ambulance arrived and pronounced her dead,' he said.

He didn't mention that he'd knelt at Chika's broken head and stroked her hair.

'Anyone else at the scene?' asked Cheney.

'There was a girl.' He looked around for Malaya's sister, but she had melted away. 'She must have been terrified.'

'I'll need a swab,' said Cheney.

Jack frowned. Cheney was superb at his job, thorough to the nth degree. 'Is that necessary for a suicide?'

'No it's not,' he reached for a plastic evidence bag, and dropped Chika's phone inside. 'But this one didn't kill herself.'

Jack felt the air being sucked out of his lungs and had to bend forward, his hands on his knees. There were dark patches on his jeans. Not from the rain.

'What are you telling me?' he asked.

'I can't be sure, until we get to the lab,' Cheney crouched next to Chika's back, 'but there are stab wounds.'

'Are you sure?' Jack skirted around the body.

Cheney pointed with a gloved finger at a blood-soaked tear in Chika's coat.

'Couldn't have happened in the fall?' Jack asked.

'Possibly.' Cheney reached under the ribbed edge of the coat and lifted it to reveal Chika's back. An inch above the fastening of a scarlet bra was a puncture wound, like a small pink mouth. 'But this wasn't caused by blunt trauma.'

'Knife?'

Cheney smoothed Chika's coat back into place. 'Almost certainly.'

The cottage was cosy. Built at a time when tradesmen chose the best materials rather than the cheapest, it was designed to hold fast against rural winters and the rain beating against it.

But Lilly knew full well it wasn't just the insulation making her pink.

'You are full of surprises, Lilly Valentine.' Karol appraised the book case in the living room, his finger moving across the book spines. 'Henry James, Thomas Hardy, Charlotte Brontë.'

Lilly perched on the end of the sofa, wine glass in hand.

'Where are your airport thrillers? Your detective stories?' he asked.

'Too much like real life,' she laughed.

He slid a volume of *Lord of the Flies* back into its place and moved to the sofa, where he sat, his arm sprawled behind his head. 'I get the impression that you like excitement.'

'That's an accusation that is regularly levelled at me,' she nodded.

'And you don't think it is true?'

Lilly pushed her hand through her hair. 'All I can tell you is that I am very glad to be no longer involved in the McKenzie case.'

'A quiet life without any thrills?' He moved closer to her.

'How about a quiet life, with thrills.'

He edged nearer still, until she could smell the blackberry tang of Pinot Noir on his mouth. The room was silent and they stared at one another intently. He was going to kiss her. If Lilly wanted to stop him she needed to say something now.

Suddenly, there was a hammering on the door. The sound crashed through the house, making Lilly jump.

Karol glanced at the clock. 'It's very late.'

Who could it be? The only person who could conceivably come this late at night was Jack.

Jack.

How would he react to the sight of Karol, comfortable in the place he used to watch the footie? She'd explain that Karol worked for her. An employee, nothing more. But the dirty dishes abandoned in the kitchen, the smell of basil oil in the air and the empty bottle of wine on the floor would tell another story.

The pounding rang out again and she heard the sound of disturbed movement from upstairs. She ran for the door and flung it open. Annabelle stood outside in the pouring rain, her hair plastered to her head.

'Annabelle?'

'I need your help,' she cried.

Sam appeared at the top of the stairs. 'What's going on?'

'Nothing,' Lilly told him, 'go back to bed.'

'I've got an exam tomorrow, if anyone's interested,' he mumbled and sloped away.

Lilly ushered Annabelle into the sitting room where she stood, dripping, water collecting at her feet.

'I'll get a towel,' said Karol and disappeared into the kitchen.

'What's going on, Annabelle?' Lilly asked.

The other woman was soaked. The waterproof jacket that should have been perfect hung off her shoulders, unzipped, the hood down.

'I'm sorry, but I didn't know who else to turn to,' she said. 'The police have come for Tanisha again.'

Lilly groaned. Please God, Tanisha hadn't breached her bail conditions already.

Karol returned and handed Annabelle a towel. Lilly cringed at the stains. The towels in Annabelle's house were pristine. Egyptian cotton, smelling of fabric conditioner. Annabelle appeared not to notice and held it to her face.

'They say Tanisha's involved in another attack,' she said. 'But this time the girl's dead.'

Lilly's mouth fell open. 'Who?'

'Chika Mboko.'

The sting of surprise hit Lilly. Only yesterday Chika had been in the witness box, larger than life. Full of life.

'You have to come,' said Annabelle. 'You have to make them understand that Tanisha had nothing to with it.'

Lilly flapped her arms by her sides. 'She sacked me.'

'Do you think she'll care about that now?'

'I have children in the house,' said Lilly. 'I can't leave them here on their own.'

Annabelle glanced at Karol who was clearing away the glasses. He looked up at Lilly.

'I could stay the night,' he said. 'Sleep on the sofa.'

Lilly shook her head. This was utter madness.

'I'll get my coat.'

Demi thunders past Gran to her room.

'Take off those wet shoes,' Gran shouts.

She doesn't pay attention and throws herself on to her bed. She's drenched, her jeans sticking to her skin. The mud she's caked in spreads on to her duvet. The cover was clean on this morning. Laundry day.

She doesn't care about that. She doesn't care about anything.

Her best friend in the world is dead. Beautiful, funny, strong Chika is gone.

She bites down on her pillow to stop herself from screaming, knowing that once again, she's all alone.

The custody suite was quiet. By midnight, the suspects had either been processed or had been bedded down for the night to sleep off whatever had got them into trouble in the first place. The only interviews that took place in the middle of the night were for prisoners suspected of serious arrestable offences, or where the prisoner was a child.

Tanisha McKenzie was both.

'Tell me this is a bad dream,' said Lilly.

Jack frowned and placed a polystyrene cup of coffee on the counter. It was dark brown, small lumps of powdered milk floating on top.

'I wish it were, Lil,' he said.

'So, what's the story?'

He sighed. Tiredness was scored across his face and there were circles under each eye, like wicked smiles.

'Phil Cheney's doing the autopsy now, but preliminary findings suggest a number of stab wounds to the back, possibly puncturing the heart, lungs or both.'

Lilly took a breath. Chest wounds were often fatal, but to catch the heart through the back took force. Whoever cut Chika clearly meant business.

'What makes you think Tanisha's got anything to do with it?'

Jack gave a tight laugh. 'Other than the victim was the only witness in the case against your client.'

'That's not enough and you know it. What evidence have you got?'

Jack flicked the cup with his thumbnail so the creamy clumps bobbed up and down. He stared into his drink, resolutely away from Lilly.

'Tonight I saw a kid die. Not a nice kid. Not a white middle-class kid from a good home and a fancy school, but still a kid. So don't lecture me about what I can or can't do.'

'I wasn't lecturing . . .'

He still refused to look at her. 'There is one person, and one person only, who is linked to the attacks on both Malaya Ebola and Chika Mboko and I want to speak to that person. Is that so difficult to understand?'

'No.'

Tanisha was sat in her usual place in the interview room, head in the crook of her elbow, on the table. Annabelle sat beside her.

'This is getting to be a habit, Tanisha,' said Lilly.

Tanisha pushed herself up and Lilly noticed her pregnancy was now showing. Had that happened overnight? Or had Tanisha simply stopped hiding it now the truth was out?

'I want you to know that I appreciate what you did for me in court and I appreciate you coming here tonight.'

It was obviously rehearsed and Annabelle beamed like a proud mother whose young child had just delivered her first lines in a school play. Lilly smiled all the same.

'Why don't you tell me your movements today,' she said.

'Not much,' Tanisha replied. 'I signed on at the police station, went shopping in between.'

'This evening?'

'Home.'

'All night?' Lilly asked.

'I ain't stupid, you know, if I bust my curfew they're gonna throw my arse back in jail.'

'I can vouch for her,' Annabelle added.

Lilly chewed the end of her pen and studied them. 'The thing is, ladies, we've been here before haven't we? You telling me you were nowhere near the scene of a crime, me going in there and making a prize twat of myself.'

'It was different then,' said Tanisha.

'How?'

'I panicked that time, just denied everything.'

'And now?'

'I don't need to panic,' said Tanisha. 'I got you.'

Jack angled the camera at Tanisha. It was like *déjà vu*. Only it wasn't a trick of the mind caused by lack of sleep, they really had all been here before, playing this same scene.

'I'll get straight to the point.' His jaw was stiff. 'Where were you tonight, Tanisha?'

'At home, watching TV.'

Annabelle leaned forward. 'I can confirm that.'

'So you were together?' Jack asked.

'No,' said Tanisha, 'I was in my room.'

'I can't stand those reality shows the young people seem to love,' said Annabelle.

Jack ignored Annabelle, kept his eyes trained on Tanisha. 'And you stayed in your room all night?'

'I was in there when the feds came for me, wasn't I?'

He'd checked the notebooks of the uniform who had arrested her. There was no doubt they'd found Tanisha in her bedroom.

He wasn't wearing a tie to smooth so he rubbed his palms along his thighs. The trousers were an old pair he'd found at the back of his locker. Tired grey joggers with a hole in the knee. He'd had to hand in the jeans he'd been wearing earlier to forensics. They'd test the blood and check them for anything else that might have leaked on to him while he held Chika in his arms.

Anger boiled under his skin. 'Did you stay up in your room all night?'

'Yeah.' Tanisha paused. 'No.'

'Which is it?'

'I came down once for something to eat. Annabelle wasn't there, so I grabbed an apple.'

'You remember that clearly, do you?' Jack snapped.

'Yeah, cos I don't really like them, but Annabelle says I should eat all that healthy shit for the baby, so, you know.' She shrugged. 'I chopped it up and took it back upstairs with me.'

Jack whipped his head at Annabelle. 'Where were you?'

'I don't know,' Annabelle said. 'Bathroom, study perhaps.'

'It's a big house,' Lilly interjected.

'So you can't be sure then, that Tanisha was there all night,' said Jack.

Annabelle spluttered. 'What?'

He tried to check his building rage. 'In this huge house of yours, you can't know for certain that Tanisha hadn't left. She could easily slip out and you'd just presume she was upstairs.'

Annabelle shook her head. 'It's not like that. I check on her all the time.'

He slammed his hands on to the table top and all three women gasped. 'Tonight, Chika Mboko died and I need to know if Tanisha killed her.'

'I didn't,' Tanisha whispered.

He breathed out though his nose and raked his hands through his hair, dragging his fingernails into his scalp. He had nothing. In fact, he had less than nothing. He had a witness who would swear that Tanisha was at home eating fruit. He needed to change direction.

'Why did you and Chika fall out?'

'Huh?' Tanisha moved back in her chair.

'You used to be friends, but you fell out,' he said. 'I want to know why.'

Her answer was instant and mechanical. 'She said I stole her phone and I never.'

'See, that just doesn't ring true to me.' He folded his arms. 'All that bitterness over a phone.'

'I've known grown men fight in the pub over football,' Lilly commented.

'The thing is, Chika intimated that it was about much more than that,' he said.

Tanisha narrowed her eyes. 'What did she say?'

'That it was complicated. Those were her exact words.' Jack rubbed his nose with a finger. 'And a row over a phone doesn't sound that complicated to me.'

Tanisha leaned right back in her chair, folded her own arms so that she and Jack were in mirror positions.

'I arranged to meet her so that she could tell me exactly what did happen between you,' he said.

'She wouldn't have told you shit,' Tanisha laughed. 'She would have dragged you over there and made up some crap.'

'I guess we'll never know,' said Jack. 'Which, from where I'm sitting, looks bloody convenient for you.'

The house is in darkness, except for the winking LCD light of the alarm. Trick cranes his neck to look through the window and lets out a whistle.

'You ain't winding me up? This is really your gaff?'

'Shush,' Jamie puts a finger to his lips. 'You'll wake my parents.'

Trick is still shaking his head in disbelief as Jamie puts his key in the lock, and taps in the alarm code. Jamie's never considered his home to be particularly posh. All his schoolmates live somewhere similar. Many of them have another house as well, in Norfolk or, more often, France. The way Trick is acting you'd think it was a mansion or something.

He shuts the door as gently as he can, but Trick is already crashing through to the dining room.

'For fuck's sake keep quiet,' Jamie hisses. 'If my dad catches us we're dead.'

Tricks nods his understanding and slips inside.

'My old man's a right bastard as well,' he stage whispers. 'Proper handy with his fists.'

Jamie's stunned. His dad's pretty crap, always going on, always looking at Jamie with his disappointed face, but he'd never beat him.

'One time he broke my mum's cheekbone,' Trick tells Jamie.

'What did you do?'

'Wrapped a baseball bat round his head.' Trick sniffs. 'We never heard from him no more.'

'Sorry.' Jamie pats his friend's arm.

'Good riddance to bad rubbish, I say.'

Jamie turns the dimmer switch so that the room is bathed in a low light. Enough to see, but not enough to wake his folks.

Trick's eyes are wide and he spins around like he's crossed through the wardrobe into Narnia. He lets out a bewildered giggle. 'What is this?'

Jamie would have thought it was pretty obvious, what with the table and chairs. 'The dining room.'

'You have a special room just to eat in?'

Actually, the Hollands almost never use it. His parents eat out most nights and if Jamie's home from school he'll pick at a microwaved lasagne with the telly on in the kitchen. Dad always complains that it's an easy room for their cleaning lady, Anjia, and that they shouldn't have to pay for it. Jamie doesn't want to explain any of this to Trick.

'Let's just get out of here,' he says.

They'd meant to come hours ago but the time had danced away. Hanging out with Trick is like that. Plans get made but never pursued. Hours stretch and bend and disappear. Total freedom. After a lifetime of having every moment of his existence scheduled and timetabled, Jamie has never been so happy and he would gladly stay with Trick for ever.

There are downsides of course. Trick hoovers down the powder at an alarming rate. He calls himself a meth monster and it's no lie. And there's a reckless side to him. Sometimes it's exciting, like when he rubs himself against Jamie's arse in broad daylight. Sometimes it's scary, like when he runs across the road, narrowly avoiding oncoming buses, or steals a pile of chocolate from a newsagent's.

'Stay here,' Jamie warns and leaves Trick fiddling with the candlesticks while he creeps upstairs.

The door to Mum and Dad's room is shut, but his heart still pounds as he passes. He's glad to reach the end of the hallway and his own room. It feels strange being inside. There's his duvet and posters, his wardrobe full of clothes. Was it only yesterday that this was his life? It seems like years ago. Like a fading memory.

He opens his drawer and takes out Uncle Theo's cash. Underneath are a handful of postcards, a beaded necklace he bought on a school trip to Provence, unused book tokens, an iPod and a chap stick. They don't seem familiar at all, as if they belong to someone else.

He shuts the drawer, glad to leave this existence behind. At the door, he has second thoughts, scurries back and retrieves the iPod. He's spent hours loading it with all his favourite tracks.

With any luck he can sell it.

Chapter Twelve

Carla Chapman is manning reception and she hates it. She's supposed to be a copper, not a glorified secretary, smiling at the great unwashed as they come to tell their tales of woe. She should be out there on the street solving crimes, not filling in Incident Report Sheets.

She hears along the canteen bongo drums that Jack McNally has bagged himself another SAO. A murder. What she wouldn't give to be involved in that.

Actually, she's a bit miffed that Jack hasn't been in contact. After she trawled through all those hours of CCTV footage for him and found that vital piece of evidence, you'd have thought he'd have asked her to get on board. One good turn and all that.

It could be that he assumes she's got a full work-load. Or that she's not on duty today. There's no way he would know that she's been plonked on flipping reception doing meet and greet.

She pulls out her phone. Maybe she should text him, offering her assistance. Something professional and helpful, with just a hint of the naughty. Before she's even decided what to say, a punter comes in off the street. It's a woman. Not local by the look of her, with dark hair cut and coloured in a way that smells of money. Her suit is the same. Definitely designer.

'Can I help you?' Carla trills.

The woman steps to the counter and places a leather briefcase at her feet. 'I don't know.'

Carla smiles encouragingly. The woman seems lost and nervous. Carla would place a bet that she's never stepped a foot in a police station in her life.

'My son's disappeared,' she says at last.

'When?' Carla asks, pulling out a missing person's report sheet.

The woman frowns, or at least tries to, but she's got one of those foreheads that won't move. Probably full of botox.

'I last saw Jamie on Monday morning, before I left for work.'

'How old is he?'

'Sixteen.'

Carla stops filling out the form. Teenaged boys go missing every day of the week. It usually turns out they've spent the night at their mate's and forgotten to ring home. No big deal.

'Have you tried to call him?' she asks.

'He's switched off his phone.'

'What about his friends? Have you given them a call to find out if he's there?'

'I don't know his . . .' The woman looks pained. 'He goes to boarding school and his friends will all be there.'

'What about a girlfriend?' Carla asks.

The woman bites her top lip. It's completely unlined. Botox, no doubt about it. 'No girlfriend.'

Carla tries not to sigh and pushes the form across the desk. 'Why don't you fill out the details and if we hear anything we'll get in touch, but to be honest with you, boys of that age usually turn up when they get hungry.'

'I think he might have already been back,' the woman says. 'Some of his things might have gone.'

'Might have?'

'I can't be sure.'

'Like I say.' Carla taps the form.

The woman takes out a fountain pen from her inside pocket and scans the form, writing out her name: *Mrs Sally-Anne Holland*.

'If you need to call, I'd prefer you to contact me and not his father,' she says.

'Why's that?'

Mrs Holland looks up at Carla as if pleading with her to understand. 'I haven't told him Jamie's missing.'

'Surely he's noticed,' Carla laughs.

'He thinks Jamie left for school on Monday and, as he boards, my husband simply assumes he's in school.' Mrs Holland gulps, a string of delicate seed pearls bobbing at her throat. 'I don't want to worry him, you see.'

Carla cocks her head to one side. Something doesn't ring true. This woman has come out of her way to attend a police station a long way from home, and now she doesn't want her husband involved.

'Perhaps you're right,' Mrs Holland says. 'Jamie is probably at home right now, working his way through the fridge and I'm making a fuss about nothing.'

'It won't hurt to at least log it,' says Carla.

Mrs Holland shakes her head. 'No, I've wasted enough of your time, please excuse me.'

With that, she puts away her pen and leaves. As she gets to the door, Carla notices the red soles of her high-heeled shoes. Louboutins. Six hundred pounds' worth of unadulterated sex appeal. When she makes DI she will stomp about in those every day and every copper in the station, including Jack McNally, will come begging at her feet.

The toaster was on the blink. Again. The bread wouldn't pop and black smoke was pouring out. Lilly took a knife and tried to gouge it out.

'That is a very bad idea.' Karol leaned across her and turned the toaster off at the socket.

He was wearing nothing but a pair of cotton boxer shorts, his chest vast and firm. He caught Lilly looking and coughed in embarrassment.

'I did not hear you come back last night,' he said.

'It was gone three and you were fast asleep,' she replied.

He turned the toaster upside down over the sink. 'Did everything go as you wished?'

'Well, Tanisha wasn't charged.'

Two slices of carbonized toast slid out in a flurry of crumbs.

'Common sense prevailed,' said Karol.

'Lack of evidence prevailed,' Lilly replied.

'What's he doing here?' Sam stood at the kitchen door. He too was bare chested, his pyjama bottoms slung low on his hips, further elongating the long strip of his hairless torso.

'Tell me he didn't stay over,' Sam demanded.

'I had to go out.'

'I slept on the sofa.'

Lilly and Karol spoke at the same time.

Sam eyed them both with suspicion. Lilly in her dressing gown, Karol almost naked. Together in the kitchen.

Lilly cleared her throat. 'One of my clients was arrested late last night, it was her foster-mother who woke you up when she came to ask for help. I spent the night at the police station so Karol kindly offered to babysit.'

'Do babysitters,' Sam spat out the word, 'often walk around undressed?'

'You are quite right, Sam, I will get my clothes now.' Karol headed out of the room.

'Do you have to be so rude?' Lilly hissed.

'Do you have to be so obvious?'

Lilly sighed. 'Don't you think if I'd been having a night of passion I might have opted for something a little more alluring?'

Sam took in her tatty dressing gown, with toothpaste on the lapel, and the fluffy bunny slippers.

'He still shouldn't be here, Mum, we don't know him from Adam.'

'He works for me,' said Lilly.

Sam rolled his eyes. 'As a secretary. I bet you haven't had him CRB checked. He could be any sort of weirdo or paedophile.'

'Or he could be an Al-Quaeda terrorist, or working for MI5.'

'Now you're just being stupid.'

'I'm simply making the point that sometimes we have to place our trust in people.' Lilly turned to the fridge. 'Now do you want some bacon?'

Mrs Ebola answered the door. Her face heavy with barely contained sadness.

'Is Demi there?' Jack asked.

Mrs Ebola showed him in. The flat was cold. No central heating and the gas fire was switched off.

'She is very upset,' said Mrs Ebola. 'She won't come out of her room at all.'

'Can I go up?' Jack asked.

Mrs Ebola nodded that he could and led him to the stairs.

'Please excuse the mess,' she clucked.

He smiled. The carpet was worn, the paintwork marked, but the place was spotless. His ma said exactly the same thing whenever the McNallys had visitors. She would spend hours on her knees scrubbing the floors, her fingers red and rough from the industrial quantities of bleach she insisted on using, but if a neighbour should so much as put a toe over the step, Ma would put her hand to her head.

'Don't mind us, we're in a terrible muddle.'

He climbed the stairs to the tiny landing. One door was shut tight so he tapped with his knuckle.

'Go away,' came a muffled voice from inside.

'Demi, it's Jack McNally,' he called. 'I'm the copper who was with you last night.'

She didn't answer but he could hear the sound of sobbing. He pushed the door open and stepped inside. There were two single beds. One fully made, the duvet freshly laundered and pulled tight. Demi lay on the other which was crumpled and dirty. She looked up at him with eyes swollen from crying.

'What do you want?' Her voice was a harsh rasp.

'To speak to you about what happened.' Jack kept his own voice low and gentle.

'You were there, you know what happened.'

Jack edged closer and bent down so he was at her level. His knees gave a rebellious crack. 'I'm afraid Chika had been stabbed, Demi, that's why she fell.'

Demi blinked at him. 'What?'

'Someone killed her,' said Jack. 'She was knifed in the back.'

Demi pushed herself up. The imprint of the pillow clear on her cheek.

'Do you know who did it?'

Jack shook his head. 'That's what I wanted to talk to you about. She told me she was meeting someone. Do you know who?'

'No. She got a text. I thought it was from you, about the stuff with the court case. Have you spoken to the girl who attacked Malaya?'

'She says she was home.'

'Do you believe her?' Demi asked.

'I don't know,' he replied. 'Tanisha McKenzie says a lot of things, if you get my drift.'

He stood with a groan and placed his card on Demi's tear-stained pillow. 'If you remember anything at all, call me.'

As he got to the door he remembered something Cheney had asked him to do.

'While I'm here, can I just take a quick swab?' He pulled out a plastic container.

'What do you mean?'

'Nothing to worry about.' He uncapped it. The plastic cheek scrape was attached to the lid, like a child's tube of bubbles. 'You and I were at the scene so forensics need to eliminate our DNA.'

'Okay.' Her voice was small.

'Open wide, it doesn't hurt a bit.'

From the walkway outside the Ebolas' flat, Jack caught sight of a SOCO van. He made his way over and flashed his badge at an officer who was methodically labelling evidence bags.

'There's a lot of crap covered in a lot of blood up there,' said the officer.

'Cheney around?' Jack asked.

The officer nodded to the stairwell at the base of the block where Chika lived. *Had lived*. The entrance was blocked by several strips of police tape. If the lift was broken the residents were buggered.

Jack peeled off the top strip, stepped over the others and stuck it back to the wall. The stairwell stank. Not standard issue piss and beer. It had the hot, meaty stench of death.

'Phil,' he shouted up, into the dark concrete, 'you there, mate?'

'Come join the party,' Cheney's voice echoed down.

Jack climbed the stairs to the tenth floor, sweating by the time he reached the entrance to the walkway. Cheney was on his hands and knees, measuring blood splatter patterns and making careful notes.

'You must really love your job,' said Jack.

'The ladies tell me it turns them on.'

'The sort of munters you go for, it probably does.'

Jack studied the wall and floor. The scene was covered in blood. He'd learned at the academy that the human body contained five litres of the stuff. What no one ever mentioned was how much escaped during a stabbing or a shooting. Maybe if they brought kids here, showed them the resulting carnage, they'd stay away from trouble. Maybe not.

'What can you tell me?' he asked.

Cheney closed his notebook and stood. 'There is no blood lower than this level, well only a few drops that flew out during the attack. The majority of it is here.'

'So this is where she was stabbed?'

'Almost definitely. I'd say she was here,' he placed Jack on the top step, his body turned towards the exit, 'and the assailant came behind her.'

'Took her by surprise?' asked Jack.

'I'd say so. There are no defensive wounds, only three punctures moving downwards.'

'Why down?'

Cheney stood behind Jack. 'The first cut is here.' He jabbed Jack with the corner of his notebook in the sternum.

'I'd turn immediately,' said Jack.

Cheney shook his head. 'You're in shock, in pain, your instinct is to fall forwards.'

He pressed on Jack's shoulders, so that he bent, and jabbed Jack with the book again, this time slightly lower.

'Actually if you'd managed to get away, you might have lived at this point,' said Cheney. 'The first wounds were deep but not fatal.'

'But she didn't run,' said Jack.

'No,' said Cheney. 'I think she fell forwards.'

Jack reached all the way until his hands touched the ground. He felt the edge of the book nudge him hard.

'Remember the entry site above the victim's bra strap? That was the killer,' said Cheney. 'Straight into her heart.'

'While she was down.'

Cheney didn't answer. Instead he skirted around Jack and through the exit, pointing to a faint trail of blood that last night's rain had tried to wash clean.

'Then she must have staggered along the walkway.'

Jack followed Cheney. They stopped at the point Chika fell from.

'She saw me,' said Jack. 'Leaned over to try to tell me something.'

'I doubt it, Jack. I'm surprised she even made it this far to be honest.'

But Jack wasn't the least bit surprised. Chika Mboko had been a fighter all her life. Even at the end, she had still been fighting.

They're sitting at a bus stop eating Rice Krispies Squares. They sort of melt in your mouth and Trick says the sugar rush helps his come-down.

They're not waiting for a bus. Just sitting. Watching.

Trick likes buses. He says his granddad used to be a coach driver.

'What happened to him?' Jamie asks.

'Dunno. We moved to get away from Dad.' Trick knows all the numbers and where they go. 'I've always been able to memorize timetables and that.'

'You should come to my school,' says Jamie. 'We never stop learning stuff. French verbs, lists of dates, lines of poetry. It's endless.'

'Do you think they'd have me, then?' Trick asks.

The thought of him in a blazer and tie, doing his prep, cracks Jamie up.

'I'm sure they'd be very glad to have you,' he laughs.

Soon they're both in hysterics, imagining Trick in the choir and chess club. Without warning, Trick's face drops and he mumbles something to himself. Three boys are walking towards them. Their heads are shaved under their baseball caps and they stop in the bus shelter.

'All right batty boy.' The largest, three thick gold chains swinging around his neck, kicks Trick's foot. 'This your new ride?'

The other boys laugh, showing an array of missing teeth. Trick smiles, but in the same way Jamie's mum smiles when she thinks she should, but underneath can't see what's funny.

'You got something for me, batty boy?' The boy scowls. 'Don't tell me you've forgotten.'

Jamie watches Trick's face. It's easy to know what he's thinking. What's the saying? He wears his heart on his sleeve. That's Trick. He's open, like a little puppy or a small child. And right now, Jamie can see Trick is frightened.

'I ain't forgot,' he says.

The boy bends down, his face right in Trick's. 'You sure, queer boy? Cos I'm happy to remind you, pour a little battery acid on your mum's face.'

Jamie's heart crashes around his chest. He can't believe what the boy just said.

'I said I ain't forgot.' Trick squeezes his eyes shut.

'I want the lot,' says the boy. 'You got one hour.'

Trick nods.

Satisfied, the boy straightens and moves away. When he's a few feet away, he turns. Jamie holds his breath, too scared to breathe. The boy holds up his hand, makes the shape of a gun and fires. All three laugh and leave.

Once they're out of sight, Trick leaps to his feet. 'Shit, shit, fucking shit.'

'What's wrong?' Jamie asks.

Stupid question. A maniac has just threatened to disfigure Trick's mum, and okay, he often calls her a fat slag and steals her benefits, but she's still his mum. Trick doesn't notice, his panic is too thick.

'I owe them money.' He hops about.

'How much?'

'I dunno.'

'What do you mean you don't know?' Jamie asks. 'How much did you borrow?'

'They're not a fucking bank, Jamie.' Trick is shouting now. 'There's no bit of paper to work out the interest rate.'

Jamie must look as clueless as he feels because Trick sighs. 'They gave me a few wraps on the never never. I told them I'd give them our telly.'

'And you didn't?'

'I tried, didn't I? But Mum caught me and called the police so I had to leg it.'

Jamie thinks fast. Trick owes some crazy people a telly. Right now he doesn't have a telly. But does it really matter? The boy with the ugly chains has probably got a flat-screen plasma at home, like all the rest of the scroungers. He just wants to be repaid. Jamie pulls out the cash he took from home. They've spent a bit, but most of it's still there.

'Here's forty quid at least,' he says.

Trick shakes his head. It won't be enough. In Jamie's other pocket is his iPod. He offers it to Trick.

'This has got to be worth something.'

Trick's hand quivers as he inspects it. It's a good one, the latest model.

'Let's see what we can get for it,' he says and they hurry off in the direction of Solomon Street.

Jack's stomach flipped as Phil Cheney unlocked the door to the rubbish chute and began scooping out the contents. A black plastic sack split open, spilling rotting meat bones and dirty nappies on to the road.

He put his hand across his nose. 'I'll leave you to it, mate.'

'Lightweight,' Cheney laughed.

Jack headed back to the SOCO van and looked in the foot well of the front passenger side. As expected he found a flask of coffee. Cheney might look like he lived in a yurt but his organizational skills outstripped Jack's. He would never come out on a job without provisions.

Jack poured himself a cup and took a sip. He felt bruised purple by the ferocity of the last twenty-four hours. He needed to rest. Sleep wouldn't come, he knew that, but a lie on his bed would be welcome. He'd finish the coffee and head home. Cheney would call him if he found anything.

As he drank, his eyes wandered back to the place where Chika had landed. Someone had placed a bunch of flowers next to the police cordon. They were the cheap kind that you could pick up in a garage. The sort he used to grab for Lilly on the way home from work.

A group of girls arrived. All hair extensions and PVC bomber jackets. They hovered at the tape, hugging one another. Jack guessed they'd be CBD, but knew, if approached, they'd be struck deaf, dumb and blind.

A car pulled up and hooted its horn. As one, the girls sloped over to it, peering in the window, speaking to the passenger. It was a man. Black. Young. Nothing out of the ordinary, yet something in the way the girls behaved told Jack to pay attention. He went through his pockets but couldn't find paper or pen. In the end he took out his phone and saved the registration plate in his contact list.

Black Merc DK639.

The girls were nodding now, agreeing with something the man had said. Then his window closed and the car sped off. The girls too disappeared.

Jack sighed and finished his drink. There was nothing more he could do here, he might as well get off and at least try for some kip. He shook the coffee dregs on to the road and was screwing the cap back on the flask, when Cheney materialized from the rubbish chute, his forensic suit brilliant against the backdrop of gloomy breeze blocks. He was holding something at chest height. Jack squinted. It was an evidence bag.

He jumped out of the van and the two men met in the shadows.

'This might just be what you need, Jack,' Cheney grinned.

Inside the bag was a kitchen knife, the blade, unmistakably, covered in dried blood.

Trick is talking. Non stop. It's a stream of consciousness that has lasted the entire journey and Jamie's head is breaking in two trying to keep up.

After he's paid off the nutters, he wants to take a break from all this. Get clean of the gear. It'll be hard, he knows, but he thinks he's strong enough. He's tried before. Locked himself in his house, barricaded the door. His mum had a fit about the nails and that but he explained it was the only way. After eight hours, he sold his mum's microwave for ten quid. This time, though, will be different. He'll score some benzos. Put himself to sleep for a day or two. Job done. Then he'll live his life. He'll pack his bags and take off. Get a job. Get a place of his own. Sure, he'll still have the odd dabble, but not this twenty-four seven thing he's got into.

'What time is it?' he asks.

Jamie checks his watch, forgetting he's already sold it. There's a white mark on his wrist where it should be, from his holiday in Antigua at half term.

'It hasn't been an hour has it?' Trick babbles.

Jamie has no idea. Time has stopped having any meaning.

By the time they get to Solomon Street, Jamie is exhausted. He needs to sit down.

'No offence, Jamie,' says Trick, 'but let me do the talking.'

He'll get no argument. Jamie couldn't, even if he wanted to.

The guy on the wall has been replaced. There's no pit bull gnashing its teeth, but the new man is every bit as aggressive. He's got a bandage around his foot and is rubbing it.

'Is JC in?' Trick asks.

'Don't speak to me, junkie,' the man snarls. 'Just go inside and do your thing.'

It seems best to do as he says and Jamie follows Trick up the path.

Inside, they head straight for the kitchen and knock on the door. The woman who looks like a man answers.

'What are you after? Glass?'

'Not right now.' Trick's voice is jumpy. 'We wondered what you'd give us for this.'

He holds out the iPod and JC kisses her teeth.

'This isn't a pawn shop, you know.' But she takes it.

'I think a hundred would be a fair price.' Trick wiggles on the spot. 'Or eighty at a push.'

JC ignores him and checks to see that it works. Then she bends towards a low cupboard, opening it with a key on a chain. Inside are three or four rolls of notes. She pulls off two twenties.

'I'll give you forty,' she says.

'C'mon, JC, you know it's worth more than that,' says Trick.

She holds out the notes. 'Take it or leave it, I don't bargain.'

Trick snatches the money and they leave. At the door, he takes Jamie's arm. 'Let's have a taste to clear our minds, yeah.'

There's one bag left from Jamie's watch swap, so they share it, hunched over the same piece of foil. A girl in the corner watches them.

'Let's have some of that,' she says.

They shake their heads.

'You can fuck me if you want,' she says, lifting her skirt to reveal grey knickers and a scab on her thigh.

'No thanks,' says Trick.

'Bastards,' she mutters and wanders off to find someone less choosy.

The weariness leaves Jamie's bones and he leans back against the wall as if he were sinking into a warm bath.

'Did you see all that fucking dosh?' Trick asks.

Jamie nods. There must have been hundreds of pounds. Maybe thousands. Mum and Dad have lots of credit cards but they never carry much cash.

'If we had that much, we could do anything,' says Trick. 'Get away from this shit hole. To the sea. Abroad even.'

Jamie smiles until he sees that Trick isn't joking. It's not one of his disjointed plans that even he doesn't believe. He's serious.

'We could take it.' His voice is low. 'She's here on her own.'

'What about the guy outside?' Jamie asks.

Trick shrugs. 'No dog and he didn't look to me like he could run.'

They stare at each other, neither daring to say a word. Upstairs, the floorboards are creaking. Perhaps the scabby girl managed to get herself a punter.

At last Trick speaks. 'If I stay here, I'll die and I don't want that. I want to be with you.'

'Do you?'

'Course,' says Trick. 'I love you.'

Jamie is stunned. They've known each other such a short time, and yet Jamie has never felt this way before. He gulps down his fear.

'Let's do it.'

The corridor at the lab was long and bare. The carpet tiles were grey, the walls red-brick, punctuated by white doors, each an exact copy of the one next to it. Standard issue.

Jack paced the length of it, once, twice, three times. The wait was killing him.

Cheney had personally brought the knife back and agreed to check it for prints and samples. Tests like these often took weeks but Cheney was doing Jack a favour.

He pulled out his phone. The battery was getting low. At some point he would have to get home or back to his desk to charge it. He considered calling the chief super to let him know what was going on, but thought better of it. There was, after all, nothing to tell. Yet.

Finally, one of the identical doors opened and Cheney appeared.

'And?' Jack asked.

'Definitely the weapon,' Cheney replied. 'It's Chika's blood and the serration of the blade is entirely consistent with the edges of the wounds.'

Jack let out a breath. This was good news. In so many cases the weapon was never found, making it virtually impossible to trace the killer.

'What about a perp?' he asked.

Cheney smiled and held up his hands as if to keep Jack back. 'A few prints, yes.'

'Who?'

'We're running them through the database now,' said Cheney.

'Okay.' Jack went back to marching up and down the corridor.

They nod at the man with the bandage, arms crossed to hide the iron bars inside their sweaters. When Trick nicked them from a building site on the other side of the estate, Jamie had been horrified.

'We won't need them,' Trick assured him. 'We'll just wave them at JC, you know, frighten her into giving us the money.'

It all seemed like a good idea, until now. But Jamie knows he can't back out.

They creep through the door, surveying the downstairs for signs of life. The scabby girl is in the first room, but she's out of it, curled into a ball on the mattress. Trick nods at Jamie. They've been through it, what each of them will say and do.

Trick knocks on the kitchen door and calls to JC through it.

She opens up. 'You two again.'

'Got something for you,' says Trick.

She gives a bored sigh and holds out her hand. Trick pretends to check behind him.

'Not here,' he says. 'Too risky.'

JC rolls her eyes, but just as Trick predicted, she gestures to them to come inside.

'She's like the rest of 'em,' Trick told Jamie. 'Fucking greedy.'

Once inside the kitchen, Trick closes the door with the back of his heel and stands in front of Jamie, so Jamie can slide his iron bar into his hands undetected. It's heavy and cold and Jamie nearly drops it.

'Come on then,' says JC, 'I don't have all day and I know you need your little fix.'

Trick fiddles in his pocket and pulls out a crucifix. He lets it dangle from his finger, letting it catch the light. Trick said his dad gave it to him for his first holy communion. He told Trick it was solid gold. 'But the tight bastard lied,' said Trick. 'I've tried to sell it before.'

JC squints at it. 'That isn't worth shit.'

This was always the risk. That JC would suss it for what it was and refuse to buy it.

'Just twenty quid,' says Trick, 'that's all I'm asking.'

There's a pleading in his voice that sounds fake to Jamie. He hopes JC will just smell desperation.

'Ten and that's your lot,' she says.

Trick and Jamie exchange a nervous glance. This is it. The moment of truth.

JC bends to open the cupboard with the key, her top riding up to expose a ring of wobbling fat. As her hand reaches inside, Trick pulls out his bar and presses it to the back of her head.

'Give us the money,' he says.

'Don't be an idiot,' JC replies.

As arranged, Jamie brandishes his bar so JC can see that one too.

'We don't want to hurt you,' says Trick, 'but if you don't give us that cash, we'll smash your skull to little pieces.'

JC moves very slowly, one hand reaching out to the rolls of notes as if in slow motion. Jamie pants, the bar shaking in his sweaty hand. He's never threatened anyone in his life. Despises Tristan and all the bullies at school. He tells himself that this is different. This is for Trick. Soon it will be over. They'll have what they need. And they'll escape. For ever.

In the gloom, he catches sight of a glimmer. Not the crucifix;

that's hanging half in, half out of Trick's pocket. It's something metal. It's near JC's other hand.

'What's that?' Jamie shouts.

'What's what?' Trick shouts back.

'There!' Jamie points to the gleam in the shadows.

Whatever it is, it's in JC's hand now and she tries to spin towards them. A gun. Exactly like Jamie's seen on the telly.

'Shit,' Trick screams and brings his bar crashing down on JC's head. She jerks forward then back, like one of those test crash dummies that are always yellow. Her eyes roll.

The gun is still in her hand, so Trick hits her again. This time the skin on her skull splits and blood begins to gush down her face.

'Get the money,' Trick screams at Jamie. 'Get the fucking money.'

Jamie drops his own bar and reaches across JC, trying not to look at the gaping white hole in her head. What is that? Bone?

He scrabbles for the rolls of notes, dropping one into the growing pool of blood. He plucks it out, pockets it with the rest.

'Let's get out of here,' Jamie races for the door.

'Don't run,' Trick warns.

Together they slip out of the kitchen, closing the door on the carnage behind them, and move briskly down the hall. The scabby girl is in the doorway and they push past her.

'Bastards,' she calls. 'You're all bastards.'

Chapter Thirteen

'I like Lola,' Tanisha stroked her bump, 'and Leticia, cos it means happiness.'

Lilly smiled at her client. Choosing a name for her baby was obviously important. Planning ahead to better times.

'I used to like Portia,' said Tanisha, 'but I looked it up and it means pig, so what can you do?'

Lilly recalled her pregnancy with Alice. She'd been in shock for most of it, running away from it, refusing to even discuss names. At the time she'd said it was bad luck, or that she was too busy, but now she wondered if it wasn't the relationship with Jack she was running from. Would she have even considered moving him into the cottage if it hadn't been for Alice?

The door to Lilly's office opened and Karol appeared with a smile and a tray of tea and biscuits. If he was tired after a night on Lilly's sofa, he didn't look it.

'I'll be mother,' said Annabelle and began to pour milk for everyone.

When Karol left, Tanisha gave a gravelly chuckle. 'I thought you said he wasn't your man.'

'He's not,' Lilly exclaimed.

'Don't look that way to me.'

Lilly felt herself redden and changed the subject. 'With Chika's death, I think the CPS might reconsider their case against you.'

'Oh thank God.' Annabelle coughed in embarrassment. 'I mean, I'm sorry the girl was killed . . .'

'I ain't,' said Tanisha.

'You know what I'm trying to say,' Annabelle blundered on. 'I'll just be so very glad when all this is over and we can get on with our lives.'

Lilly nodded that she understood.

'You really think they'll drop it?' Tanisha asked. 'That policeman seemed to want to send me down real bad.'

'Without Chika, their case is very weak,' Lilly explained. 'The prosecution might decide to cut their losses.'

'When will we know?' Annabelle asked.

'I've already listed the case for tomorrow.'

As Annabelle beamed and Tanisha nodded her approval, Lilly's mobile rang.

'Yes?'

'It's Jack.'

Lilly smiled. Perhaps the decision to drop the case had already been taken and Jack was giving her the heads-up.

'What do you know?' she grinned.

He cleared his throat, didn't laugh.

'We found the murder weapon that killed Chika Mboko. It's a kitchen knife.' His voice was solemn.

'Okay.' Lilly narrowed her eyes.

'We've tested it for prints.'

Lilly looked up at her happy client and her heart plummeted in her chest. 'Go on.'

'I'm afraid we've found a match with Tanisha.'

Jack met Lilly at the station entrance. He checked nervously behind her.

'Where is she?'

'Gone home to get some things,' Lilly said.

'What?'

Lilly sighed. When she'd broken the news to Tanisha, the poor kid hadn't been able to move. Annabelle had burst into tears, but Tanisha had sat in stupefied silence. Eventually, she had hauled herself from her chair, as if she were nine months gone, and announced quietly that she would need to collect her clothes.

'I ain't wearing that prison uniform like last time,' she told Lilly.

'I can't believe you let her out of your sight,' said Jack.

'I'm a lawyer, not her armed guard,' Lilly retorted.

'I told you first as a matter of courtesy.'

'You told me first because you couldn't resist it,' said Lilly. 'If you wanted the blues and twos you should have brought her in yourself.'

He muttered something under his breath and disappeared back into the nick. Lilly waited outside, scouting the street for any sign of her client.

After ten minutes, Lilly's mobile rang. She snatched at it.

'Tanisha?'

'It's me,' Annabelle sobbed. 'She's gone.'

'What do you mean by gone?'

Annabelle's voice was choked. 'We were packing a bag and she suddenly stopped, said she couldn't do it, that she can't have her baby in jail.'

Annabelle broke down again, her breath coming in miserable heaves.

'Where do you think she might be?' Lilly asked.

'I have absolutely no idea.'

Lilly hung up and made her way back to the station entrance, her footsteps heavy, as she went to find Jack.

Demi runs up the stairs to the disused flats that Danny uses as his headquarters. She wishes she could have changed out of her muddy jeans but knows better than to keep him waiting.

Rocky opens the metal door with a clang. 'He's vexed, so watch yourself.'

Demi nods and sneaks through. Unlike the first time she came here, the room is full. The CBD girls are huddled in a corner and there are several men stood around, including the card players and the man from the wall on Solomon Street. Demi wonders where he's left his dog.

In the middle is the table. Only it's not a table any more. It's in a splintered heap, scattered with broken glass. On the far side, in the knocked-through room, is Danny. He has his back to them and is holding an axe.

Everyone is silent. The only sound is the grunting that comes from Danny.

When he turns, Demi understands that he's not grunting. He's growling. The pit bull isn't necessary, there's already an animal in the room.

'How did this fucking happen?' he shouts, flecks of white spit collecting in the corners of his mouth.

No one answers. Demi assumes he's talking about Chika's death and of course no one does know what happened.

'These scumbags think they can come into my area and take from me.' Danny raises the axe and flings it across the room. It skitters into the wall, sending out a cloud of plaster dust.

So he's not irked about Chika. It's about money. Always money.

'Since this shit with Malaya and Chika, people are taking liberties. They think I can't do nothing cos the place is full of feds,' Danny roars. 'Well, they wrong.'

The audience mutters its agreement. Demi just nods.

'We get out there and we find them.' He lowers his voice and somehow that's worse. 'And when we find them, we bring them back here for me to deal with.'

Everyone begins to file out, so Demi stands too.

'You, stay.' Danny points at her.

She gulps. Why has she been singled out? She looks around her in panic. The others won't meet her eye. When they're alone Danny crosses the room to her. Up close, she can smell him. Sweat and cigarettes.

'I want you to go over to Solomon Street. The police are crawling over the house but they won't pay any mind to a younger like you,' he says. 'Speak to any junkies you can find. Someone knows who did this.'

Demi nods and backs out of the room. When she's almost out of the door, Danny narrows his eyes at her.

'And Demi,' he says, 'don't you ever keep me waiting again.'

Annabelle's cooker was spotless. Regardless, she scrubbed at it ferociously.

'Have you really no idea where she might have gone?' asked Lilly.

Annabelle reached for a bottle of hob cleaner and poured a generous amount of it on to her cloth. Her elbow moved in a frenzy as she pursued non-existent dirt and germs.

'Annabelle,' Lilly prompted.

As if she hadn't heard, Annabelle threw open a drawer and extracted a wire brush. She held it up triumphantly before attacking the cooker.

Lilly raised her voice. 'Annabelle, if you intend to ignore me then why the hell did you ask me over here?'

When Annabelle bent so that she could inspect her work at eye level, Lilly got up to leave. She needed to find Tanisha, if possible before Jack. Everything would look much worse if Tanisha had to be cornered by the police.

'I think I know who killed Chika Mboko.'

Lilly skidded to a halt. 'Come again.'

Annabelle went to the sink and rinsed her cloth under the tap. The water ran chalky white with cleaning fluid.

'I had my suspicions as soon as I heard,' she said. 'But now they've conveniently found evidence linking Tanisha, I'm almost sure I know who did it.'

Lilly remained in the doorway, immobile and slack jawed.

'I think you'd be better sit down Lilly.'

Lilly flopped into a chair, leaning her forearms on the table and letting them take her weight. Annabelle squeezed the last drop of moisture from her cloth, folded it neatly and, at last, took a place.

'Almost ten years ago I fostered a boy named Daniel,' said Annabelle. 'He'd had a particularly difficult childhood but I was confident that with love and patience he could turn his life around.' She paused as if considering how best to voice her story. 'I underestimated the task.' Annabelle swallowed. 'Nothing seemed to help and Daniel went from bad to worse.'

'A lot of foster placements break down,' said Lilly.

'It was more than that.' Annabelle's expression was pained. 'He seemed to want to destroy everything around him, to take pleasure in it. He's the only child I've ever been frightened of.'

Annabelle's words struck a chord. Wasn't that what Miriam had said about Chika?

'In the end he broke me and I didn't foster again,' said Annabelle. 'Then I met Tanisha.'

'What does this have to do with Chika's death?'

Annabelle put up a hand, begging for patience. 'Since he left, Daniel has raised his game. He's a big man these days. Drugs, guns, money-lending, you name it. He has a lot of power, Lilly.'

Lilly nodded. Whoever controlled the streets, controlled the people.

'And that's why I went to him,' said Annabelle.

'Went to him for what?'

'For help.' Annabelle put her face in her hands, rubbing her temples with her fingertips. 'I knew he ran a lot of the gangs on the estates, so I asked him to intervene.'

Lilly couldn't hide her shock. 'You wanted him to interfere with a witness?'

'I just thought he could speak to Chika. I was sure she was making the whole thing up out of spite anyway,' said Annabelle.

The temptation to chastise was hot on Lilly's tongue, but she stopped herself. Something told her that Annabelle's story was about to get worse.

'It was foolish to ask Daniel for a favour. I should have remembered that he's not the sort of person to do the right thing,' said Annabelle. 'With someone like that, you have to fight fire with fire.'

'How?'

'I threatened him.'

Annabelle sat very upright in her chair, every inch the proper country lady, with her sensible clothes and clean nails. Not a woman who had just admitted to threatening a dangerous gangster.

'I told him that if he wouldn't help I would go to the police, that I would tell them exactly what he had done.'

Lilly pressed harder into the table to support herself. Men like the one Annabelle had described didn't take threats lightly. 'What did he say?'

'He said he'd consider my offer.' She let out a laugh. 'Those were his actual words. Then one day when I was shopping, his car pulled up and he told me we were going for a little drive.'

She looked up at Lilly and even now her eyes were filled with fear. 'Daniel is a very bad person.'

'Did he hurt you?' Lilly asked.

Annabelle shook her head. 'He didn't need to. He told me about the last person who had tried to persuade him to do something he didn't want to do. That the man's wife had been found in a canal and no one ever did work out why all her toenails were missing.'

Lilly's throat constricted.

'When I heard the knife had been found, I knew it was him,' said Annabelle. 'I crossed a line and this is my punishment.'

Lilly's head whirled. None of it made any sense.

'The knife has Tanisha's prints all over it.'

Annabelle pointed to the block on the work surface. Lilly had seen her client take a knife from it and cut an apple. Now, one was missing.

'Anyone could have sneaked in and stolen it,' said Annabelle.

It seemed unlikely. And yet this was such a big house, a thief could have got in undetected.

'Someone like Daniel would certainly know enough people capable of it,' said Annabelle.

'What I still don't understand,' Lilly said, 'is why you even thought you could intimidate him. I'm sure the fact that he's a crook won't come as any surprise to the police, they just can't pin anything on him. They never can.'

'But that's the point, Lilly, I *can* pin something on him. I have cast-iron proof that he had sex with an underage girl.'

'Proof?'

Annabelle's face was dour. 'He's the father of Tanisha's baby.'

Trick and Jamie are hiding under the slide where they first struck up their friendship. They huddle together, counting the money for the third time. The blood on the third roll makes Jamie tremble. He refuses to think about JC's head and how it split open like the shell of a boiled egg to reveal the white inside.

'This is it,' Trick whispers. 'This is what I've been waiting for. We can go anywhere we want. Paris, maybe, or Las Vegas. I've always wanted to go there. See Elvis and that.'

Jamie doesn't point out that Elvis died a long time ago. Or that they don't have passports. Or that a thousand pounds won't be enough for the plane tickets.

Trick lays his head on Jamie's shoulder. 'Where would you like to go?'

'I don't mind.' Jamie can feel tears sting his eyes.

'As long as we're together,' Trick's voice drifts away. 'That's all that matters.'

Solomon Street is shut off by police cars at either end. The feds buzz around like flies, their radios humming and crackling. Demi is in her school uniform, her smile wide.

'What's happened?' she calls out to one of them.

He looks her up and down before deciding she's a harmless kid.

'Someone's been attacked,' he says.

Demi opens her eyes as if she's shocked. 'Killed?' The copper doesn't answer. 'Did you catch who did it?' asks Demi.

'No,' says the copper, 'but don't you worry, miss, we will.'

'Yeah right.' Another girl has arrived to rubberneck, her eyes hooded, her mini-skirt revealing a rash over her thighs.

'On your way,' the copper hisses at her. 'There's nothing for your sort here, now.'

She makes a face at him and moves off. Demi moves with her.

'Were you in there, then?' Demi asks. 'When JC got bumped?'

The girl eyes Demi with suspicion. 'What do you know about it?'

'I know I've got a bag of glass in my pocket with your name on it if you tell me what went down.'

The girl scratches her thigh, picking at the edges of a scab with her nail. She holds out her hand and Demi drops the wrap without making contact. She's seen impetigo before and knows it's catching.

'Two of 'em, both white,' the girl tells Demi. 'Pair of queers.'

'What?'

'I seen 'em, with their hands all over each other.'

'Do you know what they're called?'

The girl shakes her head and looks over Demi's shoulder, already bored with the conversation, desperate to use the gear.

'I seen one of 'em around, you know, here and on the estate.' She wrinkles her nose. 'Proper habit he's got.'

Demi almost laughs. Yet, if she's learned one lesson in recent times, it's that no one sees themselves as they really are.

'The other one's new. Some posh bastard slumming it.'

'Do you know where they went?' Demi asks.

'No idea,' the girl is already scurrying away, 'but I doubt they've gone far.'

Annabelle brought Jack into the kitchen.

'Tanisha's not here,' said Lilly.

'Fuck it,' Jack punched his thigh.

'I think you should listen to what Annabelle has to say,' said Lilly.

Reluctantly, Jack rested his hands on the back of a chair. He clearly had no intention of sitting.

Annabelle relayed the same account and Lilly watched Jack's reaction throughout. Nothing in his face gave him away. He just listened in silence until Annabelle finished.

'Thank you,' he said, and turned to leave.

Lilly waved Annabelle to remain where she was, and went after him. At the door, she grabbed his arm.

'I know it sounds unlikely,' she said.

'It's a pile of shite and you know it,' he replied.

'Maybe or maybe not,' Lilly still held his arm, 'but think about it for a second. If Tanisha has gone to find this man, she could be in danger.'

He didn't respond, but he didn't move. Lilly took her opportunity.

'If he thinks there's any chance that Tanisha or Annabelle would get the police involved he might decide to do away with the evidence.'

'I'm not convinced,' he said.

'You don't need to be,' Lilly replied. 'You want to find her as much as I do. If we keep her safe into the bargain, I'll be happy.'

He hesitated, then nodded and went back through to the kitchen.

'What's this mystery murderer's full name?'

'Daniel Kanio,' said Annabelle.

'Address?'

Annabelle shook her head.

'What about his car?' Lilly asked. 'You said he picked you up in a car.'

Annabelle fluttered her hands helplessly. 'I don't know. Black, I think.'

Jack groaned and Lilly knew she would lose him if she couldn't get something more concrete.

'Was it the guy I saw you with?' she asked. 'I was on the porch and you didn't see me at first. You got out of a black car and said he owed you.'

'Yes, that was Daniel.'

Lilly turned to Jack. 'Black Merc, private reg, DK . . . something.'

Jack pinched his brow and pulled out his phone. 'DK 639?'

'That's it,' Lilly squealed.

'I'll see what I can find out.' He pointed to Annabelle and Lilly in turn. 'You two stay here, and if Tanisha gets in contact, call me immediately.'

* * *

Demi trudges through the Clayhill, asking every user she comes across if they know anything. The name Trick comes up a few times, but no one knows where he is. If they've got any sense, this pair of jokers will be long gone. Then again, junkies aren't well known for their common sense, are they?

That's something Gran always says Demi has. Or used to.

When she gets to the edge of Clayhill, where Hightown begins, she knows she should go back. She may not be an official member of the CBD, but she's known. If Yo Yo's crew catch her slipping into their area, they won't stop to ask for her credentials. She looks skyward, at the Nike trainers hanging from the telephone wire. A warning that anyone with common sense should heed, but Demi pushes on until she finds what she's looking for. Sorry Gran.

An ordinary gate. To an ordinary swing park.

She pushes it open and goes inside. The place is deserted, no children playing and laughing. A prickle of recognition stings her. This is where it all began. This is where Malaya was attacked.

She imagines the scene. Chika, fit and fast, searching for somewhere to hide. Malaya, fat and clumsy, being tackled to the ground. She makes her way to the slide, where a dark patch tells its ugly tale.

'Why the fuck didn't you just do like Gran told you, Malaya?' Demi demands. 'Why didn't you just go to school and stay out of trouble?'

Something stirs. A snuffle from under the slide. A dog? Demi peers into the cubby-hole. Two figures, completely out of it, wrapped in one another's arms, blood spattered across their jeans.

Demi pulls out her phone and calls Rocky.

'Tell Danny I think I just found them.'

Chapter Fourteen

'No address, no phone number, no nothing.'

Carla Chapman smiled up from her computer. 'Sorry, Jack, but this guy's completely off the radar. Even the car's registered to some woman in Ilford who died three years ago.'

'Dammit,' Jack snapped and instantly regretted it as Carla's face fell. She was a good kid, eager to help. She'd make a good copper too, if grumpy sods like him didn't put her off.

'Don't worry about it,' he said. 'It was always going to be a long shot with this one. That's precisely how he stays untouchable.'

Her face brightened. 'And a Doctor Cheney's been trying to get you.'

Jack wondered why Cheney hadn't called his mobile. He pulled it out and discovered the battery had finally died.

'He said he'll be incommunicado for the next hour, something about a new piece of art,' she told him. 'But that you might be interested to know that he found someone else's DNA on the knife.'

Jack's chest contracted. Surely Annabelle's cock and bull story couldn't be true. But if it was, what did that mean for Tanisha? Nothing good, that was for sure. He checked his watch. It would take twenty minutes for him to get to Cheney. Twenty minutes he didn't want to waste, but right now he didn't have an alternative.

'Can I borrow your phone, Carla?' Jack asked.

She smiled and handed it over.

'I owe you a drink,' he said.

'I'll hold you to that.'

Lilly rolled a five-pence piece between her forefinger and thumb, letting it catch the glare from the spotlight above her head. She wasn't good at waiting. When her mobile rang, she rushed to answer it, gratefully.

At first, the caller didn't speak and all Lilly could hear was passing traffic in the background.

'Who is this?'

'It's me.' Tanisha's voice was small. 'I just wanted to say that I'm sorry.'

'Tanisha,' Lilly exclaimed.

Annabelle gasped and her hands flew to her face.

'Tanisha where are you?' Lilly asked. 'Are you okay?'

'I'm . . .' Tanisha paused, obviously struggling with the word *fine*. 'I've got to sort some things out. I just wanted to like, apologize, for all the shit I've put you through.'

'Never mind about that Tanisha, just tell me where you are.'

'I can't do that, Lilly.'

'I know this is all very frightening,' Lilly jumped to her feet, 'but you've got to let me come and get you. Under no circumstances should you go to see the father of your child.'

'How do you know about Danny?'

Lilly glanced at Annabelle. 'That doesn't matter right now. What matters is that you keep yourself safe.'

Lilly was about to explain why Daniel Kanio was the last person Tanisha should trust right now, but the line was already dead. She screwed her eyes shut, knowing there was no point in pressing the reply button. Tanisha had said what she'd had to say and the conversation was over.

Her mind was running in double time, fast forwarding past the possibility that Kanio had dispatched Chika like an annoying wasp, to the point where he might hurt a pregnant girl who got in his way.

'Annabelle,' she spoke slowly, 'you need to think very carefully about where Daniel took you in his car.'

Annabelle's cheeks reddened and her mouth began to twitch.

Lilly held up a warning finger. 'I said carefully.'

Annabelle nodded and gulped down her haste. She took three breaths to steady herself.

'I could probably show you.'

Jack had been very clear that they should stay put. But Lilly wasn't any better at taking orders than she was at waiting.

When Jamie wakes up he can only open one eye. The other feels wet and heavy. He tries to wipe it, but his hand won't move. It's numb and caught in an odd position behind his back. Never mind. He'll go back to sleep. He's so very exhausted.

Then he hears the squealing. High pitched and annoying. It whistles in his ear and around his brain like one of those old-fashioned kettles. Or an animal. He once watched a documentary about an organic pig farmer. It was meant to show you that his 'girls' had led a happy life, rolling around in their own shit and eating acorns. But the sound of their screaming when the farmer cut their throats put Jamie off ham for ever.

The noise gets so loud Jamie is forced to look.

Suddenly, he is thrust back into the present. He knows exactly where he is and why he can't move his arms.

Trick is lying at the other end of the room, his hands and feet bound with wire. The black guy who picked them up in the park is standing above him, the weird eye, lifeless and white, staring down. He's calm and still, and seems almost puzzled at Trick writhing around at his feet. He examines the cigarette in his hand and blows on the lit end until it glows a deep red.

'No, please, no.' Trick tries to roll away.

Jamie can see three or four angry burns on his face, each a perfect circle. He wants to say something to help but knows there is nothing to say. His few days of freedom are over and he and Trick are going to die here, in this airless place.

The guy crouches down and holds the ember millimetres from Trick's cheek.

'Please,' Trick screams, 'you've got your money back. It's all there. We didn't spend any of it.'

The guy shakes his head. 'This isn't about the money. Do you really think I give a fuck about a poxy grand?'

'What then?' Tears are pouring down Trick's face. 'What do you want?'

Poor Trick. He doesn't get it. The guy doesn't want anything. They've taken from him and now they have to pay. Simple cause and effect.

Behind him, Jamie hears a groan of disgust. He finds the schoolgirl in her uniform, squatting against the wall, playing with her tie, her mouth a repulsed scowl. He'd forgotten she was there. When he woke up in the park she was standing over him, a mixture of sadness and confusion on her face. She wore the same expression when the guy with the freaky eye kicked him in the face. What will she do when it's Jamie's turn to be an ashtray?

At last, the guy is forced to take a break when another man enters the room.

'Boss,' the second man says, 'there's someone here for you. Says it's important.'

'Who?'

The second man glances at the schoolgirl. 'Tanisha.'

'What does she want?' The schoolgirl looks up from her tie.

Both men glare at her and walk out of the room.

Trick is whispering to himself, his body convulsing.

'Trick,' Jamie calls out his name. He has nothing useful to say, just wants Trick to know he's there. That he's not alone.

The schoolgirl hits her head against the wall behind her. 'This is all wrong. Totally fucked.'

She bangs it again and again, getting harder and harder.

Lilly drove through the Clayhill.

'Do you recognize anything?' she asked Annabelle.

Annabelle gazed through the windscreen at the row of shops. A Spar, a florist and a Help the Aged were on their left.

'I remember the café.' She pointed to an all-night place, the windows misty with steam and grease. 'Then we went straight on.'

Lilly drove at a crawl, scouring the pavements for any sign of Tanisha. The car behind overtook and hooted at her.

'There.' Annabelle indicated to a quad in front of two blocks of flats. 'We definitely pulled over just there.'

Lilly parked the Mini and they jumped out. The tower blocks loomed over them, grey and uninviting, each floor as ugly and demoralizing as the last. Hopelessness piled upon hopelessness.

'Do you think Daniel lives here?' Annabelle asked.

Lilly opened her palms. ' The police avoid it, so the gangs have a pretty free rein.'

'It's horrible.'

Lilly couldn't argue. 'Let's split up. You take the left and I'll take the right. If either of us finds Tanisha, we grab her.'

Annabelle bobbed her head, zipped up her waterproof and strode to the lift. Lilly turned to the right and headed to the entrance nearest to her, where she read a sign.

Welcome to Clancy Block.

* * *

Sandwiched between a sex shop and a bookies was Skin2Skin, a so-called body art salon.

Jack pushed open the door and entered a reception garlanded in purple drapes. Candles and joss sticks burned on a low table.

'Yeah?' a woman with shocking pink hair and a matching vest looked up from a magazine.

Jack flashed his warrant card.

'What do you want this time?' The woman's vest displayed arms covered from knuckles to shoulders in tattoos.

'I need to speak to Phil Cheney,' said Jack.

The woman leaned behind Jack to lock the door and jerked her head that he should follow her through a velvet curtain hanging from a pole. The back of her vest gaped and the head of a mermaid inked in ocean greens and blues smiled up at him.

The room behind the curtain was in complete contrast. Tiled floors and walls painted white, lit by spotlights in the ceiling. In the centre was a chair, not unlike one you'd find in a dentist. Cheney was sat in it, his left arm outstretched, the bald and shiny head of the tattooist bent over it.

'Nice,' said Jack.

Cheney and the man, tattoo gun still in hand, looked up.

'Police,' the woman told them.

'It's fine,' said Cheney. 'Just work.'

The woman sloped away and the man went back to his design, the gun droning. Cheney flinched as the needle pierced his skin.

'Why?' Jack asked.

'Self-expression,' Cheney answered. 'Now what the fuck are you doing here?'

'I got a message that you'd found something else on the knife.'

Cheney looked down at the picture appearing on his arm. An outline of flowers poking through barbed wire.

'I found a small amount of blood not belonging to our victim,' he said. 'Could be our killer cut themselves during the attack.'

The bald guy looked up from his work, stared first at Cheney, then Jack. His face, too, was hairless, his brow bones smooth and protruding. Cheney twitched his biceps, nudging the guy back to the job in hand.

'Do you have a match?' asked Jack, praying it was Tanisha.

'Nothing on the database,' said Cheney.

Jack's heart sank. It was inconclusive, certainly didn't mean Tanisha was innocent, but it would give the defence another foothold. He could just imagine Lilly spinning her story about some unknown person stealing the knife and committing the crime, how she'd point a jury to the unidentified blood.

'Could it be Annabelle O'Leary's?' Jack asked. 'It's her kitchen and her knife. Maybe she cut herself before Tanisha took it.'

'Perfectly possible. Get me a sample and I'll rule her in or out,' said Cheney.

Why the hell were lifts always out of order?

Lilly puffed her way to the fourth floor, leaning against the exit of the stairwell as she tried to catch her breath. She'd never been very fit. A few lessons in martial arts, the odd lunchtime walk, but never any serious exercise.

A woman with a toddler passed, looking Lilly up and down in contempt. As they hit the top of the stairs, she took her son's hand and whispered to him.

'Never ever speak to these people, understand. They come here for bad things.'

The little boy nodded and they hurried down.

Lilly wondered what the woman meant, until she realized that in the dark, sweating and heaving, she must have looked like any other junkie after a fix. She stood straight and pushed her hair from her face.

Then she thought about it. The woman had been very quick to assume Lilly was an addict chasing some drugs. The Clayhill was full of them of course, but it was almost as if the woman had expected it.

Lilly looked along the walkway at the flats. The two at the far end were boarded up, metal sheets over their doors and windows. One had a slit cut into it, reminding Lilly of the openings in cell doors. Small enough to pass things through, too small for anyone to fit through. In prison it was to keep people in. On the estates it was to keep the police out.

A drug house.

Was it possible that this place was Daniel Kanio's? Lilly lifted her chin. There were sixteen more floors. No doubt half a dozen flats would be derelict and taken over by dealers.

She sighed. It was a long shot, but she had to try.

'Tell me what the fuck she's doing here.'

The schoolgirl has left the room and is screaming in the hallway. There's the tell-tale smack of a punch being landed and a groan that makes Jamie shiver. Then the door slams shut.

More voices are raised outside. And there's more screaming. Something very bad is going on out there, but whatever it is, Jamie knows this is his only chance.

He tries to push himself to his feet, but can't get enough purchase with his shoulder. He can get his feet flat but can't get his torso off the ground. He strains with the effort. It's no use. With his feet and hands tied, it's impossible.

Instead, he rolls towards Trick like a worm, undulating his body in the fag ends and shards of glass. He feels a sharp sting in his upper arm and gasps. He risks a glance and finds a sliver, three centimetres long sticking out of his sweater. The trickle of blood and the pain tell Jamie it's caught deep in his flesh.

'Trick,' he pants, 'you've got to help me.'

Trick is still babbling to himself, his head rocking from side to side.

'Listen to me, Trick,' says Jamie. 'I need you to concentrate on what I'm saying.'

Trick looks over, but his eyes are unfocused.

'Trick.' Gritting his teeth against the burn, Jamie holds out his hands. 'I need you to move over here and untie me.'

Another thud, followed by a scream, comes from the hallway, making Trick flinch. At least that means he can hear.

'We have to get out of here.' Blood falls from the gash in Jamie's arm.

'How?' Trick's voice is full of wonder.

'I don't know,' Jamie admits, 'but if you untie me, I'll think of something.'

Trick laughs as if Jamie's just told a joke. And Jamie accepts that it is pretty funny. He's just some schoolkid who doesn't know anything. He gets up when a bell sounds and eats what's put in front of him. He does as he's told, day in, day out. His mum still labels all his clothes and he hasn't even had the guts to tell her that he's gay. How the fuck does he think he can overpower a one-eyed mad man and his army of violent drug dealers?

'Please, Trick,' he whispers. 'Just trust me.'

His friend pauses, looks deep into his eyes, then nods.

As Lilly thumped on the metal sheet, she accepted that this wasn't her brightest idea.

Even if there was anyone inside, what were the chances of your average drug dealer entering into a civilized conversation?

Is Tanisha McKenzie in there?

Why yes. Shall I send her out for a little chat?

Still, if she had even the slightest suspicion that her client was inside, she'd call in the cavalry. She pulled out her mobile in readiness.

The vent flew open and Lilly peered inside.

'What?' said a voice from inside the darkness.

Lilly gulped. 'I'm looking for someone.'

'What?' The voice sounded angry.

Lilly coughed, but before she could repeat her strange request, she heard shouting. From the bowels of the flat, came a scream.

'If you hurt my baby I will kill you!'

Lilly recognized it instantly and lunged at the vent. 'Tanisha?'

'Lilly,' Tanisha's voice rang out. 'Lilly, is that you?'

Lilly scrabbled for her phone. Tried to stab the key pad. But before she could make a call, the metal door swung open and she was dragged inside.

Chapter Fifteen

Lilly flew through the dark space of the hallway and crashed into the far wall, where a pair of firm hands around the throat pinned her. Lilly choked for breath, her tongue lolling. She scratched out at the man's face leering at her, with a look of rage in one eye, the other quite dead.

He released his hold, so that Lilly fell forwards, gulping down a breath, before he pushed her backwards again. Her head smacked against the wall and the stranglehold began to squeeze the life from her once more.

'Who is this?' he shouted.

Behind him was Tanisha, her face aghast. And another girl, younger than Tanisha, wearing a school uniform. She looked so very tired.

'I said, who the fuck is this?'

Tanisha jumped forward. 'Put her down Danny, it's my solicitor.'

'Your what?'

'My brief,' said Tanisha. 'I'm in all sorts of trouble with the feds, you know that.'

Lilly heard the gagging sound come from her throat and felt the wet splash of saliva on her chin, but the world was becoming blurry around the edges. Her hands could no longer fight the man.

'What's she doing here?' Danny demanded.

'I don't know,' said Tanisha. 'She must have followed me.'

The man turned slightly so that he could direct his fury at Tanisha. 'And didn't it fucking occur to you, that someone could do that when you came over here?'

Lilly began to drift away to the sound of Tanisha crying. This was it, then. Her arms flopped to her sides and her eyes began to roll back in her head. Life and death were but two sides of the same coin. Heads you live, tails you die. No one gets to choose.

Fuck that.

Lilly brought her knee up into Danny's groin. Hard. With a grunt, he released his grip to protect himself and Lilly took the opportunity to ball her fist and bring it up under Danny's chin. His teeth crunched together with an audible snap and he fell backwards.

Lilly spluttered as her lungs filled with air, her shoulders heaving. She wanted to rest, let her chest expand, but she knew Danny was about to recover. She couldn't let that happen. She drew back her foot and kicked him full in the stomach, catapulting him on to the floor. He fell with a howl.

In terror, Lilly checked the hallway. There was only one way back, and that was over Danny. Behind him were the schoolgirl and the man who had answered the door, both shocked and disorientated. But for how long?

A foot away was a side-door. It wouldn't lead out of the flat, but right now Lilly just needed to put distance between her and Danny. She grabbed Tanisha's arm and staggered through the door, slamming it behind her when they were both inside.

The room was cavernous. At least twice as big as Lilly expected and empty apart from three old sofas huddled around the remains of a dismantled wooden table. In the far corner were two teenaged boys, skinny and frightened, their fingers entwined. They stared at her in fear and confusion.

'Help me,' Lilly screamed and began to push one of the sofas against the wall.

One of the boys didn't move, but the other vaulted to Lilly and heaved the sofa across the doorway, crashing it into place. Together they threw themselves at it.

'Trick,' the boy shrieked, 'get the other one.'

His companion wiggled his fingers, near his face. Lilly could see his cheeks were pitted with burns and he was evidently in shock.

'Trick,' the boy screamed, 'move the fucking sofa.'

Trick blinked back tears but did as he was told, shoving it across the room to the door.

'After three,' Lilly said. 'One. Two. Three.'

She let the boy take the weight of the door, while she and Trick lifted the second sofa and tried to pile it on top. She cursed as it slipped back down, scraping her foot.

'Tanisha, don't just stand there.' Lilly gestured to the other end with her head.

Tanisha joined Trick at the other end. Together they managed to raise it on its side so that it rested against the top part of the door.

'This won't hold.' Tanisha's voice was full of panic.

'Doesn't need to,' said Lilly. 'As soon as Annabelle realizes I'm gone, she'll call the police.'

'How long will that be?'

'Not long,' Lilly replied, with more confidence than she felt.

Jack swore as he punched in Annabelle's number. Because he was using Carla's mobile, he had to dial by hand, reading the number from a scrap of paper, pressing each key individually.

'Hello?' Annabelle sounded nervous.

'I've tried Lilly's number and it's dead,' he said. 'And I've tried your land line and it's going straight to answer machine. Tell me you haven't left the house.'

'Sorry,' she muttered.

Damn it. When would he learn that Lilly never did what she was supposed to do?

'Where is she?' he asked.

Annabelle gave a small cough. 'I'm not sure.'

'What do you mean, you're not sure? Isn't she with you?'

'We're looking for Tanisha on the Clayhill Estate,' she said. 'Lilly thought it would save time if we split up.'

Of course she had.

'Where are you now?' he demanded.

'Outside Clancy Block,' she said.

'Right. Don't move.'

Demi has no idea who the white woman is.

She's pretty old, nothing special, like somebody's mum or something.

Yet she singlehandedly fought off Danny. You've got to give respect for that. One minute, he had her pushed against the wall, his hands around her throat and she was making an awful noise. Then bam. It was like a film or something, in slow motion. She kicked him and punched him, and dived out of the hallway with Tanisha.

They're in the other room now, the door barricaded, and Danny is going completely off his head.

'I am going to fuck you up.' He kicks out at the door, the wood splintering. 'Do you hear me? You are going to wish you never messed with me.'

He takes a step back, lets out a howl and charges at the door with his shoulder. Screams come from inside, but the door holds.

Demi is rooted to the spot. She has no doubt that if he gets in, he will kill them all. The junkie with the burns over his face will wish he was still lying on the floor, getting the treatment. As for the woman . . .

'Tanisha, you hear me now,' he shouts, 'you better let me in or, God help you, I will cut that baby out of your stomach.'

Demi can hear crying from inside. As soon as she saw Tanisha and Danny together she knew it was his child. It was the way she looked at him, all pleading. And she knew that Danny wouldn't help her. Tanisha is just another girl. Like Malaya, and Chika and JC. None of this means anything to Danny. They're all disposable.

Which means everything she's done is pointless.

Danny reaches into his waistband and pulls out a gun. It's the one Demi brought to him.

'Motherfuckers.' He points it at the door. 'I will cap you all.'

He aims and his finger begins to squeeze the trigger.

'Boss.' Rocky's voice comes from the end of the hallway, near the front door. 'We gotta get out of here, man, before the five-oh, arrive.'

Danny frowns at him. Demi can see Rocky is frightened too, but the fear of being banged up outweighs his fear of Danny.

'Serious, boss, we need to go now.'

Danny's nostrils flare. Then he nods and goes to move away. Almost as an afterthought he fires into the door. More screaming from inside. He fires again.

'Quick, boss.' Rocky is unlocking the front door, his hands fumbling in his hurry.

Danny gives the door to the sitting room a last violent kick, then makes after Rocky. As he passes the kitchen he pauses. The meth factory is still bubbling away. He takes aim again and shoots. The sound of glass exploding fills the air. Then the whoosh of fire taking hold.

As they leave, they don't even look back at Demi. She is nothing.

She runs to the kitchen. The table is already engulfed in flames, chemical bottles shattering, throwing their contents over the walls where they instantly set alight. She glances at the gas canisters, the toxic smoke already making her chest crack.

She heads for the front door, her hand over her mouth, leaving the others inside.

Jamie cradles Trick in his arms, whispering his name, trying to ignore the red stain spreading across his chest. There's a gurgling noise in his throat and a line of blood spills from the corner of his mouth.

'Everyone stay down,' the woman tells them.

They'd been pushing against the sofas, desperately trying to keep the mad guy out. He'd been kicking it and swearing. At one point he threatened to hurt someone called Tanisha's baby, and the pregnant girl started to cry.

'Don't listen to him,' the woman ordered. 'Just hold this bloody door, until help arrives.'

So they did.

Then there was a bang. Or a crack, like a whip, and a hole appeared in the door. Jamie had no idea what it was, but Tanisha started to scream.

'He's got a gun.'

'Hit the floor.' The woman pulled Tanisha on to the ground. 'Now.'

Jamie threw himself on to the floor, hands over his head, but Trick didn't react.

'Trick,' Jamie yelled and yanked at his leg.

Trick looked down, puzzled, then there was another crack. Louder than the last. The woman flung an arm over Tanisha and Trick dropped like a stone.

At first, Jamie thought he was doing as he was told, then he saw the hole in his chest. At first no bigger than the burns on his face. Almost matching. But within seconds, blood pumped out and covered his jumper.

'Keep your head down,' the woman hisses.

Jamie lies next to Trick and holds him. He's still warm.

'Don't anyone move,' the woman says, and they listen intently, waiting for another shot.

It doesn't come. Jamie can hear the muffled sounds of glass breaking, and the thick sound of the rattle in Trick's throat.

'Hold on,' Jamie tells him. 'We'll be out of here soon.'

They wait. Still nothing.

Bang. Everyone hits the deck again. But this time it sounds different. Not a gunshot. Someone's knocking at the door.

'Can you hear me, in there?' It's the schoolgirl.

The woman puts her finger over her lips, warning them not to speak.

'The others have gone,' the girl shouts through the door.

'She's lying,' Tanisha whispers.

The girl knocks more insistently. 'There's a fire in the kitchen. You've got to believe me.'

'I'm telling you she's lying,' says Tanisha.

The girl on the other side of the door is coughing and Jamie looks at the woman. Her face tells him she doesn't know whether to trust the girl. What if they open the door and the mad guy is waiting outside?

Jamie takes a deep breath for courage. Then he's caught by a racking cough. A chemical tang hits the back of his tongue and the woman starts coughing too.

'Please,' the schoolgirl is frantic now, 'you're going to get trapped in there.'

Jamie and the woman exchange looks. Something beyond the door *is* burning. He can smell it and taste it. It could still be a bluff, but can they risk it? Jamie glances down at Trick. His eyes are flickering but he and Jamie are now both soaked in his blood.

He needs an ambulance. Jamie kisses Trick's head and nods at the woman. They both jump up and throw the sofas aside, flinging the door open.

The schoolgirl has her blazer pulled over her head. Behind her, the hallway is licked by flames and clouds of black smoke billow towards them.

'There's gas in there,' she chokes. 'It's going to blow up.'

The heat is intense, burning Jamie's cheeks. The schoolgirl's hair is singed. They all fight for their breath. The woman pulls Tanisha to her feet, then helps Jamie pick up Trick. They each take a bloody arm around their shoulders. His feet drag and his head falls forward.

The schoolgirl beckons them on down the hallway, her back bent against the blaze. They follow, deafened by the roar of the flames.

As they reach the kitchen, an explosion of glass, like a firework on Bonfire Night fills the air. The schoolgirl screams as glittering shards of glass fly towards her, slashing her hands and face. She stops in her tracks, the others bumping into the back of her.

Then there's a blast of hot air. It knocks them backwards with the force of a car. And a sheet of burning gas streaks towards them.

'Get back,' the woman shouts, and pulls them all back into the room they have just left, slamming the door as the fireball soars past.

'What the hell is going on?'

Jack was furious when he found Annabelle hovering at the foot of Clancy Block.

'Actually,' he put up a hand, 'I don't care. I'm taking you back home and we're calling in the station on the way so I can get a DNA swab from you.'

'Why?' she asked.

'Because I'm bloody pissed off with all this nonsense,' he said. 'Someone else besides Tanisha touched that knife and I'm pretty damn sure it was you.'

Annabelle looked horrified, opening and closing her mouth.

'Save your arguments,' Jack turned away, 'and tell me where Lilly is, so we can just get on with this.'

When Annabelle's voice came it was tiny. 'We thought Tanisha might be trying to find Daniel and we thought he might live here.'

Mary, Mother of God. What was the woman planning to do? Knock on every door in Clancy?

He gazed up at the tower block, rubbing the ache it gave him in the back of his neck. The lift was out of order and he really, really didn't want to walk up all those stairs to find her.

He was about to ask Annabelle to give him one good reason why he shouldn't arrest the pair of them for wasting police time, when he spotted something unusual. Around halfway up the block, an orange glow lit up one of the walkways. Then a woman appeared and leant over the railing.

Jack's stomach flipped as he remembered Chika in exactly the same position.

But this woman wasn't reaching out to him. She was shouting something. He strained to hear.

'Fire!'

More figures appeared on the walkways, both above and below, some peering up, some down, all focused on the orange glow.

Soon an alarm began to wail and the residents of Clancy began to evacuate the building. Jack ran to the stairwell, checking each person descending. There was no sign of Lilly. He took the stairs two at a time until he reached the sixth floor and knew by the pall of black smoke that he was at the right floor. When he opened the exit, he was hit by a wall of heat and a choking cloud of toxic fumes.

He ran down the walkway, trying to get as near to the source of the fire as he could. He held up his hand to shield his face as he reached the flat which was ablaze. He couldn't get closer than ten feet before being driven backwards. The flames leapt from the open door, dancing out and up, to the flat above. If the fire crews didn't get here soon, the whole block would become an inferno.

He ran back down the walkway, thumping on every door and window as he went.

'Fire,' he shouted. 'You need to get out now.'

He was at the flat nearest to the stairwell when the door opened and a young mum with her toddler appeared.

'We were asleep.' Her eyes were wide with fear.

'Don't worry.' Jack guided her to the exit. 'Just make your way downstairs quickly and calmly.'

She scooped up her child and headed away.

'I knew this would happen one day,' she said. 'Making drugs in there. All those young kids coming here and that gangster with his big black car.'

Jack skidded to a halt. 'What car?'

'There,' the woman pointed to a black Mercedes, parked at the far end of the quad.

Oh Jesus, no. Jack looked back at the flat being swallowed by the raging fire. The flat belonged to Daniel Kanio. Tanisha had come looking for him. And Lilly had come looking for Tanisha.

Trapped.

Lilly looked around wildly for an escape route. There were no other doors and the windows were boarded with metal sheets.

No way out.

'Lilly, look.' Tanisha pointed to the thick smoke creeping under the door.

Somewhere in the back of her mind, she half remembered that most victims died of smoke inhalation before the flames even got to them.

'Give me that.' She grabbed the blazer that the schoolgirl was still holding over her head, and stuffed it across the gap between the door and floor.

The girl stared at Lilly, her face criss-crossed with cuts from the flying glass.

'What are we going to do?' she asked Lilly.

Lilly blinked at the girl, sweat and blood trickling from her forehead, then at the boy lying on the floor with his clearly dying friend in his arms. Finally, she looked at Tanisha, anxious and pregnant.

'What are we going to do?' the girl repeated.

Lilly tried not to laugh. Or cry. How the fuck was she supposed to know?

'We're going to wrench off the shutter,' she said.

The others watched, spellbound, as Lilly crossed the room and began pulling at the metal sheet covering the window. It was bolted to the walls and there was nothing to grasp. She smacked at one of the bolts with her open palm, the force juddering through her arm.

In the middle of the room was the ruined table. Next to it, the author of its downfall. An axe. Lilly sprinted over, grabbed it in both hands and wielded it over her head. She smashed it down on one of the bolts, the impact sending waves of pain through her body. Regardless, she raised the axe and once again brought it crashing down.

Panting, she looked over at the kids. The boy carefully placed his companion's head on the floor and ran to the pile of splintered wood. He scrabbled through until he found a leg of the coffee table. Brandishing it like a club, he attacked the other side of the metal sheet. Immediately, Tanisha and the other girl joined them, all four raining blows on the metal with whatever they could find, screaming with pain and effort.

'It's no good.' Tanisha pulled at one of the bolts. 'It's not working.'

'Keep trying.' Lilly swung the axe again.

At last, one of the bolts snapped with a ping. The kids laughed in giddy delight, but Lilly knew there was no time to celebrate. She had seen the paint on the door, bubbling and popping in the extreme heat. It could only be a matter of minutes before the door caught light and the fire spread.

'Come on,' she roared, hitting another bolt with fresh energy.

The boy abandoned the table leg and reached for a thinner plank of wood. He slid it under the part of the sheet now freed from the wall, and levered it back and forth. Little by little, the metal was prised from the wall and there was a gap big enough to get his hand through.

'If we get another bolt off we can rip it away,' he said.

Lilly nodded. She could do this. She placed the axe between her legs and wiped her hands down her skirt. Sweat and ripped skin came away on the material. She didn't care. She grasped it as tightly as she could and swung in a long slow arc, letting the weight of her body carry it over. It hit the bolt with a clang, sending it spinning across the room.

'Yes,' Lilly panted, 'you beauty.'

As she let her arms fall to her sides in exhaustion, the other three began forcing pieces of wood under the metal sheet, prising it up. Putting aside the agony in her upper arms, Lilly lifted the axe and squeezed the head under the gap. She rolled it with the handle.

'It's coming,' Tanisha screamed.

Lilly glanced across to the door. The paint was now black, small blue flames appearing in pockets. It was now or never. She jammed the axe head as far under the metal as it would go and pulled the handle towards her.

With a groan, the shutter began to give and Lilly could feel the night air outside. They were almost there. Almost free.

Then came another groan. Not from the window. Lilly looked up. Above their heads something groaned again. Plaster showered down. Then a rumble like thunder in a summer storm.

Then nothing.

Chapter Sixteen

Lilly assumed she must be dead.

She had no idea where she was, or how she had got there. Her body appeared to be floating in a thick blackness and every muscle was paralysed.

Then she felt a sharp pain stab her leg.

Not dead then.

She tried to move but a heaviness enveloped her, like a dense blanket. She concentrated on her eyelids. If she could at least see, she might be able to make sense of what was happening.

Summoning all her energy, Lilly attempted to open her eyes. They refused and remained glued shut.

One at a time then.

She focused on her right eye until it flickered open. It closed almost immediately, but, undeterred, she tried again. This time, she managed to lift the lid halfway. Something gritty filled her iris and she blinked away the sting.

Seconds later, she forced her left eye to join in and squinted into the surrounding nothingness.

As a child, Lilly and her mum had often been plunged into darkness when the electricity ran out, and there was nothing left to feed the meter. Lilly would crawl under the itchy blankets on her mum's bed and snuggle up. If she was lucky, Mum might tell her the story of the Little Chocolate House before she fell asleep, exhausted by her shifts at the textile factory. Then Lilly would feel happy and safe, listening to her wheeze.

But this was different. It wasn't the darkness of childhood, punctuated by lamp-posts and car headlights. It wasn't even the darkness of the countryside where the moon would cast its pallor over the garden.

This was total. Eyes open or shut, it was the same.

Sudden panic made Lilly gasp and her mouth filled with the same dry grit that had filled her eyes. She spat it out, trying not to gag.

What the fuck was going on?

She couldn't think straight and her mind began to dance. Her breathing became faster and her pulse began to race.

Then from nowhere, there came a long creak. Not the high shriek of the last stair in her cottage, or the door that perpetually needed oiling, this was low, like a groan.

There it came again.

Lilly held her breath and listened. She'd heard that sound before.

It all came flooding back to her. Searching for Tanisha. The flat on Clayhill. The fire. The kids trying to rip off the metal shutter. Then the groan above her head . . .

As the ceiling collapsed.

In that second Lilly knew exactly where she was. She was trapped under feet of concrete slabs and bricks and dust. Pinned down like a butterfly in a collection.

Buried alive.

Terror ran through her body like a lit fuse. She opened her mouth and screamed.

Jack stood at the foot of Clancy, his hand cupped over his eyes, trying to make out what was happening.

'Is the fire out?' Annabelle grabbed his arm.

Jack surveyed the walkway. There was still a black pall of smoke hanging in the air, but the bright oranges and reds had stopped glowing.

'I think the fire crew are dealing with it,' he told her.

At last, the crew appeared from the stairwell, their faces grimy under the bright yellow of their helmets.

'Do they have Tanisha?' Annabelle was already sprinting towards them.

Jack followed. There were five men, sweating and leaning against one another, but no sign of Tanisha. Or Lilly.

'What's going on?' he asked.

'I'm sorry but all civilians will have to step back.' The chief pointed to a line being set up by uniform. 'It's really not safe here.'

Jack flashed his badge. 'I'm job.'

The ID on the chief's helmet stated he was Andy Freeman. He took it off and wiped his face with the heavy sleeve of his protective jacket. 'Didn't realize.'

'Just tell me what's happening. Is the fire under control?'

Freeman nodded and reached for one of the bottles of water being handed out to the crew.

'What about the people inside the flat?' Jack shouted.

Freeman held up a gloved hand, while he drank. When the bottle was empty he held it to his lips panting.

'Sorry,' said Jack, 'but there were people inside the flat. I have to know what's happened to them.'

'The fire's all but out,' said Freeman.

'So where are they?' Jack interrupted.

'There's been a collapse,' said Freeman. 'The entire upstairs ceiling has come down.'

'What?'

'This was more than a fire. There must have been some sort of explosion. Walls, ceiling, everything, it's all come down.'

Jack was stunned into silence.

'The load-bearing walls should have held up,' Freeman shook his head, 'but they've just gone. Like someone took a sledgehammer to them.'

Lilly screamed until the skin of her throat was ragged.

Please God, let this be a nightmare. Any moment the alarm would go off and she would drink in the daylight and kiss her children.

She closed her eyes, willing herself to wake up. Instead there was a noise. Not the stomach-churning moan, like the bowels of a ship, this was muffled, irregular. Lilly listened hard. It sounded like two notes. One high, the other lower. De-de. De-de. Lil-ly. Lilly.

Her eyes flashed open. Someone was calling her name.

'Yes,' she shouted, 'it's me, I'm here!'

Her voice seemed to reverberate back at her, as if something were blocking it. She took a breath and blew. Hot air came back at her. Whatever it was, was inches from her face. She had to move it.

Her left arm was completely immobile, tucked partly by her side, partly under her body, but the right was across her chest. Like half an angel. This was the one she had to use.

She tried to lift her hand, but something held it in place. She wiggled her fingers and was relieved to find a degree of give. She pressed them first into her chest, then up against the obstruction. She repeated the movement again and again until she could lift them at least a centimetre, then she slid her hand across her collarbone, towards the opposite shoulder.

At last it was free.

Slowly, carefully, she brought her palm level with her face, the knuckle of her thumb grazing her cheek. A fraction further and the heel of her hand met something solid. She passed her fingers along it, feeling her way in the darkness. It was rough to the touch and her nails made a scratching sound against it. Definitely not stone or wood. It felt like plaster board.

She pushed against it, grateful for the wobble it made. If she could get enough movement in her wrist, she might be able to knock it away.

She let her arm flop back and took a deep breath, then she shot out and up from her elbow, until her hand was holding the board at arm's length. Air and space slapped Lilly across the face. She laughed out loud.

'Lilly, is that you?' Tanisha called out.

'Yes. Are you okay?'

'I think so, but I can't move.'

'I'm going to try to free myself then make my way to you.'

'Be quick.' Tanisha's voice was small.

Lilly lowered her arm and let the board fall back towards her. The claustrophobia was immediate and sickening, but she knew she wouldn't be able to hold the board up indefinitely. Instead, she let her hand and fingers relax. Then she balled it into a tight fist, inhaled through her nose and punched.

A shower of dust hit her, making her blink and cough. But the board fell away to the side. She was able to wave her hand in front of her as far as she could stretch it.

'Are you out?' Tanisha asked.

Lilly rocked her torso. Even with the space in front of her free, she was still wedged in tight from the sides.

'Nearly there,' she said.

With her free hand, she reached out to either side. The cold solid mass told her it was stone. It was as if she had fallen into the tiny space between two walls. She patted her way along until she found the end of each slab. To her surprise they ended level with her thighs. That meant her lower legs were free. So why the hell couldn't she move them?

She felt down to her knees and found the answer. Something huge and heavy lay across them. The splinters under her thumb told Lilly it was a plank of wood. An extremely solid one.

'Shit.'

'Lilly?' Panic caught in Tanisha's throat.

'Don't worry,' Lilly pushed at the plank. 'I'm almost with you.'

Tanisha began to cry. 'I don't want to die here on my own.'

Lilly was about to answer when another voice spoke.

'You're not on your own.' It was the schoolgirl. 'I'm here.'

The plank wouldn't budge. Lilly heaved as hard as she could, but it wouldn't move.

'What's your name?' Lilly was panting with the effort.

'Demi,' said the girl. 'Demi Ebola.'

'Ebola?'

'Yeah, I'm Malaya's sister.'

Gran says death is nothing to be scared of. She says that Jesus takes us in his arms and carries us to His Kingdom. Demi never did believe her. Otherwise, why did they leave Nigeria? And why was she so upset when Malaya was hurt?

Funnily enough, Demi's not frightened now. Her face stings from the glass that exploded in the kitchen and her chest feels heavy from dust, but she's not worried about dying. She just feels so very, very sad.

Tanisha McKenzie is about a foot away. Demi can't see her, but she can hear her breathing, coughing back tears.

'I never hurt your sister,' she says.

Demi snorts. 'Chika said you did.'

'Chika lied.'

'Why would she do that?'

Tanisha lets out a sigh. 'Because a long time ago I let her down, and you don't do that to your friends, do you?'

'No you don't.' Demi's voice comes out very quiet, as if it isn't her own.

'And I am sorry about Malaya, believe me. I didn't touch her, but I stood there and did nothing to help, and that was a fucking evil thing to do.'

Demi doesn't answer. Standing by. Doing nothing. These things have nearly driven her crazy.

'I wouldn't do that now,' says Tanisha.

'Why?'

'Cos of the baby,' says Tanisha. 'I'm a different person.'

Demi reaches out with her hand and finds Tanisha. Her skin is hot and damp.

'Is it Danny's?'

Tanisha lets out a laugh. 'You're gonna think me a fool, but he said he loved me.'

Demi thinks about the first time she met him, how intimidated Chika had been. How he'd got her to carry drugs and a gun for him. How he had left her in the burning flat.

'He don't love nobody,' she says.

As she listened to the girls' whispers, Lilly focused on the plank across her knees. All attempts to push it down her legs had failed. Perhaps if she could lift it with her knees, she could knock it off.

The weight of it was immense and her knees were not strong, but no other plan sprung to mind.

With a grunt from somewhere deep in her belly, Lilly began to raise her knees. She strained against the wood, her teeth gritted, the sinews in her neck almost snapping. Her legs shook with the effort.

There was a movement. Tiny, but it was there. She wanted to cheer but growled instead, forcing her heels into the ground for more purchase.

The sweat poured down her face and into her eyes, making a toxic mixture with the dust. She screwed them shut and ignored the pain, until little by little, her knees rose, taking the plank with them.

Eventually, she pulled her feet towards her. Her knees were fully bent, the plank balanced on top. She knew there was no way she could hold it much longer, so with her free hand she pushed. It toppled down her shins, banging and gouging them before crushing her toes as it bounced away.

This was it. She pressed the palm of her free hand against the slab to her left, dug her heels in as hard as she could and hauled herself upright. Her left shoulder was dragged, rough edges of stone cutting through her clothes, ripping her skin. Lilly bit her bottom lip against the pain.

At last she was standing.

'Right then, kids,' she said. 'Where are you?'

'Here,' the girls chorused.

'Excellent.' Lilly made her way blindly towards the sound.

Jack looked from Freeman to the place where Lilly was trapped and back to Freeman.

'We have to get in there.'

Freeman shook his head. 'Too dangerous. Once the integrity of a building's gone, there could be another collapse at any time.'

'All the more reason to get those people out, surely?'

Freeman licked his lips. They were already cracked from proximity to the fire.

'I know it seems harsh, but I've got the safety of my crew to think about.'

'So we just leave them?'

'Of course not. We've already called in back-up to assess the situation.'

Jack placed a forefinger on each temple. 'But you said the place could collapse at any time and there are kids in there.'

'I'm sorry but we have to wait.'

Jack blinked back tears. 'The mother of my baby is in there, I can't just stand here and watch while she dies.'

Freeman and the rest of the crew stared at Jack, then looked at their feet. At last, Freeman slipped his helmet back on his head and sighed.

'Sometimes, I bloody well hate this job.'

Lilly shuffled and tripped across to Tanisha and Demi.

'Is anyone hurt?' she asked.

'I don't think so,' said Tanisha.

'Demi?' Lilly asked.

'No,' she whispered back.

'Listen, I'm sure they'll come for us soon,' said Lilly.

'Who's they?' Tanisha asked.

'Police, fire brigade, whatever,' Lilly replied. 'They know we're in here and they'll be looking for us.'

'But what if we run out of air?' Tanisha asked.

Lilly had been thinking the same thing. If there was no way for air to come in, the oxygen would be used up fast.

'We need to make our way back towards the door,' said Lilly.

'But we can't see anything.' Tanisha's voice took on a wild tone.

'We can feel our way. If we can find the outer wall, we can follow it around,' said Lilly. 'Eventually, we must come to the door.'

'But we could go completely the wrong way,' said Tanisha.

'What choice is there?' asked Demi. 'Do you want to sit here and suffocate?'

'No.'

'Okay then,' said Lilly.

She reached out and grasped Tanisha's arm, slid her fingers down to her wrist, before taking her hand.

Slowly, she pushed her right leg and arm out. When she was sure there was nothing in her way, she took a step. The girls followed her.

'What do you think happened to those boys?' Tanisha asked.

'Dead,' said Demi.

Tanisha gasped.

'Don't think about that,' Lilly ordered. 'Just concentrate on the here and now.'

The going was laboured as they navigated the bricks and planks that littered the floor, until at last Lilly's hand touched something soft. The pressure of her fingers sprang back at her.

'It's one of the sofas,' she said excitedly.

'Just what we need,' said Tanisha. 'Somewhere to sit down.'

'Don't be stupid,' Demi said. 'It means we must be near the door to the hallway.'

The air was filled with the sound of them patting.

'It's here,' Demi shouted. 'I can feel the frame.'

Lilly followed Demi's voice until they stood side by side, then she let Demi guide her hand up and down what was unmistakably the door frame. The door itself was gone, but in its place was a slab of concrete. She caught her finger on some jagged metal sticking out of it.

'Be careful.' She brought the finger to her mouth, sucking at the wetness.

'What now?' Tanisha asked.

Lilly felt along the perimeter. There were no gaps small enough for any of them to fit through.

'We push it over,' she said.

'It must weigh a ton,' said Tanisha.

'Together we can do it,' said Lilly.

Without another word, they each took a place at the corner and braced themselves against it.

'Let's do this,' said Lilly. 'Heave.'

As one, they drove their shoulders against the slab.

'Come on,' Lilly grunted.

Sluggishly at first, it began to wobble.

'Motherfucker,' Tanisha screamed.

The stone tablet tottered and jittered until, at last, it toppled on its side with a crash.

Gasping for breath and laughing at the same time, Lilly put her hands on her knees. The palms were cut to shreds but she didn't care.

'Let's get out of here,' she wheezed and the girls cheered.

They would have to step over the slab, now laid on its side at their feet, but they could hold on to the doorframe for balance.

Lilly felt for a flat foothold and was about to climb up when it came again.

She could feel her heart stop beating in her chest as time stood still and she listened.

The mournful groan of the building.

'Shit,' she shouted. 'Cover your heads.'

Then once again, the world imploded.

It took for ever to climb the stairs as each member of the crew took every flight on his own.

'What the hell are we doing?' asked Jack.

Freeman watched one of his men dart from floor five to six, then wait for them as close to the exit as possible.

'In the event of a building collapse, the stairs are one of the worst places to be,' said Freeman.

He paused, waiting and listening intently.

'They concertina,' he said. 'Anyone on them is cut to ribbons.'

Then he left Jack, taking them two at a time.

'Mary, Mother of God,' Jack glanced at the flight below and above him.

At last, Freeman gave him the signal to follow and, barely touching the steps, Jack sprinted to join him.

Freeman opened the door to the walkway. 'This is the tricky bit.'

'Was that not the cutting to ribbons thing?' asked Jack.

Freeman smiled and indicated along the balcony to the flat. 'We've no way of knowing if it's secure.'

'How do we find out?'

'We walk across it.'

Jack gulped and nodded.

'Maybe it's better if you stay here,' said Freeman.

'No way.'

Freeman appraised him for a moment then gave a tight dip of the head.

'Walk fast and light. Legs apart to spread the load.'

He turned, danced along the walkway until he was outside the flat, then waved for Jack to follow. Jack checked his urge to gag and trotted forward. His eyes were drawn into the night sky and the expanse beneath them. If the balcony fell, they wouldn't survive.

Finally, he was next to Freeman.

'I thought you'd bottle it.' He patted Jack's arm.

Together they peered into what had once been 63b Clancy. The outside was blackened from fire and smoke damage, but the inside was worse. A devastation of rubble piled high. Ceiling, walls, any sign of what it had once been, decimated.

Could anyone survive that?

'There are safe pockets inside there.' Freeman read Jack's mind. 'With any luck they've found one.'

'Lilly Valentine is the luckiest person I know,' said Jack.

He took a step forward but Freeman stopped him. 'The floor could give way, mate.'

Jack swallowed and searched the detritus.

'Lilly,' he shouted. 'Can you hear me?'

They waited for a reply but nothing came, only a creaking from deep inside.

'What's that?' Jack asked.

'This building is not a happy bunny,' said Freeman.

Jack called out again. And then again.

At last there came a shriek. But it wasn't Lilly.

'Let's get out of here,' Freeman roared.

'I can't leave her.'

Jack felt himself lifted off his feet as Freeman dragged him away from the flat towards the stairs. With his arms outstretched to Lilly and the night air rushing at him, Jack watched a crack appear on the walkway and the balcony fall away into nothing.

Chapter Seventeen

Lilly struggled to catch her breath, snatching at the air like a fish on land. Her head felt full and thick and wrong.

She opened her mouth to call out to the others, but her jaw felt loose.

A single drop of saliva fell. She waited for it to dribble down her chin. Instead it headed for her nose.

She shook her head, let another drop fall. This time it pooled on her septum.

Fuck. She was upside down.

She gyrated her shoulders until she could turn, then, no longer wedged in place, she fell. The impact beat against the crown of her head, the crack resounding.

'Christ,' she sobbed. 'Is everyone still here?'

A tiny voice scratched across the floor. 'I can't move.'

'Demi?'

'I can't move.' Her voice was weaker still.

Lilly felt her way and found Demi. Another concrete slab had fallen on top of her, pinning her by the chest to the floor.

'I'm going to get this off you,' said Lilly.

She jammed her hands beneath it and pushed. Demi let out a scream.

'Stop,' she cried out. 'It hurts too much.'

Lilly found Demi's face and smoothed the dust from her cheeks. 'Don't you worry, I'm going to get us out of here.'

Jamie opens his eyes, leans to his side and vomits. He hasn't felt this bad since that other morning in the boarding house.

'What the fuck do you think you're doing?'

It's the girl called Tanisha. He can't see her properly, can only just make out her outline.

'Sorry,' he mumbles.

'Demi?' she asks.

'No,' he says. 'I'm Jamie.'

'You're kidding me,' she says. 'I thought you two was dead.'

'Sorry,' he says again, though he has no idea why.

'Where's the other one?'

'I don't know,' Jamie says.

But he does know. Trick is beside him. Jamie hasn't let him go since the first collapse. He's not moving now. Not breathing.

'You don't sound like you belong round here,' she tells him.

'It might sound like existential angst, but I don't honestly know where I belong.'

'I have no idea what existential angst is, but I completely understand,' she says.

There's a moment of silence when all Jamie can hear is the sound of his own heart breaking.

'You and your friend,' says Tanisha, 'are you, like . . .'

'His name's Trick,' Jamie squeezes Trick's hand. 'And yes, we're gay.'

'Boy,' Tanisha lets out a whoosh of air. 'Round here that's a big thing to admit, you get me.'

'Where I'm from it's a big thing to admit, but I'm past caring.'

'Respect to you,' she says.

'It's more than that, though,' says Jamie. 'He's the only person in the world who cares about me.'

'What about your family?' asks Tanisha.

Jamie thinks about Mum and Dad and all the trouble he's caused with the bunking off, the stealing and the drugs.

'I think they'd be quite happy if I got stuck in here for ever.'

'My mum probably thinks I'm already dead,' says Tanisha. 'When it comes down to it, we're all on our own.'

'You'll have the baby,' he says.

He reaches his hand across and finds the bump in her stomach. She doesn't stop him. It's surprisingly hard, the skin stretched tight. Suddenly it jerks against his hand and he pulls it away.

'What was that?'

Tanisha laughs. 'The baby moving, you fool.'

He laughs too.

'Do you think we'll get out of here?' he asks.

'Definitely. Don't you?'

He doesn't answer, just listens to the sounds of the building complaining around him.

'Tell me what we do now?' Jack's eyes pleaded with Freeman.

They looked along the walkway from their vantage point at the exit. At least half had crumbled away.

'We wait for the crane,' said Freeman.

'What crane?'

Freeman gestured with his head to the quad below, where a huge crane made its way on caterpillar tracks through the crowd.

Was it Lilly's imagination or were things less black and more charcoal grey. She screwed her eyes closed, then opened them. Perhaps it was wishful thinking, but she could swear that shapes were appearing around her. In front of her, for example, was something large and square. She leaned towards it and her hand made a clang against it. Metal.

'Apart from the shutters was there anything else in the flat made of metal?' Lilly asked.

Demi's voice was weak. 'I don't think so.'

Lilly nodded and pressed her back against it.

'Why does it matter?' Demi asked.

'Because if this is a shutter,' Lilly steeled herself against it, 'it means there's a bloody great hole where it used to be.'

She shoved with her shoulder-blades and the shutter fell to the floor. There was the window, partially blocked by a pile of bricks and wood.

Outside it was night, but the light that poured in was blinding. Instinctively, Lilly turned away. The room around her made her gasp. The ceiling had completely gone and part of the ceiling of the next floor was hanging precariously, streams of dust and rubble raining down.

The floor was littered with broken furniture, fallen from the flat upstairs, but worse were the gaping holes. Lilly shuddered as she thought of herself and the girls, wandering blindly around them.

A few feet away, covered in a coat of grey dust, were Tanisha and one of the boys. They blinked at her.

'This is Jamie,' said Tanisha.

'Hello, Jamie,' said Lilly.

He smiled at Lilly in astonishment until Demi cried out in pain. When Tanisha caught sight of her she scrabbled over.

'It's going to be okay.' She smoothed Demi's hair back. 'We're right here beside you.'

Demi's breathing was laboured and Tanisha flicked Lilly a glance. Lilly nodded and ran to the window. She threw aside five or six bricks until she could lean out. The cold air was delicious. Then she looked down. No balcony. No walkway. Nothing.

Jack flung open the door to the stairwell and raced to the crane. He dived in front of it, waving both his arms. The driver brought it to a shuddering halt less than a foot from him and jumped out.

'What the hell do you think you're doing?' he yelled. 'I could have killed you.'

Jack thrust his ID under the driver's nose.

'Take me up.'

'You have got to be joking,' said the driver.

Jack jumped into the bucket. 'Am I smiling?'

Tanisha and Jamie joined Lilly at the window and cleared away the last of the bricks.

'I can't help but notice the sheer drop,' said Jamie.

Lilly sucked in her breath. Every inch of her was ripped and bruised. She was all out of ideas.

Then outside, a man appeared from nowhere, floating in the air, like an angel.

'Jack?'

The rest of the crane came into view and stopped a short distance from the block.

'We can't get any closer,' Jack shouted. 'You're going to have to jump.'

Tanisha looked down at the six-storey drop. 'There is no way I can do that, you understand me.'

Above them, the building gave a deep howl. A piece of plaster board fell with a crash, sending splinters around the room. Tanisha grabbed on to Jamie.

'We have to,' he said.

'I'm too frightened.'

He looked into her eyes. 'I'll go first, show you how easy it is.'

She didn't move, so he prised away her fingers and steadied himself.

'Come on, son,' Jack held out a hand.

Jamie pressed his lips together, took a step back and leapt.

For a moment he was suspended in mid-air, the next Jack was gripping his arm, hauling him into the bucket. He turned back to the flat, tears pouring down his face.

'See,' he told Tanisha, 'I said it was easy.'

Tanisha looked at Lilly. The kid was pregnant. How was it possible?

'Don't look down,' said Lilly.

Tanisha held the window frame with both hands and leaned as far back into the room as she could. She swayed backwards and forwards three times for momentum, then propelled herself into the air, her legs peddling furiously.

Like Jamie she seemed to fly. But too soon she began to drop.

Lilly watched in horror, as Tanisha began to sink, her arms above her head, reaching up to the sky.

'Catch her, Jack,' she screamed.

Jack leaned over the side of the bucket and snatched at Tanisha, taking one of her hands in his. Her weight dragged him forward so that he almost fell from the platform, but Jamie threw his arms around Jack's waist, reeling him back in.

For a moment they remained in position. Jamie holding on to Jack, Jack holding on to Tanisha, Tanisha swinging almost a hundred feet above the ground. Lilly held her breath.

Then slowly, Jack began to drag Tanisha up to the bucket, until she was able to scramble aboard. She fell against Jamie and they clung to one another, sobbing.

Behind Lilly, another piece of the ceiling fell, spraying Demi with rubble. Lilly knelt next to her.

'Did they make it?' Demi whispered.

Lilly nodded. 'We're all going to make it.'

Demi's breathing was so shallow it came in a rattle of tiny gasps. High above them came a rumble. Distant at first, then getting louder. The walls began to shake.

'Go,' said Demi.

Tears filled Lilly's eyes. 'Don't be ridiculous.'

'There's no point us both dying.'

A howl caught in Lilly's throat. Demi couldn't be more than thirteen.

'I can't possibly leave you.'

The shuddering around them worsened and cracks began to appear across the floor. Small, black spidery lines that soon began to grow and gape.

'Go,' Demi's voice was barely audible, 'and tell Tanisha I owe her.'

Demi's eyes closed as one of the cracks opened up, splitting the floor in two. Lilly threw herself at the window as the black swallowed Demi whole. The frame was crumbling in Lilly's hands. Any second it would collapse in on itself.

She looked across at Jack. He was shouting something at her but the roar behind her drowned him out. Above her was a huge expanse of night and stars. Below her, space, then hard ground.

She looked into Jack's face, saw Alice looking back at her, and jumped.

Chapter Eighteen

One week later

Lilly's suit jacket chafed her shoulders. The myriad of cuts that criss-crossed her body were healing, but she wished she'd chosen something looser.

She carried her briefcase under her arm, and winced as it pushed against her bruised ribs, but both her hands were bandaged and she found it impossible to get her fingers through the handle.

As she tried to open the door to the office with her backside, someone dashed forward and held it for her. It was Jamie. He looked pale and tired and thin, but he smiled at her.

'Are you okay?' she asked him.

He looked over his shoulder at a woman locking a Porsche Carrera. 'That's my mum.'

Lilly showed them both in.

'I'd make some tea,' she held up her outsized paws, 'but cups are a step too far at the moment. My assistant, Karol, should be here soon, though.'

'Please don't trouble yourself.' Mrs Holland crossed her feet at the ankle and placed manicured fingers over her knees. 'We don't want to take up any more of your time than is necessary.'

Mrs Holland's discomfort was tangible and she didn't return Lilly's smile.

'How's Tanisha?' Jamie asked.

Mrs Holland sighed. 'We're not here to talk about her, Jamie.'

'She matters, you know,' said Jamie. 'People like her matter.'

'Yes they do,' said Lilly, 'but your mum's right, we do need to discuss you.'

Jamie glanced at his mum, then nodded at Lilly.

'I told you what I did,' he said.

He had telephoned Lilly the day before and admitted to his part in an attack on a crack dealer.

'I want to confess to the police,' he said.

Mrs Holland pressed her lips together and cleared her throat. 'I don't think that's wise, Jamie. This other person you were with was the one who committed the act. Whatever his name, it was he, not you, who hit the woman. Daddy has spoken to his lawyer and he confirmed that it puts an entirely different spin on the situation.'

Jamie slapped Lilly's desk with both hands. 'Daddy's lawyer says whatever Daddy pays him to say. Don't you get it? He just wants this nasty business to disappear. He doesn't care about me or Trick or Tanisha.'

'I care.' Mrs Holland's voice was small.

She leaned forward and gently placed her hand next to his so that the little finger of her right hand touched the left of his.

'I care very much.'

Jamie's eyes filled with tears and he shut them tight. 'I did a really terrible thing and I should pay the price.'

'Listen, Jamie,' said Lilly, 'what you and Trick did was wrong, but you making a statement to the police won't change anything.'

'It'll set things right.'

Lilly shook her head. 'I've spoken to Jack McNally, the copper dealing with all this, and he says the victim made a full recovery and jumped on the next plane back to Nigeria.'

'What?' Jamie and his mum shouted out as one.

'She had no interest in answering any tricky questions, so as far as they're concerned the case is closed.'

'That's fantastic news,' Mrs Holland laughed.

She turned to her son and threw her arms around him.

'Someone has to pay, that's how it works,' said Jamie.

'Shush now.' Mrs Holland kissed his head. 'Didn't your friend Trick do just that?'

She held on to him for a long moment, rocking him back and forth, beaming into his hair. A woman who had almost lost her son and didn't want to let him go ever again. Lilly couldn't wipe the smile from her own face.

At last, Jamie looked up. 'What about Tanisha? Did they drop the case against her too?'

Lilly's smile slipped. 'They charged her with murder this morning.'

'But she said she didn't do it.'

'There's a knife with her prints all over it that says she did.'

Jamie shook his head. 'After everything she's been through, it doesn't seem fair.'

Kerry looked up from her prosecution files. If she was surprised to see Lilly in such a battered state, she didn't show it.

'I suppose you're here for McKenzie.'

'Well, it was either that or breakfast in bed with Brad Pitt,' said Lilly.

Kerry gave one of her curled lip smiles that showed pink gums above yellow teeth.

'I knew you'd want all the unused material, so there it is.' She nodded at a pile of papers on the end of the table.

Lilly opened her briefcase with her teeth and slid the papers into it with her wrist.

'As always, Kerry, it's been a pleasure.'

Outside, she tried to take out a handful to read, but they slipped from her outsized paw and scattered across the floor. Swearing, she knelt to collect them back in.

'Jesus woman, you're an accident waiting to happen.' Jack knelt beside her and scooped them up.

He helped her into a chair. 'Now, which do you want to read first?'

'Are you allowed to fraternize with the enemy?'

'If the chief super walks in, I'll tell him you used your voodoo powers on me,' he said. 'So what's it to be?'

'Forensics.'

He shuffled through the papers and placed a sheet on her lap, which Lilly skimread.

'There was another set of DNA on the knife?' she asked.

'Yeah, Annabelle's, I think,' he replied. 'Which is what you'd expect, given it was her knife.'

'You think it was Annabelle's or you know?'

'Cheney was doing the tests, then we all got a bit sidetracked.'

Lilly smiled. Who could blame Jack for not chasing this up? And no doubt it *was* Annabelle's DNA. But Lilly just wouldn't be Lilly if she didn't look under every rock and stone.

'Grab my phone, would you?' She held her jacket open.

Jack reached into her inside pocket and pulled out her mobile.

'Cheney's on speed dial,' she told him.

Jack raised an eyebrow.

'For God's sake Jack, he's the senior FI round here.' She shook her head in despair.

He hit the call button and held it to Lilly's ear.

'Cheney.'

'Hi Phil, it's Lilly Valentine.'

'Ha, I knew it was only a matter of time.'

'Before what?'

'Before you realized that Jack McNally is a no hoper with a small penis.' He let out a growl. 'Time to play with the big boys now.'

Lilly laughed. 'Sorry mate, my mum won't let me out today.'

'Shame.'

'Now about the knife in the McKenzie case.' She tapped the page on her knee. 'It says here there was a second set of DNA. Any match?'

'We couldn't find a sausage on the database.'

'Have the prosecution asked you to check Annabelle O'Leary?'

'Don't need to,' he said. 'Annabelle's on the database, she gave a sample when she became a foster-carer.'

Lilly felt a flutter in her stomach. 'So it's not Annabelle?'

'Give the lady a gold star.'

This was good news. Tanisha said she had not killed Chika Mboko, that someone must have stolen the knife. Now there was proof that someone else had indeed used the knife.

'Like I say, there was no match with anything stored on the database, but then we got lucky,' said Cheney.

Lilly sat very still. 'Are you telling me there is a match?'

'Yup. That old tart McNally brought it in himself. Some girl called Demi Ebola.'

Inside the court room, Lilly lowered herself gently into her chair. Every muscle in her body ached.

When Mr Manchester came scuttling in, it was all she could do to stand.

'Here we are again.' He read the charge sheet.

Kerry remained on her feet. 'Indeed, sir, only this time Miss

McKenzie is charged with an even more serious offence than before.'

Lilly glanced at Tanisha in the dock. She smiled at Lilly, resigned to her fate.

'Then let's get this case transferred to the Crown Court.' Mr Manchester gave Lilly a pointed look. 'Preferably without the three act drama.'

'If you mean a bail application, sir, then I'm afraid I can't oblige.'

He glared at her. 'Are you serious?'

'Deadly serious.'

He narrowed his eyes and dropped his voice. 'I will not have my time wasted, Miss Valentine.'

Lilly straightened her back. The scabs across her shoulders prickled and tore.

'Proceed.' He waved his hand at her.

Lilly cleared her throat. This was going to be a tough one.

'The police say, sir, that Tanisha killed Chika Mboko with a knife, yet they have no evidence apart from her fingerprints.'

'Isn't that enough?' scoffed Kerry.

'Hardly,' Lilly replied. 'Tanisha was not found at the scene of the crime. In fact she was found in her room some ten miles away.'

'She could easily have made her way back,' Kerry sighed.

'Perhaps she could, but one would expect her to take some of the scene with her. Forensic examination has found not one micro spot of the victim's blood on Tanisha.'

'So she had a wash,' said Kerry.

Lilly nodded. 'And at the same time washed her bedding, all her clothes and the walls and carpets of her bedroom, because not one hair or skin cell was found there either. Not bad in an hour.'

Kerry let out a snort that made the hair in her nostrils vibrate.

'And while we're considering the issue of DNA, sir, you might also be interested to know that not one drop of Tanisha's blood, not one hair or skin cell found its way on to the victim.' She shrugged at the magistrate. 'It's almost as if these two girls were never in the same place.'

Mr Manchester leaned forward, his chin in the palm of his hand.

'Of course the really fascinating thing about all this isn't the fact that Tanisha's DNA is not present, it's the identity of the person whose DNA is.'

Lilly paused. She looked longingly at the water jug, then at her bandaged hands.

'Go on,' Mr Manchester urged.

Lilly swallowed the lump in her throat. 'Tests have confirmed that blood and skin cells from another girl were found on the weapon.'

Every eye in the courtroom opened wide.

'The girl was called Demi Ebola, the younger sister of Malaya Ebola. I understand that she was found near to the scene of the crime.'

Kerry leant into Jack who nodded and whispered that this was in fact the case.

'Unfortunately, she died in the terrible accident on the Clayhill Estate, but it's my belief that she killed Chika.'

Silence fell on the courtroom as they waited for the magistrate to react.

When he spoke, it was slowly. 'What exactly are you asking for today?'

'A two week adjournment, sir, for the police to make further investigations. I understand that a vast quantity of evidence was collected at the scene and I'm sure they will want to test every last piece for Demi Ebola's DNA.'

Kerry groaned. The job would be enormous. Lilly contained a smile.

'In the meantime, sir, I should like my client to be allowed back to her foster placement.'

The magistrate scratched his head and looked over at Tanisha.

'I think in the circumstances that would be the only fair course of action.'

Outside court, Jack watched Lilly say goodbye to Tanisha. He had no doubt that she was right.

Demi had known that Chika had stood by while her sister was beaten to a pulp. It went against everything a gang stood for. The ultimate betrayal.

When Tanisha left, he slid over to Lilly and put a hand on her back. She flinched.

'Sorry.'

'It's not you,' she said. 'I'm just very, very sore.'

He looked at her. Even now, bandaged and broken, she was bloody gorgeous.

'Fancy a drink?'

She smiled at him, put a padded hand on his arm. 'I think I'll pass, head home for a bath.'

He watched her limp away, knowing now what he should have known an age ago. It was over between them.

'Did someone mention a drink?'

Carla Chapman appeared next to him.

'What are you doing here?' he asked.

'I've been chasing you around all week for my phone,' she laughed. 'And I distinctly remember you saying you owed me a drink.'

Jack glanced back at Lilly as she disappeared through the door.

'So I did,' he said. 'So I did.'

Back at the cottage, Lilly fumbled for her key before it dropped on to the step with a ping. She groaned and tried to scoop it up.

When a car pulled up and Karol hopped out, she couldn't have been more pleased to see him. He looked absurdly handsome in a black Puffa jacket.

'You're a sight for sore eyes,' she smiled.

He gave a dazzling smile.

'I came over to bring you these.' He placed a box of papers at her feet and picked up her key. 'Personal things that have no business being in your office.'

'You're a godsend,' she said. 'Come in for a coffee.'

Karol glanced back at the car and Lilly noticed the driver.

'That is Patrick,' he whispered. 'We are on our way to lunch.'

'Right,' said Lilly.

Karol leaned into her. 'He is a doctor.'

With that he opened the door, slid the box into the hall among the recycling and skipped back to his date.

How had Lilly missed it?

She stepped inside, closed the door behind her and sank to the floor.

Then she laughed until she thought her ribs might crack.